"Jesse," she whispered on a rush of breath.

Jesse Chapman, tall, dark, and more handsome than any one man had a right to be.

Kate took him in, absorbing his height, the brown hair that brushed his collar, the dark eyes that traveled the length of her in a way that made her breath catch and her skin tingle. He looked like a cowboy stepping out for the night, his white long-sleeved, button-down shirt tailored perfectly over broad shoulders, narrowing into lean hips and thighs encased in tight, soft Wrangler jeans that cupped his crotch like a lover.

Heat scorched her cheeks when she realized where she was looking. Quickly, she lifted her gaze, reminding herself to breathe.

"Hello, Katie. Aren't you going to welcome me home?"

Also by Linda Francis Lee
Published by Ivy Books

DOVE'S WAY
SWAN'S GRACE
NIGHTINGALE'S GATE
THE WAYS OF GRACE
LOOKING FOR LACEY
THE WEDDING DIARIES

Suddenly Sexy

A Novel

Linda Francis Lee

IVY BOOKS • NEW YORK

An Ivy Book
Published by The Random House Publishing Group

This book contains an excerpt from the forthcoming book *Sinfully Sexy* by Linda Francis Lee. This excerpt has been set for this edition only and may not reflect the final content of the forthcoming edition.

Ivy Books and colophon are trademarks of Random House, Inc.

www.ballantinebooks.com

ISBN 0-345-46271-8

Manufactured in the United States of America

OPM   9 8 7 6 5 4 3 2 1

First Edition: September 2004

Book design by Caron Harris

Cover by Sally Cato, Design Management NYC

FOR MICHAEL,
with love

To: Katherine Bloom <katherine@ktextv.com>
From: Julia Boudreaux <julia@ktextv.com>
Subject: Project Reinventing Kate

Sugar, isn't this exciting! The first day of the brand-new you. You are going to be divine. I just know it. All you have to do is follow the man's lead, act like you're enjoying yourself, and most of all, tell him he's great no matter how badly it all turns out. Do you understand, sweetie?!

xoxo, j

p.s. KTEX TV is depending on you

To: Julia Boudreaux <julia@ktextv.com>
From: Katherine Bloom <katherine@ktextv.com>
Subject: I can't believe you are making me do this

Don't sugarcoat it, Julia. You're asking me to be less than professional. You know how hard I have worked to earn respect. But you are one of my dearest friends, not to mention you now own the station, so I will do it. Though rest assured, I will do it with the competent professionalism with which I do everything.

As ever,
Katherine C. Bloom
News Anchor, KTEX TV West Texas

To: Katherine Bloom <katherine@ktextv.com>
From: Julia Boudreaux <julia@ktextv.com>
Subject: Inflexible

Stop being a stick in the mud. This is for your own good and you know it. Competence and respect don't keep you warm at night—or get you a raise. Besides, I have a surprise for you. <g> See you at the station!

xoxo, j

To: Julia Boudreaux <julia@ktextv.com>
From: Katherine Bloom <katherine@ktextv.com>
Subject: Surprise?

What surprise?! You know I don't like surprises. Julia!!!

one

Katherine Bloom told herself she could do this. She just needed to focus and concentrate on getting the job done as quickly and as efficiently as possible.

She refused to think about the fact that she didn't have much experience. Though surely it was no different than riding a bike. Once you'd done it, you never forgot how. And if this was what she had to do to keep her job, so be it.

Nerves tried to break through her raised-chin bravado, and suddenly keeping her incredibly great job as an award-winning newswoman didn't seem all that important. If she hurried, she realized, she could walk out the door and be in Mexico by lunch. She could change her name. Dye her hair. Find employment selling tacos on the street corner in downtown Ciudad Juárez. Didn't everyone need a career change at one time or another?

Groaning at herself, she shook the thought away. During the last week, she had put her reporter's skills to work. She had found magazine articles, online Web sites, and books with titles like *Make It Sizzle* and *Spice Up Your Life*.

Not one to depend on a man to think of every eventuality, she'd had the foresight to purchase a few things she thought they might need.

A bottle of wine.

Some painful-looking utensils. *Who knew things had gotten so creative?*

Condiments.

Honey.

Oil.

Plus, carrots and potatoes.

She still couldn't believe Julia expected her to cook on live television with a man referred to as the Naked Chef.

Kate took a deep calming breath, thought about the stress management techniques she had learned in the company-sponsored stress management course—which she had failed—then smoothed her apron.

Seconds more ticked by before she finally settled on a smile, taking in the pristine white-latticed window behind her, the perfect sink, the shiny oven. Even a real refrigerator. She had thought of everything when planning this kitchen.

Forget the fact that the refrigerator wasn't plugged in, the sunrise in the window was painted, and the walls were fake. Only the stove top actually worked. Regardless, the television set for *Getting Real with Kate* couldn't have looked more authentic if they had shot the segment from the cozy confines of someone's very own home.

However, none of that mattered just then. With only three minutes until airtime, the producer made her heart go still when he spoke into her earpiece.

"Kate, we've got a problem. The chef isn't here yet."

Julia had sworn the cooking segment was going to be Kate's ticket to better ratings. *"We won't have just any old chef for the launch of* Getting Real, *we'll have a sexy naked chef. Women will love it!"*

Kate wasn't so sure.

"What do you mean, he isn't here yet? He has to be here, Pete. I need him here." Her voice tried to rise, panic surging through her. "I can't do a cooking segment without a cook."

Forcibly, Kate reined in her growing concern.

Fact One: She was not a worrier.

Fact Two: If she repeated something to herself often enough eventually it became true—or so they said in stress management. Any minute now she fully expected Fact One to come true.

And most important, as she had pointed out to Julia, Fact Three: She was a competent woman who had risen to the top of her field with hard-hitting news exposés.

Unfortunately, and a very heart-skewering Fact Four: The audience thought she was too prim and too proper. The focus group had used words like *stiff, rigid, inflexible.* One person had gotten creative and called her *doggedly unbendable.* Now there was a description to warm a girl's heart.

Kate refused to give in and cringe with embarrassment. Who would have thought that strangers not liking her could make her feel so bad?

Which brought her to the mind-numbing and utterly terrifying Fact Five: Julia's brainchild of moving Kate off the morning news and putting her on *Getting Real with Kate*—an attempt to show a different side of Katherine Bloom by having her interview and get involved with "something real." This week she was *getting real* in the kitchen, her least favorite room in the house.

For years, her mother had had an on-again, off-again love affair with cooking. Kate had never known if Mary Beth Reynolds, Bloom, Fisher, Radley, Smythe, Lombardi would prepare an extravagant five-course meal or none at all. Kate had learned that it was easier to count on TV dinners and peanut butter sandwiches. Which made her ill-prepared for today's segment without a chef.

When Kate had balked at Julia's plan, she had been taken aside.

"Sugar," Julia had drawled in her thick Louisiana accent, despite the fact that she had lived in Texas since she was seven years old, "I have to tell you. In this day and age of witty banter and anchors acting like family, and now that my daddy has passed on, if you don't let those walls of yours down and show the audience that you know how to have fun, even I'll have trouble convincing the new auditors to keep you employed."

Kate's response that she didn't keep walls around herself had gotten little more than an unladylike snort from the very ladylike Julia.

The station was KTEX TV, founded and formerly operated by Philippe Boudreaux, man of extreme wealth, father of Julia. Up until the day her daddy died, Julia had meddled more than worked at the station, ensuring that her two best friends had been hired straight out of college.

Now the three of them were twenty-seven, with Chloe Sinclair serving as KTEX's ultra organized station manager and Katherine as a news anchor. Julia did her best to be there for anyone who needed her, as long as it didn't entail any actual work. Not that she needed an income.

It was widely reported that Julia, as the only heir of Philippe Boudreaux, was set for life.

With equal measures of resolve and determination, Kate swallowed back panic. With or without a chef, she told herself, she was completely ready. She had memorized the recipe so she could concentrate on asking the whole slew of "light and fun" questions she had prepared, not to mention reel off the spontaneous "witty banter" she had been working on for a week. She'd just have to do the cooking herself, *eek!*, and chat with the camera.

"Two minutes, thirty seconds, and still no naked guy," Pete squawked in her ear. "What are we going to do?"

They both breathed a sigh of relief when they heard Julia's voice as she entered the studio.

"Hello, darlings! Julia is here to save the day."

But saviors and chefs were forgotten when Kate turned around. She would have sat down on the kitchen stool if her knees hadn't fused with shock when it wasn't Julia in her high heels and short skirt whom she saw, but a man whose dominating size and presence blocked out everything else.

"Jesse," she whispered on a rush of breath.

Jesse Chapman, tall, dark, and more handsome than any one man had a right to be.

"Surprise!" Julia called out, the simple word echoing inside the cavernous studio.

Kate took him in, absorbing his height, the brown hair, almost black, that brushed his collar, the dark eyes that traveled the length of her in a way that made her breath catch and her skin tingle. He looked like a cowboy stepping out for the night, his white long-sleeved, button-down shirt tailored perfectly over broad shoulders, narrowing into lean hips and thighs encased in tight, soft Wrangler jeans that cupped his crotch like a lover.

Heat scorched her cheeks when she realized where she was looking. Quickly, she lifted her gaze, reminding herself to breathe.

"Hello, Katie."

He said her name with a deep rumble that skittered down her spine, his smile tilting one corner of his mouth. If she had needed any proof, the fact that he had called her Katie would have been enough to prove that Jesse Chapman stood before her. No one called her Katie. No one but Jesse.

"Aren't you going to welcome me home?" he asked, his smile sliding up at one corner.

Julia hooked her arm through his. "Can you believe it? Our very own Jesse has returned. I couldn't have been more surprised when I came down the driveway this morning and I glanced over and there he was standing at the curb in front of your house, Kate. Just standing. Just looking." She laughed with the same abandon she always did. "Looking like a cover model, I say. Doesn't he look great?"

Saying he looked great was like calling a blistering West Texas summer day warm, but Kate hardly heard. Jesse was here.

She had grown up next door to him since the day she was born. She was four years younger, and her very first memories were of him. It was Jesse who had always reminded her that it wasn't her fault after every one of her mother's five divorces. Jesse who had never made her feel embarrassed when a new "father" moved in. And

Jesse who had let her sleep in his bed after those new fathers inevitably moved out, leaving her mother in despair.

Chloe and Julia had been her best friends, but Jesse had always made her feel like she could survive.

Jesse was famous now. Golfer extraordinaire. More than that, her Jesse had gone wild.

Jesse Chapman had become a notorious ladies' man. His bold teasing grin gracing everything from the covers of popular magazines to weekly sports shows, he was sought out as much for his dark good looks and disreputable reputation as for his golf game. But three weeks ago, all that had changed. Bad boy Jesse Chapman had become a hero.

Pete's voice buzzed in her ear frantically. "Thirty seconds to showtime."

The words barely registered.

"Hello, Jesse," she said softly.

Conversation swirled all around, but Jesse focused on her. His eyes glittered with that famous devil-may-care attitude as he slid his hands into the back pockets of his jeans. He seemed intrigued and surprised, as if he didn't quite recognize who she had become.

The corner of his mouth hitched higher, making her heart do strange things.

"You look . . . different," he announced.

Kate blinked, coming back to reality. "Different?" Not beautiful. Not amazing.

"Different, but great," he added.

He thought she looked great!

Then she kicked herself. She didn't care what he thought. Not anymore. Not since she had seen him at her sister's and his brother's wedding five years ago, when he brought not one voluptuously beautiful date, but two. Suzanne had rolled her eyes at yet another of Jesse's wild escapades; Derek had been tight-lipped and grim. Of course, the number of dates hardly registered with most of the guests in attendance since Jesse hadn't been there all that long. As soon as the bride and groom said *I do,* Jesse had left.

Kate shouldn't have been surprised, or disappointed. Because that was what Jesse did best. He left.

Katherine jerked her attention to the line of carrots and potatoes on the faux countertop of her fake kitchen, to do who knew what without a chef anywhere near. Then Julia laughed the kind of laugh that didn't bode well.

"Oh, my," Julia enthused, "I have the perfect idea!"

"Fifteen seconds!"

"Jesse, you can cook with Kate."

"Me?"

"Him?"

"It will be wonderful, better than a chef," Julia exclaimed, then she clasped her hands together. "Though if you wanted to, you could get naked."

Alarm gasped through Kate, while Jesse's brows slammed together, every inch of his devilishly wicked grin wiped from his too-handsome face.

"Fine, fine, keep your clothes on," Julia conceded with a wicked grin of her own. "You know how our Kate is. I guarantee she knows the recipe like she knows her middle name. It will be fun."

Kate swore she was going to hyperventilate. Where was a brown paper bag when you needed one?

She glanced around, looking for Chloe, who would no doubt take her side. Shy but levelheaded Chloe with her shoulder-length bob and sensible shoes. Saving grace Chloe, Kate's other dearest friend, who would understand that throwing her a curve ball would . . . well, throw her for a curve. But the station manager was nowhere to be seen.

"Julia," Jesse stated tightly, "this isn't a good—"

The stage lights blinked on and Julia leaped off the set. Jesse and Kate froze, staring like deer caught in headlights. It was clear that Jesse didn't want this any more than Kate did. But if Julia was concerned, she didn't show it.

Just as the director came forward and started signaling the count with his fingers, Julia whispered, "Knock 'em dead, sugar. Show the world that deep down you're as fun and sweet as I know you are."

Kate felt conflicting emotions swell in her throat— none of which were helped by the impressively inventive curses Jesse grumbled beneath his breath.

Had she ever been fun?

Growing up with a mother who had been more child than adult, Kate had learned to be responsible, competent. Organized. Her mother had been all about passion and excitement—the very opposite of who Kate had become.

Regardless, she didn't see how anything she was added up to fun. Boring, yes. And, as the audience polls and focus groups had said, *unapproachable*, even *prim*. Why did the world have to change on her and expect something new and different?

Selling tacos in Mexico was sounding better by the second.

"Kate!" Her name was bellowed in her ear. "You're live!"

In that instant, she swallowed back fear, nerves, and memories. She had a show to do.

"Good morning, West Texas," she said to the camera, and smiled. "Today we are going to cook up a storm. Plus, we have a special treat. And I'm not talking about the food! Filling in for the suddenly indisposed Naked Chef is none other than El Paso's very own prodigal son and ladies' man, Jesse Chapman, who is here to show us if he knows how to do more than swing his club."

Kate cringed inwardly at the unintended double entendre. Pete bleated in her ear. Jesse pinned her with a murderous look. And just to the side of the stage, Julia chuckled.

But something else hit her square between the eyes. She had Jesse Chapman here. The man who had saved a woman's life three weeks ago.

How many times had she seen that footage on the television screen? Every national news network, not to mention a whole slew of cable stations, had carried the story. Always the same image of Jesse, his face determined and fierce as he carried the woman to the medic's tent at the Westchester Open.

Afterward, he had been quiet and humble about his heroics. Clearly the man was happy to talk about dating women, but wasn't interested in talking about saving them.

She could get him to talk about it. She would get him to share his feelings right here on *Getting Real with Kate*.

The newswoman surged inside her like a welcome friend. Panic and nervousness fled completely. She was in her element.

But she was supposed to be sweet. Kind. Fun.

Get the story? Audience approval?

The two thoughts did battle inside her head until she settled on a compromise. She'd start slow and easy, then work up to his feelings.

She smiled and asked as sweetly and as kindly as she could, "Jesse, tell us. Where have you been these last three weeks since you became a national hero?"

Jesse gave her a look that would have slayed a lesser newswoman. But that wasn't what gave her pause. It was Julia's breath hissing through the studio, followed by Pete's choking bark in her ear, "You're supposed to be cooking! Not grilling the guest."

A mental tug of war ensued. Old habits died hard and she itched to get him to say something, anything, about what had happened. But she wouldn't have a job if she messed up this assignment.

Smiling over gritted teeth, she said, "I hope you've been cooking because we are going to whip up a fabulous meal!"

Telling herself she wasn't really a wimp, she picked up a knife, deciding she'd have to do the cutting and chopping herself. But when she tried to chat and chop at the same time, she only managed to launch the front half of a carrot off the counter like a rocket. It skittered to a stop at the cameraman's black leather boot.

"Oh." She grimaced and the panic started to resurface. "Oh," she repeated, her brain stuck like a scratched record.

Jesse looked at her for one more long second before he muttered something that she swore wasn't favorable. Then he tugged the knife away with a harnessed power that she felt rippling through his forearms like an electric current.

"I'll chop, you stir," he instructed.

Her brain unlocked. She should have been relieved, but with him standing there, so competent, so in charge, while she couldn't even chop a carrot much less do her job as she wanted to, she couldn't help herself. "I know how to cook," she stated, then nervously snatched up a tomato.

He surprised her when he caught her wrist, holding her there before she could turn away. He looked at her, really looked this time, and she was sure that he saw her panic.

His expression shifted, and he seemed to sigh. After a second, he raked his dark hair back from his forehead and his slow, sweet-gin smile returned. "You, cook? I think you've forgotten who you're talking to."

That's all he said, just that, imperceptible to the audience, but all too clear to her. He had seen all those times she had tried to put food on the table when her mother hadn't.

As if the camera wasn't there, he reached out and tucked a single strand of her long curly hair behind her ear. He was tall and broad, making her feel cherished and safe. "As long as I've known you," he said only for her, "you've never been a quitter. You can make this work."

Kate couldn't believe it when her throat tightened over a foolishly poignant surge of gratitude. This was the Jesse she knew. The Jesse who didn't flaunt his bad behavior or take pride in how many notches he added to his bedpost.

But every ounce of appreciation fled a second later when he abruptly backed away from her, as if he didn't want her gratitude. He stared at her for a second before he seemed to forcefully smile his famous four-color-magazine smile. "Careful, darlin' " he added, his Texas drawl put on like a costume. "You can't be manhandling things."

She bristled, and only realized how tightly she was gripping the poor tomato when he had to pry it away from her.

"You can't toss them around or rough them up." He palmed the lush, round weight like a lover. "You have to hold them"—he ran his thumb over the tender skin in a way that made sensation hum through her body—"and take them gently."

Her mouth fell open. She choked, then hastily shuffled through her index cards of witty repartee. There was no comeback for taken, tossed, or manhandled.

She must have looked as embarrassed as she felt, because his lips quirked and he added, "We're talking about tomatoes, sweet thing." Then he winked at the camera.

Embarrassment turned to mortification. But she was given no opportunity to respond, not that she had a clue what to say, when Pete hissed in her ear that she better get the damned chicken in the pot if they planned to finish the recipe before the six o'clock news.

With a little jump, she picked up a piece of fowl, which thankfully had come cut. She handed a portion to Jesse.

"Could you heat the meat?"

Jesse raised an amused brow.

Her heart went still. "I mean, put the meat in the heat . . . no, rather, put the chicken in the fryer." God, she was pathetic. All he had to do was stand next to her and she turned into a bumbling schoolgirl. She'd never been much for violence, but she easily could have murdered him right there on live TV.

Fortunately, all he did was chuckle. He took the bird, set it in the hot oil, then reached across her, so close, so completely unaffected.

Jesse grinned easily, managing to look both competent and manly as he arranged the chicken. "You know the saying, don't you, Katie? The quickest way to a man's heart—"

"Is through his chest with a sharp object?" she shot back.

Jesse threw back his head and laughed, the sound rumbling through the high-ceilinged space. "Looks like my sweet Katie still doesn't put up with any cr—" He glanced at the camera, the entire crew holding their breath for fear he was on the verge of saying something very unmorning TV-ish—then said, "Crud from anyone."

Kate was certain that every viewer within a hundred miles could hear the relieved sigh that hissed through the studio.

If Jesse noticed, he didn't let on. He wiped his hand on a wet towel. Though any relief she felt quickly fled when he came up behind her, put his arms around her body, and said, "Let me show you how it's done."

Heat scorched her cheeks, heat that had nothing to do with the burner that was turned to high. His hands ran down her arms, that harnessed power controlled but there, before he gently put the knife into her palm. "Don't get any ideas now about heading for my heart," he said.

Kate could feel the collective amazement that rippled through KTEX TV at Jesse's smooth charm.

Then they began to chop.

"Have I told you how impressed I was with your interview of George W. last time he came through town?"

She glanced back at him, hardly registering the compliment. "When were you here?"

He chuckled and gave her a that's-not-the-point look. Though he answered with a "Have you missed me, Katie?"

Instantly she tensed. "I most certainly have not."

Pete howled in her ear, "Quit making moon eyes at that cowboy and wrap up the damned dish!"

She swore Jesse must have heard Pete, because the next thing she knew, Jesse tugged the recipe card away from her and got to work. He finished cutting, chopping and chatting like a pro. He even saw her list of witty repartee, and after little more than a raised eyebrow, he offered her the lead-ins so she could look like she was fun and funny, which had been her hope.

When they finally got to the end, if she hadn't been so unsettled by him, she would have thrown her arms around his neck and thanked him for saving her.

With just fifteen seconds to go, she turned to Jesse. "Thank you for joining me."

Jesse tipped an imaginary Stetson, then took her hand and kissed the back. "The pleasure was all mine," he said with that famous smile of his. It took her a moment to recover.

With a squeak, she turned to the camera and just about died, knowing that her cheeks had to be bright red. Her, the awarding-winning, hard-hitting newswoman, blushing like a teenager. "I hope you'll join us next week when I head out to Tumbleweed Trails for a chat with a rodeo superstar."

The light on top of the camera went off, bringing the segment to an end.

Julia rushed up. "You kids were great! Just perfect. Kate, that whole sweet innocent schoolgirl embarrassment thing was inspired! And Jesse, you devil. How about a full-time job? Just think what we could do with the two of you."

Every ounce of Jesse's good cheer evaporated, his jaw going tight. "No thanks, Jules. And I sure as hell don't appreciate you putting me on the spot like that. I came back here to get away from the press."

Julia patted his arm. "Did you? Then do you plan to hide away in a hotel room while you're here?"

He shrugged. "I was planning to stay with Derek and Suzanne, but that didn't pan out. I'm not sure yet where I'm going to stay."

"Ahhhh!" Julia exclaimed. "Say no more! I have the perfect idea to get you out of the limelight," she added, her voice as smooth as a glass of bourbon and honey warmed between two hands. "I know Kate won't mind."

Long years of experience with this woman warned Kate that Julia was up to something. Every remnant of heat and wonder, excitement and triumph, fled. Her eyes narrowed. "What won't I mind, Julia?"

"Well, sugar, the perfect solution is for Jesse to stay in the guesthouse."

Katherine went still, staring at her best friend, her heart doing a very different sort of staccato dance. "You don't have a guesthouse, Julia," she said carefully.

"I know that, sweetie. But you do. The cottage behind your house."

Kate told herself she had misunderstood. Jesse couldn't stay in the cottage—she didn't want him anywhere close to her. He had an amazingly unerring habit of disrupting her life. And just now the last thing she needed was something else to jar her world out of its carefully managed orbit. "What are you talking about?"

"Jesse should stay with you."

Not the answer she wanted. "At my house?"

"In your guesthouse."

Jesse planted his hands on the fake countertop. "Listen, Jules—"

"Jesse, you're family," Julia interjected with a pointed scowl at Kate. "Isn't he, sugar?"

Kate glanced from Julia to Jesse, from her best friend's censorious violet-eyed glare to what she would have sworn was Jesse's surprisingly vulnerable dark gaze—both of which made it impossible to do anything else but smile as best as she could.

Damn, damn, damn.

"Of course," she managed feebly. "You're welcome to stay in the cottage."

"Good. Then everything's settled." Julia took his arm. "Jesse stays with Kate."

To: Julia Boudreaux <<u>julia@ktextv.com</u>>
From: Chloe Sinclair <<u>chloe@ktextv.com</u>>
Subject: Kate's scream

What did you do to Kate to make her scream like that? Granted,
it was behind her closed door, but you know my ears. I hear
everything. Unfortunately I was right in the middle of my
quarterly conference call with the auditors, trying to explain our
low ratings. Otherwise I would have come running. And now
everyone's gone. Regardless, I won't forgive you, Jules, if you
have done something to Kate.

Chloe

Chloe Sinclair
Station Manager
Award-winning KTEX TV

To: Chloe Sinclair <<u>chloe@ktextv.com</u>>
From: Julia Boudreaux <<u>julia@ktextv.com</u>>
Subject: Wrongly accused

Why do you assume I did something? If you heard screaming,
I'm sure it was a scream of joy. And don't worry about the
auditors. I'll smooth over last quarter's numbers.

I'm working from home if you need me.

xo, j

To: Chloe Sinclair <chloe@ktextv.com>
From: Katherine Bloom <katherine@ktextv.com>
Subject: Your friend

Just so you know, I am not speaking to Julia. She has meddled
in my life one too many times.

K

p.s. I just got home from a great interview with a possible
Getting Real subject: a border patrol agent who works the night
shift patrolling the river. He has to deal with drug runners, illegal
aliens, people dropping dead. Fascinating stuff.

Katherine C. Bloom
News Anchor, KTEX TV West Texas

To: Katherine Bloom <katherine@ktextv.com>
From: Chloe Sinclair <chloe@ktextv.com>
Subject: What now?

Does your not speaking to Julia have something to do with your
scream?

As to your border patrol guy, you know how J is with this new
concept of hers. If the guy isn't interested in talking about
something other than hard news, don't even bother. Though
maybe if he's *drop dead* gorgeous, you could get him to talk
about his trials and tribulations with his shirt off. <g> That might
make it past her.

Chloe

To: Chloe Sinclair <chloe@ktextv.com>
From: Katherine Bloom <katherine@ktextv.com>
Subject: I never screamed

There was no screaming. Strangling, almost. But justifiably, since
Julia told Jesse Chapman he could stay at my house. Jesse! At
my house! I can't do this. You should see him. He looks great.
Adonis great. Seven Wonders of the World great. But I don't want
him looking great in my backyard!

K, who has some integrity left and will not ask any man of the
law to take off his shirt

To: Katherine Bloom <katherine@ktextv.com>
From: Chloe Sinclair <chloe@ktextv.com>
Subject: No!

Jesse is back in town?? Where is he? Why didn't anyone tell
me?!

To: Chloe Sinclair <chloe@ktextv.com>
From: Katherine Bloom <katherine@ktextv.com>
Subject: Excuse me!

I repeat, I can't possibly have Jesse living in my backyard. Do I need to remind you that we are talking about the man who has accumulated female conquests like golf trophies? Meadowlark Drive is a quiet, respectable neighborhood. Do you want him to turn my house into the Playboy Mansion? Okay, maybe the Playboy mansionette, but still, I really can't have him here.

K

To: Katherine Bloom <katherine@ktextv.com>
    Chloe Sinclair <chloe@ktextv.com>
From: Julia Boudreaux <julia@ktextv.com>
Subject: The only solution

Kate, Chloe has just filled me in. And I must say, where else could Jesse possibly stay? A hotel is out. He's family, for God's sake. His brother married your sister, though we all know that the real reason he can't stay with Suzanne and Derek is because they're in the middle of doing who knows what in their desperate attempt to get pregnant. (Did I tell you about the tiff I overheard them have regarding dirty magazines, closed doors, and Dixie cups?)

As to *my* house, I have more than enough men in my life to juggle as it is. And while Chloe darling hasn't dated anyone recently (recently being kinder than me saying Not in RECENT history), we are working on that. Having Jesse underfoot might give some nice young man the wrong impression. Which leaves

you, Kate dear. Even if you would finally give in and commit to
the divinely wonderful Parker Hammond, he has known Jesse
forever and will understand. So it's done. Jesse stays in the
guest cottage. And you better be nice. Besides, you seem to
have forgotten that Jesse isn't just a bad boy anymore. He's our
very own hero.

xo, j

p.s. That was fabulous TV this morning. Ratings went through
the roof. Who knew that our little Kate had it in her to heat up the
screen. Brava! Let's meet at Bobby's Place on Friday to
celebrate!

two

Kate crossed her ankles as she sat on the high stool at the girls' favorite hangout, Bobby's Place. Two days of trying to pretend that she was unaffected by the reality of having Jesse firmly installed in the cottage behind her house had taken its toll.

How could it be so hard to *not* pay attention to someone?

Of course, truth to tell, she hadn't had to work all that hard to ignore him. He had been gone more than he'd been there, his black Jeep rarely parked in the drive, his lights seldom on, at least until he would come in late, when the rest of the normal, not-wild population was sound asleep. Though she was almost certain he hadn't brought a single woman home. Both nights he had returned, gotten something out of his car, then gone for a walk.

Not that she was keeping track. Really. The first night she'd been up drinking tea when he arrived. Then last night, she'd been preparing for her rodeo cowboy while indulging in a Fiddle Faddle fest and 99-cent-special video marathon. What better way to keep Jesse Chapman out of her head than by consuming massive amounts of caramel corn and watching an entire season of *Sex and the City* in twenty-four hours?

Her stomach roiled at the memory, and she had the altogether foreign desire to go shopping for shoes—preferably high heeled and strappy.

Tonight, after leaving work, she had headed for Bobby's Place to meet Julia and Chloe. She was the first one to arrive, and she sat at the bar. She could see the door in the hazy mirrors on the four-sided backsplash. The giant Tiffany chandelier overhead cast the room in a golden light, while the sweet sounds of George Strait filled the place, wrapping around the dancers who swished and swirled by in a smooth-as-silk Texas two-step.

"I can't stay long," Julia announced as soon as she got there, her charm bracelet jangling against the bar when she sat down. "I have a date."

Chloe came in right behind her, hopping up onto a stool, looking like a little girl in a soda shop with her shoulder-length dark hair, china doll bangs, big blue eyes circled by long lashes, and a sprinkling of freckles across the bridge of her nose. "Who are you going out with tonight?"

"Roberto." Julia rolled the *r* dramatically.

"Never heard you talk about any Robertos."

"He's new."

Julia ordered a glass of wine, Chloe a strawberry daiquiri. Kate asked for the *Sex and the City* drink of choice—a cosmo. Chloe and Julia looked at Kate in surprise.

"A cosmo?" Julia asked.

"Let's just call it research."

Suddenly all three had cosmos sitting in front of them.

"To research," they said, clinking their drinks.

They were silent for a second, each lost in her thoughts. Though there was no question all of them were thinking about the same thing—or the same man.

Chloe said, "I can't believe Jesse's back. He looks great."

"Yeah, he looks great," Kate agreed.

"He always looks great." Julia stirred her drink. "I remember the first time I realized how good-looking he was. It was that day with the horrible storm. You were up in the tree house that used to be in your backyard. He went charging up there to get you down."

Kate groaned. "I don't want to talk about the tree house."

"You mean, you don't want to talk about the place where you declared your undying love," Julia teased.

"To Jesse," Chloe clarified.

"Just before he left for college," Julia added.

"Thanks for the reminder," Kate stated crisply.

"Sorry," Julia said with a smile, and she squeezed Kate's hand. "It's just too cute to remember you up in that tree demanding that Jesse wait for you to grow up."

"The fact that he didn't wait makes the memory a whole lot less cute in my book," Kate noted.

"Thank God, he didn't wait," Chloe added. "I mean, really. I adore Jesse as much as the next girl, but we all know he's trouble."

No sooner did Julia finish her drink than she glanced at her watch and said, "Look at the time. I've got to run. Roberto will be waiting."

She was out the door in a whiff of perfume and scads of long black-lacquer hair.

"We should go, too," Kate said.

"Let me run to the restroom first."

Kate pulled a lip gloss from her purse while she waited, but paused mid-swipe when Jesse walked through the door.

"Jesse!" several people cheered.

The minute she saw him her heart leaped, every inch of her skin tingling with awareness. Without turning around, she watched him in the hazy mirrors. He was beautiful in a ruggedly sensual sort of way. He wore a starched blue button-down shirt tonight, tucked into the Wrangler jeans that fit him like a second skin, molding to his strong thighs. His dark hair shimmered in the light, his smile broad and easy as he greeted the crowd.

Determined not to fall prey to Jesse's orbital pull, she picked up her drink for one last sip. But before she could get the rim to her lips, her eyes caught Jesse's in the mirror.

She saw his expression change. At first he looked confused to find her here, in a bar. Then, with their gazes locked in the mirror, he ambled straight toward her, his cocky athlete's body both graceful and filled with power at the same time, his sensual lips pulling up at one corner in a wry grin.

She gripped her drink nervously as the crush of people parted to let him through. He stopped just behind the bar stool and studied her reflection. She couldn't bring herself to look away.

Slowly, he turned her around on the swivel stool until she faced him, her head tilting back. Without a word he tugged the long-stemmed glass from her fingers and set it aside, then he took her hand and pulled her onto the dance floor.

It was like she couldn't do anything else. She stepped into his embrace—one arm hooking over her shoulders, the other extended as he held her hand—and she slipped her fingers through his back belt loop. It was the Texans' way of dancing. But the charge between them was universal, instant, and electric as she looked up into his eyes.

The slow sweet sounds of an old Garth Brooks ballad wrapped around them as he guided her along, a sprinkling of sawdust making the sound of leather-soled boots sliding over hardwood swish just below the music. With every turn they took, his thigh slipped between her own in a way that would have been considered foreplay in any other state.

"Hello, Katie," he said finally, his lips against her temple.

"Hello, Jesse."

The feel of his arm around her, of her hand gripped in his strong palm, was heady, quickening her blood like an extra sip of a cosmo.

"You've been busy the last couple of days," he said, easy amusement lacing his deep voice. "Working late."

"What do you mean?"

"Last night your light was on until two in the morning."

She told herself not to care that he noticed. "A morning television host's work is never done."

The corner of his mouth crooked devilishly as if he didn't believe a word of it just as the music came to an end. She started away but he didn't let her go. "One more."

"But Chloe—"

"Chloe's talking to Lacey and Bobby McIntyre. She's fine."

He turned her around, then guided her in a fast-paced, three-step country waltz.

Despite herself, all reservations and careful behavior fled completely. Before long she even laughed. Leave it to a man like Jesse to make a woman forget everything but his charm.

"Now see, that's not so hard," he said with a grin.

"What? Dancing?"

"No, smiling."

"I smile."

"Not very often anymore as far as I can tell."

"What do you know about how often I smile—"

He spun her out, twirling her around once, twice, a third time as they continued with the flow of dancers in a wide arcing circle, before he reeled her back, all in perfect time with the beat.

"—since you haven't been in town more than a few days."

"I've known you for as long as I can remember," he whispered gruffly.

"But haven't been around long enough in the last thirteen years to know if I smile or not."

"Let's just say it's a sixth sense I have."

"Knowing if a person smiles?"

"Knowing when a woman's unhappy."

"Certain women," she shot back. "Maybe. And then only because you're responsible for making them that way."

He actually missed a step. Then his eyes glittered appreciatively before he laughed loud and strong. Women turned to look, their gazes wistful.

With every turn and touch, Kate forgot about ratings

and viewer polls. Whether it was the music, the drink, or too much Fiddle Faddle and videos, she forgot.

"I thought your cooking show turned out all right."

She laughed again. "You have a bad habit of coming to my rescue."

"You have a bad habit of needing to be rescued."

"That's not true!"

"You just said it yourself." His eyes gleamed as he glanced down at her. "Remember the time you were in fifth grade, surrounded by those sixth-grade boys?"

"Hey, Billy Weeks said I threw like a girl."

"You are a girl."

"But I never threw like one. And I would have proven it if you hadn't interrupted."

"You were about to punch him in the nose. He would have punched you right back. Weeks wasn't opposed to hitting girls."

Kate sniffed, disgruntled, knowing he was right.

Jesse warmed to his topic. "That reminds me of another time I saved your ass. The day in the tree house."

Her mouth fell open in disbelieving astonishment. "You didn't save me. On top of which, I'm really tired of your *I-saved-you* theme."

"Funny, I kind of like it. And technically, I think that would be the I-saved-you-*repeatedly* theme." His dark eyes sparkled. "Plus, it's hard to forget you up in the tree, a storm to beat all storms whipping every plank and piece of plywood free. I came up there when no one else could get you to come down. Not Julia, not Chloe, not your sister."

Kate might have been able to explain away the other incidents, but as much as she denied that day to Julia and to Chloe and wanted to deny it to Jesse, the truth was he had come up into that tree. The wind had been blowing, prying boards away one by one, just as he said, lightning cracking open the sky. When all the other kids had given up on her and fled, it was Jesse who climbed up next to her, not caring how the place groaned beneath the growing storm. They had both looked out through the leaves, beyond their yards, the rain starting up, whipping at their faces.

Thankfully he refrained from mentioning the rest of the episode, where she had turned to look at him, then asked why he had gotten so upset the night before when she had slipped into his bed. She had gotten in bed with him dozens of times, but it had been the first time he had seemed big and grown up, so much older than she felt at fourteen. She had felt his strong body against hers, the strange planes and angles she'd never noticed before.

She had touched him and his whole body had gone still.

She realized now that at fourteen she should have known better. But she hadn't. With innocent wonder, she had traced the hair along his chest, following it down his body until suddenly he groaned, grabbing her hand. Setting her away from him, he had quickly rolled off the other side of the bed and slammed out the door.

It was like she had grown up overnight.

The next day, sitting in that tree, she had been confused and upset, and when he came up to get her, all she knew was that she wanted more of that touch. She had wanted more of him. And she had told him so, adding, "I love you, Jesse."

She had startled him—she had seen the surprise on his face as the wind and rain pelted them. Then finally he had smiled softly, gently.

"I love you, too, Katie, but I don't love you like that. Besides, I'd only hurt you. It's my job to protect you from guys like me."

"I don't want you to protect me. I want you to love me. You and me, we're meant to be together."

He had squeezed her hand, though he was careful to keep a distance between them they'd never had before, then he pulled her down from the tree. He had left for college the next morning and never returned for any length of time, proving her wrong.

Now he was back, holding her close as they danced, the feel of his hard body as thrilling as it had been that night she slipped into his bed. But what, she wondered, did she want to do about it?

Better sense told her to steer clear of this man. But all of a sudden, she was tired of better sense.

Excitement and determination ticked to life at the realization of just what she planned to do.

An hour and a half later, Jesse rolled down the long drive to the back of the house. As soon as he braked and put the Jeep in gear, Gwen Randolph leaned across the console and kissed him.

"Mmmm," the blonde murmured. "I've missed you. I hope you're not angry that I followed you to Texas."

"I haven't been here a week."

"A single day is a long time away from you. Besides, what was I to do when you weren't answering your messages? I called your dad and he didn't have a clue where you were. You haven't even returned Hal's calls, you naughty boy. I can't believe you're avoiding me, your father, and your golf coach when you have the PGA coming up. I have all sorts of media scheduled for you. Everyone is dying to talk to you about your heroics. I decided it was only good business to fly out here and tell you myself."

Hell, who would have known that being a hero would be so hard?

The fact was, he wasn't a hero. He had done what he had to do. When the woman collapsed in front of him, he had revived her instead of standing there and watching her die. Hard to think of that as heroic—just necessary. And the last thing he wanted was to talk about it. Which was exactly why he had driven halfway across the country and was avoiding his publicist's calls.

"Gwen, I've already said I'm not interested in interviews right now."

He pressed back against the leather seat, and she must have sensed that she had overstepped her boundaries. She cooed and stroked his jaw. "I'm sorry, baby. Let Gwen make it better."

Leaning closer, she put one delicate finger on his chin and turned him toward her. The long French-manicured nail trailed low as she kissed him with an expertise that was matched only by her ability to get his photograph in every major print publication in the United States and Europe. Gwen Randolph had single-handedly turned Jesse from an up-and-coming golfer in a sport that wasn't all that popular, to a media star. And it was that status that had gotten the top agents in the country interested in representing him. This despite the fact that while he had won plenty of tournaments, he had never brought home a single one of the majors' trophies.

So he owed Gwen. He knew it. But more and more, the casual affair they had started had become less and less casual, and he wasn't interested in being serious with any woman.

He started to set Gwen back, but before he could, her hand slid down his chest and then lower until she cupped him. Instantly, he hardened, his breath sucked in.

"See, Gwen knows how to make her Jesse happy."

His body came to life, and the fact was he didn't want to think tonight, not about golf or the mounting pressure for him to win the PGA Championship.

Which is why he gave in when Gwen's hand slid expertly against him. "Let's go inside," he stated gruffly.

Helping her out of the SUV, he led her into the cottage. At the door, she kissed him again—hot and wet, intense—making it easy to lose himself to the feel. But when they pushed inside, instantly the hairs on the nape of his neck rose.

Gwen glanced around, taking in the small space. "How quaint," she said, her voice filled with invitation.

He didn't respond. His eyes narrowed. But then Gwen kissed him one more time, her hands going to just the right places.

"Where can I change?"

He pointed to the bathroom door that stood adjacent to the bedroom. She took her small overnight suitcase, blew him a kiss, then disappeared.

The light burned low in the tiny galley kitchen. The ruffled drapes were pulled closed over the window. He didn't remember leaving the light on or closing the curtains. And just when his mind assimilated the small pot of tea and two cups sitting on the table, someone said, "Surprise."

Jesse whirled around and found Katie standing in the bedroom doorway. She wore a pair of shorts and a

T-shirt, her dark curls pulled up in a ponytail. Her pearl white teeth sank nervously into her lower lip, and she held a photo album close to her chest. She looked beautiful in an ethereal way.

Katie. Little Katie Bloom.

Time seemed to stand still, his thoughts momentarily frozen by the sight of her.

"I brought you some tea," she said, a wry, nervous smile tugging at her full lips. "And I pulled out some old pictures that I keep stored in the chest by the bed in there. I haven't looked at them in ages. I thought it might be fun."

The world faded away as he stared at her, his gaze traveling along her body, taking her in. Even wearing shorts and a T-shirt she looked amazing and wonderful—innocent and pure—everything that he wasn't. Everything a woman like Gwen was not.

Gwen.

Hell.

Katie's lips parted and she walked toward him. She opened the album and extended it. But just when she started to point out a picture of him dressed as Superman when he was nine, he snapped the book shut. "You've got to go."

"Go? But I thought we could talk and look at photos . . . maybe even dance one more dance."

"You and me?"

"Well." Embarrassment seared through her. "I just thought . . . at Bobby's Place . . ."

"Hell."

But then something clattered beyond the closed bathroom door. Kate stood very still as she tried to understand the expression on Jesse's face, not to mention the noise coming from the bathroom. "What was that?"

"Really, Katie," he said with determined command, "you need to leave."

She was barely aware of Jesse taking her arm. But before he could escort her to the door, a woman appeared.

"Tada! What do you think?"

Kate's mind ground to a jarring, stomach-churning halt. She staggered back a few steps and would have staggered farther if Jesse hadn't been holding her arm. A woman she had never seen before stood in the doorway, the light behind her making it clear that underneath the sheer excuse for a nightgown she wasn't wearing a thing.

The woman was all but naked!

Kate gasped.

"Who are you?" the women demanded in unison. Then they turned to the only man in the room.

He dropped Kate's arm and gave a world-weary sigh. "Katie, this is Gwen, my publicist. Gwen, this is Katie, my . . . ah, host?"

"Jesse, how could you?" both women demanded.

"Me?" he asked, practically choking on the word. "I didn't invite either one of you here. I was minding my own business, then you"—he pointed at Kate—"show up and want to serve me tea."

Kate's mouth dropped open. Gwen smirked.

Jesse focused on the publicist. "While you fly into town without so much as a word to me and want to serve me . . . yourself."

This time it was Gwen's mouth that dropped open.

Kate was mortified, though mostly because she wondered how she could have thought that a cup of hot tea and a walk down memory lane would in any way compare to the naked likes of women such as this . . . this . . . other woman.

She had offered him tea!

Kate wondered dismally if she could be any more of an embarrassment to the female race.

Turning on her flowered Keds, she started to leave.

"Ah, hell." Jesse plowed his hands through his hair. "I had no right to say that to either one of you."

She kept going.

"Katie, wait. I'm sorry. Bringing tea was very . . . thoughtful. I didn't mean—"

Thankfully, he cut himself off. She didn't need him adding anything else to the already insultingly embarrassing situation. She was thoughtful, not sexy. Sweet, not enticing.

She made it to the door without a word, since there was nothing to say other than to ask him when he was leaving El Paso. Preferably sooner rather than later, and if he needed assistance packing, she'd happily help.

Clutching the photo album to her chest like a shield, she left the cottage with as much dignity as she could muster. Then she headed into the dark, crossed the yard, and had to force herself past the swimming pool without throwing herself in.

To: Katherine Bloom <katherine@ktextv.com>
    Chloe Sinclair <chloe@ktextv.com>
From: Julia Boudreaux <julia@ktextv.com>
Subject: Truth to tell

Good Saturday morning, girls. So, Kate, is it true that Jesse showed up at Bobby's Place after I left? Did you really dance with him?

xo, j

To: Julia Boudreaux <julia@ktextv.com>
    Katherine Bloom <katherine@ktextv.com>
From: Chloe Sinclair <chloe@ktextv.com>
Subject: Urban cowgirl

She danced with him. Twice. Fortunately that's all she did.
Chloe

p.s. Since I am at the office, and I can see neither of you are here, I'm glad to know that providing home access to the office e-mail system isn't going to waste.

To: Chloe Sinclair <chloe@ktextv.com>
    Julia Boudreaux <julia@ktextv.com>
From: Katherine Bloom <katherine@ktextv.com>
Subject: Technicality

Does trying to seduce him count as *doing more*?
Dismally yours,
Kate

Katherine C. Bloom
News Anchor, KTEX TV West Texas

To: Katherine Bloom <katherine@ktextv.com>
    Chloe Sinclair <chloe@ktextv.com>
From: Julia Boudreaux <julia@ktextv.com>
Subject: Good Lord

What have you done now? You seduced him? How? Were
you naked in his bed? Naked in the shower? Naked with
flowers? Regardless, any sort of seduction with that man is
a mistake.

xo, j

To: Katherine Bloom <katherine@ktextv.com>
   Julia Boudreaux <julia@ktextv.com>
From: Chloe Sinclair <chloe@ktextv.com>
Subject: No!

Kate, tell us you're joking. Seducing Jesse will only get you hurt in the process.

To: Julia Boudreaux <julia@ktextv.com>
   Chloe Sinclair <chloe@ktextv.com>
From: Katherine Bloom <katherine@ktextv.com>
Subject: Unfortunate incident

Let's just say that I experienced a moment of sheer insanity, brought on, I have to believe, by a *Sex and the City* video marathon combined with too many cosmos. Okay, so I had only one—not even a whole one. But still. I thought I would surprise him with tea and photos. I wasn't thinking seduce in the traditional sense. I was thinking seduce him with the past. I know, I know, I really shouldn't think.
Kate

To: Katherine Bloom <katherine@ktextv.com>
    Chloe Sinclair <chloe@ktextv.com>
From: Julia Boudreaux <julia@ktextv.com>
Subject: Sex 101

Clearly you haven't a clue how to seduce a man. Though if
you are going to learn, promise me that you will not practice
on Jesse.

xo, j

p.s. Love you anyway, sweetie.

three

Jesse woke up on Sunday morning, and it took him a second to remember where he was. At Katie's. In El Paso.

It felt good to be home.

Gwen was gone, sent back to Florida on the first plane out yesterday morning. After Katie left the cottage, Gwen had seemed determined to make him forget everyone but her. Though each time she had kissed him, he had thought of Katie with her tea and photos, and Katie sitting in Bobby's Place looking sexy as hell. Both images unsettled him.

No question that *Katie* and *sexy as hell* didn't belong together—at least they didn't belong together in his mind.

When he had walked into Bobby's, he had seen her instantly. He still couldn't believe his reaction, hot and intense. He had wanted to get closer. Wanted to inhale her fragrance, run his fingers over the curve of her breast.

It had been the same during the television segment.

She had been such a surprise, a mix of sultry and innocent, those sexy lips of hers parting on an exhaled breath
when he had brushed his finger over the tomato. It had
taken a second for him to regain his control. He had
been glad as hell when the producer had screamed loud
enough in her earpiece that he heard.

From his first memory of Katie, it was as if they were
bound together. When they were young, Katie would
sneak into his bed when she was afraid or when her
mother was in a particularly bad spot—any of those
times she felt her world would crumble.

"You're my hero," she always whispered as she fell
asleep at his side.

He had grown up feeling the need to protect her, to
keep her safe from people who might hurt her. But when
he was eighteen, the year she turned fourteen, all of that
had changed—*she* had changed, leaving her pudgy little
girl's body behind.

By then he already knew more about sex than he
should have—a line of older women had been eager to
teach him all they thought he should know. And when
suddenly he saw little Katie as sexy, he had wanted to
touch her as those women had touched him.

But old habits of needing to protect Katie had deep
roots. Staying away from her had truly been the only
heroic thing he had done in his life, because he knew,
as well as he knew his own name, that ultimately, eventually, if he gave in and touched her, he would hurt her.
He wasn't the sort of man to settle down with a single
woman. He lived on the edge, and he liked it that way.
But Katie deserved more than a casual affair.

Since then, he had made a point of keeping her at arm's
length. He stayed away, had stayed away for years, only

coming back now because he needed distance from the press.

As much as he didn't want to be around Katie, who was playing havoc with his mind, he also didn't want to stay in a hotel where people stared and wanted autographs. Coming to his childhood home had seemed like a good idea. But he had forgotten that *home* wasn't his anymore now that Derek had married Suzanne. When Julia had suggested the guest cottage, it had seemed the best solution. Besides, he didn't intend to stay that long. A few more days, maybe a week, then he was out of here—his head cleared and ready to play.

Rolling out from underneath the flowery guesthouse comforter, so different from the king-sized bed and tailored bedcoverings he had in his Florida condo, he walked naked across the room. He pulled on a pair of shorts, then went to the tiny kitchen and made the worst cup of coffee he'd ever tasted. But at least it was hot.

The weather was beautiful when he walked outside into the early morning painter's sky. It wasn't until he stretched, his hand running down his bare chest, that he saw Katie standing just beyond the cottage, her hair wild, dirt smudging her face. She stood frozen, staring at him, her eyes wide, as she held a bucket of gardening tools in her hand.

Kate tried to get her brain to function, with little success.

He was gorgeous.

Like a god.

Better than Adonis.

Despite every good intention, despite the fact that she had learned firsthand that he was a ladies' man of the worst kind—*more than once!*—her gaze drifted low over his sculpted chest, following the thin path of hair that disappeared beneath the waistband of his shorts. She imagined where the path led.

Bad Kate.

A strange squeak sounded in her throat, and she nearly dropped her bucket of tools.

He took another sip of his coffee before a smile cracked his face. "Morning, sweetheart."

She raised a brow. "I believe *sweetheart* belongs to the woman from the other night. Your publicist. Gwen. Glad to know you don't mind mixing business with pleasure."

Jesse chuckled, a rumbling sound of easy confidence.

"What's the point of working if you can't have fun while you're at it?" He winked.

She reached down and grabbed a second bucket filled with potting soil. "I've got to go," she said with a shake of her head, then started for the workroom.

But Jesse stopped her. His hand on her arm startled her and her breath caught. He stared at her, yet again seeming confused by what he saw.

"What?" she asked self-consciously.

He studied her, and after a second he smiled, though all he said was, "Let me help you with the buckets."

She raised her chin. "I don't need your help."

He laughed out loud as he set his cup on the window ledge. "I don't doubt it." He took the buckets anyway.

She watched him as he headed for her back door, watched the way he moved with the sleek grace of an athlete. She was staring so intently, so mesmerized— damn it—that she was surprised when someone called out from the back gate.

"There you are!"

She whirled to find Parker Hammond.

"Parker!" she yelped, guilt ticking through her at her errant thoughts. "What are you doing here?"

The man answered with a confident smile as he pushed through the gate. "Good morning to you, too."

He held a large bouquet of light pink peonies and white roses. Seeing him standing in the sunshine, Kate couldn't deny how handsome he was, though a complete contrast to Jesse. Parker was everything light, with his sandy blond hair and green eyes, while Jesse was dark and brooding, sensuality seeping through him. The boy next door versus the boy who was every parent's nightmare.

When Parker saw Jesse, he blinked in surprise before his smile returned.

"I heard you were on Kate's show," Parker said with good humor as he came forward to shake Jesse's hand. "I wish I hadn't missed it. But it's great to see you now."

"It's great to see you, too, but you didn't need to bring flowers," Jesse joked with a grin.

Jesse and Parker had been good friends in junior high school, falling out of touch during high school when Jesse had started getting wild.

Parker laughed. "As a matter of fact, I didn't. I brought them for Kate." Parker turned to her. "I'm sorry I missed the first segment of *Getting Real*. But I hope these will make up for it. I heard the show was a hit."

"You are so sweet," she said faintly.

"I remembered that you love peonies. I've been calling all weekend, but you haven't been home."

"You brought flowers for Katie?" Jesse asked, interrupting, glancing back and forth between them.

"Yes, I did." Parker's sunny smile was wonderful and sexy at the same time. No question he was a catch. As tall as Jesse. As well defined. But where Jesse was the

bad boy of golf, Parker had continued in his path of re-
spectability and was now a responsible and successful
businessman. He was everything she wanted in a man.

"We've been going out," Parker explained, his fond
expression twisting something inside her. "Didn't she
tell you?"

Jesse skewered her with a hard gaze. "No, she failed
to mention that she was dating one of my friends."

They hadn't been dating steadily, but often enough
that Parker would think it perfectly fine to come over
this morning and bring her flowers. She knew he wanted
a commitment from her, and she knew that she was insane not to give it to him, but something held her back.

Parker glanced at her. For the first time, he seemed to
consider the situation. Jesse Chapman, notorious ladies'
man, standing in her backyard without a shirt. Kate could
see the realization dawning on his face.

"Are you staying here?" he asked Jesse.

"I am."

Parker looked to Kate for verification.

"He is," she confirmed, doing her best not to look
guilty.

"Well, of course," he said finally. "You're old friends,
grew up next door to each other. It makes sense."

Makes sense might have been a stretch, but she was
grateful he didn't make an issue of it.

Quickly, before his mind could go any further, she
said, "Would you like to come in for some coffee?"

Parker focused, then looked at her soil-trimmed hands
clutching the flowers. "Actually, another reason I came
by was to see if you'd like to join my parents and me for
brunch."

She could feel Jesse staring at them.

"Jesse, if you'll set the tools in the workroom, that would be great." Then she guided Parker back to the front drive.

"Jesse, let's get together for lunch while you're in town," he called back.

Jesse didn't answer, though she could feel his hot, piercing gaze on her back as she fled.

Once they got to Parker's car, she tried to think of something to say. He looked at her oddly. "Are you okay?" he asked.

She thought of possible answers.

No.

Definitely not.

I wish.

But decided on an "I'm fine" instead. "I've been putting a lot of hours in at work, so I've been busy."

His expression softened. "I've missed you these last few days. I really would love for you to join us for brunch."

She held out her arms, exhibiting herself, and found a smile for him. "I'm not sure this is the best brunch attire, but I appreciate the offer. Maybe next week."

He looked at her a long time, just looking. Then he reached out and took her hand. He didn't grimace over the dirt.

"I care for you a great deal, Kate." He glanced toward the house, then back at her. "Don't shut me out." Leaning forward, he kissed her on the forehead, so kind, so gentle, so perfectly right for her, then he got in his car and drove away.

She watched him until his four-door sedan disappeared around the bend in the road. He was an incredible man. And she resolved to make time for him next week.

Feeling good about her decision, she went inside to her workroom off the kitchen and found the buckets. Thankfully, Jesse was nowhere in sight. But she hadn't gotten more than the first tool cleaned when she heard the screen door open, then bang shut.

"Anyone home?"

He entered the kitchen, and she could see him through the open workroom doorway, the sun casting him in morning light.

"I'll be there in a minute," she called out.

He had dressed in a pair of khaki shorts with a polo shirt hanging out untucked, boat shoes without socks, and a Texas Rangers baseball cap that he tossed onto the counter. Anyone else would have looked unruly. Jesse Chapman looked wonderful and amazing and like more trouble than she knew how to handle.

He pulled open the refrigerator and looked inside.

"There's orange juice if you want some," she said.

"Thanks."

By the time she scrubbed her hands free of dirt, he was on his second glass.

"Can I get you something for breakfast?" she asked. "I have Cheerios, powdered doughnuts, and Pop-Tarts."

"A regular health nut."

"*Strawberry* Pop-Tarts. Plus I have granola bars."

Jesse grinned, then glanced back into the workroom. "You have plenty to do. I'll make breakfast while you finish up."

"You?"

"Believe it or not, I can make a Pop-Tart as easily as the next guy."

He didn't wait for a response. He got busy going through her cabinets and pantry. "Success. Strawberry *and* blueberry. The only other thing I need is a real cup of coffee—"

She pointed to the coffeemaker and the tin next to it.

"—and I'm set."

She nodded and then went back to the gardening tools. When she finished and returned to the kitchen, he was just serving breakfast.

"I made enough for both of us," he said.

She really was hungry. "Thanks." She debated taking a quick shower.

"Clean up later," he said, reading her thoughts. He shoved her gently into the seat, then set a premade pastry in front of her.

They ate in companionable silence, until Jesse finished. "Man, can I use a toaster."

"So much for modesty," she teased.

He glanced over at her with a wicked smile. "Modesty is overrated."

Kate rolled her eyes, then finished her last bite. Reaching across the table, she gathered their plates.

"I can't believe you're dating Parker," he said, leaning back, holding his coffee against his broad chest.

"Why? He's a fine man, even if he is a friend of yours." This time she grinned.

"Cute. But I don't like him."

"How can you say that! You were friends for ages."

"Yeah, well," he conceded grudgingly. "I guess I just don't like him for you."

For some reason, this really got to her, or maybe it was just a lot of things piling up. Him here. Looking great. Still wild. Whatever the reason, she sat back in the chair and skewered him with a scowl. "Given that you're a guest in my home, I don't want to be rude. However, I feel compelled to point out that my relationship with Parker Hammond is none of your business."

Jesse only grinned, unabashed, his corded forearms rippling as he set his cup aside and tossed his napkin on the table. He whistled, then shrugged. "You and Parker— who would have guessed?" He held his hands up in surrender. "Certainly not me, though that could be because I never really saw him as having much appeal."

"Glad you're such an expert on men. Have you switched over?"

His eyes went wide for half a second, then he gave a bark of appreciative laughter. "There's my Katie."

"I am not *your* Katie."

He sat for a long second, just looking, before he pushed up from the table and stepped beside her chair. Hot, intense emotion ticked through him and he couldn't explain why her words bothered him. She wasn't his. He didn't want her to be his.

But that didn't stop the hard, driving need that beat inside him. He leaned close to her ear, pressing in on her space, making her uncomfortable. "Then whose Katie are you?" he asked, his voice a low rumble. "Are you really Parker's?"

"I don't belong to anyone."

Her indignation amused him, and he smiled at her defiance. Then with slow, deliberate movements, he grabbed her chair and pulled her and the furniture around as if he couldn't do anything else. He leaned down and braced his hands against the hard wood arms on either side of her, bringing them face to face.

"I think I get it," he mused. "You're modern and liberated. The Gloria Steinem of Meadowlark Drive."

Something deep and indefinable pushed him on. He

tilted her back until the chair balanced on two legs. Her mouth opened in surprise, a single long strand of curling hair trailing along her cheek.

"Does that mean there's still a little bit of the old, wild Katie left underneath all that prim?"

"I was never wild," she managed to say.

"Do I need to remind you about wanting to punch Billy Weeks in the nose? Or riding your bike like the devil licked at your heels?" He let the chair drop back into an upright position. "What happened to that little girl?"

"She grew up."

He ran his gaze over her body. "I noticed."

The gold that highlighted her hazel eyes flared. But then she shook her head. "I noticed something, too."

Jesse tilted his head. "What?"

"Another woman in my guest cottage."

His thoughts jarred to a halt before he laughed out loud. "Now, Katie," he cajoled, "don't look at me like that—so condemning. Would it matter if I told you that I didn't have sex with Gwen?"

She blinked. "Sex?" she managed with a high-pitched, completely unprofessional non–news anchor voice.

"Surely you've heard of it," he teased, running the back of his finger along the line of her jaw. "Sexual intercourse. Having a little feel-good fun. The facts of life. Surely by now someone has told you about the birds and bees."

Her mouth fell open as he pulled her up from the chair and everything changed. The air around them crackled with anticipation, his muscles tightened. They were inches apart, close enough that he could lean down to kiss her. And he wanted to. He wanted to strip her naked and teach her all the things he had thought about when they were dancing Friday night. Which was crazy.

She might have grown up to be a woman who could easily turn a man's head, but she'd also grown up to be a woman with high standards and a strong moral compass, and that made it easy to resist her—okay, easi*er* to resist her.

Katie made him think about things that had nothing to do with his life. Like that damned innocence she wore like a shield. He liked experienced women. It didn't take a genius to know that Katie was not. He liked his women bold, knowledgeable. The kind who expected nothing from him in return.

But he couldn't help it when his gaze drifted to her lips. Every trace of laughter and teasing fun evaporated. "You're messing with my mind, sweet thing."

His fingertips trailed low along her jaw to the pulse in her neck. The heat was instant, intense, rushing through him like a flash fire. He stepped even closer, one boat shoe coming between those damned flowered sneakers, his thigh brushing against hers. Awareness rode him hard and fast.

He let his fingers drift even lower to her collarbone beneath her shirt. He savored her pale silky skin. Her eyes fluttered closed at the touch, one soft breath expelled. And when he couldn't hold back any longer, he lowered his head, their lips a hairbreadth apart, the sweet sound of her whimper making his blood pump.

But all of a sudden she sucked in her breath and jerked away, backing into the table edge as her hand came to her lips. "This can't happen," she whispered.

She was right. This was insane. But something pushed

him on. He reached out and took her hand. "You're right." He pulled her close regardless.

Her eyes flashed with an innocent desire that nearly undid him. With their gazes locked, he ran his palms up her arms, need licking through him, making him hard. Framing her face with his hands, he watched her lips part. But before he could dip his head and taste her, she asked, "Does this mean you're going to stay?"

His thoughts cemented, his body shuddering to a halt like he'd had a bucket of cold water tossed in his face. "Stay?"

He felt the place inside him that he kept locked away close off completely. His jaw tightened and he let go of her.

"What am I saying?" she said, pink flaring in her cheeks. "Of course you'll leave."

She stepped away from him, tripping. When he automatically reached out to steady her, she slapped his hand away.

"I told you, I don't need your help. On top of that, I have no interest in becoming another notch on your bedpost."

A nearly overwhelming urge hit him to explain it all to her—tell her about the past weeks, how his life felt like it was unraveling at the seams. He wanted to tell her about the jarring dreams that woke him every night since he had saved that woman. The memory of her lifeless body. Of his mouth over hers, pumping breath into her. The eerily startled gasp she made when air rushed back into her lungs. Then the way her eyes had blinked open and she had stared at him. Frightened. Confused.

But Jesse knew he wouldn't say a word. Sharing feelings and fears were for weak men. He had never been weak. Besides, what did any of it matter? Deep down they both knew that she was right. He would leave. He hadn't come back intending to stay. Didn't want to stay. He only wanted a short diversion from the chaos in his head. And he couldn't turn Katie into one of his diversions. She deserved better than that.

The doorbell rang, the sound seeming far away as they stared at each other, neither of them moving.

"Someone's here," he said.

"So it would seem."

They heard keys in the lock, then someone barreled inside.

"Kate," Suzanne called out, her voice an octave higher than normal. "Kate, where are you?"

Kate tore herself away completely, then hurried into the living room. Jesse shoved his hands in his back pockets, and after a second he followed. Suzanne Bloom Chapman—Kate's sister, Jesse's sister-in-law—stood in her bathrobe and slippers, an unfamiliar young boy with shaggy dark brown hair and dark eyes standing behind her.

"Suzanne, what is it?" Kate asked.

Jesse felt a low prickle of concern when Suzanne yanked her gaze back and forth between the boy and him.

His older brother Derek flew into the house, his hair still damp from his shower.

"Why didn't you tell us?" he demanded of Jesse.

Years seemed to circle back to when they were young, still at home, always at odds.

"Tell you what?"

The boy shifted his weight uncomfortably, his shirt ill-fitting, his stiff blue jeans too large.

Derek's jaw muscles ticked. "That you have a son."

four

Jesse took a step back. "What are you talking about?" he demanded. "I don't have a son."

They stood in the foyer, the gawky boy staring up at Jesse with an expression of sheer awe.

"Hello . . . Mr. Chapman," he said awkwardly, his hands tucked into his pants pockets. "I mean, ah, Dad."

Dad.

Shock rippled through the room at the word, at the reality of what that single syllable meant.

Kate could see the stunned expression on Jesse's face. He was visibly shaken.

Suzanne and Derek started talking at the same time, their voices rising in the foyer.

Kate watched, hardly able to take it in. A person only had to look at the boy to know that he was Jesse's. He had the same hair and eyes. A hint of the same strong jaw that would one day emerge from beneath the boy-hood chubbiness.

When no one seemed to know what to do about the child, she kindly said, "Hi, I'm Kate. What's your name?"

"Ah, um, Travis."

"How old are you?"

"Twelve."

Kate took in the boy and could tell his too-big blue jeans were brand-new, a belt holding them up. His blue T-shirt still had crease marks on it, as if he had gone to the local discount store on the way over here for a new set of clothes. But his boots were old and brown, with scuffs that needed polish.

Then every trace of awe and excitement on his face vanished when another woman marched in the door.

"There you are," the woman accused, one long hot-pink nail pointing at Jesse.

The boy flinched, his blush going a bright painful red that seeped up into his hairline. Kate didn't know the child, but she could tell how hard he was trying to hide his emotions as he stared at his feet.

"Travis," Kate said, "there's a pool out back. Why don't you wait for us out there?"

His brow furrowed with a much older man's worry. Then he nodded and walked carefully to the back doors that led to the yard.

"Belinda?" Jesse said the word like he wasn't absolutely sure.

"Belinda Martin, now Sanders," she stated. "Remember me? We used to date?"

She was short, with heavily highlighted blond hair, gigantic breasts, and lots of makeup. Kate had practically memorized Jesse's high school yearbooks, and she remembered that this woman had been in his class at Coronado High.

Belinda's brown eyes turned sly. "I've seen you all over the news lately, even saw you on TV here the other morning. And as long as you're in town, I figured it's time you started shouldering some of the responsibility for your son."

Suzanne stood to the side, shocked. Derek seemed his usual forbidding, older-brother self.

But it was Jesse's presence that was huge and overpowering. "If he is my son, why have you waited this long to tell me?"

Belinda fidgeted. "After you left for college and never wrote or called," she explained, "I got married. I didn't want to rock the boat. But Harlan left me six months ago, and as long as you're back in town, I figured what the heck. I thought it was time you knew. You have a son."

The alarm on Jesse's face couldn't be anything but genuine.

"That's impossible," he said. "I'm always careful. When we—" He cut himself off, then looked around them. "When we were together," he rephrased, "I used protection. I always do."

Belinda whipped out some kind of medical document that showed the boy's blood type.

"If you don't believe me, do as many tests as you want," she challenged. "But all you have to do is look at him to know he's yours."

Suzanne sighed. "This is about money, isn't it?"

The woman's eyes narrowed. "So what if I came here for money? I need a job, a good job, and I've got a chance to make something of myself in Vegas. But it takes cash to get out there to start a new life."

"Good Lord, Jesse," Derek stated, looking tired and far older than his thirty-nine years.

Jesse and Derek stared at each other, tension sliding between them. How many times had Kate seen them this same way? Two brothers who were so different, one conservative, one wild. For as long as she could remember, their relationship had been strained. But Kate had seen the deep love that served as a sort of glue that kept them from severing their relationship completely. They existed in a place of love and frustration, yearning to be close but the differences in each other's personality and lifestyle making it hard. Judgment and impatience competing with the need to accept, underlined by a true caring that even their differences couldn't completely erase. The unexpected appearance of an illegitimate son didn't help the situation.

At length, Derek exhaled sharply, then became the practical, responsible man he was. "Jesse will not be blackmailed."

"Derek, I can take care of this," Jesse stated tightly.

"Can you?"

A spark of always suppressed fury flared—a fury that Kate had never entirely understood. She wondered, not for the first time, what had caused the rift between them.

With effort, Jesse turned away, focusing on Belinda. "Let me see the document."

Belinda handed it over, along with an entire file. He glanced through it with quick competence, then he gestured for them to sit down. Suzanne started toward the table.

"Suzanne, not now." He looked at his brother. "I can deal with this from here."

Suzanne started to say something, but Derek stopped her. "Come on, love. He's right." He looked back at Jesse, his expression undecipherable. "If you need anything, you know where to find me."

The brothers stared at each other, then Jesse nodded. "Thanks."

Kate started to leave as well. But Jesse surprised her when he caught her hand. For a second he just stood there, then he looked out the window toward the pool. She could see Travis lying like a rag doll on a wooden chaise lounge, one booted foot on the ground, the other hiked up on slats. Discarded. Forgotten.

Jesse's tension was palpable before he turned his attention to the folder and began to go through the papers in earnest.

Birth records, blood reports. Report cards and baby pictures. Belinda started explaining them all, pointing out the unmistakable resemblances between the boy and Jesse.

Finally, he sat down and dropped his head in his hands. When he straightened, his gaze was drawn back to the window as if he was trying to understand something. "How long do you think it will take to find a job?"

Belinda seemed caught off guard by the question, as if she had been prepared for more of a fight. "Well, ah . . ." She toyed nervously with her hair. "I'm thinking a month, max. A girlfriend of mine works at Caesars Palace and she said she could probably get me a job if I come out and interview. She's going to let me stay with her until I find a place of my own."

Jesse waited until she was done speaking. "Will two thousand help you get started in Las Vegas?"

Belinda's eyes went wide. "Well," she said, seeming surprised by her good fortune. "Sure, that'll work."

Tension sliced through Jesse as he looked out the window again to where Travis sat by the pool. "Then I'll write you a check."

"Oh, okay. Good. Well then, um, great. If I could get that from you now, the car's packed, then I'll get out of your hair."

She started to stand.

"What about the boy?" Jesse asked, stopping her. "He'll stay with you in Las Vegas?"

"Actually, no. Not until I get a place of my own. But I have someone here who he's going to stay with."

He glanced back at her sharply. "Who?"

"A . . . um . . . friend." She became nervous.

"A good friend?" he persisted, his expression exacting.

"Okay, no. It's with a lady who lives down the street from us."

"You're leaving him with some lady?"

"Not just *some* lady. A neighbor lady. And I know her . . . sort of. At least I know her good enough, since I don't have anywhere else to leave Travis, and I can't take him with me and have him stay in a tiny apartment with a bunch of gals who work at Caesars Palace!"

Her face was red now with irritation and frustration, and probably with more than a little guilt.

Jesse pressed his eyes closed, something deep and emotional riding through him. "Then he should stay with me."

Belinda gasped. "With you?"

Kate felt surprise ripple through her. He'd just seen the boy for the first time, and now he was offering to take care of him? It hardly made sense.

The muscles in Jesse's jaw worked, a fierceness coming into his eyes that would have given any sane person pause. "Yes, with me."

"Listen," Belinda said, growing concerned, "I didn't come here looking to make you a father."

"Then why did you come?" he asked harshly. "Just for money? Is that it?"

Belinda blushed red.

"You can't walk in here, announce I have a son, then turn around and disappear. It doesn't work that way."

The woman looked at the file and shifted uncomfortably in her seat. "I thought it would work that way with you."

His jaw ticked.

Then she shook herself. "I'm not interested in giving up my boy. The arrangement with the lady might not be perfect. But it won't be for long. A month, tops. And I won't let you take Travis away from me."

Jesse visibly calmed himself. "I understand that, and I'm not asking you to give him up. I don't want you to give him up. As soon as you're settled, let me know and I'll send him out on a plane." He looked her directly in the eye. "Do you really think it's wise to leave him with some lady for a month?"

Panic battled with practicality on Belinda's once-pretty face. "Damn it all, you swear you won't try to keep him?"

"You have my word."

She studied her ex-boyfriend for a minute. "Well, maybe that could work. But I'll want him back as soon as I'm settled."

"Just tell me when you're ready."

She hesitated for one last second, before she conceded. "Okay, let me go talk to Travis."

She pushed up from the table. As soon as the door closed behind her, Jesse went to the kitchen. Kate found him at the sink, looking out the back window. She stood in the doorway for a long second, taking him in.

The unfortunate incident regarding her, a pot of tea, and the publicity queen Gwen was forgotten. She focused on this man, someone, she realized, she didn't even know anymore. He might still laugh and tease, but all traces of the boy she grew up with were gone. Standing there looking at him, she saw that his expression was no longer carefree, his smile no longer easy.

That was one of the things that always surprised Kate about Jesse—the way he walked through life with a bad boy's grace, his smiles and teasing quips making him seem as if he didn't have a care in the world. But now, looking closer, she saw something darker beneath the sunny facade.

For the first time since he had shown up with Julia at the television station, Kate wondered why he had come home. After so many years of living away, staying away, why come back now?

She walked up to stand beside him at the sink, her Keds silent on the tile, and she looked out the window with him. She watched as Belinda walked over to the boy, then sat down on the edge of the chaise. Kate could tell that neither of them said a word, but Belinda placed her hand on the tip of his boot awkwardly. Close, but still separated by a strained distance.

Was that the way it was with most families? She knew Jesse's relationship with his own father was complicated. Not as much father and son as buddies. Carlen Chapman had turned Jesse into his friend at a young age, taking him everywhere, while Derek had been left behind. She guessed that it was this that had divided the brothers. But she had never known why Derek had been left out. It would have made more sense for Carlen to be friends with the older son.

"Why, Jesse?" Kate asked quietly. "Why are you doing this?"

Jesse didn't answer for a long while. When he finally spoke, this rugged bad boy amazed her.

"What kind of man would I be if I wrote her a check and sent them away when all you have to do is look at him to know he's mine?" He shook his head. "Me, Katie. I have a son."

She was moved, her throat tightening. But she couldn't tell from his voice what he felt. "Is that a good *I have a son,* or a bad *I have a son*?"

He laughed, a scoffing, bittersweet sound, and straightened. "I came back here to *un*complicate my life. And what do I get? First you, too damn hot and sexy for your own good—"

Her mind spun at the words. Her, *sexy*? And *hot*?

"—and now this boy. It's like someone's playing a joke on me. What was I thinking when I said he could stay with me? *I* can't stay in El Paso. I have to get back to Florida. I planned to be here no more than a week or so. I don't have time for this. But the way he looked out there by the pool, lost, forgotten . . . Hell."

"You always did have a soft spot for lost little kids."

He swore. "I guess I'll have to rent a house or an apartment. When I showed up, Derek said I should stay with them. But I could feel the tension and reluctance in Suzanne."

"I can't believe my sister."

Jesse gave her a look.

"Okay," she conceded. "I can believe it. It's vintage Suzanne. But it's your house, too."

"Not anymore. I deeded my portion to Derek as a wedding present."

"You really are full of surprises today. Suzanne never told me."

He shrugged. "It doesn't matter. I just need to figure out where we can stay."

"Here."

She could do the right thing, too.

"Katie, I can't ask—"

"You're not asking. I'm offering."

"There's not enough space in the guest cottage."

"I'll put him in my extra bedroom."

He seemed to consider. "Are you sure?"

"Absolutely."

He leaned over, bracing his hands against his knees.

"A penny for your thoughts?" she asked.

He looked up at her as a single heartbeat passed. "A kid, Katie. I have a son."

This time he didn't hide the emotion he was feeling. He seemed as surprised by the whole idea as he seemed amazingly wowed.

"I don't know the first thing about taking care of anyone, much less a child."

She didn't respond at first, then she repeated the words he had said to her when she was faltering during the cooking segment. "You forget who you're talking to."

He glanced at her in question.

"You know more than you realize," she assured him, placing her hand on his forearm. "You know all about taking care of little kids, about making them feel safe."

He studied her, a lock of dark hair falling forward on his brow. Instantly she felt awkward and surprisingly shy.

"Besides," she quickly added, dropping her hand away, "it's just for a month."

"A month." He straightened and stared off into space. "A month," he repeated, the words sounding more comfortable on his tongue. "Sure, I can do a month. How hard can it be?"

To: Katherine Bloom <katherine@ktextv.com>
    Chloe Sinclair <chloe@ktextv.com>
From: Julia Boudreaux <julia@ktextv.com>
Subject: Good news

I have everything arranged for Kate's next *Getting Real* segment, which is scheduled to air tomorrow morning. I met with the good people at Tumbleweed regarding the cowboy interview. I feel confident that our viewers will love the show.

xo, Julia

To: Julia Boudreaux <julia@ktextv.com>
    Katherine Bloom <katherine@ktextv.com>
From: Chloe Sinclair <chloe@ktextv.com>
Subject: Love?

I'm still not sure what the draw is of this segment. Kate surrounded by horses and bales of hay, talking with someone none of us has ever heard of? Sounds unappealing to me.

Chloe

To: Chloe Sinclair <chloe@ktextv.com>
    Katherine Bloom <katherine@ktextv.com>
From: Julia Boudreaux <julia@ktextv.com>
Subject: O ye

___

. . . of little faith. The appeal is who Kate will be talking to. The
cowboy is a hottie. I felt it only good business to take the man
out to dinner to ensure that he was capable of carrying on a
decent conversation . . . with Kate, of course. Though really,
conversation isn't necessary. He's a true hunk.

xo, j

p.s. He's not a bad kisser either.

___

To: Julia Boudreaux <julia@ktextv.com>
    Katherine Bloom <katherine@ktextv.com>
From: Chloe Sinclair <chloe@ktextv.com>
Subject: Kissing?!!!

___

You took a man out for a business dinner and let him
kiss you? Julia, really. Though if he really is that good looking
and if we run some promos beforehand during the morning
news, we can count on decent ratings. What is it about
women that makes them susceptible to a well-proportioned
cowboy?

Chloe, disgusted . . . okay, and a little intrigued. But only in the
academic sense.

p.s. Kate, where are you?

To: Julia Boudreaux <julia@ktextv.com>
    Chloe Sinclair <chloe@ktextv.com>
From: Katherine Bloom <katherine@ktextv.com>
Subject: I'm at home

We've had a bit of a trauma here. We need to make the cowboy
interview fast so I can get back to the house since Jesse will no
doubt need help with his son.

Kate

p.s. I received the ankle weights and workout shoes you got for
Chloe and me. It's really sweet, Julia, but as I said when you
mentioned getting them for all of us, I truly can't imagine
wearing them.

Katherine C. Bloom
News Anchor, KTEX TV West Texas

To: Katherine Bloom <katherine@ktextv.com>
    Chloe Sinclair <chloe@ktextv.com>
From: Julia Boudreaux <julia@ktextv.com>
Subject: Jesse has a son?!

Good God, what are you talking about?

JJJJJJJ!

p.s. Your loss if you don't wear the ankle weights . . . the ad
guaranteed that they would give a girl a sexy little butt and

great legs in no time if you wear them regularly. I've got mine on now.

To: Julia Boudreaux <julia@ktextv.com>
    Chloe Sinclair <chloe@ktextv.com>
From: Katherine Bloom <katherine@ktextv.com>
Subject: Child

It turns out our Jesse experienced at least one moment of unprotected sex in his lifetime. And now he has a twelve-year-old boy to prove it. Travis will be staying in my extra bedroom while his mother looks for a job.

K

p.s. Sexy butt in no time? Perhaps will reconsider ankle weights . . .

To: Katherine Bloom <katherine@ktextv.com>
    Chloe Sinclair <chloe@ktextv.com>
From: Julia Boudreaux <julia@ktextv.com>
Subject: Questionable motivation

Inviting the child to stay in the house? And Jesse's child at that. Seems to me there is more to your motivation than sheer cramped quarters. Careful, sugar. I don't want to see you get hurt, and while I was never very good at math, I can add and subtract. If the boy is twelve, my calculations put his conception at just about the same time you were proclaiming your undying love in the tree house.

xo,
Julia Scarlett Boudreaux

five

J esse and Travis sat at Katie's kitchen table, staring at the breakfast Jesse had made.

"Pop-Tarts," Travis stated in a thoughtful, considering voice as the morning sun rose in the distance.

Katie had already left for work, leaving the new father and son to make heads or tails of their first day together.

"There's powdered sugar doughnuts, too," Jesse offered.

"A real health nut."

Jesse would have laughed if he hadn't been disconcerted about the fact that he had said those exact words to Katie. Had it really been only twenty-four hours since then?

He had stayed up late last night, sitting at the tiny table in the guest cottage in shock.

Travis.

His son.

He still couldn't believe it.

He didn't want a son, at least at this point in his life.

And he definitely didn't know what to do with one. He also couldn't believe he had offered to take care of him until Belinda got settled.

But it was the strangest feeling seeing this kid. Shock, yes, but something else, something that made everything else in his life seem less significant. Which he couldn't believe he would actually think.

He was on the verge of winning the PGA Championship. He had the opportunity to truly make a name for himself in this game—as a golfer, not as some bad boy whom the media loved to talk about. Which meant he needed to practice. Concentrate. Focus. But all he could do was think about the fact that he had a son. And that made him think about his own father. A place he had no interest in going.

After his mother died, it had been just the three guys—Dad, Derek, and Jesse—each trying to find a way to deal with Janie Chapman's death. He had been ten, Derek eighteen, while their father lapsed into shock.

It had been six-year-old Katie who came to Jesse the night of the funeral, slipping into his house after all the people finally left and his dad and brother had gone to sleep. She'd had her stuffed bear crammed under her arm as she climbed up beside him.

"It's gonna be okay, Jesse," she had whispered, sticking her little arm underneath his neck as he stared up at the ceiling. It was the only time he let himself cry.

He had woken up at four in the morning, that damned bear clutched in his arm, Katie curled against his side, sleeping the sleep of the dead.

As quietly as he could, so he wouldn't wake his father, he had shaken her awake, taken her hand, and led her barefoot through the lattice archway to her house. It was 4:15 by then, and when he pushed through the back door to the kitchen, her mom was sitting at the table, crying. It wasn't a secret that Mary Beth's newest husband had just moved out.

Even at that age Jesse could tell Katie's mom would be considered a beautiful woman, fiery and wild. It was like men were drawn to her in spite of better sense.

"Hi, Jess," Mary Beth had said to him, wiping her eyes, before adding to Katie, "Hey, sleepyhead."

Just that, nothing else—no lectures, no outrage that he was bringing her daughter home at that hour. She didn't even move to take Katie to her room. Instead, he was the one who tucked her into bed.

For years, Katie came and went from her house at all hours. More often than not, Jesse knew, Mary Beth was too self-absorbed, too caught up in concern over some man to notice when Katie was gone.

When he returned to the kitchen that early morning he shrugged, feeling awkward. "See ya."

"Jess?"

He stopped with his hand on the knob.

"I'm sorry about your mom. She loved you a lot."

His throat started to work again and his eyes burned. But he swallowed it back. No more crying.

"Thanks."

He raced out the door, across the yard, slipping back into his own bed just before his dad got up to fix breakfast. Carlen Chapman didn't say much to his boys for months, a strange spiraling distance widening between them until Jesse felt like he was losing his father, too. But Carlen had kept his sons fed and clothed.

Food and clothes. Two things a parent had to provide for a child.

Jesse glanced at the plate of Pop-Tarts. "You need more to eat than that."

Travis stared at his new dad. Not exactly a new dad like the new stepdads some of the kids at school got. This guy had been his dad from the beginning, though no one had known it except his mom. So really, Travis reasoned, he was a new-to-him dad.

Jesse Chapman was really tall—*please, please, please, let me get tall like him*—and handsome in a movie star kind of way, not really a dad kind of way. In fact, his dad really didn't seem much like a dad at all.

Without so much as a *What do you want to eat?*, Jesse looked in the refrigerator, and Travis could tell he was surprised by what he saw. "Eggs," Jesse said.

"Yeah, Kate said we couldn't live on Pop-Tarts alone."

"You talked to her?"

"This morning before she left for work. She got up early and went to the grocery store."

"She must have gotten up real early."

"Yep, said she didn't want to leave us here without any food." He laughed. "She's really nice."

His dad looked out the window, and the guy kind of laughed, thinking of something that made him smile and shake his head at the same time. "Yeah," Jesse said, "she's nice." Then he got back to work on all that food.

Travis sat at the table, trying to decide if he should mention the fact that Kate had stopped at McDonald's and gotten him a Big Breakfast after she went to the store. She hadn't gotten anything for herself, only had some cereal and coffee, saying, *"No more fat thighs for me."* Which, Travis reasoned, must be why she left the house wearing ankle weights.

Travis decided not to tell Jesse about the Big Breakfast or the ankle weights.

"I saw you swimming this morning," Travis offered instead, dubiously eyeing the eggs going into a skillet. "You remind me of that swimmer lady on those old movies my mom likes to watch. Esther Williams."

All that got was one dark eyebrow raised kind of funny, like he wasn't all that happy about being compared to Esther.

"Not that you look like a girl," Travis added hastily. "I just mean you're a good swimmer. Like Tarzan. Yeah, Tarzan in the really old movies. Though you swim way better than him. You put your head in the water. Tarzan does that weird above the water thing, like he doesn't want to get his hair wet. Though why Tarzan would care about wet hair, I don't know. He's hanging out with Cheetah. Do you really think a monkey cares?"

Jesse looked at him like he was trying to figure out if he was supposed to answer that. It was the same kind of look that tons of people gave him when he talked.

"Do you watch a lot of old movies?" Jesse asked.

Talking! With his dad! "They're my mom's favorite. Did you know that?"

That got more silence, and it belatedly occurred to Travis that his dad probably didn't know a whole lot about his mom, because he almost hadn't recognized her. Which couldn't be great, since Travis knew all about how kids were made.

Jesse set a plate of eggs, bacon, and toast in front of him.

"Yum." He tried to sound enthusiastic about the mounds of food.

They ate in silence, until Jesse went all still and his

head jerked up and he asked, "What do you usually do during the summer?"

"Me? I hang out."

"Doing what?"

He shrugged. "Watching TV and stuff."

"While your mother's at work?"

"Sure."

"Who stays with you?"

Travis sat up straight. "I'm twelve. Old enough to take care of myself."

Jesse tapped his fork against the rim of his plate and considered. "You can't just hang out."

"Why not?"

Jesse ignored that. "How about some kind of summer program? Something that interests you."

Great, more school, Travis groaned silently. "Like what?"

"I don't know. Archery? Maybe chess?"

"Chess?" He made a face.

"Then what about chemistry?" Jesse picked up his cup. "Mixing ingredients. Doing experiments. I used to love chemistry. Or geology. I bet they have a summer program for kids at the university."

That's when it occurred to him. Travis worried his lip, and it was all he could do to keep the excitement from spilling over. "What about golf lessons?"

His dad kind of jerked and coffee sloshed over the rim.

"I bet I'd be really great," Travis enthused. "You're a golfer. And your dad was one, too."

"How'd you know that?"

Travis blushed. "I read about you and him. There's tons of stuff about both of you. They say your dad could play, but you're the one who won all the trophies. Didn't your dad ever win?"

Jesse got another look on his face, a weird one this time. "My dad won plenty," he said. "He was a great golfer in his day."

Waiting expectantly, Travis thought there'd be more to the story. But more wasn't coming. "I read that you're about to win a really big tournament. It sounded totally great." He pushed some eggs around. "I also read that all the girls love you."

Jesse's brow furrowed.

"They say you can get a girl in your bed faster than any other golfer around. Cool."

"Cool? This conversation doesn't fall underneath the heading of food or clothes."

"Huh?"

"Nothing. Just don't believe everything you read, kid. And it sounds to me like you'd make a great reporter. Maybe Katie could get you a summer internship down at the station."

Light-headed with disappointment, Travis tried to smile. "Yeah, maybe."

When his mom had told him they were going to see his father, he'd been totally excited. He had assumed Jesse would feel the same way. Didn't dads have to be excited about that kind of stuff?

Now, sitting here, with Jesse looking at him so strangely, Travis figured that dads didn't have to be excited, or maybe they just wouldn't be excited about a kid like him. He knew he sort of blended in. Though when he didn't blend in, it was worse—way worse. Other kids said he talked too much.

"Can I turn on the TV?" he asked.

It looked like Jesse debated his answer. But he must not have wanted to have to talk anymore, either, because he said, "Okay."

This whole father-son thing sure wasn't working out like Travis had hoped.

With a turn of the switch, the tiny screen came to life. Travis sat back and was eyeing the bacon and toast in silent misery when Kate appeared on the screen.

"Good morning, West Texas!"

"Hey, look, it's Kate."

They stopped eating, or pretending to eat.

"Today I'm at Tumbleweed Trails for a chat with rodeo star Cowboy Bob."

Jesse and Travis looked at each other. "Cowboy Bob?" they said in unison.

Kate was dressed in a buckskin vest with fringe running down the sides, plus matching buckskin pants, it looked like, though it was hard to be sure since the screen cut off the bottom half of her. She stood next to a gigantic redheaded man in the biggest cowboy hat Travis had ever seen.

"She looks kind of uncomfortable," Travis mused.

"Who wouldn't be, dressed like that? It's got to be ninety out there already. I wouldn't be surprised if she faints."

"It looks like Cowboy Bob could handle her if she did."

Jesse scowled. "What's that supposed to mean?"

"Just that he looks strong enough to pick her up and carry her off if something happens."

Sure enough, Cowboy Bob swept Kate off her feet, though it had nothing to do with fainting. She gave a squeal, and the cowboy sort of staggered a little bit. But seconds later, she was sitting high atop a horse that looked as surprised as Kate did—and about as happy.

"Wow!" Travis was enthralled, his breakfast forgotten. "Did you see how he picked her up?"

Jesse wasn't nearly as excited.

Travis peered closer at the screen. "What's she doing? Looks like she's trying to hide her feet."

"Well, uh, Cowboy Bob, please tell our viewers a bit about the flora and fauna."

"She's wearing workout shoes"—Travis watched as Kate scrambled to tug down her buckskin pant legs— "and, oh man, she's still got on those ankle weights!"

"Ankle weights? What the hell—heck—is she wearing those for?"

"I don't know, but when she was walking out the door this morning, I heard her say something about needing to reinvent herself."

"What?" Jesse blurted out, before he shook his head. "Katie, Katie, Katie. It's always when she tries too hard to do something crazy that she gets herself in trouble." Then he whistled. "If she's trying to reinvent herself, let me tell you, Travis, we're in for big trouble around here."

"Do you think?"

"I know."

"You want me to tell you about Flora and Fauna?" The cowboy laughed. "I think I mighta dated a couple of gals named that. Though I can't imagine you came all the way out here to talk about them. But I'd be happy to tell the folks at home what I'm thinking about you." He whistled.

She cut him off abruptly, her lips pursing like a mad schoolteacher's. "Thank you, but that really isn't necessary."

The man leaned one strong forearm on the pommel of the saddle, winked directly into the camera, then looked at her in a way that heated the already blistering hot day.

"Did you see how he looked at her?" Jesse demanded, setting his coffee cup down with a thunk.

"*Now sit back, little lady, I'm going to give you the ride of your life.*"

Her eyes went wide. But seconds later they narrowed.

"Uh-oh," father and son said at the same time.

"*Mr. Bob . . . ah . . . Mr. Cowboy.*" She shook her head. "*Sir!*" she stated primly.

Then all of a sudden she froze and turned to the camera. Travis would have sworn she blanched white. With an amazing amount of effort, she smiled. "*Ha, ha!*" she laughed, though she didn't look like she thought anything was very funny. "*You're having fun, right, Cowboy Bob?*"

When the cowboy didn't say another word, only glowered, Kate got real nervous—and kind of panicky—then started reeling off facts and figures regarding the desert surroundings with mind-numbing speed. She even said something about the state capital of Texas.

Travis wasn't sure what that had to do with Cowboy Bob or the desert in El Paso, but he had seen his mom get that way before, saying weird things when she was trying to make up for some kind of mistake.

"Jeez," Travis said, "Kate looks so pathetic and sad and all, that it's hard not to feel sorry for her up on that mangy-looking horse."

Jesse stood and took their plates. "Katie, Katie," he mused, then chuckled as he put the plates in the dishwasher. When he was done, he headed for the back door. Then suddenly he stopped. After a long second and what sounded like a groan, he turned back.

"I guess we need to think about what you are going to do today. I'll call Suzanne."

"Like I said, I don't need anyone to watch me."

"And like I said, I can't leave you here by yourself."

"I could go with you!"

"I'm going to the golf course."

"Even better."

His dad tensed. "Sorry, but I've got to get a couple hours of practice in before the morning's over."

Travis sighed. Jesse hung his head.

"Maybe we could do something together later," Jesse offered.

The young boy perked up. "Wow! Great! You and me can do some kind of real father-son thing!"

To: Katherine Bloom <katherine@ktextv.com>
   Chloe Sinclair <chloe@ktextv.com>
From: Julia Boudreaux <julia@ktextv.com>
Subject: Seeing things

Kate, tell me I was seeing things. Chloe, have I lost my mind or was Kate really wearing ankle weights with Cowboy Bob?

Julia

To: Julia Boudreaux <julia@ktextv.com>
   Katherine Bloom <katherine@ktextv.com>
From: Chloe Sinclair <chloe@ktextv.com>
Subject: Ankle weights

I believe you're correct, Julia. Though I don't think viewers had any idea what they were. I blame you, of course, J, since you know how Kate doesn't do anything halfway.

Chloe

To: Chloe Sinclair <chloe@ktextv.com>
    Julia Boudreaux <julia@ktextv.com>
From: Katherine Bloom <katherine@ktextv.com>
Subject: Torso

Argh!!!! Chloe, you said it was going to be a torso-only shot!!!
The horse was supposed to be decoration. But I know, I know,
this isn't anybody's fault but my own. Though with all this effort
to make myself over into the new, improved Kate, I swear I'm
just making things worse! Sorry!

Katherine C. Bloom
News Anchor, KTEX TV West Texas

To: Katherine Bloom <katherine@ktextv.com>
    Chloe Sinclair <chloe@ktextv.com>
From: Julia Boudreaux <julia@ktextv.com>
Subject: re: Torso

Actually I think it was kind of cute. Getting caught wearing ankle
weights makes you very real. So don't worry about it.

xo, j

p.s. I saw Parker yesterday. All I can say is that if you don't want
him, then I wish you'd cut him loose. He really is divine.

To: Julia Boudreaux <julia@ktextv.com>
   Chloe Sinclair <chloe@ktextv.com>
From: Katherine Bloom <katherine@ktextv.com>
Subject: Parker

I'm having lunch with him today.

Kate

𝒮he needed a plan. Some brilliant idea for a show segment that would wow the viewing audience. But what?

Something without any sort of man involved—naked or otherwise.

Something that she actually enjoyed.

Something that would make her forget the fact that she had lost her mind and worn ankle weights on live television.

What had she been thinking?

Kate groaned. She hadn't been thinking. Who in their right mind wore ankle weights anywhere besides the privacy of their own home or at a gym?

She walked into the Hacienda restaurant at 1:00 on the nose. She had changed into a white cotton blouse and straight skirt to battle the heat.

"Kate." Parker stood up from the table when she approached, his warm smile instantly putting her at ease.

"I was surprised when you called," he added, holding her chair.

Standing so close, she was reminded of how tall he was, how solid and handsome. He wore a light blue pinstriped shirt with a burgundy tie. As the oldest son of the Newland Hammond family, he had taken over the running of Hammond Industries when his father had retired three years ago. He was one of El Paso's most sought after bachelors. But he had made it clear his only interest was her.

"I wanted to see you," she said.

He tilted his head slightly and nodded. "I'm glad."

After they ordered, he leaned back and looked at her. "You look great, as usual."

She almost told him that he did, too, because he did. Sun beat in through one of the hundred-year-old windows, the Rio Grande only a stone's throw away from this building that had once been a fort in the 1800s. The adobe and rustic wood reminded her of the rich mixture of Texan and Hispanic cultures in this town she loved so much.

When Parker reached across and took her hand, after a moment of surprise, she smiled with an amazed contentment when she realized that this was real life. Quiet moments shared with people she cared about.

It was astounding how easy it was to talk to him. During a meal of enchiladas and crisp tacos filled with shredded beef and lettuce, they laughed and shared stories of growing up in El Paso. When he offered her a bite of his chile relleno, she accepted, taking the morsel from the fork that he held out to her. By the end, over coffee and a dessert of flan, Kate had forgotten all about Cowboy Bob.

Parker walked her to the car, took her keys, and opened the door. She started to get in, then turned back to thank him. He was standing right there.

The sun shone against his face, his green eyes bright like freshly mown grass. And when he leaned forward, he kissed her. Soft and gentle, pleasant and warm.

When he pulled back, his gaze met hers. "I'm glad you called."

"So am I."

Driving away, she knew that she really was glad. Parker was everything Julia said. Divine, kind, and safe. No, not safe. Julia had never said safe. But somehow that was the word that kept playing over and over again in Kate's mind. Safe, unlike Jesse. Good, in contrast to Jesse's bad boy life.

She returned to the office, got some work done, then headed home. She parked in the shade cast by one of the old cottonwood trees in the yard. The smell of honeysuckle and oleander blossoms mixed with the high summer heat. When she got to the back door, she could see through the screen into the kitchen. A slow, deep breath ran through her at the sight of Jesse standing at the opened refrigerator, his forearm braced against the top as he peered inside.

He stood in profile, the deep gold afternoon sunlight highlighting the sharp planes of his face, the chiseled jaw, the nearly perfect patrician nose. Finely carved muscles emerged from beneath the sleeve of the golf shirt that hung loose from his shorts, his strong thighs braced. She sensed a restlessness in his long limbs today, like he was a caged animal ready to pounce.

There was nothing calm or safe about him.

The minute she pulled open the screen, he glanced over at her. His eyes flashed with darkness.

"Hi, honey, I'm home," she said, trying for light and fun to cover how disconcerted he made her feel.

He looked tired, every ounce of his bad boy ease gone. She studied him. "Hard day at the office?"

She didn't understand the intensity that flared on his face. His eyes narrowed, then they opened as he took a breath, and like magic, the storm was gone. A second later, his lips crooked in a smile.

"Me? Have a hard day?" He laughed, the sound deep and confident. "I think you've forgotten who you're talking to. The guy who doesn't have a care in the world."

She knew she hadn't imagined the darkness. "Jesse, are you sure there isn't anything wrong?"

He closed the refrigerator door and leaned back against it. "Not a thing. Though I'll let you make something up if it would make you feel better."

"Funny. I would not feel better."

"Good. Now tell me about your day."

She studied him for one last second before she lifted her shoulder in a semi-shrug. "My day was fine. Better than fine. In fact, it was great, couldn't be better."

His grin ticked up even higher. "I can tell." He pushed away from the refrigerator and walked over to the pantry like he owned the place. "Your mom called."

The gears in her head shifted. "How do you know?" she asked, her mouth dropping open in confusion.

He glanced back at her. "The phone rang. I answered."

"Just like that?"

"Are there new rules to answering the phone since I left Texas?" He started rummaging around in the pantry.

Kate scowled. "You can't just . . . just . . . come back here and act like everything is the same. It isn't the same as it used to be. We aren't kids anymore."

"So you're saying I shouldn't have answered the phone?"

"Be serious."

"I am." He came out of the pantry with a screwdriver in his hand. "I take it you don't want to hear her message."

A deep growl sounded in her chest as she set her purse down on the counter. "Tell me, what did she say?"

"We talked—"

"About what?"

"This and that. You know she always liked me."

"Great. You get a gold star. Now what was her message?"

"The weather's beautiful in Wyoming this time of year."

Her shoulders came back. "That's all she said? And what are you doing with the screwdriver?"

"I believe her exact words were, 'Tell my little Kate that there are plenty of hot men in this cool climate.' Suzanne had mentioned Mary Beth moved out west." He walked over to the back door. "The hinges on the screen are loose. I'm going to tighten them before they pull out all the way."

Kate gave an unladylike snort. "My guess is that my sister said something along the lines that our mother had to leave Texas because she ran out of marriageable men in the entire state—which my mother has just proved with her message." She glanced over at the hinges. "You don't have to do that. You're a guest. I'll call a handyman."

"As long as I'm here, no need."

"Jesse Chapman." She couldn't help her smile. "Golfer extraordinaire and good with tools. Who knew?"

"And don't you forget it." He chuckled deeply and reached up to the top hinge, his stance slightly parted. His triceps flexed with each turn of the screw. "Your mother asked me to pass the message along to Suzanne as well. I got the feeling that Mary Beth didn't want to call Darling Daughter Number One herself." He moved to the next screw. "They never did see eye to eye, as I recall. Though I guess there were a lot of people who didn't understand your mother."

Kate knew what he said was true, and deep down she agreed. But this was her mother, and instantly she felt defensive. "She has a creative spirit and she needs to be free to create."

He dropped his arms and turned back. He surprised her when he reached out and ran his finger down one of her long curls, round and round, slowly, hypnotically. When he stopped, he touched her, tilting her chin until she met his gaze. Sensation raced through her, settling low, flaring when his eyes drifted to her mouth. The world around them seemed to disappear. She felt disconnected from everything but this man, floating in a dream like madness sought. Which was exactly what wanting Jesse Chapman was. Madness.

"She doesn't deserve you, Katie, never has. Mary Beth's a flake. A great flake, no question, but nonetheless—"

"A flake."

"You got it."

"If you are so reproving—"

Abruptly, he dropped his hand. After a second, his teasing smile resurfaced and he returned his attention to finishing off the hinge. "You must have had a rough day. You've dragged out the big words. Where's the dictionary?"

"Amusing, Mr. 4.0."

"3.8. I got a B in Spanish."

"That's right," she teased. "Your attempt to date Senorita Gonzalez didn't work out."

The last top screw didn't want to go in. His concentration focused as he undid it, straightened it, then screwed it home.

"It didn't, did it?" she gasped with a half laugh.

"Let's just say that I probably deserved a C. I never was all that good at conjugating verbs."

"No, you just like conjugating."

He glanced over his shoulder. "Did you just tell a joke?"

She might have growled.

He laughed softly. "I like it when you get all hot and bothered."

"I am not hot, and I am certainly not bothered."

"Sure you are." He secured the last screw on top, then squatted to do the same to the bottom.

A horn sounded outside. Neither of them did anything about it until it sounded again. Curious, Kate walked through the house and went to the front door, peering out the window.

A car had pulled up in the drive, and Kate recognized Madge Lehman's sedan. Kate opened the door.

"Hi, Kate!"

"Hi, Madge."

No one said another word, though Kate could tell her neighbor was waiting expectantly for something.

"I came to pick up Lena."

Belatedly, Kate remembered Travis.

"Oh, well . . . just a second, Madge."

Kate turned around. Jesse was there.

"Travis already met someone in the neighborhood?" she asked.

"If so, I'm not aware of it. Plus, he's at Suzanne's."

They glanced to the side and saw an unfamiliar back-pack sitting in the foyer next to one they both recognized as belonging to Travis.

"Are you sure he's at Suzanne's?"

"I just got here right before you did." Jesse's brow furrowed.

"Oh, great. He must be here. In the house. Alone with little Lena, unsupervised."

Deep down, she knew she was overreacting. But she wasn't a parent, didn't have that ease mothers and fathers learned over long years of adjusting to their kids' behavior. She was new at this, and there was a real parent sitting outside thinking her child was here, safe, sound, and no doubt supervised.

Jesse didn't look any happier about the situation than she felt.

They darted through the house, finding no sign of Travis. But when they came to his bedroom, the door was shut, and they could hear the radio playing.

Kate froze, panic flaring. "What do you think they're doing? He is your son, after all. I wonder if sexual precociousness is genetic."

Jesse swore, then clicked open the door to find Travis and a girl about his same age kneeling by the side of the bed.

"Are they praying?" Kate whispered.

"He better be praying," Jesse bit out.

"This one's really good," Lena said, tilting her head to get a better view.

"Yeah, maybe." Travis flipped a page of not a Bible, but rather a glossy magazine. "But this one's better."

"Says who?" Lena demanded with a scoff.

"Says . . . I don't know. It just is. Guys are much better golfers. Everyone knows that."

Lena leaped up, planting her hands on her hips. "You're such a toad. Guys are not better."

"Toad? You're calling me a toad?"

"What's going on here?" Jesse demanded, his tone accusing.

Not textbook-perfect parenting technique—even Kate knew that—but it got the kids' attention.

Travis and Lena whirled around.

Lena waved. "Hi, Miss Bloom!"

"Hi, Jesse!" Travis said. "You're home! Are we going to do a father-son thing now?"

"What do you two think you're doing?" Jesse asked crossly.

The girl's smile evaporated. "Ah, maybe I should go," she stuttered. "See ya later, Travis."

She bolted for the door and was out of the house before they could say another word.

Kate, Jesse, and Travis stood staring at one another.

"You're supposed to be at Suzanne's," Jesse stated.

Travis shrugged. "I got bored. When she got on the phone, I went for a walk. That's when I met Lena. She's really cool and she helped me come up with a whole bunch of father-son stuff to do."

"There are . . . are . . . rules about this kind of thing," Jesse added, grasping for what to say.

"Rules about looking at magazines? Talking to Lena? Or about father-son sorts of stuff?" Travis asked. Then he got excited again and extended one of the magazines.

"You should see the pictures in here. Look at this! You're right there!"

Kate peered closer, and indeed, it was a shiny, color, freeze-frame photograph of Jesse doing a victory sign as a ball rolled straight for the hole.

"Wow," she said.

"Isn't it cool?" An old edition of *Golf World* hung from Travis's fingers as he went to the middle of the room. "I can do the same thing." He lifted one knee and pulled his crooked arm down like a semitruck driver honking a horn. "See! I'd make a great golfer. I bet there's no chess guy who could do that."

"Chess?" Kate asked, confused. "Golf?"

Tension rippled through the older male as he took the magazine away. "Doing victory dances is not high on the list of good golf qualities—"

"Not according to that *Star Magazine* article I read about you."

Jesse's lips thinned.

Kate shook her head, still confused. "What are you two talking about?"

"I've been reading about Jesse and golf. I know I'm supposed to be figuring out something else I can do this summer besides golf. But golf sure sounds fun, and I read that Jesse's been playing since he was about my age." Travis smiled knowingly. "It also talked about him having a way with girls. Kinda like me, too," he said with a gloating smile. "Lena's cute, huh?"

"Last I heard"—Kate sliced a look at Jesse—"sneaking girls into a boy's bedroom wasn't considered an extra-curricular activity."

Jesse's jaw tensed. "You're grounded."

"Grounded?" Kate gasped.

"Who, me?" Travis asked.

"Yes, you," Jesse snapped.

"For reading golf magazines?" Travis wanted to know. Kate and Travis exchanged a look.

"For . . . having a girl in your room," Jesse stated, then he turned and walked out the door.

"Well," Travis mused, "I guess grounding is a father-son kind of thing. I just thought we'd do something more fun than that."

Kate shook her head and realized she wasn't the only person around here who was having a hard time adjusting to a new set of circumstances. She had worn ankle weights on TV and Jesse had just grounded his son for no real good reason. Jeez, they were a pair.

To: Katherine Bloom <katherine@ktextv.com>
    Julia Boudreaux <julia@ktextv.com>
From: Chloe Sinclair <chloe@ktextv.com>
Subject: Date

How was lunch with Parker?

Chloe

Chloe Sinclair
Station Manager
Award-winning KTEX TV

To: Julia Boudreaux <julia@ktextv.com>
    Chloe Sinclair <chloe@ktextv.com>
From: Katherine Bloom <katherine@ktextv.com>
Subject: Great

Amazingly great! It was wonderful! He really is dreamy. Also, I
had an idea for a new segment that will show viewers that I'm

not a complete idiot and that shouldn't turn me into a blushing
fool. I was thinking about something with pets?

Best,
Kate

Katherine C. Bloom
News Anchor, KTEX TV West Texas

To: Katherine Bloom <katherine@ktextv.com>
   Chloe Sinclair <chloe@ktextv.com>
From: Julia Boudreaux <julia@ktextv.com>
Subject: Animals

Hmmm. I actually like the idea. And I'm thrilled that you had a
good time with Parker. I can't believe after all this time both you
and Chloe had dates.

xo, j

p.s. Let me think more about the pet thing.

To: Julia Boudreaux <julia@ktextv.com>
   Chloe Sinclair <chloe@ktextv.com>
From: Katherine Bloom <katherine@ktextv.com>
Subject: Dates

Chloe had a date and no one told me? Who, when, where?!!!!

K

To: Katherine Bloom <katherine@ktextv.com>
    Chloe Sinclair <chloe@ktextv.com>
From: Julia Boudreaux <julia@ktextv.com>
Subject: Setups

I arranged the date for Chloe, but you know how she gets. All
nervous around men. Awkward. But I've sworn to cure her since
she is too sweet and wonderful and amazing never to have been
in love. I'm going to find her a man if it kills me.

xo, j

To: Katherine Bloom <katherine@ktextv.com>
    Julia Boudreaux <julia@ktextv.com>
From: Chloe Sinclair <chloe@ktextv.com>
Subject: Gander

Jules, I know you mean well, but he's not my type. I mean, really,
he named his car. Goose. Have you ever heard of anyone out of
high school who names his car?

Chloe

To: Chloe Sinclair <chloe@ktextv.com>
    Katherine Bloom <katherine@ktextv.com>
From: Julia Boudreaux <julia@ktextv.com>
Subject: What's in a name

So he calls his car Goose. He probably named it after that fellow in *Top Gun.* The guy who moved on to *ER.* If I were you I wouldn't be so picky.

xo, j

To: Julia Boudreaux <julia@ktextv.com>
    Katherine Bloom <katherine@ktextv.com>
From: Chloe Sinclair <chloe@ktextv.com>
Subject: Naming names

I don't care if it refers to the goose that laid the golden egg. If he names his car, what else has he christened? I shudder to think.

C

To: Chloe Sinclair <chloe@ktextv.com>
    Katherine Bloom <katherine@ktextv.com>
From: Julia Boudreaux <julia@ktextv.com>
Subject: Ooooo . . .

Do you really think he has named his penile appendage? Hmmm . . . Igor? King of the Jungle? I guess it might be hard to do anything really wild or wicked like going down on a dick with a name. Oh! He's named it Dick!

xo, j

To: Chloe Sinclair <chloe@ktextv.com>
   Julia Boudreaux <julia@ktextv.com>
From: Katherine Bloom <katherine@ktextv.com>
Subject: Tom Cruise

Penile appendage? Good God, Julia. And Chloe, my guess is if your date named his car Goose, he probably named his penis Maverick. Kind of a *Top Gun* theme.

K

To: Julia Boudreaux <julia@ktextv.com>
   Katherine Bloom <katherine@ktextv.com>
From: Chloe Sinclair <chloe@ktextv.com>
Subject: Unglued

Have the two of you lost your minds? Movie character body parts, and I am not going down on anyone's anything, regardless of what it is called. And I don't want to hear any of that prude business. It is only good sense. Now both of you leave me alone so I can work in peace.

C

seven

It was nearly midnight when Kate turned off the computer. Earlier, Parker had called and they had talked on the phone like teenagers. Instead of pulling further and further away from Parker since Jesse's arrival, she had felt more comfortable being around him. It had been fun and she had hung up feeling a little bit giddy by this unexpected turn in her world.

Retrieving a printout, she left the house and walked across the yard to slip the single page under the guest cottage door. She wanted Jesse to have the information first thing tomorrow morning.

Crouched on the flagstones, the paper halfway under the door, she was startled when it opened. From her vantage point, all she saw were incredible hard-muscled legs with a dusting of dark hair disappearing up into a pair of khaki shorts. Then a shirt, just pulled off, bunched in his hand as if she had interrupted him undressing.

She scrambled to stand. "I have information for you,"

she said as smoothly as she could over the flutter in her chest.

His lips tilted at one corner. "Hello to you, too."

"I found this on the Internet. It's the perfect solution. If you'd like, I can go over it with you."

"I assume that means you want to come in."

Her mouth fell open when he didn't wait for an answer, slung the tee over his shoulder, and walked back toward the tiny kitchen.

Kate had to focus her thoughts, though she hadn't managed to do it before he stopped, looked back at her, and said, "Are you going to stand there, or are you coming in?"

"Oh. Well, fine," she replied with a firm nod of her head as she stepped inside.

But the minute she entered, she knew it was a mistake. She didn't remember her guesthouse feeling so small. Jesse seemed to fill the place, all heat and hard muscle, leaving no room for anything but his presence. Three different types of putters were propped against an overstuffed chair, while several white balls were scattered on the rug around an empty, washed soup can that was tilted over on its side. More than that, however, she couldn't help notice that her teapot and cups were still sitting on the counter like an embarrassing rebuke.

Fortunately she caught sight of her hair in a decorative mirror, distracting her. She grimaced at the sight. Her curls looked like a full head of Medusa snakes.

His gaze, however, drifted lower, touching her everywhere, then he whistled appreciatively. "Nice legs."

The ankle weights were working!

Though just as quickly she reminded herself that she

didn't care. After only a second more, she remembered why she was there. "Travis."

That wiped the smile off his too-handsome face.

He turned away from her and went to the tiny refrigerator, pulled out a beer, and popped the tab. Just before he took a sip, he hesitated. "Do you want one?" he asked.

"No, thank you."

"Are you sure? You could use a little loosening up."

"I am plenty loose," she stated stiffly.

Fresh amusement surfaced in his eyes, though fortunately he didn't comment.

"I'm here about Travis. I think it's a great idea to enroll him in a summer golf program."

The beer can stopped halfway to his mouth. She could see emotion trailing across his face. Then it was gone and he shrugged. "If you want him to play golf—"

"*He* wants to play. It's a great solution to keep him busy while I'm at work and you're doing . . . whatever it is you do. That is, unless you have a problem with golf."

That darkness flared, then he visibly tamped it down. "No problem. Like I started to say, if he wants to play golf, it's fine with me."

"Earlier I made a call and found out that the country club is in between sessions. But I've also learned that there is an afternoon program in Canutillo on the public course. A van picks kids up right here at the corner."

"Just tell me who to write a check out to, and I'll take care of it in the morning."

"Oh." She had expected an argument. Clearly this man was more than generous with his money. It was just his emotions he kept to himself.

After a startled second, she handed him the printout.

He glanced over it, and when he finished, she was still there. "Did you want something else?" he asked.

"No. No. There's nothing else." She started to leave, should have left, but stopped at the last minute. "Though there is the whole thing about the grounding."

That broad smile of his reappeared, this time a little sheepish. "I know. I didn't handle that so well."

"True. Maybe in the morning when you mention the golf, you could say something about that, too."

He didn't respond.

"Travis needs more from you than money, Jesse. Paying for lessons is a great gesture, but don't withhold everything else. I'm pretty sure he wants to play golf to have something in common with you."

He studied her, then finished the beer in one last swallow, crumpled the can in his fist, and tossed it into the trash. He turned to face her and she didn't like his expression at all. His midnight eyes narrowed and he took a step toward her.

"Wow," she said weakly, "two points."

When he didn't stop, she took a step back. "What are you doing, Jesse?"

"I wish to hell I knew."

He pulled his belt from his shorts with a single jerk, the leather snapping in the hot summer night.

"Ah, I'd say you're . . . undressing?"

"Good eye."

"Meaning?"

"You all but said that I withhold everything but money, and I don't appreciate it."

"Now, Jesse, when I said that, I wasn't trying to be hurtful. Not at all."

He tossed the belt aside, his eyes brooding like a storm. Sexual awareness rippled through her. She hated how her breath rumbled low in her chest, just as she hated the way she felt the same unsettling tightness she had felt five years ago when she had walked in on him while he was getting dressed for Suzanne and Derek's wedding.

Her mind drifted back to that day years earlier. Jesse had just gotten out of the shower at his house. Her own home was filled to overflowing with bridesmaids and wedding people putting on the ceremony in the backyard.

Not realizing Jesse had returned, she walked into his bedroom to get away, only to find him just out of the shower. She must have made a sound because he turned. He stood before her, naked and amazing, his sex thick and large, hanging in a soft fullness between his thighs that made her mouth go dry.

"Oh," she had whispered.

She had been twenty-two, just out of college, and settling into who she wanted to be. There was that young Kate who had been adventuresome, battling with the newer Kate who had spent too many years taking care of her wildly passionate mother. Jesse made her forget them both.

"You're beautiful," she had added.

He watched her. And when she boldly looked at his soft fullness, he grew hard. He muttered a curse, and started to turn away. But good sense fled. She took the steps that separated them in the tiny bedroom, then she touched his back. She saw the way his body tensed, saw the flexing muscles that ran along his spine, disappearing into his slim hips, so white against his tan.

"Kiss me," she had whispered.

She had never wanted anything so badly. Just when she thought he'd tell her to get the hell out of there so he could get dressed, he turned.

"Katie," he said with a mix of jaw-ticking restraint and incredible kindness. "You're innocent—"

"I don't want to be." Conviction rushed through her in equal measures to desire.

He almost reached out like he had so many times before, as a friend, as the boy who kept her safe. But then his expression changed, his nostrils flaring, and he dropped his hand. "You might not want to be, but I want that for you. Some guy is going to come along and sweep you off your feet. You deserve that."

"I want you, Jesse. You know that."

"You deserve better."

That was what she had never understood—why he thought she deserved better than him. And why he never believed her when she told him how great he was.

That night, when she stepped even closer and whispered, "I deserve *you*," he groaned one last time before something inside him let loose and he pulled her to him.

Their bodies came together, her palms flattening against his skin. His lips came down on hers, teasing and tasting with an expertise that should have given her pause. He showed her passion with his body, as if he had been waiting for this moment.

The sensation was heaven. She ran her hands up his torso, then down along his spine as he kissed her, feeling his groan shudder through his body.

He clutched her to him like he sought something more from her than just the kiss as he buried his face in her hair. "God, Katie," he choked.

She could feel his tight control slip a notch, felt the

way he nearly trembled when he kissed her again, this time running his tongue along her mouth. When she opened to him, he tasted her deeply, suddenly savagely, as if his control had broken completely. He lined her face with his strong hands, tilting her to him so that he could kiss her temple and eyes, across her neck to the shell of her ear.

When she felt his palm slide underneath her shirt, drifting higher until he grazed her breast, every nerve ending came alive. She wrapped her arms around his neck, holding on as he coaxed her, she meeting his demands as he brought her body to life, making her want more.

"Katie," he breathed. Then he swore an oath and tugged her T-shirt over her head.

She felt air hit her skin at the same moment he dipped his head and opened his mouth over her breast. Her head swam as his hands slid low, cupping her hips, pressing her against his need.

"God, you're beautiful," he whispered reverently. "Beautiful and pure."

Then all of a sudden he froze. After a second, he tore himself away. One minute she felt the hardness of him against her, his hands and mouth exploring her intimately, then the next he set her aside with a feral groan.

His breathing was deep and labored, and his eyes narrowed as he grabbed her shirt and pulled it over her head, then tugged her arms through the holes as if she were a child. "You've got to leave," he said. Nothing more.

"But—"

"Damn it, Katie, get the hell out of here."

That day she had been upset and mortified when she raced out of Jesse's room and had run straight into Derek.

"Kate? Are you all right?"

"I'm fine," she answered, tears spilling over, before she hurried out of the house.

Two hours later she'd been crushed when Jesse showed up at the wedding with not one date, but two. Both of the women glowed with the same kind of passion and fire her mother cast out. Kate had felt betrayed when he hadn't even said hello—then devastated when after angry words with Derek, Jesse had taken his dates and left.

Kate swallowed now, all these years later, when Jesse took a step toward her in the guesthouse. She took a step back, bumping into a small table. The memory of him always did battle with the man he had become. Sinful, but still incredible. Wild, but she couldn't deny that he had stepped up to his responsibilities to his son. As always, he was a mix that was hard to understand.

He kicked off his boat shoes one by one. Her heart surged and her pulse rushed through her veins.

She cleared her throat. "I realize that you're to be commended for taking care of Travis. But I hope you'll give him more than simply a place to stay. He is dying for a scrap of your attention. He deserves that from you."

"I'm going to send him to golf school."

"I'm talking about giving him some of your time."

He inhaled sharply, raking his hands through his hair. "You might look sexy as hell in those workout clothes—"

This time she inhaled sharply.

"—but you're still a pain in the ass," he added with a mix of irritation and bemusement.

"I'm only trying to point out what's right," she managed to say. "Is it so bad to have high expectations?"

She could tell he took pity on her when he smiled. "No, little Katie, it isn't. But I didn't come back here to be parented by you, or to be a parent. I'm going to take care of Travis while his mother gets settled. But that's it. So don't try to make this trip something that it isn't."

"Then what is this trip about?"

He didn't answer. His gaze drifted to her lips as he took the last step that separated them, bringing them close enough that if he wanted to, he could touch her. His shirt was gone, only his shorts separating him from the way he looked that day when she had walked into his bedroom.

Despite every warning, heat raced through her, centering at her core, hot enough that she felt the need to press her legs together against the thought of what she wanted him to do to her. Touch her. Kiss her. Finish what they had started five years ago.

She would have closed her eyes as she sucked in a breath of anticipation if his burning gaze hadn't been locked with hers.

But she didn't think she could take it if he touched her again, then left. It had taken her five long years to hammer her life into an order that didn't revolve around the hope that one day they would end up together.

"Listen," she blurted. "Whatever the reason is that you came back, it's time we spelled out in plain English what the deal is while you're staying here."

"The deal?"

With effort, she planted her hands on her hips and did her best to look authoritative and commanding. "No sex. There isn't going to be any sex between us."

"Interesting. Why's that?" One dark brow rose in challenge, his lips tilting in an aggravating tease.

"You don't agree?"

"Actually, I do, but I'm still curious why you have to make a rule about it."

"Well, for starters"—she raised her chin—"you're leaving."

He conceded with a nod. "True."

She could have done with a little less straightforward bluntness. "For another, I'm not your type."

"I don't have a type."

She couldn't help snorting in disbelief. "Though more important, you have a son to think about."

This really made him grin. "I can't have sex *and* have a son?" he teased.

She rolled her eyes. "Someone should have had that birds and bees talk with you."

He laughed out loud, then reached for her, awareness and desire leaping through her like a flame.

Those traitorous thoughts she always had when Jesse was near fought to the surface. Kissing. This man. And maybe, just maybe, it wouldn't be so bad to give in to a little fling.

She nearly scoffed out loud. Giving in? A little fling? Like those women he brought to the wedding?

Like her mother.

The thought cut through the desire licking through her body.

"No sex!"

He hesitated, though for only a half second before his smile turned wicked and he grabbed something off the table behind her. Too late she realized he must have been going for a towel the whole time.

"Can't take a shower without this," he stated.

Embarrassment flashed through her, wiping out every bit of desire. She should have been relieved, and yet again she should have left well enough alone. But she couldn't help herself when her mind circled back to the question that had been plaguing her.

Maybe it was her pride, or maybe the reporter in her couldn't be held back any longer by dictates to be sweet and affable, but she asked, "Jesse, if you're so determined to keep distant from your past, then really, why did you come back?"

His body went taut. Seconds ticked by before he said, "Everyone needs a vacation."

"Seems to me that most people go to the Bahamas or Tahiti to get away."

"Not when they're trying to avoid the media."

"Is it really so hard to be a hero? Do you really have to fight off so much attention that you had to run away?" She was on a roll and couldn't seem to stop herself. "Why do I think there's something you aren't telling me?"

She could see his jaw start to work, the towel gripped between his two hands.

"Because you were always filled with dreams inside a head that you fooled everyone into thinking was sensible." He secured the terry cloth around his neck. "Now, unless you want to hang around and get the sort of show that I'm beginning to think you secretly want, I'd suggest you head on back to your house. Wouldn't want you breaking any of those no-sex rules of yours."

To add muscle to his point, he unzipped his shorts, the khaki slipping low on his hips, his thumbs hooking under stark white Jockeys. And just when she turned to make a hasty retreat, she caught a glimpse of his beautifully chiseled anatomy as he tossed his shorts aside.

To: Katherine Bloom <katherine@ktextv.com>
From: Julia Boudreaux <julia@ktextv.com>
Subject: Getting your wish

I've thought about it, and I agree that a pet show for the next segment of *Getting Real with Kate* will be perfect. I even have a great idea. It's fresh and original. You are going to love it, as will the audience!

xo, j

To: Julia Boudreaux <julia@ktextv.com>
From: Katherine Bloom <katherine@ktextv.com>
Subject: Thank you

I appreciate this, Julia. Pets are much more me than naked or wanting-to-get-naked sorts of men. I promise I'll do the station proud this time.

Now, tell me a bit about whom I'll be interviewing. I want to be prepared and have a list of proper questions to ask. Maybe I should go over to the library and get a few books on pet care so I'll look knowledgeable.

Many thanks,
K

Katherine C. Bloom
News Anchor, KTEX TV West Texas

To: Katherine Bloom <katherine@ktextv.com>
    Chloe Sinclair <chloe@ktextv.com>
From: Julia Boudreaux <julia@ktextv.com>
Subject: Girl Scout

Kate, sugar, I think it's best you go in unprepared. It's all your Girl Scout sort of planning that gets you in trouble. Think of this segment as a time to relax and have fun. Then on Thursday, the night before, let's go out and have a pre-show celebration. Just the three of us. I promise not to end the night early with a date. It will be fun.

xoxo, j

To: Julia Boudreaux <julia@ktextv.com>
    Chloe Sinclair <chloe@ktextv.com>
From: Katherine Bloom <katherine@ktextv.com>
Subject: Unprepared!

How can I go in unprepared? Though maybe you're right. Perhaps it's best if I just let it flow. It's only pets after all.

As to Thursday night with the girls, I would love to, but Travis has his first day of golf camp and I want to be at home to see how it went.

K

To: Katherine Bloom <katherine@ktextv.com>
    Chloe Sinclair <chloe@ktextv.com>
From: Julia Boudreaux <julia@ktextv.com>
Subject: Hmmm

Aren't you the little domestic these days. Staying home to make sure all is well in the domicile. Though it's fine. Turns out Roberto called after all.

xoxo, j

To: Julia Boudreaux <julia@ktextv.com>
    Katherine Bloom <katherine@ktextv.com>
From: Chloe Sinclair <chloe@ktextv.com>
Subject: Bad boys

Admit it, Jules, for someone who keeps telling Kate and me to find someone to settle down with, you sure keep yourself distant from any truly marriageable men. The only guys you date are passionate artists and rugged cowboys who make it clear they aren't interested in settling down.

Chloe, the observant

To: Chloe Sinclair <chloe@ktextv.com>
From: Julia Boudreaux <julia@ktextv.com>
Subject: Snippy

You're not observant, you're making things up. I am only twenty-seven, young enough to date anyone I choose. Now get back to work. You have Kate's pet show to arrange. I sent my ideas in a separate e-mail.

xo, j

e i g h t

"**S**anders, Travis!"

"Here."

Travis looked around the small group of other kids who stood on the driving range of the Canutillo Golf School. A big burly guy who didn't look like he knew the first thing about golf, much less had the ability to hold a club due to his girth, called roll.

A group of boys stood off to the side. Travis could tell on sight that they were the cool kids. Uncool kids had a second sense about these things. Normally, he would have steered clear of the group, but he had the next few weeks, if that long, to show his dad what a great kid he was. And didn't great kids have cool friends?

Once roll call was done and their coach said to get into foursomes, Travis drew up his nerve and walked over to the three coolest guys.

"Hey," he said, shuffling his feet, his hand flying up nervously as he waved.

The kid who must have been their leader shot him a scowl. "What do you want, twerp?"

"Ah, you know. A foursome."

"You pervert!"

The boys laughed.

"What's so funny?" the coach asked.

"Nothing, sir," one boy said with exaggerated politeness.

Coach considered them, grumbled, then went on. "Sanders, I'm putting you with Hartman, Puskus, and Fisk."

Great. One glance and any idiot could tell they were not cool at all. Proof came when the cool guys announced variations of their names. None of them good. At least Travis didn't have a name that could be twisted into anything embarrassing.

"Hey, perve," they whispered at him.

Okay, so they didn't need a name to contort.

The rest of the afternoon didn't go much better. The clubs assigned to him were old, and when he did manage to connect with the ball, a metallic shudder raced up through his arms into his shoulders, sparking a headsplitting pain.

"No, Sanders, don't slap at the ball. Stroke it," Coach said.

Though what exactly that meant, Travis didn't know, since whenever the man swung the club he looked more like a baseball player than any golfer Travis had ever seen.

But he tried nonetheless, determined to make inroads with the cool guys.

After hitting a few balls, it was someone else's turn to step up to the tee. Travis fell back.

"You can swing pretty good," he told the number one cool guy.

The compliment didn't go unappreciated, though it didn't get a response.

"My dad would probably be impressed."

Still nothing. Okay, time to go in for the kill.

"Yeah, my dad, he can really play golf. Everyone says so."

"Like who?" Jimmy, the head cool guy, begrudgingly asked.

Travis shrugged, his heart pounding hard. It was happening. They were talking to him. And in a second when they found out about Jesse, his place would be secured.

"The newspapers and stuff. They write about him all the time."

"Who is your dad?"

"Jesse Chapman."

For half a second awe simmered through their eyes, then they burst out laughing. "Yeah, sure. You related to Chapman? No way, perve."

"It's the truth. Everyone says I look just like him."

"He isn't even married." Then Jimmy got sly. "What are you, some kind of accident?"

Travis's fluttering heart turned into a heart attack. He hadn't thought about that part. He hadn't realized where this would lead.

"You are!" the boys screamed in glee, laughing.

"You're a perve and a bastard."

They really thought that was funny.

"Is your mom a whore? Is she expensive? Can we afford her?"

It had never happened before, but standing there in the heat and dirt with tiny tufts of grass here and there, he snapped. All his good cheer and optimism shattered. He hardly knew how it happened, but suddenly he lunged at Jimmy. Years of being a kid with no real father, since Harlan had never liked him much, welled up until he felt tears streaming down his cheeks with every strike of his fist. He punched and hit, but after a second of surprise, Jimmy quickly moved out of the way, and the boys only laughed harder when Travis swung one last time, missed, and landed in a patch of dry desert sand face first.

They laughed for a while longer, then left him there. He wanted the ground to open up and swallow him whole. He stayed that way for what seemed like forever. Then suddenly Coach's big meaty hand grasped him by the shoulder.

"Here, Sanders, don't let 'em get to you," the man said, helping him up. "And don't ever let 'em see you cry."

The man dusted him off, then shoved a club in his hands. "You're up again. And this time put all that anger into your swing."

The van dropped Travis off at the corner of Meadowlark and Vista del Monte. He'd had to sit right by the bus driver in order to survive the short trip from the golf school. When he hopped down, the rental clubs he'd been assigned banging against his legs, he could hear the other kids' taunts as they drove away.

Travis didn't move. He watched the van until it disappeared down the street, then he turned and walked across to Kate's house.

Kate was really nice. Heck, she worried about him way more than his mom did. But he wouldn't think about that. Kate wasn't his mom, and soon he'd be leaving for Las Vegas. He wondered if Jesse would miss him, then he scoffed. His dad would probably jump up and down for joy.

He was surprised when he walked down the drive and saw Jesse by the pool. He had some tools and he was fixing one of the lounge chairs. Seemed like Jesse was always fixing something around here, always had some tool. Though Travis had seen that at night Jesse read all kinds of books about golf. Strategy books, books on how to play. He even watched videos of golf game after golf game on Kate's machine. It was like the guy was looking for something.

Given the totally crummy day he'd had, Travis wasn't in the mood to talk. He tried to slip by without being noticed. But Jesse must have heard him, because he turned around.

"Hey," Jesse called out, standing up with a hammer in his hand.

Travis gave a quick wave, but he didn't stop.

Inside the house, he found something to eat. He felt a spark of pleasure at the sight of a plate lined with real sugar cookies, not hard ones out of a box, with creamy icing on top. He managed to pour a glass of milk and head for the table with the entire plate.

He couldn't have been more surprised when a few minutes later Jesse actually came into the house.

"So," his dad said, all cheery. "You found the cookies. I made them."

"You?"

"Yeah. I used to love those things."

Amazingly, his dad looked like he really cared what Travis thought about the cookies. "They're good."

Jesse beamed. "How was golf camp?"

Not nearly as good. But Travis wasn't about to admit that maybe he wasn't cut out for golf after all. He forced a smile and said, "Great! It was really fun!"

Jesse looked at him kind of funny. "You want to tell me about it?" he asked.

"Nothing much to tell. We learned about the clubs, hit some balls. Tomorrow we're going to learn to putt."

Great. Tomorrow he'd have to go back.

"Who's teaching?"

"Coach Peters."

"Gary? You're kidding me. He's a great guy and all, but he's a baseball coach."

That would explain his peculiar form of hitting the ball. Travis answered with a shrug.

They both turned at the sound of tires on gravel. Seconds later, Kate came into the house with a gigantic smile on her face.

"Hi, T. How was camp?"

T. She had started calling him T. A fun nickname that showed he was part of the crowd. He felt stupid tears burn in his eyes.

"Great," both he and Jesse said at the same time.

She glanced between them, then said, "This is wonderful news. What have you learned so far?"

Travis pushed up. "Just stuff. But I'm kind of sweaty, so can I go for a swim?"

"Well, sure."

Travis headed out before they could ask him any more about golf. Nope, he'd have to spend some time coming up with some answers about that. And boy was he glad he was heading out because just as he was leaving the kitchen to go to his room to change, Derek came to the back door.

He looked really mad, but the minute he saw Travis he kind of worked up a smile. "Hi, Travis."

"Hi." He flipped up a wave, then bolted for his room.

Jesse studied his brother through the screen door. Derek came into the kitchen without being asked.

"Kate," Derek acknowledged with a nod. "Can I speak to my brother for a moment?"

"Oh, sure." She gathered her purse, then followed Travis.

Jesse could tell by the look on Derek's face that he wasn't happy.

"What's up?" Jesse asked, leaning back against the counter, crossing his ankles.

"I had a visit from Daniel Lehman today."

"I take it I'm supposed to know who Daniel Lehman is."

Derek's jaw ticked, but he kept his voice level. "He is a neighbor, a colleague at the bank, and the father of Lena."

Lena. That sounded familiar. Then Jesse remembered the little girl in Travis's room. Great.

"And?"

"He was not happy about the fact that his daughter came over to play with Travis without an adult in attendance."

"It won't happen again. We've already talked about it. Besides, all they were doing was looking at golf magazines."

"Just the sort of response I would expect from you. It doesn't matter what they were doing—"

"It doesn't?" Anger surged up despite the fact that he was trying to keep it at bay.

"What matters is providing guidelines for a child and setting good examples. You haven't the first clue how to do either."

Jesse pushed away from the counter. "What the hell is that supposed to mean?"

"Don't play naïve with me. We both know you don't have a clue what guidelines are or boundaries for proper behavior. Travis is a kid, and he needs boundaries whether you had them or not."

That's all it took. One minute they were standing there, the next minute years of frustration spilled over and Jesse pinned his older brother to the wall. "You don't know what the fuck you're talking about."

But Derek was frustrated too. "Don't I? When did you start smoking? Eleven? And drinking? Twelve?"

He pushed Jesse away, gaining release only because Jesse felt like he'd been punched in the gut. His breath grew labored.

"How about the first time you had sex?" Derek pursued relentlessly. "Thirteen?"

"I don't have to listen to this."

"Or how about the time that you should have done the decent thing and stayed away from an innocent young woman who loved you so much that she'd let you take advantage of her?"

"What the hell are you talking about?"

"Kate."

"I've never taken advantage of Katie."

"Haven't you? The night of my wedding?"

"I've told you before, and I'll say this one last time: I didn't take advantage of her that day."

"I can't believe you still expect me to believe that nothing went on between you two in your bedroom. I saw her. I saw her come running out crying."

"Fuck."

"Ah, yes, isn't that what you do best?"

The fury exploded, and he had his brother up against the wall again, his own demons wrapping around him like a vise. This time Derek cursed, then sighed wearily, pulling a deep breath, calm returning with effort.

"Damn it," the older Chapman stated, shaking his head. "I'm sorry. I shouldn't have said anything. That's the past. I came over here about the future."

Jesse pushed away. "What are you talking about?"

"Face it, Jesse, do you really think you can take care of Travis? Don't you think he deserves a place to stay where two mature adults can care for him?"

"What are you saying?"

"I'm offering to take Travis off your hands. I know you. You're champing at the bit to get out of here. So go. Leave Travis with Suzanne and me."

Jesse's eyes narrowed. "I see why you're doing this now. You can't have kids, so you decide you'll take mine instead."

Where physical blows hadn't hit their mark, that did. Jesse knew he shouldn't have cared. But he felt like a jerk for having said it anyway. That was how it worked with them. Fury pushing them on, each of them saying things that wounded deep. It had been that way for too many years to count. Old habits that were hard to change. Years of each of them disappointing the other.

"Hell. Just go, Derek. Travis is my responsibility. I've arranged for golf camp."

"There's more to taking care of a child than golf camp. You have to guide and mold and care."

Jesse remembered Katie telling him a version of the very same thing. And that's when the idea hit him.

"I am going to do more. I've come up with a plan so Travis and I can spend more time together." As soon as he said the words he couldn't believe it. But he was too far in to turn back. "We're going to rebuild the tree house."

"What?"

"The one that used to be in Katie's old cottonwood. Travis and I are going to rebuild it together."

n i n e

*R*ebuild *the tree house.*

What the hell was he thinking?

Travis and Kate were fixing dinner, and Jesse left the house. He wanted to punch something. He wanted to get out of town. Just as Derek had said.

Jesse thought of his father.

Decades ago, it had been at the golf course where it had all started. His father had taken him and Derek to hit a few when Jesse was eleven, Derek nineteen. Derek had hated the game. But the minute Jesse had felt the club face connect with that tiny white ball, he was hooked. The sensation was amazing. The feeling of power that he hadn't felt with anything before or since. More than that, it had been the first time in months that Jesse felt as if he could traverse the divide that had grown between father and son. It was the first time something had sparked in Carlen's eyes. A sign that there was still life inside him, that maybe Jesse wouldn't lose him after all.

Golf was also the most frustrating game ever invented.

It was a day-to-day challenge no matter how good a player became. On a good round, golf made him feel like a king. During a bad one, he wondered why he bothered. But those days when he experienced that heady rush of success, that sensation of pure connection, was what brought him back.

But Carlen and Jesse shared more than just golf. Once the bond had started, Carlen had shared his entire world with his younger son. The drinking, the women—as Derek had said, since he was eleven.

That was the demarcation line, the before and after. Before, when their father was in shocked despair over their mother. Then after, when slowly, bit by bit, vice by vice, the man had made his younger son his friend. Carlen Chapman had been alternately moody and arrogantly selfish, and Jesse had never known how to say no, causing his innocence to end early, though so gradually that he sometimes didn't remember being any other way.

After a year of having a broken father, Jesse hadn't known how to decline when Carlen offered him his first drink. He wanted his father back, in whatever capacity was offered. The wildness had become the only life he knew. But Jesse had always done what was right when it came to Katie.

On the day of Derek's wedding, he had wanted nothing more than Katie. Her innocent touch had nearly undone him, just as it had years earlier when she was fourteen and had run her fingers down the path of hair on his chest.

That seemed to be their pattern. Katie seeing something in him that no longer existed, and Jesse trying to do the right thing—at least when it came to her. Because he was not an innocent. And he knew if he made her his, then moved on as he knew he would, Katie would always be considered one of the women who couldn't keep him.

Jesse got in his Jeep and started to drive, then found himself pulling through the tall, black gates of the El Paso Country Club. His fingers tightened on the steering wheel at the sight of the sprawling red brick building at the head of an old-world circular drive shaded by ancient cottonwood trees.

He sat for a second, staring beyond the building to the course. He wondered if he could afford to take a chance on pulling out his clubs and trying to hit a bucket of balls. Would the driving range be crowded? Would people circle around, closing in on him?

He had been honest when he said he had come to El Paso to get away from reporters. He didn't want to talk about the hero business. But it was more than that— there was more that he had a hard time admitting even to himself.

He'd been on fire all year, coming close to winning nearly every tournament he played. Now, with the PGA Championship looming in August, what he really couldn't afford the press getting wind of was that he hadn't been able to swing a club without breaking into a cold sweat since he saved that woman.

He took a deep breath and told himself he could solve the problem here, on this course where he had fallen in love with the sport. He would pull out his clubs, empty his mind, and work out the glitch in his game.

He put on a pair of soft spiked shoes, then pulled a putter, nine iron, and driver out of his bag. As he walked toward the pro shop, heat simmered off the black tarmac, the sky overhead an almost painful blue, without a cloud in the sky. To his left, he could hear kids splashing in the complex's swimming pool. To his right, the felt-wrapped rubber whack of a tennis ball volleyed over the net on the courts.

The minute he pushed into the air-conditioned confines of the golf shop, everyone stopped what they were doing.

"Jesse!"

Golfers crowded around, shaking his hand, glad to be there for his return. Others whom he had never met before hung back, smiling that hopeful smile the more dignified fans got when they wanted him to notice them. Most people assumed this was his favorite part of the game given the sheer amount of media attention he had garnered over the years. But in truth, he hated it.

"Welcome home," the pro said, coming up and shaking his hand. "Good to see you here."

Jesse tried to concentrate on what the man said as they caught up. They discussed rankings and some new up-and-coming talent. It seemed like forever before he was able to continue on through the shop to the other side, coming out onto the putting green.

With measured movements, he set his other clubs aside, then took the putter and a handful of balls. For one long moment he just stood there. His heart felt like it was lodged in his throat, his palms clammy.

Relax, Chapman.

Focus.

He could see through the trees to the towering heights of Mount Franklin rising up into the wide-open West Texas sky. The golf course spread out before him like a carpet, huge willow trees and cottonwoods lining each fairway. This was the world he had known his whole life. This was the solution to the glitch in his game. It had to be.

Dropping the balls onto the velvet green, he took his stance over the putter, swung a few times in practice. He glanced at the mountains one more time before he blocked out the world, breathed deep, pulled the putter back, then swung through. The connection simmered through him as he watched the ball roll toward the miniature flag. He concentrated so hard that he could make out the ball maker's name circling round and round until the ball fell into the hole.

His breath came out in a rush, and he pressed his eyes closed. Good.

He sunk the next two in a row.

The tension that had wrapped around him eased a notch. Barely, but enough that it felt good to be here out on the course. No cameras circling around. No fans with expectations that were impossible to meet.

Stepping up to the last ball, he took a deep breath. He heard someone say his name in the distance. For a second he froze. But then he blocked it out. He swung the club ever so slightly, felt the solid clink of connection, sending the ball running up toward the hole, looking a little left, before it caught the break, circled the rim, then fell into the cup with a gratifying clatter. Success. Five for five. It was a start. But the short game hadn't been the problem. That lay ahead on the driving range.

Before anyone could come up to him, he gathered his belongings and headed over to the ball machine and got a bucket of balls. Concentrating, he told himself he could re-create the same sensation with his driver and nine iron as he had with the putter.

He ignored the other golfers, his grip tight on the metal handle of the wire bucket, and headed for the range. But escape wasn't in the offing. Within minutes, a crowd circled around, closing in on him, making it hard to breathe. And when someone hollered out, demanding that he go for the trees beyond the three hundred–yard marker, the sound startled him. The ease of El Paso was forgotten. The hope for a simple cure on this course was lost.

For nearly as long as he could remember, he had lost himself to women, to sex—and to pushing to the edge, adrenaline and satisfaction pumping through his body, emptying the constant circling in his mind. For a few minutes, a few hours, he forgot the innocent life he had known before. Oddly, it was his father who had taught him about that, about the forgetting. First with a cigarette. Next with a drink after father and son started playing golf together. One drink then two at the infamous "nineteenth hole."

But it was the night of his thirteenth birthday that had changed him completely. His father leaving him alone with one of the older man's many girlfriends. She giving him the sort of present that made his body come to life. It seemed that he had been heading toward that night for the preceding two years.

Derek had been furious when the woman had walked out of Jesse's bedroom. Their father had laughed. Jesse hadn't known what to do. But he knew that he had to protect his father. What would happen if Derek told the people who came by trying to make sure all of them were okay after their mother died? Would they take their father away, leaving them with no one? How had it happened that the world Jesse participated in so that he wouldn't lose his father had suddenly become yet another way that could cause another loss?

Whatever the answer was, Jesse had been protecting his father ever since.

Jesse whirled around. Several people waved. Women smiled that smile he had come to hate. An invitation. A promise of what they wanted to give him.

He knew he didn't dare try to swing because if he did, even here, he realized, he very well might shank the ball. And he couldn't afford for anyone to see that his game was off.

Fuck.

With effort, he smiled and bowed gracefully.

"Sorry, folks, but I just remembered I have someplace I have to be."

People started to grumble, but Jesse didn't stop. He left the full bucket of white balls on the grass, bypassed the pro shop this time, then headed for the parking lot, the club shafts banging against his leg as he went.

Swearing, he carelessly tossed his clubs into the back of the Jeep. The minute he slid into the driver's seat, he shifted into gear and had to force himself not to floor it.

Instead, he drove with careful precision through the open gates, then straight down Country Club Place to Country Club Road, away from the course, away even from Katie's house and the old neighborhood. When he got out of sight, he pushed the accelerator hard, losing himself in the speed, as if he could outrun the terrifying thought that maybe even El Paso couldn't put him back together again.

To: Julia Boudreaux <julia@ktextv.com>
    Chloe Sinclair <chloe@ktextv.com>
From: Katherine Bloom <katherine@ktextv.com>
Subject: Construction site

I'm worried that Suzanne is panicking over not being able to get pregnant. Derek came over and wanted to take Travis. Jesse could have done the easy thing and said yes. Instead, he decided to rebuild the old tree house.

He's already started drawing up plans, making lists of all the things he'll need. He says it's a project that he and Travis can work on together. Travis, unfortunately, didn't look nearly as excited. He made some comment about him and tools not being particularly compatible. But I suppose it's a great way for the two of them to bond.

K

p.s. Maybe at some point down the road we should think about a pregnancy show.

Katherine C. Bloom
News Anchor, KTEX TV West Texas

To: Katherine Bloom <katherine@ktextv.com>
   Chloe Sinclair <chloe@ktextv.com>
From: Julia Boudreaux <julia@ktextv.com>
Subject: Soap opera

It's a shame to hear that all that scheduled sex and ejaculating
into cups hasn't paid off for Derek and Suzanne. I can only hope
that when I finally find a man worthy of having my child, I'll be
able to.

xo, j

p.s. I refuse to do a show on pregnancy, but a *fun* show on *how*
to get pregnant isn't a bad idea. Though first let's get through
the pet segment.

To: Katherine Bloom <katherine@ktextv.com>
   Julia Boudreaux <julia@ktextv.com>
From: Chloe Sinclair <chloe@ktextv.com>
Subject: re: Construction site

Are you telling me that not only has Jesse's little vacation been
extended due to his son, but now he's going to play handyman in
the backyard when he has a huge tournament coming up?
Though I guess you're right about the two of them spending time
together.

Anyway, Kate, tomorrow's show is set. Though, Julia, are you
sure about this?

Chloe Sinclair

Station Manager
Award-winning KTEX TV

To: Julia Boudreaux <<u>julia@ktextv.com</u>>
   Chloe Sinclair <<u>chloe@ktextv.com</u>>
From: Katherine Bloom <<u>katherine@ktextv.com</u>>
Subject: Sure about what?!

What is there to be sure about regarding a pet show???

K

t e n

First thing the next morning, Kate pulled up to the back of KTEX TV and pressed the call button at the rear entrance. She didn't have to wait long before she was buzzed in by security.

The morning news team talked and laughed on air before cutting to an advertisement. Sitting on the brightly lit set, they didn't even notice Kate as she walked past, since the anchors and the weatherman were busy pulling concealed powder out of news desk flower arrangements and weather station props to pat on noses that never got a chance to get shiny.

KTEX was an award-winning station, but like much of the local media, it didn't have a staff for hair or makeup. The on-air talent did their own, fishing blush and compacts out of table decorations between each segment.

Kate did the same thing—had for years. But in addition to primping, she included massive amounts of prepping. Today would be the first time ever she had gone on the air without a clue about her subject. She prayed Julia was right that having a more free-flowing style would make her loosen up.

Before she gave another thought to the pet show, there was something else she wanted to do first. She bypassed her office and continued down the hall to the sports department.

Vern Leeper sat in his office.

"Good morning, Vern."

The ex-football player of about sixty leaned back, the springs of the 1950s vinyl and metal chair squeaking in protest. He was the sports editor for the station, and despite his old boy facade, he was a virtual repository of all things pertinent to sports. Anything he didn't know he was happy to research.

"Good morning, yourself, good-looking."

He also thought he was a charmer.

"What can I do for you?" he asked.

"What do you know about Jesse Chapman?"

Vern whistled. "El Paso's very own prodigal son. What exactly do you want to know?

"Anything. Everything."

"Don't you read *People* magazine?"

"I'm not interested in his love life." At least she wasn't about to admit it to Vern. "I want to go deeper than that."

"Let's see." He leaned forward, planting his elbows on the desk. "He's a damn fine golfer. Could be one of the best. Though we'll see how good he truly is in August when he competes in the PGA Championship."

"What do you mean?"

"The PGA is the last of the four major tournaments of the year. Every golfer knows that if he wants a legacy that goes beyond having made a good living, he's got to win at least one of the game's four majors. So far, Jesse hasn't been able to do it."

"All the great golfers win them?"

"Not all, but there's more pressure on Jesse to succeed than some others. I have no doubt that he's good. But you see, he gets a lot of attention—and there are those who say he gets it because of his pretty-boy good looks and his antics with the women, not because of his talent. But what I have always admired about Jesse is that he never succumbed to the taunts or innuendos. He has lived his own life, played his own game, and now he's on the verge of proving the naysayers wrong. That's what makes this tournament different for Jesse. If he can win one of the majors, he'll prove that he's not just a pretty face."

She remembered the darkness that crept into Jesse's features. The tension that flared only to have him firmly wipe it away. Was he really less at ease being a bad boy than she had thought?

Vern steepled his fingers. "Jesse's coming up to a big tournament. The pressure's intense and every sports writer is going to be watching what he can do in August. This is a huge game for him. He really needs to win. He needs to keep his head clear and his focus tight. How better to do that than going back to his roots?"

"And you think that's why he's come back here? It's a place where he can have space and no worries?"

"Exactly."

But his son had arrived, turning his world upside down. Regardless of everything that rode on this single tournament, Jesse had taken responsibility for Travis. Kate felt a sharp stab of amazement and respect. No wonder Jesse hadn't seemed himself lately.

"Morning, Kate."

She turned and found her director standing in the doorway.

"Hi, Pete."

"Are you ready for the show?"

She extended her arms, showing off the casual slacks and sweater set she had worn. It seemed a good balance between buckskins and her normal business suit.

"You look great," he said. "See you on the set."

By the time she left Vern's office, she forced herself to forget about Jesse for now. She had a show to do, a show she needed to make shine to help her stay employed.

But an hour later, when she walked onto the set for *Getting Real,* her heart went still.

Jesse and Travis pulled into the driveway in the black Jeep.

"I think we found everything we need," Jesse said.

"And then some."

Jesse laughed. "Yeah, maybe I got carried away. But there's just something about a lumber store that makes me want to buy things."

Travis looked at him like he was crazy.

They had gotten to the Home Depot at seven-thirty that morning, then spent a couple of hours there, Travis trailing along, trying to look interested. In the saw section, the kid had gotten fidgety. "Are you sure we should get one of those?"

"We've got to cut the wood somehow. You're not afraid of saws, are you?"

After a long second of apparent debate, he said, "Me? Nah. Love saws."

Now the back of the SUV was loaded with most of
what they would need to rebuild the tree house Jesse remembered as a child. Everything else would be delivered.

The minute Jesse turned off the car, Travis leaped out.
"It's time for *Getting Real with Kate*! Quick or we'll
miss it."

"You go ahead."

Travis didn't wait. He raced inside. Jesse hesitated,
not sure he wanted to see any more of Kate, getting real
or not. But as if he couldn't help himself, he dropped off
some tools, nails, small rungs of wood for ladder steps,
and a saw in the backyard, then went inside. He told
himself he was thirsty.

The television in the kitchen blared, Travis leaning
forward as the opening music and credits rolled.

Then there was Katie herself, looking sweet and wonderful in her new outfit. She sat on a sofa, smiling. But
Jesse could tell she was panicked. She looked at a note
card, and her eyes filled with dread before she said,
"Please welcome Mistress Reynalda." A long, painful
pause followed before she added, "Pet psychic."

"Pet psychic?" Jesse demanded.

"Cool," Travis enthused.

No question this had Julia written all over it.

A woman dressed in a long flowing caftan and a tur-
ban came out onto the stage like a Middle Eastern queen
entering her court.

"Hello," she said in a heavy accent. Sort of *Arabian
Nights* mixed with a barely disguised Mexican flare. She
held two big white fluffy cats, one underneath each arm.
"*Tank* you, Mees Kate, for having me."

The woman arranged herself on the sofa, then extended one of the big fluff balls to Kate. Kate's smile wa-

vered, her eyes going wide with panic when the cat put out its paws like it was putting on the brakes. Jesse could all but hear her thinking that even animals didn't like her.

For half a second, Kate held the cat at arm's length, then seemed to remember the camera.

Fighting for her smile, she brought the animal as close as she could, but the feline wasn't too happy about the arrangement. It started to squirm, trying to get away.

"Now, now, Mees Kate," Mistress Reynalda said in a soothing, if condescending, voice. "Relax. You must be at ease with your pussy."

Kate froze, her fingers clutching the cat in a death grip of shock, making it squirm even more. Jesse dropped into a chair like a piece of lead.

"Mees Kate, please," the woman added as the cat hissed. "You must pet your pussy."

Even on the small, twelve-inch screen, Jesse could see Kate turn a bright shade of red. Then suddenly she started patting the cat. Not gently, not soothingly, but rather with a frantic, flat-palmed pat, pat, pat on the head, its eyes squeezing shut each time.

"No, no! Not like that. Here, let me pet your pussy for you."

With that, Kate jerked up off the sofa, and the cat bolted, flying straight for the cameraman. Though this time it wasn't a simple carrot that rocketed across the set. The cat must have attached itself to his leg, because the camera whirled to the side until all Jesse and Travis could see was the regular news team on their set, dabbing their faces with makeup as they waited to go back on air. Instantly, the co-anchors went stiff and drudged up bared-tooth smiles before the screen went blank. Seconds later, an advertisement for Herb Harts Auto Parts whirled to a frantic start.

Travis clicked off the television, then the two males who looked so much alike sat in silence.

"Wow," the twelve-year-old finally said. "I didn't think anyone could get so red. And over a cat."

"Maybe we shouldn't mention it to Katie when we see her."

"Really? Why not?"

Good question. Jesse wasn't interested in explaining the pussy problem because he had no idea what the boy did or did not know about a woman's anatomy and the slang sometimes used to refer to it. And he had no interest in finding out. That really didn't fall under the heading of food or clothes.

"Most artists don't like talking about their work."

It sounded lame, even to him.

"Why not?"

"Listen, Travis, we have a tree house to build."

The second the show was over, Kate walked straight off the set and grabbed her handbag from her office.

"Kate!" Chloe called after her.

"Not now."

With measured movements, mentally reeling off the name of every president since George Washington, she left the building. Although as soon as she stepped out into the bright sunshine, she realized she had no idea where she could go. Certainly not home, since the last person she wanted to see was Jesse.

So she went to the mall. Not the Sunland Park Mall close to the house. She drove across town to the Cielo Vista Mall.

She didn't want to think—not about ratings, television shows, or cats. She couldn't remember the last time she had shopped or indulged herself with a hot dog on a stick.

But the minute she walked inside the air-conditioned expanse, she heard the first whistle.

"Look, it's Meeeees Kate!"

That got a few cheers. Though it also got more than a few less-than-funny comments alluding to the episode.

"That's some kind of pussy you have, Meeeees Kate" was just a taste of the critique that came her way.

Had everyone and their brother watched that show of all shows?

She was tempted to drown herself in the sparkling fountain in the middle of the mall. Unfortunately it was empty for repair and if she dove in she would only give herself a good knock on the head. Though maybe with luck amnesia would follow and she could forget pussies and pet psychics and start a new life as a fry cook in a truck stop diner. Too bad she couldn't cook.

"I'm the laughingstock of West Texas," she muttered, returning to her car.

She took herself to lunch at Louis's Barbeque Palace, the darkest place she knew, where customers couldn't possibly recognize her in the dimness. If they did, they didn't mention it. She ordered a gigantic plate of tangy meat, coleslaw, and potato salad and the largest size Coke they had.

But before her food arrived, the door opened, sunlight brightening the interior. She cringed and tried to hide when she saw it was Julia and Chloe.

She considered diving under the table, but her shoes kind of stuck to the floor and she really didn't want to ruin her new pants.

"We knew we'd find you here," Julia announced, sitting down across from her in the booth, her Tiffany charm bracelet jangling against the Formica tabletop.

Chloe sat down next to Kate, as always looking sweet and endearing in her bangs and sensible clothes. "Are you okay?" Chloe asked kindly.

"I'm great, never been better."

"You're talking to us, sugar," Julia announced. "And you've just been through a rough day at work. Who knew that Mistress Reynalda was going to go on like that about pussies?"

Kate groaned, Chloe bit her lip, and then suddenly a laugh bubbled up and Kate dropped her head into her hands. "A pet psychic wanting to pet my pussy."

Then all three of them were laughing until tears streamed down their cheeks.

"It's really not funny," Kate chastised through her laughter.

"See, you're better already," Julia added, calming down. "Next time, we'll come up with something different, something better." She smiled at her. "We're the Three Musketeers, remember? We stick together."

Kate felt her throat swell with emotion and gratitude for her friends. "I sure miss the old days when life wasn't so complicated."

"No offense, sweetie, but life has never been all that uncomplicated." Julia waved a waitress over. "Two more of whatever it is that she ordered. Thank you." Then she turned back. "Where was I? Ah, Kate's revision of history by saying that life didn't used to be so complicated."

"I haven't rewritten anything."

"Need I bring up your mother and her revolving door policy regarding husbands?"

"Julia," Chloe reprimanded.

"What? We both know that Kate refused to learn new stepfather's names until they made it past the six-month mark."

"That's not true!"

Julia leaned forward. "How many names did you learn?"

"I learned them all." Then Kate wrinkled her nose. "I just wouldn't *use* their names until they made it past the six-month mark."

"Ah, yes," Julia stated wryly, "not complicated at all."

Kate knew it was true. Growing up with Mary Beth was anything but easy, or normal. Though the truth was, until Kate had been seven years old, when Julia and her family had built their mansion next door, changing the neighborhood forever, she hadn't realized that there was any other way to live. Chloe hadn't moved in until a few months after that. Not that Chloe or her life had been normal.

It had been seeing Mrs. Boudreaux that had opened Kate's eyes. The beautifully ordered woman had made Kate realize that other mothers didn't stay in bed for days at a time. And Julia's pretty white ruffled bed always had sheets on it.

Mrs. Boudreaux wore fancy suits, making her look like Nancy Reagan. Kate's mother dressed in flowing garments that fluttered like gossamer draperies caught in a breeze. Mary Beth had always been like a fairy-tale princess, disconnected from reality. Kate had acted as the bridge, tethered to her mother by the fiery brightness and love that Kate forced herself to remember all those times when the brightness dimmed and the love seemed to disappear. As much as Kate hated all the men, she had learned that a new man always meant the love returned, doled out unselfishly to everyone in the house.

As the years went by, Kate took care of Suzanne, learned to pay the bills, ward off bill collectors when money ran low, and call the divorce attorney when a father moved out.

All these years later, Kate couldn't have been more thankful when their meals arrived, distracting her from her thoughts.

"Jeez, you could feed all of China with this," Julia proclaimed. Though that didn't stop her from digging in—with all the delicate grace and finesse that was Julia.

Between Kate's friends and every bite of the best barbecue in town, the memory of the pet psychic began to fade. Emotion welled up, and she reached out and grabbed each of their hands. "You are the greatest. I'm glad you found me."

"You know we couldn't let you hurt like that," Chloe said.

Julia pulled away. "Don't you two go all sappy on me. Of course we would find you."

"Remember my braids?" Kate asked. "Remember how I was the laughingstock because my mother insisted that I wear them?"

"They called you Swiss Miss," Julia said.

Chloe nodded her head in memory. "Kids can be so mean."

"I hadn't thought of your braids in years," Julia mused, after finishing a bite of her meal. "Your mother should have been shot. The only plus to your mother's episodes of self-involved melodrama was that at least then she didn't make you do crazy things. Her idea of motherhood must have been learned from a how-to book written by the old woman in *Hansel and Gretel*. Did Mary Beth ever try to put you in the stove?"

"Julia!" Chloe and Kate barked their surprised laughter.

"Fine, just wondered."

"Anyway," Kate continued, "you took one look at my hideous hairdo and the merciless teasing I got, then the next day you came to school with the exact same style."

Julia waved the comment away. "I wanted to make a fashion statement."

"You wanted to make a statement that I was your friend. No one would dare make fun of Julia Boudreaux— or me either after you took me under your wing. I wish everyone knew what a big heart you have underneath all those feathers and glitz."

Julia busied herself by stirring her Coke with the straw. She had never been all that comfortable with people's kind words and sentimentality. "You must be hormonal or overwrought, Kate." She glanced up and smiled almost shyly. "But a sweet, wonderful mess of overwrought hormones."

All three of them had tears burning in their eyes by the time they had cleaned their plates. And when they got out into the parking lot, Julia reached out one last time. "I'm glad you're feeling better, sweetie. Now go home. Take the rest of the day off to regroup. Then tomorrow we'll come up with something new."

Chloe gave her a big hug, then the two of them were off in Julia's Lexus.

Feeling better and hopeful, Kate thought she'd surprise Parker and stop by his office, concentrating on the thought of his sweet and gentle kiss, the soothing flutter she felt when he held her hand.

But he wasn't in, and by four in the afternoon she had little choice but to go home.

The minute she pulled up she noticed Travis's rental clubs set up against the side wall. She could just make out a hint of the boy and Jesse high up in the old cottonwood. They really were rebuilding the tree house. A rough-hewn floor had already been secured to the old notches in the limbs that were still there.

The sight raised her respect for Jesse even more. It was unsettling to think that bad boy Jesse Chapman might care more than he let on. Did she really know him at all anymore?

Travis and Jesse worked up in the tree. Rather, Jesse worked, and Travis sat cross-legged, his fingers curled around the branches to keep him secure.

It seemed impossible to take her eyes off of Jesse, who was working with a confident precision. His concentration was intense. He held nails between his lips, before he took them one by one, hammering them home with three dead-on hits. If she hadn't known he was a golfer by trade, she would have assumed he was an experienced carpenter.

But it was the distinct contours of his body that held her attention. No shirt, bronzed skin covered with a light sheen of sweat. Hips slim beneath the soft jeans he wore.

Shaking the image away, she went inside and changed, intending to get on the computer to work from home. Instead, she ignored the phone messages, didn't check her e-mail. She returned to the backyard. With her thoughts still beating through her like a drum, she crossed the grass to the tree and climbed the newly hammered-in rungs.

"Where's Travis?" she asked when she reached the top. "I saw him just a second ago."

Jesse looked at her for a moment, sexual heat competing with the punishing Texas sun, before his eyes narrowed as if he was frustrated with himself, and he looked away. He gestured toward the garage. "Getting more nails."

Without waiting for an invitation, Kate sat down on the secured plywood. Wrapping her arms around her knees, she stared out into the distance. Jesse went back to hammering.

"Did you see the show?" she asked carefully.

"What?"

"*Getting Real with Kate.* Did you see it today?"

He seemed to debate, then sat back on his heels. She felt awkward under the intensity of his gaze.

"Does it matter if I did?"

"Well, no."

"Good."

Travis climbed up, holding on carefully, cringing until he sat with some security on the floor.

"Hi, Kate. What do you think of this place?"

"I'm impressed."

"Yeah, Jesse says it's going to be the best ever—even better than the one that used to be here where you threw your arms around him and kissed him silly."

Kate's mouth fell open. "I did no such thing."

Jesse raised a brow.

"Okay, I might have. But I never would have thought of you as the kiss-and-tell type."

"You did the kissing, not me."

Jesse chuckled. Kate muttered.

"Jesse said you were a pistol when you were young."

A pistol, she mouthed at Jesse.

"Said you were a pistol today on the show."

She whipped around just in time to see Jesse trying to cut Travis off. "You saw the show?"

"We saw it, all right," Travis said with a nod of his head and a snort of disbelief. "Those were some cats you had. And who knew they had thoughts? But Jesse made me turn off the TV. Did we miss the part where you actually talked to them?" Then suddenly the boy stopped, his face scrunching up as he glanced just beyond Kate. A second later, his eyes went wide and he looked back at her. "Though maybe that was something else we were watching. Not you at all. It was . . . *Pet Detective*. With Jim Carrey. That's it." He cringed. "I'm starved. I think I'll go get a snack," he added, then gingerly climbed down out of the tree.

Kate dropped her forehead to her knees. "Admit it, I was horrible."

"Horrible? You're exaggerating."

She narrowed a glance at him.

"It was entertaining. Interesting. I bet you money not a single soul turned you off today."

"You did!"

"Look at it this way. Good or bad, talk is talk, and no doubt people will be talking after that show."

"Great, just what I want. All of West Texas talking about me."

"Not necessarily about you, wild thing. About your pussy."

"Argh!"

He leaped out of the way and down the rungs before she had a chance to pick up the hammer.

To: Katherine Bloom <katherine@ktextv.com>
From: Julia Boudreaux <julia@ktextv.com>
Subject: Good news

Ratings went through the roof during the pet segment. The audience loves you when you get all red and embarrassed. Which is why I've decided on the next show. "The Lover's Lesson." A show about sex products, just like you suggested.

Julia Boudreaux
Owner
KTEX TV West Texas

To: Julia Boudreaux <julia@ktextv.com>
From: Katherine Bloom <katherine@ktextv.com>
Subject: No way

Don't you dare go all owner on me!! I will not do a show on sex products. I suggested a pregnancy show!! A perfectly respectable segment on women getting pregnant.

KCB

Katherine C. Bloom
News Anchor, KTEX TV West Texas

To: Katherine Bloom <katherine@ktextv.com>
From: Julia Boudreaux <julia@ktextv.com>
Subject: Perfectly boring

. . . and you know it. The pet psychic was *not* boring. The look on your face alone when Mistress Reynalda instructed you to pet that cat was priceless. Though surely we can find a balance between too prepared and not prepared enough. I'll send a whole slew of products over so you can have a look this time. Get all prepared, if you have to.

xo, j

eleven

Jesse walked out of the guest cottage, intent on getting a few clubs and heading across the street to the seventeenth fairway of the country club. It was dark, after midnight, and he was guaranteed to have the course to himself.

But when he saw Katie in her kitchen, he stopped because she was pacing. With a lamenting sigh, he set his clubs up against the wall, then went to the back door.

Katie stopped and whirled to face him when he entered. She wore a white tank top tucked into drawstring pink pajama bottoms rolled up at the ankles. Her hair was loose and curly, like she had been running her hands through it over and over again, and the tea she had made sat on the counter untouched. She looked half wild, half hot as hell.

"What are you doing?" he asked bluntly.

"I'm trying to decide what to tell Julia when I quit."

After she had jumped through hoops to keep her job, this came as a surprise. He was too confused to reply.

She threw her hands up in the air, the tank top pulling tight across her breasts. She didn't have on a bra. The cotton outlined the sweet fullness, her nipples showing through the material, making heat sizzle through his body. Jobs and quitting them were forgotten, and he felt an urge to take her to the guest cottage and peel the pajamas off so he could run his tongue along each breast, then lower.

"Great!" she bleated. "Just great! I know what you're thinking!"

"You do?" He grimaced, refusing to feel any sort of guilt because thinking and doing were two separate issues. Just because he was thinking about breasts, tongues, and Katie in the same scenario didn't mean he was going to do anything about it. He wasn't.

He eyed the door and knew that tonight he'd be in for a cold shower.

"See, you're antsy to get away from here. You're embarrassed to be seen with a woman who can't look at a cat, hear someone call it a . . . a pussy"—she shuddered—"without turning bright red, like a freaking cherry."

All this talk of pussies and cherries wasn't helping.

"I heard that!" she yelped.

"Heard what?"

"You groaned. You're tired of hearing about it. Me and my job. You're thinking that I should just go out there and find other employment because I'm not cut out for TV."

"Ah—"

"Oh, sure. Stand there and be all judgmental."

"Okay—"

"I knew it! You think I'm making a fool of myself, and if I had any balls at all that I wouldn't put up with it. I'd stand up and say *no*! I refuse to become the laughingstock of West Texas!"

He sighed and shoved his hands in his pockets. "You're venting."

"Venting?" she all but hollered, her arms extended, her hair wild, her breasts playing havoc with his mind. "Do I look like I'm venting?"

"Actually—"

"Don't answer that. Tell me if I'm venting after you see this."

Jesse felt more confused by the second and was doubly wishing he had kept going down the driveway instead of stopping in here. He loved women, loved being around them—except when they turned into raving lunatics.

"Katie, you're upset—"

"You bet I'm upset." She started pulling things out of a brown paper bag. "I'm upset about this."

She slammed down a handful of plastic-wrapped multicolored grocery items.

"You're mad about Fruit Roll-Ups?" he asked, things not getting any clearer.

She yanked out something else. "Fruit Roll-Ups and these!" She shook a plastic-wrapped package of oversized dice.

"I still don't get it," he said.

She didn't bother to explain. She continued on, pulling out a board game. On closer inspection, he realized that it was some kind of golf entertainment.

Then she upended the bag and a whole slew of other items tumbled out. It took a second for them to register. Then he started to laugh.

"This is no laughing matter, Jesse Chapman. Julia has

lost her mind. She has sent me a bag of sex games and tells me I am going to do a show about them." She picked up a fruit roll and tore it open. "Tell me, what could this possibly be used for?" She ripped off a piece with her teeth and started to chew.

"Edible underwear."

She gasped, then spit it out. "What? How can this be used as underwear?"

"If you really want to know"—he couldn't help but grin—"you unroll it, cut two long strips, cross them between your thighs, bring them up and secure them at your waist with a ribbon or a belt."

She blinked about half a dozen times. "Like X marks the spot?"

"You got it."

"I'm appalled."

He shrugged with a devilish nonchalance. "You asked."

"How do you know these things?" she demanded.

"You'd be surprised what a guy can learn on the golf circuit." Jesse grabbed the golf game and chuckled. "Now this is inventive. *Fore!* Play. A combination of the sex and golf term wrapped up in a single bedroom game revolving around golf. Clever."

"It's sick."

"So you're not a golf fan." He grinned. "But admit it, you love the dice."

She glared at him as he ripped the oversized cubes from the package. But she didn't wait for more enlightenment. She started pacing again. "Everyone wants me to be some new Kate. I don't know how to be a new Kate. I can't even decide who this new Kate is supposed to be. I can't concentrate. Though I could if . . . if . . . if *you* weren't distracting me. That's it. You're the one throwing me off."

"Me? What did I do?" he asked with a choking laugh.

Instantly, she stopped and groaned. "You're right. You haven't done anything. But you're here and you're easy to blame, what with all your wild distracting ways, great body, incredible hair, and that damned sexy smile—"

"You like my smile?"

"I hate your smile. It's enough to make the smartest women alive lose their concentration. Heck, they write about it in *People* magazine!" She sighed dramatically. "Though my problems aren't your fault. It isn't you. I know that. But if my not figuring this out isn't about you, then I have to accept the fact that it's about me. Which means that I have to fix *me*. And I haven't a clue how to be anyone else."

All the vigor and anger drained away, leaving her spent. Unable to do anything else, Jesse touched her chin, making her look at him.

He smiled at her.

She scowled. "Your sweet talkin' ways aren't going to work on me this time," she stated stubbornly. "I'm unhappy and miserable and you aren't going to make me feel better."

His smile spread. "I'm not sweet talkin', sweet thing. I'm just telling the truth. You've never understood how great you are, how you have always been good enough just as you are."

"Tell that to Julia, or all those viewers who think they're critics."

"I've never thought of Katie Bloom as a whiner."

"Exactly! This is what *getting real* has done to me."

He ran his thumb along her jaw. "You can do it, Katie. You can win. But you can't give up."

He saw the pulse in her neck flutter. He watched as her hazel eyes flared with green before her lips set in a firm, forbidding line.

He put his hands up in surrender. "Fine, see it your way, Miss Award-Winning News Anchor. You, Miss Highest Weekly Ratings for KTEX since the station started airing *Getting Real with Kate*."

She shot him a glare. "Great. Next the infamously bad Jesse Chapman is going to launch into a lecture on honor, morals, and respect."

His lips tilted. "Is that a rock group?"

Her eyes narrowed, then she couldn't seem to help herself. She laughed.

"You're bad, Jesse Chapman."

"I try."

She breathed in, then exhaled long and slow. "Why are you being nice to me?"

"I want to see you happy," he said softly.

As sudden as a summer storm, every trace of suspicion in her expression fled, replaced by a hint of tears that welled in her eyes. "Really?"

"Really."

The moment was intimate and caring, and it made him feel uncomfortable. He might want her happy, but he didn't want this, not the emotion or the intensity. He couldn't handle it—the hope and need he saw in her eyes for him to be correct that she was good enough as she was. He dropped his hand and moved away.

"You're leaving?" she asked, her nose wrinkling. "If you stay, I promise to play nice," she offered with a sweet, hopeful smile. "I might even have a beer in the re-frigerator."

His gaze ran down her body. Despite everything he had been telling himself about this woman and all that she represented, heat and desire flared. Without ever taking his eyes off her, he knew he couldn't walk out when she had that look on her face.

Then without thinking, he picked up the worded cubes, and rolled them.

Her appreciative smile turned to concern. "What are you doing, Jesse? I said I promise to play *nice*, not dice."

There was a quaver in her voice.

"Hmmm," he teased. "Lick showing on one die, and Lips on the other."

He came toward her.

"Now what are you doing?" she asked nervously.

"Showing you how to use the dice. It's the least I can do. I know how much you like research."

Then he licked her on the lips. "Mmmm, cherry Fruit Roll-Up."

He saw her uncertainty as she touched her lips. What had started out as a teasing game suddenly didn't seem like a game any longer. He wanted to do more than lick her, at least more than lick her lips. He wanted to lick the lines and creases of her body.

"Why do you keep doing this to me?" she whispered.

As if he could do nothing else, he tossed the dice again. "Kiss and Face."

Alarm brightened her cheeks. But combined with alarm, she breathed in deeply, her breasts rising. "I'm not going to play," she stated without much conviction.

"I dare you."

"I'm not six years old anymore."

"Chicken," he teased softly.

He saw that old competitiveness surge, and more than anything he felt relief that his old Katie was back. The despair gone, the uncertainty erased.

"I am not chicken."

"Bauck, bauck," he whispered.

She growled, then leaned forward as fast as a chicken and pecked him on the cheek. "I did it."

"You never could resist a dare."

"Like you could?" She snorted.

His smile turned wicked. "Okay, I accept." He rolled again.

"I wasn't daring you!"

"Sure you were." He peered at the dice. "Touch and Foot."

Kate looked relieved until he said, "Mmmm, this might take some inventiveness," then told her to sit on the counter.

"Absolutely not!"

He lifted her with ease, her body sliding up against his before he set her down on the tile.

"Now, Jesse."

She bit her full lower lip, making it glisten, and he wished the dice had come up as Lick and Lips once again.

Instead, with his gaze never leaving hers, his hand skimmed down her pajama pants until he came to her ankle. It was slim and delicate. He started to take hold of her foot, but she gasped, then hurriedly brushed off the bottoms.

He raised a brow.

"I wanted to make sure they were clean."

But every ounce of resistance evaporated when he ran

his palm over her arch. Their eyes were locked together, her chin slightly raised to meet his gaze, and her lips parted in a silent intake of breath.

Katie had always been cute with her wild curls and big hazel eyes. But sitting here now, she was changing before his eyes. Day by day, bit by bit. She had grown into a beautiful woman.

It had become harder and harder to see her as little Katie whom he had known forever. And when his hand drifted over her ankle and underneath the flannel pant leg, he wasn't thinking about friends.

His pulse drummed through his body as he ran his palm up her calf, pulling up the soft baggy material as he went. The gold in her eyes flared as his other hand slid beneath the flannel on her opposite leg. He lingered at the sensitive spot behind her knees before nudging them apart and stepping closer. He curled his fingers around the backs of her knees, then slowly he pulled her round bottom to the very edge of the counter.

Leaning close, he kissed her temple, running his hands up underneath her T-shirt, along her spine, her skin smooth like silk. The heat in the room seemed to grow, but her nipples pulled into tight buds beneath the thin cotton as if it were cold outside.

She trembled, and when he leaned down and gently kissed her, she sighed against him. Desire exploded, but he kept it in brutal check. He knew women, and he knew Katie wanted him. But he didn't want to scare her, and when he brushed his lips over hers, her hands fluttered for a second as if she didn't know what to do with them before they settled on his chest.

He was sure she must feel his pounding heart, and he groaned quietly, dropping light kisses along her lips.

"Open for me," he whispered.

After a hesitant second, she did, her hands curling into his shirt when he found her tongue, pulling her closer. With the V between her legs no more than an inch away from his cock, he wanted to press her against his hard length, then sink inside her. He could almost feel her warmth surrounding him, hot and slick.

Letting his control slip a bit, he pressed his arousal against her. Her body tensed at the feel of his insistent need, but she gave a soft moan at the same time. Running his hand down her spine, he pressed her body to his, slowly, over and over again.

When he lifted his head, she was breathless. He wanted nothing more than to lift her shirt, capture her arms above her head, and take each nipple into his mouth. And he would have, consequences be damned. But without warning, her breath seemed to freeze in her chest, her eyes going wild. Then she caught him off guard when she pushed at his chest, ducked beneath his arm, and scrambled down from the counter.

She hurried away without a glance, though he would have sworn she was chanting, "No sex, no sex, no sex," as she disappeared out the door.

Kate, Parker called last night to ask me what your favorite restaurant is. I probably shouldn't be telling you this, but I have yet to understand the dynamic going on between you, Jesse, and Parker. I felt it was only sensible to give you a heads-up. Why is it that I feel like I'm in seventh grade again?

Chloe Sinclair
Station Manager
Award-winning KTEX TV West Texas

p.s. I told him you loved ribs and coleslaw at County Line. He insisted on something fancier, which left me wondering why he called at all.

How is it possible that I am the only living human being who actually liked seventh grade? Dissecting frogs, finally getting books worth reading, the first opportunity to take an elective. I'm still not sure that I made the right choice between French and Debate. Who knows where I'd be now if I had taken a foreign language. Maybe in France!

Katherine C. Bloom
News Anchor, KTEX TV West Texas
a.k.a. Miss Debate Team, Zach White Junior High

To: Katherine Bloom <katherine@ktextv.com>
    Chloe Sinclair <chloe@ktextv.com>
From: Julia Boudreaux <julia@ktextv.com>
Subject: What's this I hear . . . ?

Going out with Parker for a romantic dinner? Does this mean there's going to be something wilder than crème brûlée for dessert? Pshaw, what am I saying? Kate doesn't know the first thing about wild, and forget about her doing anything crazy.

xo, j

To: Julia Boudreaux <julia@ktextv.com>
    Katherine Bloom <katherine@ktextv.com>
From: Chloe Sinclair <chloe@ktextv.com>
Subject: Bad Julia

Jules, really, don't egg her on. You know how Kate gets when you all but dare her to do something ill-advised.

Kate, don't listen to Julia. You know we love you just as you are. Crème brûlée is all you need to think about for dessert.

Chloe

To: Julia Boudreaux <julia@ktextv.com>
    Chloe Sinclair <chloe@ktextv.com>
From: Katherine Bloom <katherine@ktextv.com>
Subject: Bad KATE

Hey, I can do wild. I can even do crazy, thank you very much. In fact, I have a feeling Parker's in for the night of his life.

Crazy Kate Bloom

To: Julia Boudreaux <julia@ktextv.com>
    Katherine Bloom <katherine@ktextv.com>
From: Chloe Sinclair <chloe@ktextv.com>
Subject: re: Bad KATE

Oh, dear . . .

twelve

A day later, at nearly seven in the evening, Jesse sat at one end of Kate's sofa, Travis at the other. Katie was nowhere to be seen, but Jesse knew she was in the house.

He had avoided the golf course for days, hadn't picked up a golf book or even considered watching an instructional video. The television was on, and they stared in mindless fascination at *Buffy the Vampire Slayer* reruns on cable.

"I can't believe this is really a show," Jesse said with a grimace, but he couldn't stop watching.

"My favorite character is Xander. He's really great," Travis offered. "But he's kind of a nerd."

Jesse glanced between the television and Travis. "If he's a nerd, then he's a cool nerd."

"Really? A nerd can be cool?"

"You bet they can. Take Bill Gates. He's one of the richest men in the world."

"I like Riley, too."

"The commando guy? I guess he's okay."

Then silence until the next advertisement came on.

"Where's Katie?" Jesse finally broke down and asked.

"Getting ready for her date."

Jesse pushed up straighter. "Date?"

"Yeah. She's going out with Parker. He's taking her to Café Central."

Jesse's mind clamped down. He knew it shouldn't bother him. Hell, he should be thrilled. But for reasons he wasn't interested in examining, it really ticked him off.

Travis whistled, sort of. "He's going to spend some money in that place." He never took his eyes off the television. "Since Harlan moved out and my mom started dating, it's her favorite place to go. She says it means the guy really likes her if he takes her there. But usually they only take her to places like Carlo's Canteen and Melville's Mexican. Melville doesn't seem very Mexican to me, but the little flags you raise whenever you want something from the waiter are really neat." He glanced over at Jesse, who stared at him. "What?"

"How do you know where Parker's taking Katie? She hasn't mentioned any of this to me."

Travis rolled his head back and focused on the screen. "I don't think she likes talking to you much. Whenever you're around, she gets all red in the face. Sort of like how she got when Cowboy Bob lifted her into the saddle. Or that day with the cats. Not so good, I'm thinking. But me . . . she likes talking to me. When she was ironing her clothes for tonight we talked."

"About what?"

"Stuff."

Jesse told himself to keep his mouth shut. "What kind of stuff?"

"I don't know, just stuff like she said she was going to wear a suit. But my mother says you should never wear a suit on a date."

"Did you tell Katie that?"

"Yep. She was real glad to hear it. I told her she should wear a skirt to show some leg. My mother says—"

"Your mother isn't here," Jesse stated mulishly. "And I think Katie should wear the high-collared shirt and long flannel pants."

"It's summer. I don't think she's going to."

But Jesse wasn't listening. He pushed up from the sofa.

"Where are you going?"

"To find Katie."

At the end of the hall, he knocked once on her door, then turned the knob. She whirled around, her short, cropped cotton top swirling. She wore a pair of terry cloth shorts, and her hair was wrapped up in a towel.

"You can't just walk in here like that!"

"Travis said you have a date."

She gaped, then gave him a look of exaggerated patience. "Maybe you didn't understand. I said"—she pointed at herself—"*You can't just walk in here like that.* A correct response from you"—she pointed at him—"would be something along the lines of *I'm sorry,* or even *I didn't mean to barge in on you. I'll just be moseying along.*"

"I don't use words like *moseying.* Besides, I've already seen you naked. You're dressed now. What's the problem?"

"You have never seen me naked!"

"Think back—"

"Great, another one of your *think backs*."

"—to the day you were at my house and you stripped naked. You said something about wanting to try out a new kind of bubble bath."

"I was three!"

"See, you admit it. But that's not what I'm here to talk about." He clicked the door shut and walked across the room to stand in front of her. "You said you didn't like Parker."

Disbelief at his unabashed audacity made her mouth fall open. "I never said that."

"Sure you did. We were standing in the kitchen that day when he came over with the flowers. You were streaked with dirt from gardening."

"You said *you* didn't like him."

His lips quirked at one corner. "I knew someone didn't like him."

She rolled her eyes. "Jesse, what do you want? I'm running late as it is."

"I think you should cancel."

"I am not going to cancel."

He heard his own frustrated growl. "Then you should go to a place like Melville's Mexican."

"Why in the world should I go there?"

"They have these little flags you can raise when you want something." Even he knew he was acting insane, but the thought of his Katie—yes, his, damn it—going out with one of his old friends made his blood boil.

Her chin rose a notch. "I don't see a restaurant with little flags as the ideal place to have a romantic dinner."

His jaw went tight and he eyed the tip of her chin, elegant, beautiful, like the rest of her, and stubborn—also like the rest of her. The thought brought him back to his senses. What she did or didn't do wasn't any of his business—and she wasn't his. More than that, and as much as he hated to admit it, a man like Parker Hammond would be good for her. She deserved someone like Parker, who was a responsible pillar of the community. A man who would never hurt Katie—even unintentionally. Jesse knew that no one could say the same about him.

Suddenly, he had no idea why he was standing there in her room, in her house. Hell, in El Paso.

He headed for the door with a curse. He stepped out into the hallway just as the front bell rang.

"Kate!" Travis called.

She gave a little jump, then pushed Jesse the rest of the way out the door. "That must be Parker. Will you get it?" she asked. "And be nice to him until I'm ready. Thanks!"

She slammed the door in his face.

Five minutes later, Jesse, Travis, and Parker sat in the den, each of them sitting forward in his seat, elbows on knees. Conversation was strained.

"Did Kate say she'd be long?" Parker asked.

"She didn't say," Travis answered.

Jesse just gave a cold stare as a few more silent minutes went by.

"So, how is it being back in El Paso?" Parker tried again.

"It's all right."

"Have you seen any of the old gang?"

"No."

Parker nodded his head. "We've all lost touch."

Then more sitting in silence.

Finally, Kate came out, and all three males leaped to their feet, relieved. Though every ounce of Jesse's relief evaporated at the sight of her. She looked gorgeous, hair done up and kind of wild, and wearing a silky blouse that shimmered. And a skirt—a damned skirt that showed off the most incredible legs.

"Wow, Kate," Travis enthused. "You look beautiful."

Her smile was shy but pleased.

Parker looked rapturous at the sight of her. Despite his reasoning about what Katie deserved, Jesse hated that he felt a slow beating . . . fury? Yep, fury, he reassured himself. The kind that any good friend of hers would feel over how she looked like a damned fine seductress. It had nothing to do with jealousy. He didn't let himself think about the fact that fury made little sense and should hardly be more acceptable than jealousy.

The couple headed out the front door, but just before she escaped, she looked back and whispered, "Wish me luck."

The plank of oak thudded closed. Jesse and Travis stared.

"Luck?" Jesse asked. "What does she need luck for?"

Travis turned to him with the seriousness of a priest. "My guess is that she's going out to have sex."

"Sex?"

"Yep, she's acting an awful lot like how my mom's been since she started dating."

Jesse didn't want to think about Travis being aware of his mother's . . . extracurricular activities, just as he didn't want to think about what he felt regarding the possibility of Katie on her way out the door to have sex.

And yet he couldn't stop thinking about it. "Let's see what else is on TV," he grumbled.

Dinner was divine.

Kate sat back against the upholstered chair and drank in the surroundings. The lights burned low; music played softly in the background.

Parker reached across the table for two and took her hand. "You are the most beautiful woman here."

She felt the blush sting her cheeks, and it felt good. She realized that she felt happy, even if she wasn't filled with crazy excitement. This was what life was about.

Squeezing back, she said, "Thank you. Everything has been perfect."

Lulled by the same contentment she had felt with Parker at lunch and when they spoke on the phone, she decided that if she wanted to stop living on the sidelines of life, this was her opportunity to take drastic measures. It was time she moved forward toward a new future.

She also thought about Julia's e-mail.

"I thought we could go back to your place," she blurted out.

His eyes filled with desire, his voice lowering. "I'd like that."

They drove to his house on Rim Road. She had seen it once or twice. It was a showcase of tasteful furniture and artwork. Which meant it looked nothing like the eclectic mix of Kate's adobe house with its terra-cotta tile roof, the overstuffed sofa, and multicolored hand-painted kitchen chairs.

"Can I offer you a glass of wine?"

She agreed, sat on his ultramodern chaise, her skirt fluttering around her knees, then sipped the full-bodied cabernet, hoping for liquid courage to keep her from bolting. She tried to make herself think *wild* if not *crazy*, but it only made her heart hammer harder.

Parker turned on the stereo, pressed a button that opened the living room drapes, and she saw the city spilling out below their perch on the hill.

"It's beautiful," she said, meaning it.

He sat down next to her without answering, then ran the backs of his fingers along a single loose tendril of hair that curled down her cheek. She waited to feel a tingle of sensation, a shiver of longing . . . something, anything.

"I have always loved your hair," he said, his voice ruggedly deep.

She mentally rolled her shoulders, took a deep breath, and let him kiss her.

His lips met hers, gently coaxing, and when she couldn't quite bring herself to open up, he ran his hand down her spine with sensual prowess.

She brought her arms up and slipped them around his shoulders, making him moan in pleasure. Then suddenly her mouth was open, and his tongue tangled expertly with hers as he pushed her back into the cushions.

Her pulse raced, though it was a panic born not of fear of Parker, but fear that no other man but Jesse could make her feel anything. This time, with this man, she didn't feel anything. She felt nothing for him other than a warm, comfortable friendship.

With effort, she concentrated, trying harder to lose herself in the moment. She wanted to have sex. She was going to have sex.

She relaxed into the kiss. She ran her hands up his arms. But still she couldn't drum up more than a blip on the Thrill Chart.

Okay, she told herself, *you can do this.*

But when his hand drifted up her midriff, and she realized he was headed for her breast, she couldn't take it anymore. Feeling like at any moment she would cry with aggravated frustration, she pulled back.

Kate squeezed her eyes closed, embarrassment racing through her, then opened them again. "I'm so sorry," she said. "I never should have started this."

Parker looked like he didn't know what to think, much less say.

"It's too soon," she added, hoping that this was true. "You are so wonderful and I don't want you to think less of me for being so forward."

"I don't think less of you, Kate."

She wanted to strangle him for understanding. She wanted him to rant and rave and tell her that she didn't know what she wanted and that he wasn't going to wait around forever. She wanted him to stand up to her, not put up with the runaround she constantly gave him.

Then he surprised her.

"This is about Jesse, isn't it?"

Her mouth fell open in disbelief, then she groaned silently. She didn't know how to answer.

"Of course it is," he said. "Everything changed when Jesse showed up in town. Next thing I know you're calling me, wanting to go to lunch. The other night you called for no other reason than to talk." He took her hand. "I was flattered. You are an amazing woman. You're beautiful and smart. But you're also kind and caring. It's an incredible combination." He studied her fingers. "I even thought that maybe you'd come around and really see that I'm not half bad."

"Oh, Parker. You are a wonderful man." Disappointment seared through her at the realization that this wasn't enough for her. "Any woman would be lucky to have you."

He smiled ruefully. "But I'm not wonderful enough to capture your heart."

She opened her mouth to say something, deny his words. But she couldn't lie. As much as she didn't want to admit it, to him or herself, she knew he was right. He wasn't enough to capture her heart.

He stood. "Come on, I'll take you home."

Feeling horrible and wistful for what might have been, she let him guide her to the car. They drove through the dark streets silently. Kate pressed back against the leather seats and wished desperately that she could love him.

At her house, she started to invite him in, but he touched her hand.

"Good night, Kate."

She nodded, then slipped inside, waiting quietly with her back against the closed door until his headlights shone against the house as he pulled out of the drive. Then she sighed, every ounce of energy and determination flowing out of her, leaving her weak, utterly spent, and not at all happy.

She felt frustration push at the wistful longing. Everyone wanted her to change—the audience, the auditors, Julia—everyone, that is, except Jesse, who wanted her to remain some figment from his past. She couldn't quite do either.

Thinking she'd fall face-first into bed, she went to her room. But when she craved a cup of chamomile tea, she changed quietly into a tank top and shorts before heading to the kitchen. As if deep down she had known he would be there, she found Jesse sitting at the table in the moonlight.

As always, the sight of him made her body come to life. His dark hair was raked back from his forehead to fall against his neck in gentle sleek, shiny waves. His elbows were planted on either side of a placemat, his biceps showing from beneath the edges of his soft cotton T-shirt. For long seconds all he did was look at her when she entered, like he hadn't a clue why he was sitting there.

"Is something wrong?" she asked.

"Yeah," he answered finally. "Just about everything. But that's beside the point. How was your date?"

She came into the kitchen and flipped on the light switch. "It was great."

"You don't look so great."

"Okay, it was less than great, not perfect." Then her voice cracked. "It's over."

"What?"

She sat down at the table, dropping her head in her hands. "Parker and I aren't going to see each other anymore."

Good, Jesse thought.

Fortunately, he didn't say it out loud, though he did feel the all too familiar need to protect her.

"It's over, finished." She swallowed hard.

He couldn't help it. He muttered an oath, then scraped his chair closer and placed his hand on her head. "Ah, Katie. Tell me what happened."

"I can't do anything right these days," she whispered, her voice cracking again as she fought back tears.

"That's not true." With infinite care, he pulled her into his arms as one tear slid down her cheek, then she buried her face in his chest and cried. "You do plenty right," he whispered, rubbing her back.

"No, I don't. And tonight I failed."

"Failed at what, sweetheart?" he asked patiently, rocking her gently.

She pushed away with a start. "At sex."

Jesse's mind took a second to adjust. "Sex? You had sex?" Hell, just as Travis predicted.

"*Failed* at sex, and failed at having a boyfriend."

"You were barely dating." He set her back in her chair and pushed up from the table. "I want to get back to the first part. Are you saying you had sex with Parker?"

"Tried? Yes. Had? No. I went to his house with every intention of sleeping with him. That's what led up to calling it quits."

Staring at the top of her head, he was foolishly pleased.

She jerked up her chin, fire burning in her eyes. "I couldn't go through with it! I went to his house ready, willing and able. And . . ."

He started to pace. "And what?"

"And then he kissed me and I didn't feel anything, at least not anything as good as when you kissed me, which made me want to run in the opposite direction and not have sex even though I was telling myself it was high time I had some and—"

Shuffling footsteps came down the hallway, catching their attention.

"What's going on?" Travis stopped in the doorway, his hair disheveled with sleep, his eyes squinting against the overhead light.

Kate tried to smile. "Nothing's wrong, T. Everything's fine."

"Bad date?" he asked knowingly.

All of a sudden, her lower lip quivered.

"Thought so," he added.

Without a word, the boy walked over to the freezer, reached up on his toes and pulled out some Häagen-Dazs, found a spoon, then returned to the table. Peeling off the top, he set the ice cream in front of her, then offered the utensil.

"What are you doing?" Jesse wanted to know.

"It's a cure. Chocolate's better, but all Kate's got is strawberry."

"Don't tell me," Jesse said with a grimace. "You learned this from your mother."

Travis smiled.

Kate didn't smile, but she took the ice cream. She started to eat. Jesse realized he was extremely pathetic if a twelve-year-old kid was the only person around here who could deal with situations. "I'll get a bowl."

Travis shook his head. "No bowl. For some reason, using a bowl doesn't help anyone feel better nearly as well as eating straight from the carton."

Both males stood side by side, arms crossed, peering at her like she was some kind of exotic animal at the zoo as she ate bite after bite. After a while, Travis nodded his head in approval. "She's really eating now. A sure sign of recovery. I'm going back to bed."

Travis left them alone, and Jesse sat down next to her. He could see that indeed she was feeling better. In fact her hazel eyes started firing with green. This, he could tell, was a sure sign something was up.

The spoon went still and she glanced over at him. Then she set it down with a decisive bang. This really couldn't be good.

She licked her lips, though it kind of looked like she was trying to be sexy. He realized yet again, and with the same astonishment, that she was a twenty-seven-year-old woman with very little experience. Hard to imagine in this day and age. But it pleased him more than it should have.

She pulled the clip out of her hair, and the long curls fell in a tumble.

"Katie," he asked carefully, "what are you doing?"

She bit her lower lip and looked at him through lowered lashes. "I was just thinking—"

"Maybe you shouldn't think after so much sugar."

She leaned close and smiled with the excitement of someone who had just come up with an ill-advised plan. "Have sex with me."

Jesse's jaw dropped and his spine straightened.

"You're bad boy Jesse Chapman. You can't go all prim on me. You'll ruin your reputation."

"You're the one who made the no-sex rule."

"I take it back. In fact, why bother with rules? I feel wild. I feel crazy."

"You and I aren't having sex," he said, his tone warning.

"Why?"

"Because."

"Now there's a great answer."

"You want a better one?" he demanded. "How about this? I'm not interested in a commitment at this point in my life. And despite your attempts to be modern and forward, you aren't interested in sex without a commitment—

which, by the way, were you planning on marrying Parker?"

He expected that to stick in her craw, make her get indignant and storm out of the room. Instead, she smiled at him. A real sexy smile, and he knew it wasn't a good sign.

This time when she leaned close, she kissed him. Heat raced along his senses. He wanted her.

He pulled away. It didn't matter what he wanted. She wasn't someone whom he could lose himself in for a mindless space of time. "No, Katie. I can't afford this," he whispered. "And neither can you."

"How can it possibly hurt?" She kissed him again, softly on the lips, and she could feel sensation shudder through him.

"My reputation alone will hurt you."

"I don't care about your reputation, at least not now."

"Damn," he groaned.

But when he would have gotten up and left, she wrapped her arms around his shoulders.

"We're both damned, I suspect," she murmured. Then she kissed him. No sisterly peck. No awkward nip.

"You make me crazy," he whispered one last desperate time, before he captured her mouth with his own.

His hands ran down her back. She could feel his barely held patience war with the hard-driving lust. He showed her what he wanted, molding her mouth to his. She sighed softly.

Her breath shivered through her and her mind reeled. The feel of his lips on hers was exquisite, warm and heated, gentle but demanding. Her eyes closed, and she exhaled like she had been waiting. Waiting to breathe, waiting for this—this deeply heavenly touch that made her body come alive in a way that she hardly understood. When his tongue grazed her lips, coaxing them to part, she stopped thinking.

She thought she heard a soft mewling sound and refused to concede that it had come from her. Though that became difficult to do when the next sound she heard was his deep, rumbling growl of satisfaction.

He ran the tips of his fingers along her skin, drifting low over her throat, then down farther to the scooped neck of her tank top. His gaze trailed low as well, and suddenly she remembered that she wasn't wearing a bra.

The fire in his eyes flickered brighter, then his fingers ran along the edge of the thin cotton, back and forth, teasing, before he gently tugged the material up, exposing her breasts.

The expression on his face was sheer awe as he outlined the fullness with his hands, stopping just before he touched her nipple.

Her breath caught, and she felt a yearning pressure build between her legs. She wanted him to touch her there, cup her, spread her with his lips like she had dreamed, then fill her.

He circled one breast with his finger, avoiding the nipple, that heat inside her growing. She had the decidedly embarrassing desire to move her hips toward him. She wanted to feel the hardness of him between her thighs. Then finally he touched the taut aching peaks, and she moaned in ecstasy as he gently pinched.

Then his mouth came over hers and it was a tiny piece of heaven. She felt an amazing sense of power when he groaned. Their tongues twined, then he slowly impaled her mouth, over and over again, so intimately, showing her what sex would be like with him. Hot and wet, slow and sweet.

Relishing the feel, she curled her fingers into his cotton shirt. And passion exploded.

He pulled her into his lap, her bottom cradled between his thighs, as his mouth claimed her once again. The sensation was hot and enveloping, mind spinning and exhilarating. She felt herself melt into him, his strong arms capturing her against his massive chest.

When their tongues touched, fire burned through her, his lips brushing gently at first, then with demand, his strong thighs spreading just enough so that she could feel the unmistakable hardening of his body. Wrapping her close, he consumed her. He tasted dark and dangerous, like a slippery slope between sanity and decadence, making her want more. Making her want to give in, forget right from wrong, lose herself in the intensity of emotion.

"Kate? Jesse?"

The words came from just beyond the door. Mortified, Kate tried to jerk free. But Jesse held her secure, shielding her as he discreetly tugged down her shirt before he let her go.

"Jesse?" Travis came to stand in the doorway between the hall and kitchen, looking as serious as a nun. "Could I have a word with you?"

"Now?" Jesse asked.

"Well, ah, yes."

Jesse hesitated for a second before he pushed up, calming his raging desire. Feeling a tiny bit of what he was afraid might be fatherly concern, Jesse followed Travis out into the hallway. "What is it?"

The boy glanced back to make sure Kate couldn't hear. "I understand the whole wanting to kiss her thing."

Jesse choked.

"But I really don't think it's a good idea to give in and do it."

"What are you talking about?"

"She went out on a date and had a bad time. Then she comes home and starts kissing you on the rebound."

"I'm not a rebound," Jesse said indignantly. Though deep down he knew the kid was right. He had seen it often enough and had steered clear of it. But tonight, with Katie, better sense fled. Her innocence made that jaded part inside him crack open and feel a lightness he hadn't known in years. Not since he was eleven.

"We both know that's what it is," Travis added all too insightfully. "I've seen it a thousand times with my—"

"Mother." Jesse hung his head.

"If you continue . . . doing what you're doing, she'll hate you in the morning. And while she pretty much hates you already, she'll hate herself, too. I was thinking that she's way too nice to start hating herself on top of all the work stuff she has going on."

Jesse stared at the boy long and hard. "Go to bed."

"Promise you won't take advantage of her."

"I am not going to take advantage of her," he replied tightly.

"Promise you won't kiss her again."

Jesse's narrow-eyed gaze must have made Travis think better of pushing him, because suddenly the boy said, "Okay, okay, I'm going."

He disappeared down the hall.

With his body pulsing and his mind raging, Jesse returned to the kitchen. Whatever his sins were, he had never taken advantage of a woman in his life.

"Is everything all right?" she asked.

"Yes," he stated coldly. Then he took a deep breath. "Yes, everything's fine. But it's late and we both need to get some sleep."

"Sleep!"

Yes, sleep, at least for tonight. He wouldn't pursue this to the logical end that his body craved. If he looked at her again, at the confusion and desire mixing on her delicate features, he was afraid his conviction would desert him. "Good night." He headed for the back door.

He wanted her, and he didn't want to think. He wanted to lose himself in her sweetness, consequences be damned. He thought of how he could lean her back, pull off her panties, and lick the sweet center of her, gently sucking her clitoris until she came. There were so many ways to pleasure a woman. He had pleasured more women than he could count.

Pleasure. Katie.

The words shot through his head like a shiver. He wanted to. But then he remembered Katie sweetly curling against his side, counting on him to keep her safe.

That was the problem. This constant seeing her as young and innocent, remembering the bond between them. Not exactly a sister, but not someone he could think about in a sexual way.

But he could no longer pretend that things hadn't changed. Whether he liked it or not, things had shifted between them. There was no going back. He had to finally face the reality that little Katie was the past. A sensual, grown woman had taken her place. A woman who made him crave and long for something he had thought long dead inside him. And he wanted her.

Only one question remained. What did he plan to do about it?

He turned the knob, then pushed out through the screen. A summer breeze drifted in, bringing the smell of honeysuckle and roses.

At the last second, he looked back at her. "Did I mention you're too good for Parker?"

"No."

"Well, you are."

Then he let the screen slam as he headed for the guest cottage.

To: Katherine Bloom <katherine@ktextv.com>
    Chloe Sinclair <chloe@ktextv.com>
From: Julia Boudreaux <julia@ktextv.com>
Subject: Tell all

So, how crazy were you on your date with Parker?

xoxo, j

To: Julia Boudreaux <julia@ktextv.com>
    Chloe Sinclair <chloe@ktextv.com>
From: Katherine Bloom <katherine@ktextv.com>
Subject: Dessert

Well, we went to his place after dinner, but no one got lucky. Though I did try, Julia. You would have been proud. Afterward, however, I felt the distinct need to throw myself in a body of water. Preferably one with sharks. It seems to be a recurring theme with me these days.

Kate

To: Katherine Bloom <katherine@ktextv.com>
    Julia Boudreaux <julia@ktextv.com>
From: Chloe Sinclair <chloe@ktextv.com>
Subject: Rumors and water

It must be something in the air, since there's a rumor floating around regarding Julia and a certain pool.

Julia, tell me it isn't true that you dove into the hotel pool at the Symphony League's Black Tie Gala.

Chloe

Chloe Sinclair
Station Manager
Award-winning KTEX TV West Texas

To: Katherine Bloom <katherine@ktextv.com>
    Chloe Sinclair <chloe@ktextv.com>
From: Julia Boudreaux <julia@ktextv.com>
Subject: No comment

You can't believe everything you hear about me. But you can believe that Kate's love products segment is scheduled for tomorrow.

Enjoy!

xoxo,
Julia Scarlett Boudreaux

To: Julia Boudreaux <julia@ktextv.com>
    Chloe Sinclair <chloe@ktextv.com>
From: Katherine Bloom <katherine@ktextv.com>
Subject: Hmmm

I'm starting to think that a show on love products isn't such a bad idea.

Kate—formerly known as an award-winning news anchor

thirteen

Hot-pink lips. Check.

Curls left long, brushed out just enough to make them full and wild. Done.

Stretchy top cut low, the neck lined with marabou feathers and glittering with sequins. Perfect.

Skirt cut high and tight. Probably too high and too tight. All the better.

High-heeled pair of red hooker heels.

Kate just about swooned as she looked at herself in the mirror—the bad kind of swooning, as in passing out, and she most definitely wasn't a swooner.

At any second, she fully expected her heart to burst out of her chest because it was pounding so hard. Or maybe she'd hyperventilate.

She glanced around the KTEX makeup room, looking for a brown paper bag. Finding none, she tried to remember the stress-management techniques. But it seemed like she hardly remembered the class she had taken, or

the instructions they had given. She settled for rolling her
shoulders.

"Buck up, Katherine," she whispered to her reflection. "You can do this. You are going to do this."

With three minutes to showtime, she stood up from
the chair, thought sultry—prayed she knew what sultry
was—then nodded her head and left the room.

Walking down the long, narrow hallway, she ignored
the startled gasps, just as she ignored the niggling thought
deep in the back of her mind that hooker heels didn't
do a whole lot to make her seem friendlier. Today she had
something else to prove, and it pushed her on like a general's command sending her into battle. Forget the fact
that said general must be a demented fool fighting an
imaginary foe—or worse yet, a hopelessly unwinnable
war while wearing stilettos.

She almost managed a smile over all the *w*'s.

She strode past Chloe, the clang of the station manager's metal clipboard hitting the cement floor the only
sound she made. Even Julia took one staggering step
back at the sight of her. Since Kate hadn't wanted to
mention that she and Parker had broken up, she had
avoided both Chloe and Julia. They would have asked
more questions than she had answers to, and she wasn't
about to admit that he had said the reason for the
breakup was none other than Jesse Chapman. No, that
would require way more discussion time than she was
interested in giving.

So Kate avoided them all, including ignoring them
now as they stood in shock as she headed toward the set.

She tucked in her earpiece as the introductory music
came up, the visual of the sun rising over the horizon in
bright shades of red and orange filling the monitor she

could see below the camera. Then she smiled just as Pete signaled that she was live.

"Good morning, West Texas!"

She told herself she could do this, and she prayed that her heart would calm down.

"Today we have a delightfully fun show that will give us all a few tips on how to make these hot Texas nights *even hotter.*" She flipped her hair over her shoulder, but only managed to get a puff of marabou in her face.

The clipboard clanged again.

Coughing, Kate picked a feather from her slick and shiny lip gloss. But she did it with what she hoped was a lusciously sensual smile.

The cameraman actually came out from behind the camera for a moment to stare in dumbfounded disbelief.

Pete did that bleating thing in her ear.

Rather than be deafened, she pretended to play with her curls, and popped the plastic piece from her ear.

Like a cat on a hot tin roof, she walked to the first product lined up on the counter, thinking sexy, really sexy, while at the same time doing her best not to trip. With game show pizzazz, she whipped out her hands and announced, "What better way to spice up your life than with a fun pair of dice?"

Chatting away, she rolled the cubes a few times, making sure she showed only the tamest variations, regardless of the fact that what she had actually come up with was far racier than Kiss and Cheek, Lick and Ear. She did have half a brain left. She didn't want the show to be jerked off the airways for being profane.

"And for all you golf aficionados, how about a little *Fore!* Play? You know that shout golfers make when the ball is headed straight at some poor unsuspecting soul?

Fore!" She laughed loudly. "Well, get yourself this game, my friends, and I guarantee you'll be shouting, all right. But I don't think it will be *Fore*! If you find yourself a strapping man with a fine, strong putter and a good set of balls, I'm betting you'll be shouting: More!"

She wasn't positive, but she thought Julia might have fainted just beyond the set. Either way, Kate was on a roll.

She moved on to a game she had found in a shop in downtown El Paso. Earlier, she had hung it up on the fake wall in her *Getting Real* kitchen. It was covered by a small drape. With a flourish, she tugged the satin free, revealing a dartboard, the round circles leading up to the bull's-eye filled with boldly printed instructional targets that would have made Hugh Hefner blush.

Picking up a dart, Kate gave it a good hard throw. But it missed completely, flying off the set.

Someone yelped in the distance.

Kate looked straight into the camera. "I guess it's just like they say. *Love hurts*."

Jesse paced back and forth across Katie's kitchen. He was going to wring her neck the second she arrived.

Even hours after *Getting Real with Kate* had aired, he still couldn't believe what he had seen on morning television. His Katie on the screen, sexy, sensual, and— Good God, he couldn't believe those shoes. When she had come around from behind the counter and the camera got a full shot of her, he had spit out a mouthful of Cheerios.

He swore she did it just to drive him insane. She'd no doubt be pleased to learn that it was working. And who wouldn't be going over the edge when faced with this constant battle? One minute he wanted to protect her and keep her safe, then the next he wanted to pound hard and deep inside her.

Yes, he had lost it. He was losing his mind over a woman he didn't want to want.

The front door creaked open, then closed with a whispering click. Then silence as someone tiptoed across the entry hall as unobtrusively as possible. As well she should, he thought grimly at the memory of today's segment of *Getting Real*.

But the *she* he expected wasn't Katie at all. Travis stood in the foyer, frozen at the sight of him, his golf bag still hanging from his shoulder, surprise, guilt, and a suspicious red welt playing havoc with his face.

"What happened to you?" Jesse asked with sharp concern.

"Me?" Travis asked gingerly. "What happened to me?"

Jesse could practically see the gears in the boy's head working fast to come up with a story.

"You've got a red mark on your face."

"Ah, I . . . fell. Yeah, that's it! I fell."

"On your head?"

"Well, I was . . . getting a ball from the pond."

"Oh, really?" Did the kid think he was born yesterday?

"Yeah, you see, I didn't want to lose the ball. So I reached and reached and the next thing I knew I fell in."

"But you aren't wet."

His nose wrinkled. "It happened hours ago. I'm dry now."

Jesse stared at the boy, then sighed. "Travis, you can talk to me if something is wrong."

"Really?" Travis asked, not looking convinced as he headed to the kitchen.

"Really."

"Okay. I want to quit golf."

"Quit?" His head spun as he tried to think like a father. Not a natural task for him for many reasons. "So soon? You've hardly given the game a chance."

"I bet I'd be better at chess than I thought," the twelve-year-old said with complete seriousness. "Or that chemistry stuff you mentioned. Experiments, mixing ingredients. Sounds like fun."

"You can't just quit," Jesse stated, walking over to the pantry to get Travis a snack.

"Why?"

Good question. His first instinct was to say, *I said so.* But that would rank right up there with grounding for no good reason. So he tried to think like a good father, but he hadn't a clue what a real father would do. He could hear his own father. *"You want to quit? No problem."*

But Jesse had learned a person couldn't be a quitter, at least not if he wanted to amount to anything. Just like he couldn't quit now as the PGA Championship approached. He had to force himself back out to the course; he couldn't use Travis or Katie as an excuse not to persevere.

"Why don't you tell me what's really wrong, Travis? Is it harder than you thought? Is the coach bad? Hell, I don't know how he can be any good if all he knows is baseball. I'll talk to him. In fact I'll call him Monday morning."

"Oh, that's okay. No need—"

The quiet click of the front door opening again caught their attention. Someone else was trying to sneak in.

"What is this?" Jesse asked, glancing at the ceiling like he was looking for guidance. "All of a sudden everyone decides to come in the front?"

Jesse returned to the living room and found a second person tiptoeing toward the back hallway.

"It's about time you got home."

Katie froze, then pivoted to face him. She smiled a big guilty smile. But Jesse knew it was an attempt to cover nerves.

"All I want to know," he enunciated carefully, "is what the hell has happened to everyone around here?"

Jesse didn't know how to explain the frustration that raced inside him. His concern for Travis that he didn't know how to show. His feelings for Katie that he didn't know how to deal with.

He watched as every ounce of Katie's nervousness whisked away.

"Nothing has happened," she shot back.

"Nothing? You were talking about foreplay! On TV. Good God Almighty, Katherine, I can't believe you said *Find yourself a strapping man with a fine, strong putter and a good set of balls.*"

Travis gasped. "Oh, man, I can't believe I missed it."

Red flashed up Katie's face and disappeared into her hairline. But a second later, her eyes narrowed dangerously. "It is none of your business what I was thinking, or what I was doing for that matter. I had a show to do and I did it."

Jesse shook his head. "First you talk about sex on TV, then Travis wants to quit golf."

Katie instantly cocked her head, her own problems forgotten. "You want to quit, T?"

"Well, I was thinking about it," he admitted.

"Nobody's quitting anything," Jesse announced. "Not yet, anyway."

"Well, well," she said with a superior smile that really

got his goat. "Haven't you become the arbiter of proper behavior."

"You better believe it. Someone around here has got to have a clear head."

"What are you going to do?" she asked, her voice overly sweet. "Ground us both this time?"

His eyes narrowed. "I'm thinking grounding isn't such a bad idea after all. But no, that isn't my plan. I have something better in mind. On Sunday the three of us are going to play golf."

"Us?" Travis groaned. "The kind of *us* that means me playing, too?"

"Golf?" Katie demanded. "Why in the world would I do a thing like that?"

"Because Travis needs to loosen up and remember he's just a kid. And you"—he pointed at Katie—"need to get your head out of the studio and stop worrying that you're not good enough as you are."

He saw the minute the anger drained out of her and she swallowed hard. But that age-old stubborn streak in her wasn't as easily squashed.

"And you think a round of golf will solve that?"

"A round of eighteen holes solves a lot of things."

"Golf isn't a cure-all, Jesse."

"Maybe not. But it's the only cure I know."

The sun had set, the big, wide-open West Texas sky dotted with stars, when Kate heard the sound of splashing water as she returned from a walk. A single dive into the pool, followed by silence in the summer night.

She still couldn't believe the *Getting Real* segment she had done that morning. Despite her denial to Jesse, she had lost her mind. Yet again! She shuddered when she remembered the line about the putter and balls. Though truth to tell, she also had to suppress a smile. Bad Kate.

She came through the back gate and saw Jesse's sharply defined body cutting through the pool, his form smooth and economical, barely causing a ripple on the water's surface while he swam laps. As always, awareness shimmered through her. His arms glistened in the moonlight with each stroke they took. When he came to the end, he flipped easily, then started back across.

She really didn't like this awkward dance they played. Awareness mixed with restraint. Her body itched for his touch. But as much as she had tried to be Ms. Modern *Sex and the City,* when push came to shove and sanity was in residence, she still couldn't get around the fact that she didn't want to be another in the long line of women who chased after him. She wasn't meant for Parker, but she wasn't meant for Jesse, either.

She would have bypassed the pool and gone into the relative safety of the house, but when she started for the door, he stopped.

He rose up to stand in the shallow end, his hands coming up to clear his eyes, then rake back his hair. Every time he did that, his arms up, his fingers to his head, tangling in the dark strands, she felt that frustrating sizzle of sensuality.

"Couldn't sleep?" he asked.

She shrugged, taking in the faint outline of his body partially lit by the pool lights. She didn't know how to put into words the unrest she felt. The constant careening back and forth between wanting to live freely and the old fears that any sort of wildness would ruin her.

"Neither could I," he said. He walked to the side of the pool, his movements exaggerated by the water's resistance. "The temperature is perfect. You should stick your feet in."

She told herself to go inside. She walked toward him instead.

At the edge of the pool, she kicked off her sandals and stepped on to the top step, leaning her hip against the chrome handrail running down the center, the water rushing around her ankles. She looked at him until she had to look away.

The old cottonwood was visible against the moonlit sky, the sides of the tree house seeming like alternating teeth cut out of a Halloween pumpkin.

"We should finish sometime next week," he said, following her gaze.

"It's going to be great and long lasting, this time. Most regular houses aren't built so well."

He laughed out loud, the sound echoing in the night. "We have some long hours to go before it's secure in the tree. At this point, a bad storm could send it tumbling. Though I know Travis will be happy to be done with it. He's not crazy about the saw, the hammer, or even the nails."

"Then why are you doing it?"

He came up the steps, one at a time, stopping one below her, and he looked down into her face. "He's twelve but acts and talks like he's thirty. Like I said earlier, he needs to have some fun. Regular, kid fun," he quickly added. He hesitated. "Besides, I thought that when we were finished, after he saw what he had made, he'd be proud. You know, give him some confidence."

Her heart lurched, and she crossed her arms on her chest. "You have the potential to be a good father."

He laughed again. "No, I don't, and we both know it. But he's a good kid."

"You seem to have adjusted to the reality of fatherhood."

"The thought of it still rattles me." He hesitated, then glanced at the tree house. "And as much as I keep telling myself life is going to go back to the way it used to be, it's not. Now I have to figure out what to do about it long term."

He turned back to her then, and curled his fingers around her bare arms.

Instinctively, her hands came up, her palms flattening on the hard planes of his chest—intending to push free. His skin was hot and cold, like electrically charged marble, and she couldn't seem to move away.

"What do you want to do?" she asked, her voice unsteady.

"To hold you."

The words were like fingertips grazing down her naked spine. She drew a breath. "I'm talking about Travis."

He focused on his hand curling around the skin on her arm, running his thumb over her flesh much as he had done in the cooking segment in what seemed like a lifetime ago.

"Truthfully, I don't know," he answered her. "I wish everything wasn't so . . ."

His words trailed off, but she understood what he meant. "Complicated," she finished for him. "I know the feeling."

"Maybe so," he conceded, his voice a gruff whisper. "I want things to be simpler. But there aren't any simple answers."

He watched the progress of his fingers as he ran the backs of them against her arm. Then he surprised her when he asked, "Why did you do the love products show?"

She didn't respond at first, because she didn't have a clue how to explain. "It seemed like a good idea at the time."

Water glistened on his body, and she watched a single drop run down his torso to the wet swim trunks that molded to his hips and crotch. He brought his finger to her chin, forcing her to meet his gaze. When she did, she could tell that he didn't believe her.

"Okay," she admitted, "I wanted to be sexy." Which was true. But all she had managed to do was feel like a traitor to herself. With every move she made these days, she wasn't getting real, she was getting farther and farther away from anything that had to do with reality.

His strong arm came around her body and pulled her close, her thin cotton shirt absorbing the water on his skin. Instantly, she felt the hardness of him and her breath fluttered.

"Doing things like talking about sex on television isn't what makes a woman sexy," he said, his strong hand drifting lower to the small of her back. "When a woman feels powerful, that's sexy. When a woman isn't afraid to be herself, that's incredible. It's as simple as that."

Kate felt her temperature rising, sexual desire riding through her. "You said yourself nothing's simple."

His hands slid down her back to curve against her bottom, cupping her, bringing her up against him, holding her secure. The need she felt was exhilarating and a little frightening.

"What I said," he corrected her, his eyes darkening,

"was that there are no simple answers. There's plenty else that is simple and straightforward."

He leaned close then, and she knew he was going to kiss her. She wondered for one fleeting moment if this was why she had gone for the walk, not to get away, as she had told herself, but so she could return and find him here, to feel his hands on her, to taste the pleasure of his lips against her mouth.

She could feel the hard beat of his heart, felt the intensity of his desire. He wanted her, even if at some deeper level he held himself back.

She told herself to push him away, to latch on to the fluttering tails of sanity as it fled. Instead, her arms curled around his neck, unwilling to let him go.

"God," he breathed against her, making her feel alive. Desired and wanted.

Pulsing need shimmered through her veins with an intensity and boldness that made her heart trip. She felt consumed by his gaze, hot and unmistakably sensual, and when he widened his stance and tucked her close between his thighs, she relished the sound of his deep rumbling groan as he leaned down to kiss her.

Just a kiss, she reassured herself. Just a simple kiss.

He nipped at her lips, sucking gently and biting, until she opened to him. She shivered when he pressed her against the hard ridge of his erection.

"I want you," he whispered. "I want you in a way that I have never wanted a woman before."

And suddenly she realized that despite what he said, there was nothing simple about this.

fourteen

Jesse shuddered at the feel of Katie's softness press-ing against his cock. He strained against his swim-suit, wanted nothing more than to slide hard and deep inside her.

Unable to do anything else, he kissed her again, brush-ing his lips back and forth, as he tried to rein in his desire. But when she kissed him back, clinging to him, innocently mimicking his movements, it was hard to think of anything but quenching the driving need he felt pulsing through him.

He understood in that moment, with Katie in his arms, the inevitability of the path they were on. He had tried to do the right thing and stay away from her. But the fight had been futile.

Pulling back, he framed her face with his hands, forc-ing her to meet his eyes. Katie, his Katie, had grown up to be Kate, a sensual woman who hid beneath serious reporter's questions and respectable business suits. Katie with plain hazel brown eyes that suddenly smoldered with a nearly erotic golden green, fringed by long lashes.

"I've fought it, but I can't any longer," he said to her. "We are going to make love, Kate."

He watched the heavy-lidded desire in her eyes burn away as understanding dawned. He could tell that his bold declaration made her nervous and thrilled her at the same time—the wildness fighting, as always, with the need to be responsible.

"We can't."

She tried to push away, but he held her firmly against him.

"Why?" he asked.

"We have a rule—"

"You tossed the rules out the night you asked me to make love to you."

Her eyes flickered and danced as she tried to come up with a response. "It was a moment of insanity, just as this is insanity. You were right earlier when you said I lost my mind. I am losing it, starting the moment I wore ankle weights on TV, then exploding full blown the other night when my head was spinning from a really bad date and . . . and . . . too much sugar."

He watched her lush mouth move, then gave in and leaned forward to taste her again. "You are sweet, but that has nothing to do with it and you know it. You can't deny what is happening between us any more than I can."

She inhaled, her head coming back ever so slightly, her eyes lighting with fire. "I've reconsidered my request from the other day," she said. "And I now completely and utterly deny that I want to . . . well, you know."

"Have sex?"

"Whatever."

He lifted his hands to her hair, running them through the fullness of her curls, slowly stroking, the very tips of his fingers gliding along the sensitive flesh behind her ears. She sighed, her mouth parting, her lips naked of lipstick, wet and pink on their own. Then he took her hand and pressed it to the evidence of just how much he wanted her.

Her pulse leaped in her neck, her eyes widening, and after a second, he could see the primness that reigned inside her losing its battle. "I disagree," he stated. "I'm hard and hot and I want you. And I'm willing to bet that if I slipped my fingers inside those high-waist panties I can see outlined beneath your shorts—"

She gasped.

"—when I touched you, you'd be wet"—he gently nipped the corner of her mouth—"and hot"—he ran his tongue along to the opposite side—"and slick."

A soft sound escaped her throat as she opened to him, followed by a shuddering sigh when he slowly slid his tongue between her lips. She reacted instinctively, sliding her own against his. She tasted sugary and delicious, like a decadent sin.

The innocence in her touch stirred both a deep need to protect and a desire to conquer what he felt clear down to his groin. He hadn't lied when he said he wanted her as he had never wanted a woman before. No question it was the same sort of lust, but this time it was more intense, a driving need that, as hard as he had tried, he couldn't shake.

"That's it," he encouraged as her fingers cupped his erection for one fleeting moment. The second she did, her breath stuttered.

If there had ever been a moment when he could have pulled back from this insane path, it fled the second he felt her hand through the wet swim trunks.

Giving in, their mouths slanted together. He meant to start out gently, get her used to the sensual pleasure. But instantly their mouths came together in a way that was primal and all consuming. Her kiss was as hungry as his, as if neither of them could get enough. Her breath came in ragged little gasps as he pressed her back against the sturdy handrail, her thighs lacing with his as she circled his shoulders with her arms.

Sliding his palms down the curves of her body, he cupped her hips before skimming lower to her bottom. She moaned into his mouth as he drew her fully against him.

This time he moaned over her willing eagerness. He gently nipped her lower lip as she arched closer, his cock hard and pulsing against the small curve of her abdomen. Lifting her up with ease, he carried her into the house. He didn't stop until he came to the kitchen. Setting her down on the countertop, he moved closer to stand between her thighs.

The smell of honeysuckle and oleander followed them inside, mixing with the scent of Kate, innocent and sensual, wrapping around him, making him hot and tight and aware of what he really wanted to do . . . bend her over the sink and slide into her.

He kissed her with a slow, heated passion, his palms just barely grazing over her, trailing down, his lips skimming to the pulse that throbbed in her neck. She gasped when his hands ran along the sides of her breasts, nothing separating his touch from her except her thin cotton top.

Desire pulsed through him like lightning, electric in a black sky, not civilized, not cautious. Her head fell back against a cabinet as his thumbs swept over her nipples beneath the thin material, bringing them to taut peaks, then circling before one hand drifted to the long line of buttons that ran down the center of her shirt. One by one they gave way as his fingers worked the tiny fastenings.

He stopped at the button just above her shorts, then peeled back the material, revealing her breasts. Jesse silently marveled at the beauty of her.

"I dream of you," he whispered. "You fill me with a need that wakes me at night. It's been hard as hell to stay in the cottage and not cross the yard and slip into your bed."

He saw an answering boldness rise through her. And when he caught her hands, pinning them behind her, then bent his head to taste, he could tell she forgot—propriety, responsibility, their past.

Her suppressed hunger surfaced and he sensed her careening flight toward satisfaction. She arched to him as he dipped his head again, capturing first one taut nipple, his teeth gently nipping, then the other.

It was hard to imagine how they had come to this point. After years of seeing her as sweet little Katie, a constant in his life, he found it difficult to reconcile how this would change his world. But he wasn't a man to deny something once he understood the inevitability of it. There was no question in his mind that he and Kate were on a heady sensual ride that wasn't going to stop until they reached some kind of conclusion. He accepted that now. And he would make sure she accepted it, too.

A flash of concern raced through him over the thought of where this would end. But he brushed it aside. They would find the sexual pleasure and satisfaction they both sought.

Suddenly, he released her. They came face to face, her eyes heavy-lidded with passion and growing confusion.

"If I don't stop now, I won't be able to," he said, reining his body in with fierce control.

Her skin was flushed, her lips slighted parted, and a satisfying disappointment flickered across her features.

"You liked that, didn't you, Kate?" he said with a grin.

Dazed, she could only touch her lips.

"There's so much more that I am going to show you."

Her gaze started to clear over his arrogant announcement. He knew that was all it would take to set her passion in check. And if he hadn't, he wasn't sure he wouldn't have given in and picked her up and carried her to the guest cottage and made love to her then.

She opened her mouth to protest, but he pressed his forefinger to her lips. "I'm going to kiss you and stroke every inch of your naked body. I'm going to spread your thighs and taste your hot sweet center until you understand what being sexy really is. Then make no mistake about it. I am going to make love to you. Not tonight, because I know you're not ready yet. But we will make love, I promise you that."

To: Chloe Sinclair <chloe@ktextv.com>
From: Katherine Bloom <katherine@ktextv.com>
Subject: Memo

Dear Chloe:

I have read your parking memo and am in full agreement that each of us should be more considerate not to park carelessly, taking up more than one clearly marked spot. Rest assured, I will do my best to be a part of the solution to KTEX TV's parking problem.

Yours sincerely,
Katherine C. Bloom
News Anchor, KTEX TV West Texas

To: Katherine Bloom <katherine@ktextv.com>
From: Chloe Sinclair <chloe@ktextv.com>
Subject: What gives?

Kate, you've never in your life responded to one of my parking memos. While I appreciate your interest, I know you well enough. Something's up.

Your friend,
Chloe

Chloe Sinclair
Station Manager
Award-winning KTEX TV

To: Chloe Sinclair <chloe@ktextv.com>
From: Katherine Bloom <katherine@ktextv.com>
Subject: Truth

Okay, the truth is, I turned on e-mail in hopes of having a note from Julia regarding the love products show. Surely she's not too upset since really, it was her idea to do it in the first place. Plus, she is totally into all the sexy stuff. You'd think she'd be over the moon about it.

K

To: Katherine Bloom <katherine@ktextv.com>
From: Chloe Sinclair <chloe@ktextv.com>
Subject: Hard to say

I haven't heard from her, either. But maybe you should give her some time just in case. I've never seen her faint like that.

Chloe

To: Chloe Sinclair <chloe@ktextv.com>
From: Katherine Bloom <katherine@ktextv.com>
Subject: Wow

She really fainted? I had hoped that I was just imagining things. And how can she turn into a prude so easily. Errrrr! How is it that I keep having to deal with these crazy things? First the audience reaction, then Jesse's surprise arrival, and now the thought of having sex?! I can't take it anymore!!!

Kate

To: Katherine Bloom <katherine@ktextv.com>
From: Chloe Sinclair <chloe@ktextv.com>
Subject: Explain please

I hate to be the one to break it to you, but being sexy and being over the top are two different kettles of fish. And what is this about the sex? I thought you chickened out with Parker. Tell me you haven't been making nocturnal visits to the guest cottage.

C

To: Chloe Sinclair <chloe@ktextv.com>
From: Katherine Bloom <katherine@ktextv.com>
Subject: No!

No sex. I swear. And there will be no sex! And really, C, don't you dare breathe a word about this to Julia. Promise me! I never should have mentioned anything. I was half venting, half thinking that if I spelled it out, it wouldn't seem so bad. But it is bad. The truth is, I *want* to have sex with Jesse.

As to sexy vs. over the top, I know you're right. I can understand it if Julia never forgives me.

Kate

To: Katherine Bloom <katherine@ktextv.com>
From: Julia Boudreaux <julia@ktextv.com>
Subject: Hanky panky

What is this about you having sex? With Jesse? I must hear every detail. How far did you go? Was he as good as the newspapers make him out to be? And how about his body. Delicious? I expect a full report pronto.

xoxo, j

p.s. I considered never speaking to you again, but I decided to reconsider when, drumroll please, yet again the ratings went crazy. Bigger than big! Who knew you had it in you to be wild *and* crazy? Brava! We will ignore all the crazed fan mail you're getting from prisoners who want to take private lessons.

To: Julia Boudreaux <julia@ktextv.com>
    Chloe Sinclair <chloe@ktextv.com>
From: Katherine Bloom <katherine@ktextv.com>
Subject: Unforgiven

Chloe, I cannot believe you told Julia!! Now I won't hear the end of it. For everyone's information, I DID NOT HAVE SEX!!!! And what is this about prison mail?!

Katherine Bloom, formerly known as a respectable news anchor and upstanding citizen, who is expected to play golf—*golf*— early this coming Sunday morning.

p.s. Speaking of prisons, thanks for the pardon, J.

To: Katherine Bloom <katherine@ktextv.com>
    Chloe Sinclair <chloe@ktextv.com>
From: Julia Boudreaux <julia@ktextv.com>
Subject: You say tomato

You might not have had a good old-fashioned fuck, sugar, but I can read between the lines. You'll be having one soon. As to golf, I guess you were right about finding yourself a big strapping man with a fine, strong putter and a great set of balls.

xoxo, Julia Scarlett Boudreaux

p.s. That wasn't a faint you saw. I was laughing so hard I collapsed.

fifteen

*J*esse needed to clear his head, find his focus. But all he had been able to do since last night was think of Katie.

Kate.

Hell. It hadn't just been since last night. It had been since he drove across the city limits.

He had become obsessed with her, her beauty—the innate sensuality that she was just beginning to discover. But it was more than that. Kate was beautiful in a way that went deeper than the surface. As much as her idealism and determination drove him crazy, he also admired her willingness to do whatever it took to make something happen. She wasn't a quitter. And she wasn't afraid to show that she cared deeply and unabashedly for the things she considered to be important in life.

He had taken responsibility for Travis as much because he couldn't stand to see her disappointed in him as because he didn't know how to do anything else. It was the right thing to do—he knew that—and he saw it that way because so often in his life he found himself looking at issues as if he were looking at them through Kate's eyes.

He cursed the affliction even though he knew it had saved him more than once.

But he had to set thoughts of Kate aside. At least for now.

Starting today, he planned to spend his mornings concentrating on his game. In the afternoon, once Travis returned from golf camp, they'd work on the tree house. And at night, he would concentrate on Kate.

He got hard just thinking about all the things he would show her. The pleasure he would give her. But that was for later.

He had allowed Travis and Kate and the tree house to become an excuse not to deal with what was really wrong. His game was falling apart. He was unable to take a driver in his hand without breaking into a sweat. He'd always had nerves of steel. But now his heart pounded just thinking about having to play in the PGA Championship. Was he choking now that he finally was considered a favorite to win?

And then there was his son. Jesse didn't really know what it was about Travis that made him want to make space for the kid in his life. Was it because the boy was something he had created—even if it was unknowingly, much less unwillingly? Something beyond himself, beyond the total consumption by golf that had been his life?

The boy was naïve in so many ways, though far older than his years in others. Jesse wasn't sure what he was supposed to do about the kid, but he knew he needed to do something—give something to the boy beyond the memory of a tree house they had built together. Something that would provide him with a foundation of faith in himself, a confidence that he didn't have.

There was no denying that Travis wasn't happy and wanted to quit golf. This was after the boy had all but begged him to be able to play. Something wasn't right, and Jesse had every intention of finding out what it was.

And when he should have turned right to head to the country club to work on his swing as time ran out before the PGA Championship, he turned left and headed for Travis's golf camp.

His own game would have to wait.

Travis stood as far away from the group as he possibly could. The sun beat down so hard that there wasn't a green piece of grass as far as the eye could see. Stretching out before him was a long, mowed field with more grass roots than actual grass since the hard-packed and dried earth refused to allow anything to burrow deep.

When he took a step, a fine powdery dust puffed around his sneakers. He felt like Pig Pen from the ancient Charlie Brown cartoons that his mom liked so much, and just as much an outcast.

He would have skipped camp altogether if Jesse hadn't been watching when the bus showed up. That morning they had started out like usual. They ate breakfast—his dad was obsessed with feeding him. But then they didn't do any work on the tree house. Which was fine with him since he couldn't handle the tools very good. No matter how many times Jesse showed him how to use stuff, he couldn't quite get everything to connect right. Once he nearly smashed his own thumb, but Jesse had reached out real quick and grabbed the hammer just in time.

Travis shuddered just thinking about the potential pain.

But not even that compared to the very real pain of dealing with the bullies at golf camp. He'd rather be hanging out with Lena Lehman, who was pretty cool, even if she was a girl and a real know-it-all.

One day the two of them had snuck onto the golf course and played a few holes. The chipping and putting had actually been fun. And while he might not be all that great at the whole game, he had impressed her with his putting.

But then Jimmy and his sidekick Walter from golf school had shown up and hadn't been happy to see him. The last thing Travis wanted was to be embarrassed by those two in front of Lena, so he'd said he had to go home, and escaped.

Lost in his thoughts, he shoved his hands in his jeans pockets and hoped that Coach would forget to call on him. He didn't realize trouble was brewing until it was too late.

"Hey, perve," Walter taunted, pushing him in the back. Jimmy didn't say a word, he just glared.

"Ah, hi," Travis said, flipping his hand up, then turning as fast as he could and heading for Coach, who was way over at the other end of the makeshift driving range, helping some other hapless camper with his swing.

But Walter and Jimmy circled in front of Travis, blocking the way. The only thing Travis could do now was yell. And he wasn't that big of a baby.

"Where you going so fast, fat boy?" Walter pushed him into Jimmy.

Jimmy pushed him back. "We have some talking to do."

"Talking?" Travis asked with a traitorous shake in his voice.

Walter shoved him up against the chain-link fence edged by prickly bushes, scraping his arms. "Stay the hell away from Lena. She's mine."

"Oh." Lena had said she hated Jimmy and Walter. "How can she be your girl if she doesn't like you?"

That's when he got the big push. But since there was nowhere to go, the only thing that happened was that the air got knocked out of him when he slammed harder into the fence. Travis realized too late that he shouldn't have said that to a bully.

"Stay away from her, piss face," Walter hissed.

Air rushed back through his body, making him dizzy. He thought he just might barf all over Jimmy's and Walter's fancy golf shoes.

"No problem," he said. "I won't talk to her ever again."

They laughed in his face and shoved him again. Travis tried to get away, but he only ended up in a cloud of dust and gravel when they threw him to the ground.

"You're a freakin' bastard, remember, perve breath," Walter added.

Walter and Jimmy laughed at that, but all of a sudden their laughter cut off like a guillotine had slammed home.

It was the shadow that Travis noticed next—the harsh West Texas sun blocked out. Thank God, Coach had arrived to save him from certain death or, at the very least, the loss of a few teeth.

"What's going on here?"

The voice stopped him cold. Not Coach.

Travis glanced up and felt his heart cease to beat in his chest. It was bad enough to think of Lena seeing Jimmy and Walter pick on him, but he thought he would die over the idea that his dad would see him looking like a wimpy moron, eating dust.

"Travis?" Jesse asked, his eyes narrowing as he took in the situation. "What's going on?"

Walter and Jimmy made a big production of pulling Travis up, dusting him off, and putting their arms around his shoulders. "You're all right, Travis, aren't you?" They laughed self-consciously. "He's our good buddy."

"Yeah, I'm fine. Really." Travis gestured to Jesse to follow. "Come on, I think we should go."

The boys didn't need any more than that. They turned tail and ran toward the campers who were lined up firing golf balls into the parched field.

It wasn't until Walter and Jimmy had slipped into their spots in line that had been held by their clubs that Jesse glanced at Travis. "What was that all about?" he asked.

"Nothing."

Jesse considered him for a minute. Travis didn't worry that he'd pursue it. He never did. Using the simple word *nothing* had proved to be a great answer to get Jesse to leave him alone.

"Are they beating you up? Is that why you don't like golf?"

Okay, it had worked in the past.

It didn't take more than a second for Jesse to realize he wasn't getting anything out of the kid. He remembered the welt on Travis's temple. Suddenly the boy's desire to quit golf school took on a whole new dimension.

Jesse's first instinct was to do whatever it took to make things better for Travis. "I'm going to talk to your coach."

Travis grew agitated and his eyes went wide. "No! Please don't. There's nothing to say, really."

Jesse's own father leaped to mind—the way the man constantly embarrassed him. One minute laughing like a boisterous fun guy, then next glaring with the fury that settled in his eyes so easily and at so little provocation. Derek had responded by becoming cautious and staunchly conservative. Jesse had become just the opposite of his older brother—careless and intentionally wild—and he had done it with relish. But careless and wild, he had learned, had consequences. The kind that was standing right in front of him with dust and gravel sticking to his skin.

Jesse wanted to do this right. He didn't want to embarrass his own kid.

His own kid.

The words hit him all over again.

"Really," Travis added. "It'll only make it worse."

Jesse stared silently for a second, then he bent down on one knee. "I want to make things better. Tell me why they beat you up."

Travis grimaced, looking despondent. "You really don't have to do the dad thing. You're not very good at it. But thanks." He headed toward the parking lot.

Jesse wasn't about to give up that easily. "Travis, I'm trying. Give me a break."

This time Travis groaned and hung his head.

"I'll fix things for you, T." That nickname that Kate used for Travis. Jesse had never wanted anything more than he wanted to fix this for the boy. "Tell me what's going on."

Travis sighed wearily. "I guess they think I'm a nerd. You know, kind of like Xander on *Buffy.*"

"You're not a nerd," Jesse stated indignantly.

He got a snort for an answer.

"I mean it. You're a great kid. And all you have to do is be yourself and not worry."

"Being myself is what gets me into trouble."

"No way. I bet you get around them and are nervous, or you try too hard. You really are a great kid. And you don't have to take any crap from those guys."

"You're saying I should fight back?" The twelve-year-old gasped. "Like fist fighting?"

Jesse couldn't tell if Travis was horrified or thought it was cool. Not that it mattered either way. Jesse could just imagine how Kate would respond if she found him giving the boy fighting lessons. Though his initial instinct was to do just that.

"No. No fighting." He racked his brain for an alternate idea. "But you have to stand up to them."

Now there was a useful plan, Jesse thought disdainfully.

"That's easy for you to say. You're cool. And you wear cool clothes."

"I'm not so cool," Jesse admitted. "I'm just a kid in adult clothes. Ask Kate."

Travis finally smiled, giving a snort of laugher. "Yeah, you make her crazy."

"Maybe a little."

Another snort. "I think you make her a lot crazy."

"Okay, okay, I get the point." He grimaced. "But I think she's coming around."

Suddenly they both smiled, the image of Kate clearly in each of their heads.

"Come on. Let me talk to your coach. Then we'll figure out how to deal with golf camp."

The minute Jesse headed for the opposite end of the driving range, Gary Peters noticed.

"Jesse Chapman!" the big burly coach called out.

"Hello, Gary."

The men shook hands.

"I was hoping you'd stop by sometime," Gary said.

Jesse turned to Travis. "Go get your clubs, T."

The minute Travis headed away, his feet scuffing in the dirt, Jesse refocused on the coach. "I wanted to talk about Travis."

"He's a good kid."

"I know that, but when I drove up a few minutes ago, he was getting pushed around."

Gary sighed. "I've been trying to keep my eye on him, but you know how it is with a boy like Travis."

Jesse's eyes narrowed. "No, I don't."

Peters shifted his weight. "Like I said, he's a good kid, but he's had a hard time fitting in. He's kind of awkward. I wish I could do more. Travis could be a decent golfer. His short game is pretty damn good and he putts better than anyone in the class. I'll hand him that. Hell, if the sports programs had a lick of money to spend, I'd have an assistant and it wouldn't be me alone trying to keep twenty-five kids in line. What we need is money. Then I could do something with a kid like Travis. And it's the same all over town."

They talked for a while longer. And by the time he and Travis were leaving, Jesse had an idea where to start to help his son.

First thing Saturday morning, Jesse strode into Kate's house like a drill sergeant, waking everyone up so he could tell them his new plan.

"Shopping?" Travis and Kate asked in unison.

"You need some new clothes," Jesse told Travis.

At ten sharp, they drove to the Sunland Park Mall. Going from store to store, Kate sipped a cup of coffee as they went. But coffee or no, it quickly became clear that none of them knew what constituted cool clothes for the junior high set. Thankfully there was a teenage sales clerk working at one of the stores who was full of advice.

When they finished, Kate didn't mention that Travis looked like an urban thug, with his crotch down to his knees. She'd never seen the boy look so happy as he was now in his ill-fitting jeans and gigantic Nike trainers— not sneakers, as she had mistakenly called them. Jesse looked as happy as his son.

Once newly attired, Travis walked or strutted around the shops. On the way home, they stopped at the grocery store. Jesse had announced halfway through their mall excursion that he was going to cook dinner that night. When they pulled into the drive, the Jeep loaded with groceries and cool clothes, every ounce of darkness that had been in Jesse's eyes when he had arrived home last evening from Travis's golf camp was gone.

After Kate put the groceries away, she went out to the guest cottage to talk to Jesse. The minute she walked in the door, her palms felt moist. No matter how many times she saw him, he did that to her.

"You were wonderful with Travis today," she said truthfully, her gaze drifting to his lips.

He smiled a lopsided smile, his hair falling forward, making him look like an errant schoolboy. "You were great. Thanks for coming with us."

He took a step toward her, reaching out. But his hand froze when they heard the back screen door slam.

"Hey!" Travis called, barreling inside. Then he stopped. "Jesse? Kate?"

She blinked and leaped back, her cheeks red-hot with guilty embarrassment at what she had wanted to do. Let him touch her. Touch him back.

After one look at them, the boy smiled and nodded knowingly. "Has he been showing you that putter of his?"

Kate thought she would collapse. Jesse's brows slammed together. Unperturbed, Travis went straight over to the club in question and rummaged up a handful of balls. For the first time she noticed the makeshift putting course set up around the guest cottage.

"Look at this," Travis announced. Then he proceeded to putt into a soup can over and over again with astounding accuracy. "I've been practicing."

Jesse stood there, a grin turning up one corner of his mouth. "I can tell," he said.

Kate felt amazingly relieved as Jesse and Travis straightened the putting course made from cans and man-made hazards. Travis had not been referring to her love products show.

After they putted a few rounds, Jesse suggested they go for a swim. Travis was all for it. Kate wasn't nearly as enthusiastic. It wasn't the swimming part that bothered her—though she couldn't remember the last time she had actually ventured into the pool—but rather the idea of putting on a swimsuit that gave her pause. After the Cowboy Bob debacle, she had sworn off the ankle weights.

But the next thing she knew she had changed into a one-piece Speedo that she'd had since the days when she thought she'd get in shape by swimming laps. When she came out of the house with a towel wrapped around her torso and secured under her arms, Jesse whistled.

Kate blushed.

Travis said, "There's that look again."

"What look?" she asked.

Jesse gave a quick shake of his head.

Travis answered anyway. "The one you got when you did that cat interview."

Jesse groaned. Kate would have returned inside except he caught up to her and steered her back around just as Travis did a cannonball.

"Oops," Jesse said as she stood there dripping, though there was barely a trace of repentance on his face. And even less when he tossed her in the pool.

"I take it that was another accident," she said when she came up for air.

"Nope, that was on purpose."

For the rest of the afternoon, they swam and played. At dinner, Jesse and Travis cooked everything. They laughed and joked, and Kate felt a poignant squeeze that she didn't want to examine when Jesse reached across the table and ruffled Travis's hair.

The day was idyllic in many ways, at least until much later when Kate realized that spending hours outside that afternoon had left her with a sunburn to beat all sunburns.

"Ouch, ouch, ouch," she moaned after she pulled herself out of the bath.

Drying off was more of a patting affair, each touch making her grimace. Gingerly slipping a robe on over her cotton nightgown, she went to check on Travis. The boy was sound asleep. The sheets and covers were half thrown off, half tangled around his ankles, his Spiderman pajamas too small and so old that she knew they were something that he hadn't yet wanted to give up.

She allowed herself to go into the room to straighten the covers. She adored the boy, but knew better than to get too attached. He'd be leaving in the next couple of weeks. Would Jesse still leave then, too?

The thought caught her off guard.

Frantically, she worked to shore up her defenses. He would leave. He wouldn't stay. She told herself to remember that.

Clicking the door shut, she went to the kitchen. In jeans and a T-shirt, Jesse stood by the counter, staring out into the dark yard. She made no noise, just stood for a while looking at him, taking him in.

After a moment he turned. He didn't say a word at the sight of her but simply leaned back against the sink, his hands hooked over the edge behind him. His gaze was at once confused and sensual as his eyes ran the length of her.

"You're up late, even for you," he said, his voice both rugged and sexy.

"It's not so late."

The clock in the hall rang the hour. Two in the morning.

"Maybe a little late."

Pushing away, he came toward her. Her heart stilled before it jarred to a start in her chest. Her pulse leaped and her palms grew moist, and she was thankful she had worn more than a nightgown.

She couldn't say a word for him to stay where he was, nor could she bring herself to flee. He didn't stop until he stood before her, his gaze drifting to her lips, then lower.

Her nipples pulled into tight buds in response to nothing more than his gaze, taut and aching for him to brush his palms against them as he had done before.

Reaching out he touched her, his fingertips drifting along her collarbone, then down her arms, which made her remember why she wasn't in bed.

"Ouch."

"What's wrong?"

"Nothing."

"Ah, more *nothing*s. Did you learn that from Travis?"

Despite herself she smiled. "All right, if you must know, I'm sunburned."

He stepped back, not far, but enough so that she could breathe. At least she could until he tugged at the edges of the robe.

"What are you doing?" she asked, her voice a high-pitched squeak.

"Taking off your robe."

"**M**y robe?" she stammered.

He answered by pulling the material back, revealing the bright white skin that ran like a ribbon through the painful red sunburn. "It's too hot for a robe."

He felt the shiver of desire that raced through her, saw how her hazel eyes flashed with green fire. Her breath caught and fluttered. Instinctively, she tried to cover herself when he ran his finger down the unburned, delicate white skin, his hand drifting lower until he came to the curve of her breast, safely hidden away beneath her prim robe.

She was beautiful and innocently vulnerable. With every day that passed, he wanted her more. His body ached to find hers. But he wanted her to trust him, he realized. He felt a nearly unrecognizable determination to be patient, to woo her.

The thought made a beat of wolfish pleasure pound through him. He'd always been a man to take what he wanted, when he wanted it. But with Kate, he wanted to lead her to a place where she could truly accept her own desire. Because while one minute she wanted to be free and modern, in the next, long years of being responsible surged.

It was a battle for her. He understood that. And he would guide her slowly to what he conceded they were destined to share. Passion, their bodies.

"Let me see your burn." He claimed her hand, gently running his fingers over the pulse in her wrist.

"My burn?" she managed, pulling her robe back around her.

He smiled at her. "Yes, your burn. That's all."

She bit her lips, but didn't protest when he tugged her hands away, and after a second she let them drop. The small gesture was an act of trust. His chest felt like it would explode with simple pride. It was amazing what she did to him, how she could wipe everything from his mind but her.

He felt her tremble when he parted the material again, but there was no fear, and his pride grew.

Her skin was a mix of flawless pearl juxtaposed with angry red. "I've seen worse, but it has to hurt. I have some ointment that will help." Careful of the burn, he secured her robe, then tugged her out the back door and across the pool deck to the guest cottage.

Once inside, she made a point of remaining in the tiny living room when he let go and continued on into the bathroom. She stood with her robe tied tight and her arms crossed securely. She heard him rummaging around in a drawer.

"Where are you?" he called back to her.

"I thought you could bring whatever it is you have out here."

"I'm not going to jump your bones, Kate."

Kate grimaced. "O ye of honeyed words."

When she marched into the bathroom, he didn't respond, only started to pull the robe away. Out of habit, her hand leaped to the closure. "I'll do it," she said.

After a second, he handed over the plastic tube in surrender. "Fine."

She could tell he was trying to help, but he was also showing her that he would take this at the pace she wanted—as if he had no doubt whatsoever that indeed they would make love.

The realization made her mad, but it also made sensation surge between her legs. Whether he stayed or whether he left, more and more she wondered what she wanted. To take a chance? To stay safe? To wear caution and virtue like a badge of honor?

She didn't know.

She took the ointment, debated for a moment, then left the cottage, only to return five minutes later. He hadn't moved an inch.

"Yes?" he asked, his dark hair brushed away from his face, his eyes filled with a predatory gleam barely masked by a kind patience.

"Well, I can't get it on."

Though she had given it an amazing try. But her attempts had yielded only marginal success given that it was next to impossible to reach her back without stretching the very skin that the sunburn made scream in pain.

"I'm happy to help you *get it on*." His smile turned into a teasing grin.

Kate rolled her eyes, though truthfully it was easier to sort through her feelings for this man when he was teasing rather than when his dark gaze smoldered in a way that caused her heart to block her throat, making it hard to breathe.

Jesse chuckled, pulled her robe away before she realized what he was doing, and tossed it aside.

Every trace of humor melted away. She became aware of the sheer nightgown she had worn beneath the sensible cotton. He looked at her with something she could only term awe. Wariness began to fade beneath the heat of a traitorously bold pleasure.

He turned her until her back was to him. She trembled in anticipation. Then all he did was smooth the thick lotion over her shoulders like a calm professional. But even that felt amazing.

A tiny—she told herself it was tiny—moan escaped her lips. Jesse murmured wordlessly, sliding his palms along her skin, pushing the straps of her gown to the side.

She wiggled her shoulders. "Maybe a little more to the left."

This time there was a chuckle mixed with the rugged sensuality of his touch. But she reasoned that a girl needed a little attention now and again, and while in the guise of a sunburn rub, what could it hurt? She half believed herself. The minute it turned to something else, she'd put a stop to things.

Though more and more she began to wonder why she had thought her no-sex rule was such a good idea. All he had to do was look at her for her limbs to go weak and a strange staccato dance to start up in her chest.

Starting at her shoulder blades, his hands slid up, then down, in a deep stroke. But the second time his palms swooped up they didn't stop. Her body began to hum when the tips of his fingers spread the ointment along her collarbones.

"How long has it been since you've had sex?" he asked.

Surprise rippled through her, and she tried to be incensed. "One, that's none of your business, and two, it hasn't been that long."

"I don't believe you. I think it's been a long time . . . if ever."

Her chin rose defiantly. "So sue me. I will not be my mother."

The words burst out of her, seeming to come out of nowhere. She cringed.

His strong hands paused, then came up and gently squeezed her shoulders, pulling her back toward him, his breath against her ear. "You've never been your mother, Kate. You never could be."

She pivoted to face him, her gown slipping low when the tiny straps fell farther down her arms. "Oh, really?"

She couldn't explain why she felt insulted. As always when she was around him, she felt skewered by the double prongs of reason and desire. Nothing ever seemed black or white. Too much gray, making her vacillate from one need to another. She didn't want to be like her mother, tangling with men in a way that left her as nothing more than a twisted knot on the floor. But there were other times, like now, that Kate wanted to be seen as passionate and wildly desirable. But she also knew that her feelings were more than that. Deeper.

"I know that no one would ever confuse me with my mother, because she's so vibrant and beautiful that men can't help but fall in love with her. She's like a bright flame that draws people—especially men."

Kate knew she was being ridiculous, even childish, but couldn't seem to stop herself.

His gaze burned and his jaw went taut as he took in her body. Then he tilted her chin, forcing her to meet his eyes. He was so tall, so commanding, and she looked up at him and saw the intensity of his emotions.

"You have it wrong, Kate. You could never be like your mother, not because you aren't full of passion, but because Mary Beth has always been selfish. She uses men to fix her life. And when the excitement pales and the real world sets in, she moves on to the next poor unsuspecting soul for a new fix of excitement to chase reality away. You, Katherine Bloom, have always faced up to the truth, no matter how difficult it is. I've always admired you for that."

She bit her lip. His words touched her deeply, but they also frustrated her.

"Maybe I'm tired of people's admiration," she stated. "Maybe I just want to feel alive for a change, without worrying about what happens next or what the future holds. But whenever I start to give in, I think of my mother. One minute I'm trying to be wild, then the next I can't hear the word *pussy* referring to a simple cat without flushing crimson with embarrassment. Then in order to prove that I am not the prude I've just proved myself to be, I swing back the other way, acting like a possessed person as I did with that love products show. It's a vicious circle. Be responsible so I'm not like my mom, but then lash out for having to be so responsible all the time. The night I asked you to make love to me, I wanted to feel free and wild. All of a sudden, I had this overwhelming urge to forget everything and feel sexy. Me, suddenly sexy." She shook her head at how ridiculous it was. She snorted. "But then my mind swirls back, and I can't follow through."

His finger drifted along her jaw to the pulse in her throat. "You are sexy, Kate. Not suddenly, after you put on some short skirt or because you asked me to make love to you. You've been sexy for years—sexy in all the best ways. Hell, you were even sexy clutching that photo album to your chest, with that pot of tea sitting on the table next to you. You were hot and beautiful but I couldn't afford to see you that way."

Their eyes met and held, her breath shuddering painfully inside her. It flashed through her mind that he might pull her to him, capture her against his chest, their mouths slanting together in hunger. But none of that happened. No moment of startling passion, no music soaring to a crescendo in the background.

"Now let me get a better look at that sunburn," he said.

Disappointment made her sigh. She was thinking passionate sound tracks and he was thinking medicine.

But then very carefully he slipped his forefingers underneath the straps, pulling them farther down, and then down even lower, revealing her breasts.

Her sigh caught in her throat, and her heart pounded. She tried to reconcile a friend's concern with the heated look in his eyes.

He peeled the gown away with an infinite slowness until it fell in a puddle around her ankles. She stood still, her pulse ragged. The heat in his eyes flared, then his lips tilted at one corner.

This is your chance to be sexy.

The words flitted through her head. But it wasn't a matter of being suddenly sexy, not even outrageously sexy as she had been on the love products show. But truly sexy, in a way that for once was real. She could be powerful. She could be confident.

Like a bad habit, embarrassment tried to push through the power when he just stared at her.

"What?" she asked nervously when he stood there and only looked.

"New panties?"

Sheer bikinis with tiny pink roses trimming the edge.

A foreign, beating confidence surged through her as he turned her back around and pressed her spine to his chest. He ran his palms up her bare midriff, stopping just below her breasts before trailing low again, making her shiver with longing.

"And matching toe polish," he murmured against her ear. "I like it." Then he splayed his hand over the curve of her abdomen, pressing her even closer, the proof of his desire hard and insistent against the small of her back.

"Do you feel that?" he whispered hoarsely. "Do you feel how much I want you?"

She could barely speak as the tips of his fingers brushed the very edge of her panties. With a groan, he ripped his shirt over his head in one clean stroke, then pulled her back.

Dropping featherlight kisses along her neck, he cupped her breasts, pushing them high. Her breath slid out in a moan when he wouldn't let her turn around, only gently squeezed her nipples between his thumbs and forefingers. She felt on fire, burning for something she could hardly name. But deep inside she knew this was what had been missing from her life. Sex and need. Passion.

No, she realized. It was Jesse who had been missing from her life.

It was crazy, insane. Two people drawn together despite the fact that she wanted all of him and he wanted distance.

She didn't know why he needed distance, needed a wall built securely around him. He was comfortable when he was in control, when he was teasing and playful. But ultimately the smiles hid something deeper that she didn't understand. But maybe, just maybe, she could crack through that hard armor. Maybe, by staying with her instead of leaving town or even going to a hotel, he wanted her to try.

The thought filled her with hope and excitement. When his arm came across her collarbone, holding her secure, one hand still cupping her breast, pressing her high, she leaned back into him. Her skin felt hot, but not from the sunburn. And when his fingers slipped beneath the elastic band of her panties, her body shuddered.

Nudging her feet apart, he widened her stance. She obeyed willingly, only to gasp when his fingers found the curls between her legs. With one slightly calloused tip, he parted her.

Her mouth fell open in a silent *ah* of sensation.

"You're wet," he whispered against her ear.

His finger traced the sensitive edges. She made an incoherent sound.

"You're hot," he added. "Your passion is amazing."

He circled and teased, but his finger didn't slip inside her. He turned her to face him, his blue eyes darkened with satisfaction. His hands curled around her elbows, pulling her back to him.

Heat rushed through her, and she inhaled just as he bent his head to kiss her. It was as if he breathed her in, his lips sucking at hers, his teeth gently nipping. She could have lost herself in that simple kiss forever.

When he took her hand and tugged her toward the bedroom, she followed. Her heart pounded in anticipation, but he wasn't headed for the bedroom. He pulled her into the bathroom and kicked the door shut. When he leaned over and turned on the water in the tub, he still didn't let her go.

"A bath?" she asked.

"A bath," he confirmed.

He rummaged around in the cabinet filled with an assortment of things she kept there for guests. The plastic bottle of Vitamin E bath oil had never been opened, speaking to the number of guests she'd had.

Jesse poured some into the water. "It will help your sunburn."

Ah, back to the sunburn. Though she wasn't sure how a bath would help after the ointment had already been applied. But who was she to argue? she reasoned over the loud drumbeat of her pulse in her ears.

When he hooked his fingers beneath the very thin edges of her panties, she let him, her eyes closing on a soft exhale as he carefully pulled them down.

He did nothing for a moment, and she opened her eyes to find him kneeling before her like a splendid knight.

"You're beautiful," he said.

He was no longer the charming bad boy of golf. He was an amazing man with desire written in his eyes. Then he leaned forward and pressed his lips to the curls between her legs. Instinctively, she gasped.

"Never be embarrassed in front of me," he commanded as he rose, his lips trailing up her body.

She allowed herself to relish every touch. When he stood before her, she melted into him.

Hesitantly, she kissed him. She felt as much as heard the groan that rumbled when she slid her hands along the chiseled contours of his body, her palms savoring the well-defined muscles of his back. Then around to the front, her fingers circling his nipples. For a few incredible moments, he let her maintain control. She touched and kissed, explored as she wanted.

Then suddenly this strong man had had enough. "Careful, Kate," he said, his voice ragged. "If your hands get any lower, you're going to find yourself in my bed, on your back, with me sliding inside you."

She realized in that second that if he tried, she wouldn't say no. The last remnant of her no-sex rule was gone. Finally, completely. And suddenly she felt wild and free.

He guided her into the tub, his hand holding her arm securely so she couldn't slip in the oily water. The water was warm and soft against her skin as she allowed him to lay her back. She sighed with pleasure and closed her eyes, sinking down until the water lapped at her chin.

She looked up at him towering next to the bathtub, his chest bare, his button-fly jeans riding low on his hips, the top button left undone. She could see a glimpse of that place where his tan gave way to untanned skin, the narrow trail of hair running down his abdomen disappearing from sight.

"You're amazing," she murmured.

His smile crooked at one corner as he sat down on the floor next to her. She watched him watching her, his fist

resting on his bended knee, his chin on his fist. Then his
smile disappeared and he dipped his hand into the water.

Anticipation raced through her, mixed with a start of
nerves. "Jesse?"

"Shhh," he whispered, his palm gliding through the
water, then slowly over one breast, then the other, bringing her nipples to taut peaks.

Clearly his intent wasn't for her to relax. Proof came
when his hand dipped lower, down along the curve of
her belly, then lower still, before he parted the curls between her thighs once again.

This time he didn't stop.

He touched her intimately, circling gently.

"Yes," he murmured, nudging her thighs apart a little
more, before sliding one lean, slightly calloused finger
inside her, and she moaned.

The invasion was both hot and heady.

"You're tight. Relax," he commanded gently. "Spread
your legs for me, sweetheart."

She wanted to, though her mind instinctively whispered of wantonness. He stroked her then, and her brain
lost control, her body overriding any concern.

She whimpered in a way that made him pause. Which
only made her whimper even more.

"Is this too much?" he asked, his finger gliding slowly.

"Yes," she groaned.

But when he started to pull out, she clutched his hand.
Helpless to fight this need, she didn't care about being
proper. She wanted this, needed it in some primal way
that was beyond words.

His low chuckle was ripe with arrogant satisfaction,
but she didn't care about that, either. And when he slipped

a second finger inside her, hard and deep, she shuddered with her own pounding pleasure.

She couldn't seem to help herself when she shamelessly arched her hips to him. His touch taunted and teased, circling her.

Her body reached for what he wanted to give her.

"That's it, Kate."

Her body shimmering with passion, her eyes fluttered closed.

"That's it," he whispered, boldly stroking, pulling out until the tip of his finger touched her most sensitive spot, circling, then sliding deep once again.

"Lift your knees for me," he instructed, his voice low and passionate.

When she looked at him again, his expression was filled with a wealth of emotion. "Open to me, Kate."

Her heart pounded, then slowly, dragging in her breath, she did as he had instructed. She lifted her knees until her feet were planted on the bottom of the tub, offering more of herself. He studied her face for one last, long second, then he nudged her legs even farther apart, leaning forward and kissing her wet knee. "Yes, sweetheart, just like that."

A shiver of heat ran through her as he pulled the drain plug, allowing the water to escape, then he slid his hand down the inside of her thigh to the core of her. His palm briefly cupped her before he ran his palm up her other thigh, the water draining, draining, the waterline slowly, maddeningly, lowering against her body.

It felt like the water licked at her. Then his hand, sliding lower and lower, parted her, and he slipped his finger deep once again.

Composure and common sense were lost, and all she wanted was more of what he was giving. When she thought she couldn't feel anything better, he slipped a second finger inside her. She squirmed, seeking something that she knew of but had never experienced.

His fingers delved deeper, stroking long and slow, his thumb expertly finding the tender nub. Needing to hold on to something, she brought her hands up, clasping the porcelain sides, and she refused to think about how she tilted her hips to give him more of her.

"Yes," he murmured, stroking faster, bringing her closer and closer to something that she wanted.

His tone was so tender, every ounce of dominant male arrogance replaced by awe. She felt a true sense of sexiness that went far beyond her earlier attempts.

She felt the need to buck. She was vaguely aware that her head rolled from side to side, vaguely heard how his breathing was thick with his own desire. She wanted to reach out to him, touch him, but when she would have he held her secure with his touch.

"You're almost there," he whispered. "Reach."

And she did, thrusting her pelvis against his sliding fingers. And when his thumb and forefingers closed ever so gently on her clitoris, her world exploded, shuddering through her like a lightning bolt. Blue and electric. Intense and all-consuming.

He cupped his palm to her mound, helping her to manage the shock of sensation, her entire body tense.

It wasn't until her orgasm spun itself out that every ounce of tension evaporated. The next thing she knew, Jesse had her out of the tub, cradled against his chest, as he carried her out of the bathroom and laid her like a precious gift on the bed.

She saw his primal satisfaction that he could make her feel such intensity. She had never let go completely before. But now she was with the man she had dreamed of for a lifetime. She didn't care about right or wrong. She understood that she could touch, feel, revel, and he wouldn't think less of her. Suddenly she understood that this man would allow her to let go of inhibition and she would not have to feel guilty afterward.

That's when she knew what she wanted—to make him feel the same spiraling need he made her experience again and again when he touched her. He always kept himself under a cast-iron control—potent and all-consuming. Even after his bold proclamation that they would make love, he had maintained a safe distance between them. And she was tired of it.

Surprising him, she rolled to her feet to stand before him. His gaze turned wary, as if he sensed the shift in her.

"What is it?" he asked.

She didn't answer. With her heart pounding hard, she reached low and undid the remaining buttons on his jeans.

"Kate, what are you doing?"

Kate knew that she had never needed a man before, but she understood now that she needed to share her love for this one. She had tried before, but he had always turned her away. She wasn't going to let him turn her away again. Because she did love him—not because he was the boy she had cherished while growing up. But because he had grown into a man who was good and kind, only he kept that goodness hidden beneath a facade of wild boy charm.

He had scoffed when she said he was trying as a father, but only a good man would have put everything aside to do what was right. And he had been that sort of man from the day he arrived and saved her from looking like a fool during the cooking show.

Again and again, he saved her. Now she would do whatever it took to save him in return.

She would kiss him, she would cherish his amazing strength. He had said they would make love. She realized he was correct. And she also realized that it didn't make her like her mother.

But before they could share that ultimate bond, she had to find a way to break through the barriers he had erected around himself. She had to make him feel.

She realized in that second that Jesse was all about making other people feel. Making other people smile and laugh. But he didn't allow the same for himself. He didn't allow himself to let go. Didn't allow himself to give his heart.

He had been through a string of lovers without ever giving more than pleasure.

Her eyes implored him when she started tugging at his jeans.

"I'd be careful if I were you, Kate. You're playing with fire."

She only tugged harder until he had little choice but to step free of the denim or push her away. She saw the war that raged—the vulnerability that flashed in his eyes. But he did step free, the simple action not so simple, one brick in his wall chipped away.

He stood before her like a man sculpted from granite, hard and solid, no doubts left that he wanted her. She didn't care that she was naked, damp from the bath. She felt alive as she never had before.

"Kiss me," she whispered.

She didn't wait. She reached up. A breath shuddering through him, he leaned down, giving in, and brushed his lips over hers, once, twice, before he pulled her to him.

Both of them naked, their kiss turned hard and rough, hot and wet. She couldn't get close enough. When she grew impatient, he didn't laugh or grin. He groaned like a man lost before they fell onto the bed and he captured her hands above her head.

"I want you, Kate," he murmured, sucking one nipple deep in his mouth. "I want to make love to you."

"And we will, just as you said," she promised, her body arching to him for more.

He nipped and kissed and laved her nipples with his tongue. Her body yearned again. But this time it wasn't about her.

"But not yet," she added.

She felt the entire length of his body tense with confusion. She rolled off the bed. He followed, but didn't get farther than the edge of the mattress before she stopped him with her hand against his chest.

"What are you doing, Kate?" There was a tremor in his voice.

"I'm going to make you feel," she whispered.

Wariness flared in him, proving to her that she was right. This strong man didn't allow himself to feel. But she wasn't about to give up.

She pressed her hand to his chest, leaning into him. He sat, his gaze still formidable. But heat mixed with danger when she kneeled before him.

"Kate," he said, his tone warning.

"What, Jesse?"

"You seem obsessed with proving that you've grown up. Let me assure you that there's nothing left to prove."

He sounded so stern, so forbidding, and she bit her lower lip with a sudden spurt of nerves. But something more powerful than that urged her on, pushing at her fears.

Hoping he couldn't tell how she trembled, she boldly ran her palms up his naked thighs. His body shuddered, his erection straining, his pulse visible in his neck as he tried to keep control of himself.

Without a word, willing him with her eyes, she tugged at his knees. But he didn't budge, his breath growing ragged.

"Spread your legs." Just as he had said to her.

When he didn't move, his every muscle taut, she whispered, "I want this."

Jesse felt his body's need, along with the need not to give up control. He had never felt so on fire for a woman in his life. But he didn't want to taint the one person he knew who was nothing but pure goodness.

Making love to her was one thing. Letting her go down on him was another.

Taking from Kate seemed impossible. But when she leaned forward and began kissing a path up his thigh, he didn't know how to maintain his defenses.

After long ticking seconds, he spread his legs with a desperate groan. She moved between his thighs and looked at him one last time, her gaze filled with an emotion so genuine that he felt tears burn in his eyes as she finally, inevitably lowered her head, gently taking his hardness in her mouth.

Instantly, sensation like he had never experienced before exploded through his body. She moved on him, her hot, wet, slick mouth gliding over him with an innocent desire that made his blood pound relentlessly.

Jesse wasn't sure how long he could take the sweetness of her. She took him back in time to innocence and purity. Even as her lips circled him, her inexpert motions bespoke that innocence, sending a shiver of unadulterated need coursing through him.

His head fell back, and though he told himself to move her away, his hands only guided her, taught her what his body wanted, what it started to demand.

Sensation built, control became harder to maintain. He arched over her back, running his palms down her spine to her hips.

A deep moan rumbled in his chest. Kate heard it, he could tell, because she grew even more bold.

She reached low, cupping his balls, taking his length deeper in her mouth, hot and wild, wet and sweet.

He knew that if he didn't do something, he was going to come. And he didn't want that. Not now. So he tried to pull her away.

But when he pulled her up, her eyes glittered.

"I want this, Jesse," she said, hardly seeming like Kate at all.

Their eyes locked.

"Let me in," she added, her voice nearly cracking with emotion. "Let me inside those walls you keep around yourself."

She broke his grip, circled his cock with her palm, then slowly, divinely, lowered her head once again.

With that there was no turning back. His body overrode better sense. Conceding a bacchanalian defeat, he felt his legs spread wider. His hand fisted in her hair as his body shivered—making him lose control.

And he did. Lose the reins of that tightly held control. His body peaked as she took him deep one last time, and it happened. He shuddered with his release at the exact moment he ripped her away. He pulled her up to him, clutching her to his chest, his seed spilling over her body, his dick pulsing, throbbing, until he felt like he couldn't breathe.

It was then that he felt the wonder in her as she clung to him, and he felt as well his throat tighten and his eyes burn. When his heart finally settled back, he tipped up her chin. She was smiling. She was happy. Then she moved away and kissed him on the forehead, planting her hands on his thighs, bringing them face-to-face.

"I love you, Jesse Chapman. I've loved you my whole life. But this is a different love. A mature love that has nothing to do with bandaged knees and rescuing. And I'm not going to let you lock me out anymore."

Then she pulled on her clothes and left him sitting there wanting to reach out, but refusing to do so. His age-old need to maintain distance was still there, but it fought with the very real need and desire to pull Kate close. More than that, could he afford her love? He didn't know. He only knew for certain that he didn't deserve it.

To: Julia Boudreaux <julia@ktextv.com>
    Chloe Sinclair <chloe@ktextv.com>
From: Katherine Bloom <katherine@ktextv.com>
Subject: Beautiful Sunday

Good morning, my lovely friends! I hope everyone is having a very nice weekend!

xo, Kate

To: Katherine Bloom <katherine@ktextv.com>
    Chloe Sinclair <chloe@ktextv.com>
From: Julia Boudreaux <julia@ktextv.com>
Subject: !!!!

Why are you using so many exclamation marks? Don't you realize how obnoxiously cheerful they are? And this from a woman who mere days ago was lamenting her situation regarding some sort of sexual act or non-act. Hmmm, sounds suspicious to me.

j

To: Julia Boudreaux <julia@ktextv.com>
    Katherine Bloom <katherine@ktextv.com>
From: Chloe Sinclair <chloe@ktextv.com>
Subject: Very suspicious

And did you notice we even got an xo, too?

Chloe

Chloe Sinclair
Station Manager
Award-winning KTEX TV

To: Chloe Sinclair <chloe@ktextv.com>
    Katherine Bloom <katherine@ktextv.com>
From: Julia Boudreaux <julia@ktextv.com>
Subject: Allergies

I would guess she'd had sex if, one, it hadn't already been a far-fetched guess the first time I made it, because two, Kate and sex have become allergic to each other. At the rate she is going, she will forget how to do it. In fact, isn't there some new trend out there regarding revirgination? Kate certainly would apply.

xo, j

To: Julia Boudreaux <julia@ktextv.com>
    Chloe Sinclair <chloe@ktextv.com>
From: Katherine Bloom <katherine@ktextv.com>
Subject: Wonderful news

Hold onto your hats, ladies. I think things between Jesse and me are going to work out. Things are changing between us . . . and of course there is the whole issue of how well he is dealing with being a father.

K

To: Chloe Sinclair <chloe@ktextv.com>
From: Julia Boudreaux <julia@ktextv.com>
Subject: Oh dear

Kate believing things can work out with Jesse can't be good.

xo, j

To: Julia Boudreaux <julia@ktextv.com>
From: Chloe Sinclair <chloe@ktextv.com>
Subject: You're surprised?

Excuse me, but HELLO!! I hold you responsible for this, Jules. If it hadn't been for you forcing Jesse to stay in the guest cottage, none of this ever would have happened. She's never fallen out of love with him, and you know it. Regardless, don't rain on her parade. I haven't heard her this happy in weeks. Give it some time and hopefully it will work itself out. If not, we'll figure out a way to make things better.

Chloe

To: Katherine Bloom <katherine@ktextv.com>
    Chloe Sinclair <chloe@ktextv.com>
From: Julia Boudreaux <julia@ktextv.com>
Subject: My fault

I kick myself. As Chloe said to me, this is all my fault. I never should have told Jesse he could stay with you. But you know we love you, sugar, and you know we are only thinking of what is best for you. So when I say be careful, you know it's only with the best intentions. He is Jesse Chapman, after all—the man as famous for leaving women as he is for his good looks and golf swing. I don't want to see you get hurt, which is exactly what I'm afraid is going to happen here. Because Jesse will leave.

Your friend,
jules

To: Julia Boudreaux <julia@ktextv.com>
From: Chloe Sinclair <chloe@ktextv.com>
Subject: Excuse me?

And that's not raining on her parade how?????

Chloe

"*Jesse will leave.*"

Kate tried to ignore Julia's e-mail. Julia didn't know how things had changed, didn't know Jesse as well as she did. But when he walked into the kitchen the next morning and merely looked at her, his expression dark, Kate felt a bead of doubt form.

Fortunately, the doubt evaporated the minute he closed the distance between them and pulled her close. He kissed her forehead, the tip of her nose, then her lips—a long, lingering kiss that made her knees go weak.

But when he pulled back, he didn't say a word about last night. Unfortunately, Travis bounded in behind him right then, giving Jesse no chance to say anything else. Though he would have. Surely.

"Hey, Jesse. Hey, Kate," the boy said happily.

"Morning, T," Jesse said, smiling broadly. "Are you ready to play golf?"

Travis grimaced. "Oh, yeah, I forgot."

"Come on. It'll be fun," Jesse assured him.

Jesse turned back to Kate and raised a brow. "Why aren't you dressed? We have a tee time in forty-five minutes."

Golf. Oh, dear. The last thing she wanted to do was get out on the course for eighteen holes. She hadn't played in years.

"Sorry, really, but I don't have golf clubs, and I know the country club doesn't rent them, so I can't play. How about I go to the store and make a big dinner for you and Travis when you're done?"

Jesse chuckled. "No way." He left, returning a few minutes later with a practically new, top of the line set in tow.

"They're your sister's," he explained.

"Oh, wonderful," she managed. "And I appreciate it, really. But the truth is, it's a beautiful day and I have tons I need to get done before the week starts."

He ignored her comment and shoved a pile of clothes into her arms. "I got these from Suzanne as well just in case you try to use the 'I don't have anything to wear' excuse."

She silently conceded that it had been next on her list.

Thirty minutes later, she stood outside the El Paso Country Club pro shop. Travis and Jesse stood next to her, Jesse amused, Travis about as happy about this round of golf as she was.

"Neat clothes," the boy offered.

Neat hardly began to describe the horror that she wore. A short red skirt that was dotted with golf balls sitting perfectly atop a colorful array of tees. Her requisite collared shirt was sleeveless and tucked into the skirt, with one big ball over her right breast. If she'd had a single other comfortable sports shirt with a collar she would have worn it. She felt like a cross between a cheerleader and a fool.

"Thank you, Travis."

Jesse, on the other hand, and unfairly in her opinion, didn't have multicolored golf paraphernalia dotting his clothes. He wore a gray-blue golf shirt tucked into form-fitting navy pants, and easily could be mistaken for a cover model.

Her gaze met Jesse's. His dark eyes were penetrating as he studied her, as if trying to understand something.

"What?" she demanded.

He only studied her a moment longer, then glanced at his watch. "We're up."

Before they could get in their golf carts, Lena Lehman ran up to them, adorned in miniature golf clothes of her own and sporting bouncing pigtails. "Hey, Travis!"

Travis was visibly surprised and pleased, though he glanced around a little nervously.

"You wanna play with us?" the girl asked. "Ned Greenley didn't show, and we're having a putting tournament over on the green. I know you're really great at putting."

"Ah," he stammered. "Well, I'm playing with my dad."

"But it will be soooo much fun. Please!"

Travis glanced back and forth between Jesse and Lena, his face wrinkled with indecision.

"Do you want to play with the other kids?" Jesse asked kindly.

"Not if you don't want me to," he answered.

Jesse kneeled down until they came eye to eye. "I want you to be happy," he said softly. "I want you to have fun."

"It'll be great fun!" Lena cheered. "Besides, I need you on my team."

Standing, Jesse turned his attention to the little girl. "How are you getting home?"

"I'll walk. Travis can walk with me."

Jesse squeezed Travis on the shoulder. "That sounds like fun," Jesse said. "Go ahead and hang out with the kids."

Travis didn't look like he knew what to do, but when Lena boldly took his arm, he followed.

"Are you sure that was the right thing to do?" Kate asked.

"Hanging out with kids his own age seems the best to me."

"I guess you're right."

Which was how she ended up heading for the number one tee box on a sunny Sunday morning, about to set out onto the course with no one but Jesse. Too bad it involved playing golf.

As soon as they were in the cart, he started telling her about what he had seen at the golf camp the day before. He was tight-jawed and grim about the other kids picking on Travis. Then he finished up with how the coach had said the program didn't have enough money to allow him to deal effectively with so many campers.

"I just wish Travis could be confident enough to be himself," Jesse said.

"He's twelve."

"That means he can't be confident?"

She shrugged, thinking about the fact that even at twenty-seven she wrestled with the same issue. One minute confident. The next feeling like a fish out of water.

He drove the cart with ease, bypassing the men's tee.

He didn't put on the brakes until they reached the bright red women's markers.

"But what about you?" she asked. Then she sat up straight when it finally dawned on her that he hadn't brought his clubs.

He shifted his weight uncomfortably. "I hurt my shoulder and didn't think I should play."

She remembered last night and how he had picked her up out of the bathtub, then carried her into the bedroom. "That didn't seem to be a problem about ten hours ago."

A wickedly sly smile curved on his face. "Just hit the ball."

She held up her hand in surrender. "Fine."

She got out of the cart, retrieved the driver, then froze when she became aware of Jesse sitting behind her with a very clear view of her butt and legs.

Raising her chin, she poked her tee in the ground, set her ball on top, then lined up the club face. She could feel Jesse's eyes on her back—or butt. She had no choice but to spread her legs to take her stance.

He had the audacity to whistle.

"Letch."

"Prude."

She glanced at him over her shoulder and smiled wickedly. "I hardly think that applies anymore after last night."

Though every bit of hot and sassy was no doubt ruined when she felt a heat wave of embarrassment flash in her face.

One corner of Jesse's mouth ticked up in amusement. "You've got me there." He looked back toward the clubhouse. "Unless you want the foursome behind us to stare at your butt, too, I'd suggest you tee off."

She noticed the four men in the distance gathering

clubs into the next cart. With a squeak, she addressed the ball, swung, and was too frantic to give it a thought that she might miss. As a result, she had never hit the ball so well.

"Wow," she said, impressed, as her shot sailed through the blue sky.

"Not bad," Jesse added.

She strutted over to the cart. Jesse rolled his eyes, then they took off down the fairway.

"Have you been playing?" he asked.

"Not since high school."

To prove her point, her next shot wasn't nearly as good.

"Stop thinking," he stated.

"That might be easy for you to do, but some of us don't have an on-off switch in our brains."

"Funny," he grumbled, but at the same time he wished like hell it were true.

What he'd give to stop thinking—especially about the sense of ease he felt growing in his chest.

He couldn't believe it. For the first time since he left El Paso thirteen years ago, he felt what he was beginning to suspect was the urge to stay.

Preparing for her third shot, Kate placed the club face behind the ball, her stance widened, and heat sliced through him. He had the urge to cup the sweet V between her legs. The thought couldn't be erased, and he pushed out of the cart and came up behind her. His fingers itched to touch her. He wanted to wrap his arms around her and pull her into the evergreen trees.

Marshaling his thoughts and shoving his hands in his pockets, he said, "I'd use a seven iron for that shot if

I were you. If you connect, it should put you on the green."

She straightened, then scowled. "But that's the thing. You aren't me. And I want to use a nine iron." She started to readdress the ball, then suddenly she whirled back. "Don't you have anything to say to me?"

He made a production of looking confused. "A nine iron will leave you short?"

"Noooo. Something *else* you want to say to me."

He knew she was talking about last night. When he had said that they would make love, he had half wondered if taking her to bed would once and for all get her out of his mind. But just the memory of Kate going down on him made him go hard so fast that it hurt. He had never known a woman who had wanted nothing more from him than to give him pleasure. Though that wasn't exactly true, he conceded. Kate wanted a piece of his heart. And after she had given to him so unselfishly last night, he was afraid that he'd never be able to live without her.

Was it possible to start a new chapter in his life? Could he get his swing back together before anyone got wind of the fact that his game was falling apart? Could he win the PGA and prove that he was a true golfer?

Could he let Kate into his life? Could he deserve her love?

He didn't know.

"You want me to say something?" he asked. "Then how about, 'You're amazing.' "

Her eyes went wide. "Oh," she whispered.

"Now swing."

She blinked, then turned to focus on the ball like she was standing on a shooting range instead of a golf course. Clearly trying to hit the ball really hard, she jerked the stroke. Instead of sending the ball rocketing toward the green, she sent it up into the air. By the time it returned to earth, it landed only about thirty yards in front of them, ninety yards from the pin.

They stood there and stared. The sun was making its steady ascent, but not yet blazing, the sky a cobalt blue without a cloud to be seen. An egret swooped down, its wings wide and majestic, before it settled into one of the towering cottonwood trees that lined the fairways.

"*Now* you can use your nine iron," he said with a chuckle, then headed back to the cart before he could touch her.

Kate walked the short distance, made her shot, impressively well this time, managing to land the ball exactly as he predicted. She was on the first green in four strokes. Not bad for someone who hadn't played since high school. She leaped up and cheered, and Jesse couldn't help his smile.

After a decent two-putt into the hole, they moved on to the second tee box.

For the first time in weeks, Jesse felt a low burn of desire to pick up a club. Nothing forced, as he had felt every day that he went to the course. He almost did it, but decided to wait until tonight when he could slip through the fence across the street from her house to practice. No sense in trying if he wasn't sure he could succeed.

During the next three holes, they hardly spoke, Jesse lost to his thoughts, Kate lost to her own. On number six, he realized that something had eased in Kate, as if she was slowly unwinding with every stroke she took.

Concentrating on her shot, she lined up with the flag,

aiming directly for the pin. He noticed that she had the habit of biting her lower lip when she concentrated. Even that seemed sexy when she did it.

So much about her seemed sexy now. The way she walked, and even the damned feathered pen she kept hidden in the kitchen desk drawer. It was like Kate was ruining him for any other kind of woman.

When she duffed a chip shot into a hazard, he laughed and surprised himself when he took her sand wedge. For a second he went still. But no one was around, the foursome well behind them.

"Stand back," he said, feeling a competitive surge, "and let a pro show you how it's done."

Kate smiled as he chipped out of the trap, the ball rolling within inches of the hole. He even putted it in to give her a par. "Saved your cute little backside from yet another bogey or even worse," he announced with teasing pride.

She conceded with a nod, but her eyes narrowed with determination when she stepped up to the next tee box. Not to be outdone, she concentrated and swung her driver with a good amount of proficiency considering that she rarely played. She worked each shot after that.

Jesse hung back until halfway up the number eight fairway. The need to swing a club ticked through him. And when she walked up for a short shot onto the green, Jesse dropped a ball next to hers.

"I'll give you a two-stroke handicap," he said.

"Are you suggesting a competition, Mr. Chapman?"

"You bet."

Though who knew Kate could be so competitive? She rubbed her hands together and chuckled wickedly until he laughed and snatched away the pitching wedge. "Watch and weep," he quipped.

But just as he started to make the shot, she belted out a whooping scream.

In some deep recess of his mind he understood she was playing with him. But another part, a more recent part, responded with a fierce wildness as he remembered that day barely a month ago on the driving range in Westchester, the tournament scheduled to start the next day. It was the moment when Jesse's game had started falling apart.

Memories of that day swam to the surface. Early morning, the sun not yet up. He had wanted some time alone on the driving range before anyone arrived so he could hit practice balls in peace. But peace wasn't to be had. His father had already been there on the range, the sky still purple, not yet brightened by the sun that threatened on the horizon. Carlen Chapman had been angry as he hit ball after ball, smelling of alcohol, upset because Jesse hadn't introduced him at the players' dinner the night before.

But Jesse had been just as furious. He'd had enough— of his father's antics, of his father's demands. In that moment, he'd had the same blinding tunnel vision as his father, so they were both taken by surprise when everything changed.

It all happened so fast. The woman appearing, crying out his name as so many women did. *Jesse!* Followed by the accident that no one had seen in that early morning dimness—just as she hadn't seen the club face swinging when she leaped out at Jesse. He knew that as long as he lived he would never forget the club striking her in the chest. The air knocked out of her in a strange whoosh, those ticking moments of startled shock before she collapsed in front of him.

By the time a man with a camera raced onto the scene, Jesse was giving her mouth-to-mouth resuscitation. And when word got around about the incident, the story was that he had saved a woman's life.

That night, he hadn't been able to sleep, watching news report after news report recounting his golf career— recounting some larger-than-life bad boy of golf they were now calling a hero. The next day he had walked to the first tee box, the crowds circling around, and he'd had the sudden realization that he wasn't sure he could play.

He hadn't quit as he had wanted to. He had gone out on the course—but it was the worst round of his life. He hadn't been able to play since. With less than two months before the PGA Championship, he felt desperation start to pound in his temples.

Anger, fear, and frustration made him whirl around on the El Paso Country Club golf course. For half a second he didn't even realize he was facing Kate. When finally his mind cleared he could do little more than demand, "What the hell are you doing?"

Blood rushed through his veins in a way that he couldn't begin to explain to her. Nor could he let her know how much she had affected him.

"Oops," she said with feigned innocence. "Did that hurt your concentration?"

The impudent smile and those white teeth sinking seductively into her lip made the warrior's fierceness fade— thankfully—to be replaced by a stirring of desire. He nearly laughed in relief at the heat, at the distraction from the turmoil in his head.

Sucking in a deep breath, he concentrated on payback. But his teasing retribution wouldn't involve noise.

The minute Kate bent over for her next shot, he did what he had been dying to do all morning. He slid his hand down over her butt.

Kate yelped, missing the ball completely. "You!" Then she came after him with the pitching wedge.

"Serpentine," he called out, zigzagging as he ran, keeping just beyond her reach. The memories faded completely, and he ran with a child's careless abandon. Kate had distracted him.

Yes, she had distracted him from the reason he had returned here—to find his game. She had managed in the space of a few minutes to set the churning muddle of his life aside. He let her catch him in a thick cluster of trees. The minute she reached his side, he circled his arm around her waist.

They came face to face, slightly out of breath from fun. But then everything shifted. Fun was replaced by driving need. He wanted her—needed her. Wanted to find release from the hell in his mind.

"You truly are amazing. As long as I live," he whispered, "I will never forget last night."

Her lips parted.

"You wanted nothing more than to give to me. Without a thought for yourself."

He backed her against the tree, the pitching wedge hanging from her hand. The moment his mouth came down on hers, the club dropped to the ground, and she clung to him.

The kiss instantly turned to fire, their hands frantically searching, unable to get enough. The world beyond the trees disappeared.

"I've wanted to do this since you walked into the kitchen wearing that goofy skirt."

"What?" she demanded as he kissed the line of her neck. "I thought you golfers loved this stuff. Just this morning I saw Hal 'Ribbons' Ribmore wearing a pair of orange-and-yellow plaid pants that made the sun squint."

He nipped at her ear. "I think any man who willingly lets people call him Ribbons is answer enough regarding his choice of apparel."

He pulled her up, pinning her against the craggy bark. He wanted her with a passion that burned through thought and reason.

With tantalizing attention, he lowered her feet back to the ground, then lowered himself, kissing a trail down her body until he kneeled before her. He sensed that she was half hesitant, half aroused as he pressed his lips against each of the insane multicolored tees and balls, his hands riding up her bare legs, under her skirt.

Pulling her close, he kissed the ball centered just over the juncture between her thighs, and her hands fisted in his hair. Slowly, he tugged the skirt higher. She dragged in a ragged breath when he found her panties and pulled them low.

He nudged her feet apart, her red-and-white saddle oxford golf shoes looking like candy canes lying forgotten in the green grass. He kissed her again, his lips trailing to the sensitive flesh of her inner thigh.

Her body began to tremble, desire winning out completely. But when reality had faded so thoroughly that he would have pulled her down and made love to her in the trees, their bubble burst as a golf ball from the foursome playing behind them landed with a solid plop on the green.

Kate and Jesse froze, then her eyes went wide, and she started scrambling to get away.

"Oh, my gosh! What are we doing? We're on a golf course, with people everywhere."

Straightening her skirt, she rushed out, only to stop dead in her tracks when the foursome pulled up, looking startled when she popped out of the trees. But startled turned to amused knowing when Jesse followed.

Kate was the brightest shade of red he had ever seen. Jesse smiled calmly, held up a ball, and said, "Found it."

The men glanced at his pant knees, which he noticed were marked with sprigs of grass and pine needles. Jesse quickly brushed them off with a laugh. "Amazing how you have to crawl around to find these tiny little things. Guess I should have called it a lost cause and moved on."

With their eyes focused straight ahead, Jesse and Kate leaped into the cart, then zipped over to the number nine tee box.

Kate teed off, then they didn't speak during the rest of the hole. They made good time since Jesse didn't hit another shot. Though every few minutes they burst out laughing when they remembered the looks on the foursome's faces.

But when they pulled up to the back nine turn-around to head back out for the second round of nine holes, things changed.

"Hey, Jesse!"

A guy who clearly didn't belong on the course came over to them.

"Jesse," the man said. "How's it going?"

He wore a short-sleeved business shirt that was a decade old if it was a day. Pens lined his pocket, from which he pulled a small spiral notepad.

"Tommy," Jesse said, his voice clipped.

The man looked Kate up and down. "Hey, babe, I'm liking your new show."

"And you would be?"

"Tommy Davis."

"The *El Paso Tribune* sportswriter?"

"The one and only."

Tommy Davis was known to be caustic, not a man to honey coat his words. He also reported any rumor he heard swirling. If it turned out to be untrue, he shrugged it off. *"You win a few, you lose a few,"* he had been quoted as saying.

Kate felt the tension that rose through Jesse. This was a different tension than what she had sensed coming from Jesse earlier.

Tapping a pencil on his pad, Tommy glanced at their golf cart. "I've been thinking about doing an article on you. El Paso's very own hero."

"I can't imagine there's anything very interesting in that," Jesse replied.

The reporter smiled, his lips thinning. "I suspect everyone 'round these parts would love a Jesse Chapman exposé."

Then Jesse changed. He sat back in the cart and took on a casual, devil-may-care attitude. Tension fled and he turned into the Jesse Chapman she had read about a thousand times in *People* magazine.

"If you want a story, then call my publicist. Gwen Randolph."

He called out the woman's phone number by memory, and Kate hated the taste of jealousy.

"I'd rather deal with you," Tommy persisted. "In fact, maybe I could tag along for the back nine."

Jesse chuckled. "Sorry, my friend. But I'm giving Kate a lesson."

"Really?" The reporter considered Kate for a long second. "You gonna do some golf on *Getting Real with Kate*? It's not a bad idea."

She hated this man just as much as she hated this new Jesse. Cool and suddenly a star.

"But a lesson is even better," Tommy persisted. "It'd make for a great angle. A Hero Always Helping." The reporter got a strange, considering look on his face. "You are a hero, aren't you, Jesse?"

That tension flared, and a slow-burning, barely detectable panic surged in Jesse, like he was a hunted man.

She glanced back and forth between the two men, then, regardless of how Jesse was acting, she knew what she had to do. "I've had enough golf for one day," she interjected.

A palpable relief sparked in Jesse's eyes, she was certain, before he shrugged with nonchalance. "Got to do what the woman wants, Tommy boy. Call Gwen. She can get you whatever you need."

They drove away, neither saying a word, though Kate would have sworn that Jesse didn't relax an ounce until they returned the cart to the pro shop, gathered her clubs, then finally closed themselves inside his Jeep. She searched for something to say, but hardly understood the quietly contained rawness in him that she felt simmering against the rugged leather interior like heat coming off tarmac in waves.

He put the vehicle in gear, leaving the parking lot, driving with controlled precision until they arrived at her house.

"Hey," she said, touching his arm, "are you okay?"

The minute she touched him, she felt the battle of tension and ease rush through him like an electrical current. She saw a restlessness, a frustrated dissatisfaction in his eyes, before a smile filled with yearning pulled at his face.

"I'm fine. I've just been distracted lately, and I need to get some things done. I need to be playing and practicing, and whether I like it or not, with the PGA coming up, I'm going to have to start dealing with reporters."

He didn't wait for her to respond. He reached across her, his strong arm brushing against her. For half a second they were so close that he could kiss her. It was like he could do nothing else when he gently pressed his lips to hers. Then he smiled, this time genuinely. "I'll see you later." Then he reached even farther across and pushed open the passenger door. "I promise."

Not knowing what else to do, she got out of the Jeep. The minute she shut the door, he drove away, controlled patience spent, the car going too fast as if somehow Jesse was howling at a too bright sky, pushed to that precarious edge he had been flying toward for as long as she could remember.

Julia, the auditors are still unimpressed with our ratings. They are pressuring me to make scheduling changes. I'm afraid it's time we take a long hard look at our lineup.

Chloe Sinclair
Station Manager
Award-winning KTEX TV

Did they mention specifics?

Julia

To: Julia Boudreaux <julia@ktextv.com>
From: Chloe Sinclair <chloe@ktextv.com>
Subject: Specifics

Yes, a few, including *Getting Real with Kate*. The truth is, the ratings for *Getting Real* are all over the place. One day they're up, the next they're down. While it's had some great ratings, the rest have been dismal and advertisers are wary of the show.

Chloe

To: Chloe Sinclair <chloe@ktextv.com>
From: Julia Boudreaux <julia@ktextv.com>
Subject: e-mail

I've been reading through several viewer e-mails and reviews of the show. Apparently no one knows what to expect. One minute Kate is trying to be sexy, then the next she's ultraprofessional. I thought this was the perfect answer to Kate's image problem. I'm afraid I've only made it worse.

Julia

To: Julia Boudreaux <julia@ktextv.com>
From: Chloe Sinclair <chloe@ktextv.com>
Subject: Solution?

What do you propose we do?

Chloe

To: Chloe Sinclair <chloe@ktextv.com>
From: Julia Boudreaux <julia@ktextv.com>
Subject: Sigh

Let me speak to her.

To: Katherine Bloom <katherine@ktextv.com>
From: Julia Boudreaux <julia@ktextv.com>
Subject: Meeting

Kate, sugar, could you come to my office?

Julia

To: Julia Boudreaux <julia@ktextv.com>
From: Katherine Bloom <katherine@ktextv.com>
Subject: re: Meeting

Julia, give me a second. I have a quick e-mail to send. Then I'll be there.

K

To: Vern Leeper <vleeper@ktextv.com>
From: Katherine Bloom <katherine@ktextv.com>
Subject: Golf tournament

Dear Vern:

As I recall, Jesse Chapman played in a tournament several weeks ago. The Westchester Open, I believe. Could you get me any video of Jesse at that event?

I'd greatly appreciate it.

Best,
Kate

Katherine C. Bloom
News Anchor, KTEX TV West Texas

eighteen

"Kate, I'm really sorry about this."

Kate felt dizzy as she absorbed the words.

"But we have no choice but to cancel *Getting Real with Kate.*"

Pride forced Kate not to clutch the arms of the chair while she sat through every long ticking minute of explanation as to why her show was being canceled. "I know you are, Julia," she managed.

"The auditors were breathing down my neck—"

"Julia, really, you've explained. And I know you wouldn't do this if you didn't feel it absolutely necessary."

Her best friend sat across from her, looking worried and equally devastated by the turn of events. Thankfully, the phone rang, and when the owner of KTEX TV answered it, Kate used it as an excuse to leave.

She stood and walked with measured control out of the office, only hesitating when she saw Chloe. The station manager looked at her with concern. Chloe had known. Kate saw it in her eyes.

Feeling a flash of betrayal that they had been talking about her behind her back, Kate headed for the door, not stopping when Chloe called after her.

Deep down Kate understood that the owner and station manager would talk business, had to talk business. But not quite so deep down, at a shallow place, she felt like the odd man left out.

Wanting a distraction, needing a distraction, she whispered the names of the presidents.

"Washington, George. Adams, John." Concentrating on the names, she caught her not-so-sensible high heel in a crack in the parking lot, then fumbled with her key in the car lock. She got to "Monroe, James" before she fell into the sensible velour bucket seat of her sensible, no-nonsense vehicle—like falling back into the place she had been before Jesse came home.

It had finally happened. The cut swift and startling, though ultimately not surprising. She really had failed. The viewing audience hadn't liked her when she was serious. They liked her even less when she was *un*serious. Which left her with the not so great thought that they didn't like her at all.

She refused to sink into self-pity, so she forced herself on to listing state capitals. She started with Alaska—both for its geographic location and its appealingly ordered first letter of A. She wouldn't go to a mall or smother her misery in a huge plate of barbecue and cole slaw. She would go home.

She needed to get her thoughts in order. Because she realized that Julia hadn't said anything about what would come next. Had the pity in Chloe's eyes been because it

276 Linda Francis Lee

was more than just canceling *Getting Real*? Were they firing her?

Kate thought she might get sick right there in the parking lot. But she wouldn't go down without doing everything in her power to survive. There had to be something that could save her job. And the only way to do that was to come up with an alternate plan. Something that she could do and that would work on local television.

Her fingers curled around the steering wheel as she stared beyond the windshield, not seeing anything but the churn of thoughts in her mind. What would El Paso want to see? What did she know enough about to showcase convincingly? Who could she find that met both of these criteria?

It hit her then, bright and clear like a West Texas summer sky. She understood what she could do.

Her answer.

The solution, and it lay with Jesse Chapman.

A shiver of concern raced through her when she thought about the fact that she had told Jesse that she loved him—and he hadn't responded. Was she deluding herself that things could work out?

She couldn't worry about that right now. She had a job to save.

Sliding the sedan into gear, she wheeled out of the KTEX TV parking lot, taking I-10 instead of Mesa Street, making it home in record time. But when she pulled into the driveway, Jesse's Jeep wasn't there.

She threw the gearshift into reverse, then drove to the golf course. When she didn't find him there, she drove to a golf supply store. She even wheeled through the Home

Depot parking lot, looking for his black Jeep. But Jesse was nowhere to be found.

With every mile she drove, she thought of how Jesse had told Travis that he needed to be himself. And that was exactly what she needed to do. *She* had to be herself. As silly and trite as it sounded, that was exactly what she had to start doing.

She felt almost giddy at the realization that she had to stop trying to be sexy or smart or any of the things she wrapped around herself so she didn't have to dig deep to find out who she really was. Kate Bloom. A newswoman who could give Julia her ratings, help Travis with his friends, and at the same time give the public sports programs the funding they deserved.

She just had to convince Julia. She also had to convince El Paso's very own prodigal son of the part she needed him to play in her plan.

Julia! I have an idea. A great idea for a new segment. Something that will please us all. Just give me one last chance and I promise to deliver.

Kate

Katherine C. Bloom
News Anchor, KTEX TV West Texas (Hopefully still)

Chloe, I just heard from Kate. She hasn't gone off and done something drastic, as you feared, but she actually sounds

excited about some new plan of hers. Can you buy us some time
with the auditors?

Jules

To: Julia Boudreaux <julia@ktextv.com>
From: Chloe Sinclair <chloe@ktextv.com>
Subject: Excitement?

About what? Whatever it is, don't screw it up, Jules. And yes, I
can eke out a bit of time.

Chloe Sinclair
Station Manager
Award-winning KTEX TV

To: Katherine Bloom <katherine@ktextv.com>
From: Julia Boudreaux <julia@ktextv.com>
Subject: Idea?

What is it, Kate? What kind of idea? If you want to talk in person,
why don't we go to dinner tonight?

xo, j

To: Julia Boudreaux <julia@ktextv.com>
From: Katherine Bloom <katherine@ktextv.com>
Subject: Can't

... do dinner, but thanks anyway. Too much to do. As to my idea, I mentioned it because I didn't want you writing me off too soon. Let me put it together first. Then I'll surprise you. Also, have you heard from Jesse recently? I've looked all over for him, but can't find him.

To: Katherine Bloom <katherine@ktextv.com>
From: Julia Boudreaux <julia@ktextv.com>
Subject: Fine

I guess I'll be the one who has to endure the surprise this time. Serves me right. <g> As to Jesse, I heard he was meeting with Bobby Mac today at Bobby's Place.

Keep me posted.

xo, j

nineteen

Kate wheeled along Mesa Street. She drove up the undulating hills as fast as she could. Mount Franklin rose to her left, craggy and beginning its afternoon turn to red as the sun started beating into it. To her right, she could make out Mount Cristo Rey, with its towering cross peak, and the Sierra Madres in Mexico just beyond, forming a valley that cradled the west side of El Paso.

Turning into the parking lot of Bobby's Place, she threw the car in park, then hurried to the door. She saw Jesse the minute she stepped inside.

A rush of heat mixed with a settling calm washed through her at the sight. He sat with Bobby Mac, Jesse's shoulders wide and braced as he leaned forward, his elbows on the table, a beer in front of each man. Both men were handsome, but it was Jesse who filled her mind and her heart.

Jesse hadn't come home last night before she had gone to bed, but his Jeep had been there when she woke in the morning. Though he had left again by the time she got out of the shower.

Now he looked tired, as if he hadn't slept at all. His expression was grim as he talked to Bobby Mac. But when he looked up and saw her, he smiled. Just that, enough to reassure her that everything was going to be all right.

She all but ran over to the table.

"Kate," Bobby said, surprised, as he stood.

Jesse studied her for long seconds before his smile broadened and he rose slowly. "Kate," he acknowledged.

She wanted him to reach out and take her hand. But he didn't. Instead, he held her chair like a perfect gentleman.

"I hope I'm not interrupting," she said, and even she could hear that she sounded like a giddy schoolgirl.

"You're not," Bobby said. "Jesse and I were just talking about how being a father isn't so easy. Kids don't come with instruction books."

"Jesse's doing a better job than he realizes," she defended.

"I'm sure he is."

Jesse just shook his head.

"What can we do for you?" Bobby asked.

Kate blinked as his question sank in, or rather as a single word sank in. *We.* As in Jesse and Bobby.

The unexpected insight cleared her thoughts, and suddenly her plan shifted and expanded. Not only was Jesse a professional golfer, but Bobby Mac was an ex-quarterback for the Texas Lone Stars. This would be great.

"I have a proposition to make."

Jesse's smile quirked devilishly. "You? A proposition?"

Kate felt embarrassment rush to her hairline as the men appreciated the humor. "Funny."

"I try."

She leaned forward, planting her elbows on the table in her enthusiasm. "I've been thinking about the fact that Travis's golf camp needs money. I did some research on the Internet and made some calls before I drove over here. I learned that most public sports programs in the area need help. No surprise really, and I wanted to do something about it."

Bobby chuckled. Jesse did not.

"What did you have in mind?" the ex-football player asked.

"Well . . ." She glanced back and forth between them. "I was thinking of a golf showdown of sorts."

The smile on Jesse's face froze. "And who did you see *showing* down?"

"Well, um, you and Bobby Mac."

The change happened so quickly that it felt like her head spun. Jesse's jaw visibly tensed and his grip on the beer mug tightened so hard his knuckles went white. Confused, she rushed on.

"It makes all the sense in the world! El Paso's two most famous sports stars playing for charity. Jesse Chapman versus Bobby Mac McIntyre. It would be great."

"You know," Bobby said with a laugh, "now that I'm not out on the field, I've been playing some serious golf. I wouldn't mind a friendly matchup for charity."

Jesse still hadn't moved. His forearms were still planted on the table, the muscles taut and well defined. She felt light-headed from keeping herself from reaching out to him.

"It's not a bad idea," Bobby continued.

"It will be great!" Kate cheered, as much for the distraction as for the idea that Bobby was on board. "Not only will the proceeds go to public programs, but it will bring more awareness to the problem. And the two of you will prove that you truly are hometown heroes."

She realized that she sounded no better than Tommy Davis, who wanted to do an exposé on Jesse. But this was different, wasn't it? Granted, it would save her job, but it would help a good cause in the process. If she told him how much this meant to her, how she needed this to stay employed, surely he would agree.

"What's in it for you?" Jesse asked.

Not exactly the response she was looking for.

"Fair enough." She clasped her hands in front of her. "I want to tape the event for *Getting Real with Kate*. And yes, I need this, I admit it. But it also showcases both of you and helps the sports programs. I'll televise the event. Of course, it won't be a full eighteen holes. We'll come up with a mini version of the game that will be fun and competitive. I'll walk along with a cameraman and a mike and interview both of you as we go. Then I'll edit it in the studio to fit a one-hour format."

Bobby considered. "Where will the winner's money come from?"

"The whole thing just came to me today. So I don't have all the details ironed out yet. But as I see it, we get local businesses to sponsor the event. They get great exposure, plus goodwill in the community and among viewers who are going to go out and buy their products, all in return for delivering a big check to the winner's chosen sports program. For example, Bobby, you could play for football programs. Jesse could play for golf programs. Whoever wins, wins for their particular activity."

"And whoever loses?" Bobby persisted with a chuckle. "What happens to him?"

"Second place will get money as well, just not as much. A win-win for everyone!"

Kate glanced at Jesse, who sat back. He hadn't agreed, but he hadn't said no, either. Optimistically, she plunged ahead.

"It won't be anything fancy, and it will have to be soon since I think it has to be done in the summer to highlight summer sports programs. If you agree, I'll start making plans immediately. I'm sure I can get the El Paso Country Club to let us use the course. It will be great!"

"I like it," Bobby pronounced. "What do you say, Jesse?"

Jesse stared not at Bobby but at her with an unfathomable darkness. "I don't know how I can say no."

"Then it's settled," Bobby stated, and pushed up from his chair. "Let's go back to my office and start working out the details."

Jesse stood up as well and shook Bobby's hand. "Can't. I've got to go. But thanks for lunch."

Bobby slapped him on the back. "I'm going to give you a run for your money, my friend."

With a tight smile, and without a single glance at Kate, Jesse started to leave.

"Jesse?"

He turned back, his eyes blazing. But after a second he relaxed, and his smile grew genuine. "You have plans to make. I'll see you later."

Then he was gone.

To: Katherine Bloom <katherine@ktextv.com>
    Chloe Sinclair <chloe@ktextv.com>
From: Julia Boudreaux <julia@ktextv.com>
Subject: Fabulous!

Kate, so sorry that I had to pressure you for details regarding your idea. But, alas, the auditors needed more than my word. I completely respect that you didn't want to tell me yet, that everything wasn't pinned down, but I'm so thrilled that you let me know what you're putting together. A golf-off is inspired. I read your proposal this morning, and it's utterly dee-lish. The auditors are impressed as well. Jesse v. Bobby Mac. I knew I could count on you not to let me down. But two weeks? How can we put this together in two weeks?

xo, j

To: Julia Boudreaux <julia@ktextv.com>
    Katherine Bloom <katherine@ktextv.com>
From: Chloe Sinclair <chloe@ktextv.com>
Subject: In agreement

I have to agree with Julia on this one, Kate. Great idea, but not enough time to implement. How about we do it in September? I'm sure I can get the auditors to give us that much time.

Congrats!
Chloe

Chloe Sinclair
Station Manager
Award-winning KTEX TV

To: Julia Boudreaux <julia@ktextv.com>
    Chloe Sinclair <chloe@ktextv.com>
From: Katherine Bloom <katherine@ktextv.com>
Subject: Golf-Off

September is too late! We have to pull this together in two weeks, because I want to showcase Travis and the kids at the golf camp. And camp will be well over by September.

Given that, we need to move into high gear. Chloe, you're the best, I know you can put it together. Advertising should be a cinch since every local sponsor in town will want in on this. And with publicity spots running on heavy rotation between now and then, we'll have no trouble getting local companies to donate money for both the winner and the runner-up. Not only will they get free publicity, but the money they donate is a tax write-off. Plus, we need only one camera crew since the whole show is Jesse and Bobby Mac.

The good news is I already have the golf course for the event. It's going to be a ratings smash!

Kate

288 Linda Francis Lee

To: Katherine Bloom <katherine@ktextv.com>
    Julia Boudreaux <julia@ktextv.com>
From: Chloe Sinclair <chloe@ktextv.com>
Subject: Fine

I say we go for it. I've jumped through hoops before, and I can do it again to get everyone assigned. What do you say, Julia?

C

To: Katherine Bloom <katherine@ktextv.com>
    Chloe Sinclair <chloe@ktextv.com>
From: Julia Boudreaux <julia@ktextv.com>
Subject: re: Fine

I say we have a golf-off to produce. But we can't afford any mistakes.

xoxo, j

To: Julia Boudreaux <julia@ktextv.com>
    Chloe Sinclair <chloe@ktextv.com>
From: Katherine Bloom <katherine@ktextv.com>
Subject: Not to worry

Everything is going to be great! Nothing's going to go wrong!

I'll keep you posted.

Kate

To: Vern Leeper <vern@ktextv.com>
From: Katherine Bloom <katherine@ktextv.com>
Subject: Westchester golf tournament

Dear Vern:

Sorry I didn't get by your office, but have you found any footage of the Westchester Open yet? I'd really like to see anything you can find ASAP.

Best,
Kate

To: Katherine Bloom <katherine@ktextv.com>
From: Vern Leeper <vern@ktextv.com>
Subject: re: Westchester golf tournament

Dear Kate:

The tournament was not covered nationally. However, I have a call in to the local affiliate who must have some footage for highlights to use on their news. As soon as I hear anything, I'll let you know.

Vernon Leeper
Sports Director, KTEX TV West Texas

twenty

othing's going to go wrong might have been a tad
optimistic. And she hated that she'd had to show
her hand to Julia before she was certain that all was
okay with Jesse. Sure, he had agreed to do it at Bobby's
Place, but she couldn't deny that she was worried.

To compound her concern, Jesse had avoided her for
the last two weeks as she worked on the Public Programs Golf-Off. Arranging something of this magnitude
would have been challenging under the best of circumstances. Doing it so quickly really kept her on her toes.

But the sheer amount of logistics and arrangements
wasn't what gave Kate nightmares. Since the day Travis
had arrived in El Paso, Jesse had put the boy first. Now,
with the golf-off looming, Jesse had shifted his entire
focus onto his game. She felt bad for Travis. And she
couldn't help but wonder why Jesse was avoiding her.

Because he now saw her as nothing more than a reporter who wanted something from him?

She was concerned that it was something more. Something bigger that she was missing. But when she tried to talk to him, he was busy, on the cell phone, just leaving, or, more than once, simply hadn't answered the door. No discussions, no more shared meals. But most of all, no more talk or even hint of sex. She hated how that bothered her the most.

One night she woke and was surprised to find Jesse asleep in the chair beside her bed, that old photo album open on his lap. Getting out of bed, she had quietly knelt before him, allowing herself to trace the tired lines of his face. He didn't wake when she pulled the album away. She waited for him to stir while she sat on the floor next to his chair, looking at pictures of them growing up. His family and hers. Jesse, young and laughing, his mother next to him, smiling and clearly proud. Then another of him with his father, years later, standing in front of their house, Derek caught standing off to the side, left out. Or was it that Derek wanted no part of his father's and brother's escapades?

After Mrs. Chapman died it was like Carlen Chapman had needed Jesse—sort of like how Kate's mother had needed her. But in her case, the child had become the parent, while in Jesse's case, the child had become a buddy.

When she got to the end of the photos, Jesse was still asleep, as if he hadn't slept in weeks. Finally, she covered him with a blanket, then went back to bed.

He was gone in the morning, the blanket tucked around her. He was drawn to her, but avoiding her as well, she realized. It made her feel both hopeful and despairing of ever breaking through those walls of his.

The day before the golf-off, with a West Texas summer storm brewing, huge billowing clouds starting to fill the sky, all of El Paso was buzzing about the event. Travis sat in the kitchen, elbows on the table, face in his palms, staring at the TV that wasn't turned on.

Kate came inside the house through the back door. She tossed her keys and purse on the counter. "Hey, kiddo."

"Hi." He didn't look over at her. "Aren't you supposed to be at work?"

"Aren't you supposed to be next door with Suzanne until the golf van shows up?"

That got a half smile out of him, a smile so like his father's that Kate felt her heart twist.

"Yeah. But Suzanne is 'shampooing' her hair and said she'd call when she was done. Though she's really dyeing it and thinks I'm clueless and couldn't tell the difference. She said you've left every emergency phone number known to man so I'd be safe for the few hours it would take to do her hair. Plus, I'm going over to Lena's in a few minutes to help her with some stuff."

"Is her mom at home?"

"Yeah. And I swear we won't look at a single golf magazine."

The looked at each other, then started to laugh.

"So what's your excuse for being here?" he asked.

She shrugged, trying to look nonchalant. "I was over at the golf course, making sure everything was in order for the big day tomorrow."

"You were looking for Jesse, huh?"

Her hand went still in the middle of pouring a glass of orange juice. Then she rolled her eyes. "Am I so transparent?"

"Yeah. But that's okay."

He turned back to face the empty screen. "Is everything okay with my dad?"

Kate's pulse leaped with anxiety. Travis had been so excited when he learned about the event.

She busied herself putting the carton back in the refrigerator. "Sure, he's fine."

She wished she was as certain as she sounded. Had she been so focused on her own concerns that she hadn't given enough attention to the warning signs that had been there all along? His return to El Paso? Diving into the tree house project instead of playing golf when he had the biggest tournament of his life coming up?

And what had Tommy Davis meant when he'd said, *"You are a hero, aren't you, Jesse?"*

When she thought about it, she realized there had been an odd tone in the reporter's voice. A question.

Wheels on gravel caught Kate's and Travis's attention. They stared at each other in hope, neither realizing they were holding their breath until they saw the black Jeep and they exhaled in a rush.

"It's him."

"He's here."

She had to force herself not to fly out the back door right behind Travis. Instead, she stood at the kitchen sink, praying for calm. Praying that she was wrong and Jesse was all right.

"Hey, Jesse!" the twelve-year-old called when he came through the back gate.

Jesse stopped and looked toward the house. "Travis," he acknowledged.

Kate could see him through the window. He pulled off his golf cap, his hair matted from sweat, a bright white stripe across his forehead making the burn on his face more apparent. His expression was as dark as the gloomy sky.

Travis raced across the yard to see him.

Kate could make out only a few of the words that carried on the wind that began to stir through the leaves. Travis must have said something about the unfinished tree house because they both looked up.

Pushing open the screen door, Kate came out into the yard. Jesse stopped mid-sentence and looked at her. His expression became even darker, more unfathomable.

"Hey," she said softly.

He shoved his hands in his back pockets. "Hey."

Travis put his hands in his back pockets as well. "I was just telling Jesse that we need to finish the tree house. We're supposed to put a railing up to hold the sides secure. If we don't, the wind will probably wreck it."

As if to prove the point, a gust of wind shuddered through the tree's limbs, and the planks of wood gave an ominous creak. It was like a replay of all those years ago, the wind tearing apart something that she cherished.

"When do you think we can do it?" Travis asked Jesse. "Probably better do it soon. Though I guess we can't do it tomorrow, since you have the golf-off."

The wood creaked even more, but Jesse didn't respond.

Travis looked at him curiously, and with more than a little concern. "You're playing, aren't you?"

Simple words, though the meaning not so simple, put out there so boldly, asking exactly what Kate was afraid to. Half of her expected Jesse to toss off an easy *"Sure."*

"Travis, I'm sorry. But no, I won't be playing."

Wind rushed through the yard, through the tree house, stressing the boards, rustling their world.

"What?" Travis choked.

"It turns out I have to leave town in the morning."

Kate's breath expanded painfully in her chest. Jesse focused on her. "I'm sorry about the late notice."

A thousand questions sped through her mind. How could he possibly disappoint Travis? Or El Paso? Concerns about the actual tournament barely registered.

"It can't be helped," Jesse added.

Travis blinked, then blinked again. "I gotta go," the boy said, his voice strained.

"Travis," Jesse said, stopping him. "I'm really sorry, T."

"No problem. I really gotta go. Lena's waiting for me."

When Jesse would have questioned him, the boy turned quickly to hide his sudden tears. Then he dashed away, and the sound of the back gate banging closed echoed through the quiet neighborhood.

Kate and Jesse stood there for a second before Jesse cursed, then headed for the guest cottage.

"Jesse!" she called after him, then followed. "What is going on with you?"

He kept walking, and when he started to slam into the cottage, she was there, her palm planted against the plank.

"What is wrong?" she demanded.

He raked his hands through his hair, his dark eyes wild. "Nothing's wrong," he all but yelled, turning away and continuing inside just as lightning cracked open the sky.

Kate stood there, stunned, the rain starting, the wind

growing harsh and punishing, until the first board wrenched free, tumbling down into the bright green summer grass.

Shaking herself, she followed him, slamming the door shut behind them. She counted to ten. "Jesse, damn it, once and for all, talk to me."

Pivoting on his heel, he came back to face her. "What is there to talk about? I came home to work on my game, and I've done everything *but* work on it."

"You've done nothing but work on it for the last two weeks."

"For all the good it's done me. All I can do is think about you." He took a step toward her.

Despite her having known him a lifetime, every instinct she possessed screamed he was dangerous, and a frisson of concern raced through her. When he took another step closer, his expression grim, she took a step back. Suddenly standing there pushing him didn't seem like such a smart idea.

"Jesse, really, clearly there is something bigger going on here. Let me help."

"God," he groaned, "I'm beyond help. I'm beyond sanity. You drive me insane. I want you to be the little Katie Bloom that I've known forever. Sweet, kind, uncomplicated. Not this wild woman who . . . who . . ."

"Who what?" Her shoulders came back.

"Who has a body meant for sin."

Her mouth dropped open. "You're upset because I grew up? What kind of insanity is that?"

He plowed his hands through his hair. "Exactly. I am insane. I can't stop thinking about you naked in my arms."

Her breath snagged painfully in her chest.

"But don't you see, there's no future for us. We are so different. We want different things. My life isn't here. My life is on the circuit, and in Florida. I can't be pure and innocent and everything you deserve in a man. I know that, and you know that. . . ."

She hated how her throat tried to squeeze closed.

"But still, all I can think about, all I can dream about, is you." He took a step closer. "You going down on me, making me burn with an innocent desire I have never felt before."

Her mind whirled as he came closer, backing her up against the small counter in the kitchen. "I said we were going to make love. I told myself that I didn't care that you were distracting me. But I have to care. I have to care about golf—it's what I do. It's the only job I know. Just as television is what you do."

The edge of the Formica bit into the small of her back. Jesse stopped directly in front of her, his gaze burning.

She didn't know what to say, or think. All she knew was that her body tingled from nothing more than his proximity—and from the fact that she plagued his dreams as much as he plagued hers.

"Every night I want to cross the yard and slip into your bed," he whispered, his voice gruff with accusation, "when I should be concentrating on making sure I keep in shape. I eat Pop-Tarts with relish. I stay up late without a thought."

"But you're known for late nights."

"Not anymore. I can't afford that life if I am finally going to win one of the majors. And now I have the chance to win one of the most prestigious tournaments in golf, and I've hardly seen a golf course since I got here. I haven't focused. I'm squandering an incredible opportunity. And that, at least for now, has to be my priority."

He started to move away, but she caught his arm. "Stop running, Jesse."

He went still, his tautly held control practically vibrating through him.

"Touch me," she persisted.

"Kate, you don't want this," he stated, his voice tortured.

"But I do. I want whatever you can give me. I don't want innocence. I don't want purity. I want the man that you are."

Tension rode him hard, she could see it.

She curled her fingers into his shirt, tugging him back. "Please, Jesse."

Then suddenly, like a dam breaking, he clutched her to him, his mouth coming down on hers hungrily. She responded with the same intensity, matching his movements when he sucked her lower lip, grazing his teeth along the tender flesh of her throat. This time there was no gentle coaxing, no teasing prelude. He undid her shirt, then dipped his head.

Instinctively, she arched to him when his tongue returned to her nipple, circling the outer edge. A moan escaped on an expelled breath as he tugged up her skirt. He slipped his palms inside her panties, cupping her bottom. He buried his face in her shoulder, the tips of his fingers sliding low until they brushed the core of her.

A deep shuddering breath expelled from her lungs, and her body tensed.

He stroked her softly. "You undo me."

He kissed her temple and her forehead, gentling her.

Then in one controlled but powerful yank, he ripped her panties free.

She bit her lip, but he ran his tongue along the contours, savoring her. She couldn't seem to help herself when she closed her eyes and moved her hips ever so slightly to experience more of his touch.

"That's it," he crooned. "Let me touch you."

With one hand at her back, holding her secure, he cupped her mound, moving erotically as he nipped her ear with his teeth. "You are so sweet," he whispered, his breath warm against her skin.

She felt pleasure coming from every direction. Hot and intense. She felt carnal and primal. Then his thumb parted her moist center, brushing against her tender nub, and she felt her body shudder. He made her feel wild and wanting at the same time. She wanted everything he could make her feel.

"Let go," he commanded.

And she did. She tugged at his shirt, and in seconds his clothes were gone. When he lifted her up, setting her on the counter, she felt the cool tiles against her bare skin. Leaning her head back against the cabinet, her body sought what he wanted to give.

Unchecked desire made her legs weak as he ran the edge of his thumb along the delicate seam beneath the tight curls. Then slowly he tugged her forward, her legs spreading wider. And when he pulled her gently from the counter and onto the hard head of his manhood, she gasped and clung to him, her legs curling around his waist.

He moved her carefully on the plump head, and he groaned into her neck. Then slowly, gently, he guided her hips as she slid down the hard, full length of him.

He cried out her name when he had impaled her completely. But he was big, too big, and she gave a small mewling cry.

"Damn," he said, his voice ragged.

With amazing strength, he pulled her free, then set her on her feet. When she would have touched him, he turned her around until she braced her hands on the counter.

"I won't hurt you," he promised. "But I can't stop."

He peeled away her skirt entirely. She felt aware of herself as she had never been before. Naked and daring.

He ran his palm up her spine. His touch whispered around, over her ribs, until he found her breasts. Her nipples puckered even tighter, a tiny moan escaping from deep in her chest. His palms pushed the mounds high, his thumbs circling, making her body pulse. And when his hands drifted down and around, they didn't stop until they came to her bottom.

"You are amazing," he murmured, palming each round cheek, parting her ever so slightly, then pressing his hard erection against her. "You turn my thoughts upside down, twisting my mind until all I see is you and all I want is to slip inside you until I come."

He took her hand and guided her back to the bedroom. But he didn't take her to the bed. He had her sit on a small love seat. Her breath caught when he kneeled before her, then gently spread her knees.

"I want to touch you and kiss you everywhere." Her chest rose on a deep breath. "Your eyelids"—he kissed her there—"your ear"—he brushed his lips along the delicate shell—"your mouth." He gave her a fleeting kiss, taking her hands and stretching them out along the back of the love seat.

"Don't move your arms," he commanded gently.

Then he cupped her face with his palms and he kissed her again.

She inhaled deeply, and he tasted her mouth. He circled and probed. Instinctively, she sucked as he slid his tongue into her, and when she started to move her arms, he stopped. "No moving," he reminded her, his voice gruff against her lips as he kept a tight rein on his desire.

She cried softly in frustration as he began to kiss her skin, exploring. She moaned when he pulled away, but the moan shuddered when he touched her nipples with the pads of his thumbs, and her head fell back, her wild tresses cascading in a tumble of curls.

"I burn to feel you," he said. "Here." He squeezed ever so slightly, then took her in his mouth, sucking her nipple deep, tonguing the barely perceptible indentation in the very tip before drifting to the soft underswell. His breath rasped in his chest, his body straining toward her. "Here." He trailed lower over her abdomen, and then lower until his lips grazed her tight V of curls. Her head came up, but her arms didn't move when he nudged her knees farther apart. Their gazes met. "And here," he whispered.

Without looking away, he touched the sweet tender flesh between her thighs, parting her with his finger.

Instinct flared, and she tensed against him.

"Let me touch you."

Then she eased just a bit, enough so that he could glide his finger along the wetness on her secret folds.

"I said I was going to touch you everywhere. I've barely begun."

She bit her lower lip in that way she had that drove him mad.

"Trust me," he said, his body pulsing, barely patient enough to show her pleasure, show her the very intensity her body could experience. He wanted to lay her back and give in to the driving need he felt to be inside her. But not yet.

Her knees jerked apart in tiny increments as he began to run his fingers through the tight curls. When finally she exhaled a sighing breath, he slid first one finger inside her, then two. Her hips tilted up to him as he stroked. When he dipped his head and licked her, she was lost, and did little more than open farther to him.

He licked and sucked, stroking her. She gave in completely, threading her fingers in his hair, her body arching over his head as he trailed his lips along her curves. Then suddenly they were on the carpet, their bodies tangling together.

They rolled, each hungrily trying to get closer. Frantic, until they rolled again, bringing him on top.

Supporting his weight on his forearms, he framed her face. Her innocence and love shone up to him. Then she moved against him, and he needed to be inside her.

He guided himself to her and instantly he realized that despite her being wet and wanting him, he'd have to be careful, go slowly.

Sharp need stabbed through him, but he concentrated on Kate and her pleasure.

He kissed her patiently, wooing her, pulsing against her opening, teasing her flesh into easing. But Kate groaned in frustration, whipping her head from side to side.

"I want you inside me, all of you."

"I don't want to hurt you again," he managed to say over the shuddering desire that threatened to consume him.

She slid her hands down his back to his naked hips. "You won't." Then she pulled him to her, and he couldn't hold back any longer.

He gave in to the full strength of his need, and a deep groan escaped him. He nipped and sucked, unleashing desire as he sank deep. Her mouth fell open on a silent gasp. But when he tensed and tried to pull out, she said, "No!"

"You want this? You want me?"

"Yes! Yes!"

She rolled her head on the carpet with each syllable. Pleading. Demanding.

He pulled her close, his heart pounding against his ribs, and he felt her entire body trembling as she adjusted to him.

"Wrap your legs around my waist," he instructed her.

The minute she did as he asked, he sank even deeper, and this time he gasped at a woman who could take all of his length—as if this woman, Kate, was meant for him. Had always been meant for him.

"Damn," he whispered thickly into her mouth. "You're mine."

He began to move slowly until he felt her passion surge again. She panted as he stroked her slickness with his sliding shaft, bringing her up toward orgasm, kissing her, his tongue mimicking his lower body. And just when she cried her release, he plunged deep and captured her mouth with his, slipping his tongue into her hot wetness and feeling her shuddering tremors as his own. Then the tremors were his, his body erupting and arching into her, convulsing with a sheer aching intensity that he had never experienced before with any woman.

He whispered her name three times as his passion spent itself.

They clung together for what seemed like hours, neither wanting the bubble around them to burst. When he finally pulled up onto his elbows, he saw that her cheeks glistened.

"Why are you crying?" he asked, his voice ragged.

She smiled at him, then reached up and touched his face. Her fingers came away wet. "They're your tears, Jesse, not mine."

twenty-one

"**J**esse!"

Someone called out, causing Jesse and Kate to freeze.

"Jesse! Where the hell are you?"

"Fuck, it's Derek," Jesse stated.

"Did you lock the door?"

"You were the last one in."

Kate gasped, and they broke apart. Like guilty teenagers, they raced back to the kitchen and started scrambling to pull on their clothes. Jesse was done in no time, but Kate fumbled with her buttons.

Jesse gently but assuredly moved her hands away. "Let me."

"There's no time!"

"Exactly," he said, amused when he gestured to the mess she had made.

He worked the fastenings with ease. "There."

Kate gasped when she saw the ripped edges of her panties on the floor. "No! Over *there*!"

"Damn. How do you forget underwear?"

She started to argue.

"This isn't the time, Kate."

Which was true. But neither of them could retrieve the slip of material before the older Chapman burst into the guest cottage.

"What the hell is this?" Derek asked grimly, his hair and shoulders wet from the rain that had started to pour. He shook the afternoon edition of the *El Paso Tribune* in the air.

Every trace of vulnerability in Jesse disappeared. "Hello to you, too, big brother."

"I don't need any of your smart mouth. What the hell is this article?"

"What are you talking about?" Jesse asked, his voice dangerous.

Derek waved the folded newspaper. "The front page of the sports section."

Tension raced through Jesse's body fast and quick. For long seconds, he didn't move. It was Kate who reached for the *Tribune*.

Jesse was frozen on the spot, his face a mask of stone.

As the two brothers glared at each other, she unfolded the section and was immediately hit by the headline.

It's Hell Being a Hero

Or so it would seem for El Paso's prodigal son Jesse Chapman

By Tommy Davis

Jesse glanced over her shoulder and saw it, too. With a jerk, he turned away, bracing his hands against the counter.

"Jesse?" she started to say.

"Read it to him, Kate," the older Chapman said. "He needs to hear what is being said about him."

Not knowing what else to do, she began to read. *"Rumor has it that Jesse Chapman hasn't been able to play since he saved a woman's life."* She glanced at his back. "Tommy Davis is that reporter we saw that day on the golf course, isn't it?"

"The one and only," he said coldly.

She went on. *"Is he really a hero, or is he still the bad boy of golf who took to the wild life like a duck takes to water? My guess is that if Jesse wasn't such a pretty boy, there wouldn't be a sports person around who would have heard of him. Will he change that this August at the PGA Championship? Does he have the talent worthy of the attention he's given?*

"But more than that, is Jesse Chapman really a hero—or just a wolf in shining armor? Because this reporter has learned that the only reason the woman collapsed that day on the Westchester driving range was because she was hit with a golf club. Did Jesse hit her, then save her in turn? Hard to know, because no one is talking, including Jesse Chapman. What is our local bad boy hiding?"

The article went on, detailing Jesse's life for the last decade. The minor tournaments won. The press coverage gained.

Shock rippled through Kate. When she glanced up, Jesse had turned around, facing her.

"Is it true?" she asked. "Did you hit that woman?"

"Did you, Jesse?" Derek demanded.

Jesse's jaw cemented.

Derek closed his eyes as if praying for patience. "What

the hell have you done that a guy like Tommy Davis
would question whether the reports about you being a
hero are true or not?"

Kate watched that shift in Jesse that she had seen before. On the set of *Getting Real*, on the golf course in
front of Tommy Davis. And now.

Suddenly the smiles returned. "I'm no hero, big
brother," Jesse said with his bad boy smile. "You of all
people should know that. Haven't you made that clear
to me for years?"

Derek's eyes narrowed, only then the patience evapo-
rating. "Damn it, Jesse. What pushes you to do these
things? Drinking at age eleven—"

Jesse held up his hand in an exaggerated attempt to be
helpful. "You've got it out of order. First smoking, then
drinking."

Kate watched the exchange with growing horror.

"Don't worry, I didn't forget, Jesse. Just like I didn't
forget the present Dad gave you when you turned thirteen. A whore and a birthday fuck. Was she good? Did
you enjoy it?"

Kate felt like she had been punched.

"You and Dad," Derek continued, "with your drinking and your women."

Kate couldn't believe what she was hearing, and she
also could feel that Jesse was losing his tight grip on his
bad boy smile. He was about to break.

"You're a broken record, Derek. Let me make it
easier. Drinking, whoring, irresponsibly fathering a son.
What else?"

Dark eyes glared into dark eyes, inches apart. Then
something caught Derek's attention. He glanced over to

the kitchen floor and saw the ripped panties. After a second, he glanced between Jesse and Kate.

"What else, you ask? How long have you been screwing Kate?"

Instantly, Jesse had his brother pinned against the wall. "I've never done anything to hurt her."

"Yeah, right. You keep forgetting the day of my wedding. Screwing her in your bedroom. And don't you know all of El Paso is talking about her being your newest plaything while you conveniently stay in her guest cottage? Looks to me like that's just what's been going on."

Jesse slammed him against the wall again, knocking Derek's breath out with a guttural gasp.

"Jesse! Stop!" Kate raced forward, breaking into that dark place where Jesse had gone. After a second, he jerked away, Derek bending over to catch his breath.

She had never seen any man look so ravaged as Jesse did then. With a growl of pain, he banged out of the cottage, into the rain, and was gone.

She wanted to follow, but didn't. She turned to Derek, staring at him as she tried to understand. "Regardless of what you believe, I threw myself at Jesse the day of your wedding—and Jesse told me no."

Derek straightened, confusion slowly giving way to a reluctant knowledge, a single frown line of guilt marring his features. "Maybe I'm wrong about that, but not about the other things. Jesse has been wild and irresponsible for as long as I can remember."

She looked at this tall, strong man, so like his younger brother in looks, but lacking a flare for life and laughter that had come to Jesse so easily. Her voice was soft when she spoke. "I think you're jealous that your father has always paid more attention to Jesse than to you."

His eyes narrowed. "I didn't give a damn if Jesse had his attention."

"Didn't you?"

"My father and Jesse had plenty in common. Let the two of them be wild and ruin their lives. I wanted no part of it."

She bit her lip as she considered his words. "Is it possible for a grown man to have 'plenty in common' with a child? Or does the adult teach a boy the ways of a man?"

She saw Derek's eyes flicker, and just then something occurred to her. "You were, what, nineteen when Jesse was eleven? Wouldn't you have made a better drinking buddy? Why *did* your father turn to Jesse instead of you?"

He shrugged with a nonchalance that Kate could tell he didn't feel. But he didn't respond.

"Did he ever ask you to go drinking?" she persisted.

"Yes! And I said no. But Jesse didn't."

His burst of anger made her head jerk back, and she blinked in surprise. "Derek, why are you so angry? Don't you see?" she said with kind insistence. "You want points for saying no at nineteen, and condemn Jesse for not turning him down at eleven. You, an adult, versus Jesse, a boy?"

Derek's thunderous gaze wavered.

"I don't know what really went on in that house of yours," she added, glancing out the window as she remembered the past, "but I do know that on the night of his thirteenth birthday, he came to me, fighting back tears, and he wouldn't let me touch him. He never let me touch him again."

As if he had been hit, Derek took a step back, and this time his face darkened with something other than anger.

She met Derek's gaze. "Did it ever occur to you that as the older brother, you should have at least tried to protect Jesse from the very attention you blame him for having?"

Derek's nostrils flared, and she could see understanding finally, completely, sink in. "Hell," he bit out.

"Sounds like it was," she said. "For both of you, I'm sure. But you never thought to help Jesse find his way out of it."

"Hell," he repeated, dragging his hand through his hair in a way that made him look so much like Jesse.

"He needed a father and a big brother. Do you see how he didn't get either?" Reaching out, she laid her hand on his arm. "I'm not trying to blame you, Derek. Really, I'm not. I'm just trying to point out that Jesse doesn't deserve blame, either. Your father deserves that."

"Hell," he said one last time, before he left the cottage.

She didn't know what he would do. All she knew was that she had to find Vern Leeper and learn what had really happened at the Westchester Open.

To: Julia Boudreaux <julia@ktextv.com>
    Katherine Bloom <katherine@ktextv.com>
From: Chloe Sinclair <chloe@ktextv.com>
Subject: Weather

I can't believe it's raining. It can't be raining. Or if it's going to rain, it has to stop by tomorrow morning. Everything is set. Promos running every hour. The phone lines are ringing off the hook. Kate, you were absolutely right. It's like every citizen of El Paso wants to be at this event. So it has to stop raining.

Chloe

p.s. Kate, Vern was asking for you. He has some videotape he said you wanted. I told him to put it on your desk.

Chloe Sinclair
Station Manager
Award-winning KTEX TV

To: Chloe Sinclair <chloe@ktextv.com>
    Katherine Bloom <katherine@ktextv.com>

From: Julia Boudreaux <julia@ktextv.com>
Subject: Worry

Chloe, darling, you worry too much. Though I suppose that's what you get paid for. Regardless, you know how these summer storms are. They blow themselves out by evening. Tomorrow is going to be glorious. Everything is perfectly in order on our end. How about you, Kate? Everything set?

xo, j

p.s. What videotape?

To: Chloe Sinclair <chloe@ktextv.com>
From: Julia Boudreaux <julia@ktextv.com>
Subject: Kate

Have you seen or heard from Kate? She's doing her disappearing act again. I'm a little worried that something has gone awry.

j

To: Katherine Bloom <katherine@ktextv.com>
From: Chloe Sinclair <chloe@ktextv.com>
Subject: Busy

Kate, I know you have your hands full. But please give me an update.

Chloe

To: Julia Boudreaux <julia@ktextv.com>
    Chloe Sinclair <chloe@ktextv.com>
From: Katherine Bloom <katherine@ktextv.com>
Subject: Update

Everything is fine. I'll see you both at the course in the morning.

K

To: Chloe Sinclair <chloe@ktextv.com>
From: Julia Boudreaux <julia@ktextv.com>
Subject: Kate

Why do I get the feeling that everything isn't so fine?

twenty-two

It was dark when Kate pulled up to the station, her wipers slashing back the rain. The employee parking lot was empty except for the skeletal night shift. The security guard stood under the eave of the roof, trying to escape the brunt of the storm.

"Hello, Ms. Bloom," the man said. "Surprised to see you here this late."

"Hello, Mr. Vasquez. I need to pick something up."

"I'm looking forward to the big golf-off tomorrow," he added excitedly.

Kate wished she felt even an ounce of excitement. Instead, all she had was dread of the impending disaster. Regardless, she had to see the videotape Vern had left for her, praying it held the answers.

The guard used his key and let her into the building. She waved at the night crew as she headed for her office. Flipping on the light, she entered. Her desk was perfectly organized. Books were lined neatly on the shelves. The videotape was lying on the blotter, *Westchester* printed boldly in black Magic Marker on the label. A stick-um note was attached.

> *Kate,*
> *This is the file footage the local Westchester station took. An old friend from my days at NBC got it for me. There's not much here relating to Chapman. It wasn't one of his better tournaments. But the whole hero episode is on it, which happened the day before the tournament started. Then there's some footage of him teeing off for the tournament. Not much, but that's the best I could do.*
> *Let me know if you need anything else.*
> *Vern*

Taking the cartridge, Kate went to the video room, popped the tape in, and pressed Play. White, gray, and black static filled the screen before images whirled to an abrupt start, as if someone had turned the camera on suddenly, and she was hit with Jesse's image, bouncing, as if the cameraman was running toward him as he turned on the tape.

It was hard to see anything in the early morning dimness. Just the black velvet golf course as the sky started brightening to purple. She realized that Jesse was standing on a driving range, his face ravaged, shocked, his father there with him. The sight of Jesse always made her body hum with electricity, but this time her eyes narrowed, her heart slamming into her throat. She realized that something had already happened before the video started to roll.

Her heart raced as she watched the scene unfold, the frantic tension in Jesse's body. A close-up of his face, his eyes wild. But his voice was fierce and commanding as he yelled, *"We need help here!"*

She couldn't see anyone else around, no one to help but his father and the cameraman.

Kate's stomach clenched as the camera panned down and she saw that a woman was crumpled at Jesse's feet. No blood, just her lying there like she was asleep on the ground next to the golf clubs, a tipped-over bucket spilling a few remaining brilliant white golf balls onto green grass, and a perfect pair of men's golf shoes waiting to be put on. The scene would have been peaceful if it hadn't been for the odd angle of the body.

Kate watched, her palms damp, her heart pounding in her ears as Jesse bent over the woman, his athlete's body powerful as he started resuscitation. He worked like a machine, mouth breaths, then chest compressions. Again and again.

And his barely audible words. *"Come on, come on. Come back."*

If sheer will could save her, Jesse could do it. Then suddenly breath rushed into the woman.

Kate could see the relief that surged into Jesse. Then he swept her up, his strength clear in every movement, and moved away. The cameraman followed as Jesse carried the woman to a medic's tent. Then static after the flimsy door slammed shut.

Kate sat staring at the sizzling fuzz on the screen. This was what had made Jesse a hero, she knew that. He had breathed life back into that woman.

Before Kate could absorb it all, the static cleared, and the next image she saw was the camera panning up at the dark, stormy sky. It had to be the next day, when the tournament began, the winds picking up. Then a pan of the crowd, golfers, officials. And Jesse.

In the distance, someone yelled, "Yo, Jesse, you're a hero!"

But Jesse hadn't wanted to talk. He was focused, ready to start playing, he said.

Kate pressed Fast Forward, speeding through the sort of footage a sportscaster would use to highlight his or her report on the evening news. Clips of other golfers as they teed off. Putts being sunk. She didn't slow until Jesse returned to the screen. He didn't joke with the gallery as was his trademark; he was quiet. Worried. She could see the stress in his expression. Then he teed up. The sheer perfection of body and motion as he practiced his swing. Then stepping up to the ball. But his shot wasn't nearly as perfect. Jesse, the man known for his swing, shanked the ball off into the rough.

Kate continued to watch, but he must not have gotten better because the rest of the video clips focused on the tournament's top golfers, one of whom was a rookie who was playing out of his head, gaining the attention.

The remaining clips on the tape didn't show anything useful. But something bothered her, and she couldn't leave it alone.

She pressed Rewind, then started again at the beginning. Leaning forward, her concentration intense, she viewed the opening sequence over and over again until she had memorized the images. It was just before she gave up that she finally understood.

Stunned, Kate pressed Stop, her hand shaking. She sat there, just sat, until she realized that she had to find Jesse.

After a quick good-bye to Mr. Vasquez, she flew home,

careening up and down the undulating hills. At red lights, she waited impatiently, praying that Jesse would be there when she arrived. With every mile she drove, the rain lessened, the storm winding down. By the time she got home, the stars and moon were trying to work their way through the clouds. And the Jeep stood in the drive.

Her relief was short-lived when she saw the tree house lying in a shambles on the ground after all their hard work.

When she banged into the guest cottage, then the house, both were empty. But she knew where he was.

She all but ran down the drive and across the street. Feeling like she was twelve years old again, she slipped through the chain-link fence, careful not to get snagged. The minute she came around the pump house, she saw him. He stood on the tee box, hidden from the street. He was beautiful, his driver in his hands, the long seventeenth fairway stretching out in front of him.

She could have watched him forever.

"I knew you'd find me," he said, the words barely audible, but he didn't turn around. "You always found me. Ever since you were old enough to get out your back door."

She could just make out a hint of a smile tugging at his mouth before it hardened into a firm line. She took the remaining steps between them, stopping in front of him.

He crossed both of his hands on top of the club's grip, like he had to keep himself from touching her.

"I remember when your mom brought you home from the hospital. I wanted nothing to do with a baby, especially not a girl. I managed to avoid you for a while— hell, a couple of years. But then one day I was playing in the yard and I heard you crying. My mom was at some meeting, and when you wouldn't stop I figured I better check things out. Even back then I sensed something wasn't right with Mary Beth."

Kate had never heard this story.

"I went to your back screen door and knocked. But no one answered. So I got myself inside and followed the noise."

"Wasn't my mother there?"

"She was. Sitting on the floor in your bedroom, crying just like you."

This time Kate looked away.

"Somehow it didn't scare me," he added. "I walked over to where you were on the bed and sat down next to you." He reached out on the dark golf course and turned her chin back toward him. "Little imp, you stopped crying the second you looked up and saw me. You stared up at me with these gigantic eyes, and hell, you even smiled."

"Why didn't you ever tell me that?"

He shrugged. "I hated to add proof that your mom didn't know the first thing about raising kids. Besides, I never wanted to admit that maybe we were bonded somehow. I especially didn't want to admit it to you."

"I guess I was kind of tenacious."

"Very. Do you remember sneaking into my room?"

She cringed. "Which time?"

"Exactly. There were dozens."

He was right. She knew it. But he had always been her refuge from her mother's instability.

"I'm talking about the time I'd had a big fight with Dad," he explained. "You came marching into my room. When I told you to go away, you didn't so much as flinch. You laid down next to me, dressed in jeans and a Too Cool T-shirt, and told me to scoot over."

"I don't remember the Too Cool part."

"The next thing I know I'm telling you all about it, about how I had to work harder if I was ever going to be a truly great golfer, but my dad didn't believe I could do it. Me, fourteen, you ten, and I'm spilling my guts to a little girl."

"I do remember that," she stated. He had been serious about golf from the beginning. "You were number one on the varsity golf team at fourteen, but you said you weren't good enough."

"I wasn't. But I didn't know that until I played in the junior tournament in Albuquerque. There were guys there who were incredible. And they made me realize I wasn't good enough. If I wanted a scholarship, I had to be better. So I asked my dad to help me. When he said he was too busy, I asked to take lessons from the pro. He said no to that, too. But do you remember what you said?"

"Not exactly."

"You said that with or without my dad's help, I was going to be the greatest golfer who ever lived." His expression grew intense. "You and those damned eyes, always making me believe I could be anything I wanted to be."

"Because it was true. It still is."

He stood there forever. "Every kid deserves to have someone who believes in them—really believes and proves it. I wish I could have figured out how to do that for Travis."

"You did."

"Not in a way that makes a difference. Not in a way that will sustain him his whole life."

"Then you will. You still can." She could tell that he didn't believe her. "You're a good man." She hesitated, searching for a way to make him understand what he had at the core. "Don't give up on Travis, or yourself."

"Give up?" He laughed bitterly. "My game has fallen apart. Can you believe that, Katie? Me, who has had a club in my hand since I was a kid? Now I break out into a cold sweat whenever I'm on a tee box. That's why I can't play in the golf-off tomorrow."

"I know."

The mixture of clouds and stars trying to break through lit the night enough that she could see Jesse flinch. Then he pivoted around to look at her. "What are you talking about?"

"I saw some videotape of Westchester."

She had never seen any man look so vulnerable. His jaw worked, the cords in his neck bulging with tension—and maybe with a little hope that he didn't have to keep his secret anymore.

She couldn't do anything else when she tucked herself close to this strong man, hugging him tight. For half a second, he let her hold him, though his arms hung at his sides. His breath was ragged, dragged in sharply, harshly expelled. After an eternity, a haunting groan broke out of him loudly enough to startle a small flock of sleeping birds out of the overhanging tree. Then he wrapped his arms around her and buried his face in her shoulder.

"Oh, Jesse," she whispered, and pressed her palms to the broad planes of his back as if she could somehow heal him. "Why won't you talk about it? You saved her life. I saw how you wouldn't give up. You really are a hero."

He broke away from her. "I'm not a hero. Davis was right. She never should have needed to be saved."

"He also implied that you hit her with the club."

"Fuck."

"Tell me what happened, Jesse. I want to hear the truth from you."

He grabbed her arms desperately, like giving in, finally letting the words rush out of him. "It was nearly dark and she came out of nowhere, screaming and screaming at me. *Jesse!* She ran onto the driving range right in the middle of a swing. The club caught her in the chest and she went down."

That was what the camera hadn't captured, the moments that led to the collapse.

"You said yourself that *she* ran out, Jesse. She got in the way. You can't blame anyone for that."

He closed his eyes, no doubt remembering.

"Jesse, you *did* save her."

"Again, like Tommy said, she never should have needed to be saved. Then the next thing I know, everyone's calling me a hero. But for the first time I really saw who I had become. Who I was. I watched news report after news report showing me and my life. Thirty-second spots. Sixty-second spots. Three- and four-minute exposés on Jesse Chapman over the years. It was like I saw myself crystallized, distilled down to the essence of who I really was. The bad boy, the wild guy. And I didn't like who I saw. On top of that, I realized I was everything Derek says I am." He shook his head. He even half laughed, a bitter sound wrenched from his chest. "Derek *is* right. I have been drinking and screwing women for longer than I can remember."

"Maybe that's really why you're a hero."

He looked at her as if she had gone crazy. "What are you talking about?"

"Despite the life your father led you to, you survived. And despite your dad being anything but a father, you've done lots of things right. Heck, look what you've done for Travis when you easily could have given Belinda money and washed your hands of the situation. Or take me. You have always tried to do right by me. And that woman, no matter what happened, you saved her . . . and you're willing to let people believe you hit her when it wasn't you at all."

His entire body went still.

"Your father hit her, not you, but just like you've been doing for years, you protected him."

He started to pace. "You can't know that."

"Sure I can. You're not saying a word about what happened to the press or anyone because if you did, you'd have to say that your father hit her. You're protecting him just as you protected him when you were young and people were concerned that he wasn't being a good enough father. When teachers questioned you, you said how great he was. You made up all sorts of great, normal, father-son things that you said the two of you did together, instead of admitting the truth. I remember, Jesse. I heard you say plenty of stuff about your dad that I knew wasn't true. And just minutes ago I watched that video of Westchester over and over again. Then it finally dawned on me. Your father was holding the club. Not you."

"Dad with a club doesn't prove anything."

"Doesn't it? I'm willing to bet that you never even picked up a club that morning." Her toned softened. "What professional golfer hits almost an entire bucket of balls in street shoes?"

He stared at her hard, cornered.

"Once I realized that, I went through the tape one last time, and that's when I finally looked at your father—standing there, holding the club, his face white, scared. He was the one hitting balls that morning. He was the one who hit her, Jesse. Not you. And you can't spend the rest of your life trying to protect him."

"Is that how you plan to save your career? By reporting that? If that's the case, let me add to your story. Carlen was furious because I hadn't acknowledged him at a players' dinner the night before. His dream was of being like Tiger Woods's father, getting the gratitude, getting the kind of hug Tiger gave his dad after he won the Masters. How many times has the world seen that video clip? How many times has my father said that would be us one day? But that night when I got up to speak, when I had a chance to acknowledge him, he was drinking, making a scene as usual. I stood there at the podium and all I felt was a bone-deep weariness. I was tired of it; I was tired of him. So I didn't say a word of acknowledgment." He groaned, then cursed. "I left him sitting there, then I went home with that woman—"

Her shoulders stiffened in surprise. "The one you saved?"

"Exactly. Do you like that part for your story? Is that sordid enough for you?"

"Jesse, stop doing this."

"What do you mean, stop? You're the one who came out here wanting to talk. So I'm talking. I left my dad at the dinner. Went home with that woman. Then I left her before she woke in the morning." His eyes were damning. "Is that heroic?"

She didn't know what to say to the pain in his voice.

"I went straight from her house to the driving range. I didn't want to see anyone. But Dad was already there, drunker, angrier. And looking for a fight." Jesse dropped his head in his hands. "Dad was furious, telling me he could have been a better player, that he had been a better player. But that I'd been lucky. He had already gotten my clubs out. With every accusation he spat at me, he hit a ball, wild, out of control. I've never felt so tired in all my life. But angry, too. I started yelling back, which only made him angrier, swinging wildly, ball after ball. Then out of nowhere that woman came barreling up, mad as hell that I had made love to her, then left her. I might not have hit her myself, but whatever happened out there that day, I caused it as surely as if I had swung the fucking club."

With angry movements, he snatched up his ball and tee, then his clubs. When he straightened, his face was ravaged, and it tore her apart. She reached out to him, touching his face. "I love you, Jesse—and you have to stop blaming yourself."

He didn't move, but he closed his eyes when she trailed her fingers down his cheek to his neck, before she placed her hand over his heart.

Somewhere in the distance, she heard a car drive by. But the world was blocked out by trees, bushes, and the gently humming pump house.

He bowed his head, and she could feel the strong beat of his heart. He didn't move, and she felt a stab of hope.

But when she stepped closer, he straightened and looked her in the eye.

"You've always loved me, whether I deserved it or not. But don't stand there and tell me I'm a hero. I'm not. And no matter how much you want to believe that I am, I never will be."

"That's where you're wrong. You are a hero. And there are plenty of people who know it. Stay, play in the golf-off, and prove it to yourself. You deserve that. And so does Travis."

"You don't understand, Kate. I can't play. Not for you. Not for Travis."

"But you have to!" Her eyes narrowed, her brow furrowing. "You have to try."

"I'm sorry. It's not going to happen. Not with me. Besides, you don't need me." He looked at her forever, then leaned forward and kissed her on the brow. "You're going to do great."

Then he disappeared through the chain-link fence. Kate stared after him, too filled with dread to move.

twenty-three

Dear Katie,

I've made arrangements with Derek to make sure Travis is returned to his mother. Please tell him that I'm sorry.

Knock 'em dead, my sweet little Katie. All you need to make your golf-off a huge success is your charm and Bobby Mac on the course. I called Harvey Mendle and got him to take my place.

Forgive me.

Jesse

He really had left.

She knew he told her he couldn't play, that his game had fallen apart. But in quiet moments she had hoped, believed, prayed that he wouldn't really leave her. Deep down, she understood that her pain wasn't about the game. This wasn't about the golf-off. It was about the fact that yet again the one person she had always loved had left her.

"No," she cried, crumpling the note in her hand as she raced out the back door into the early morning darkness, then across the yard to the guest cottage.

Somewhere in her mind she registered that the Jeep was gone. But it wasn't until she pushed inside the tiny house, saw his belongings missing, that she couldn't hope any longer. *Jesse was gone.*

"Not again."

Kate whispered the words, closing her eyes, the note still clutched in her hand. Her chest tightened, her throat working as she held back the burn of tears. "We could have worked something out. We *were* working it out. We could have worked this out together."

But that wouldn't happen. Not now.

With a jerk, she slammed out and returned to the main house. She reeled off the names of presidents; she went through every state capital. But New Mexico stumped her. She never missed New Mexico. New Mexico was easy. But the capital eluded her.

She sat down hard, dropping her head into her hands. *Jesse was gone.*

The sun had just started to turn the black to a deep shade of purple, and she covered her despair with anger. It was easier that way, like pushing dirty socks and jumbled clothes into the closet and closing the door—making it possible to believe that the room was neat and tidy, organized and orderly.

Soon the sky would brighten, and all of El Paso would be waiting to see Jesse Chapman take on Bobby Mac McIntyre—a match between the city's heroes. Two men who had made them proud. But Jesse wouldn't be there.

She felt sick at heart—for herself, yes, but as reality

began to sink in, she remembered that she wasn't the only one who would be hurt by Jesse's leaving.

"Kate?"

The sound of Travis's voice brought her head up with a start. He stood in the doorway, still wearing his pajamas.

"Is something wrong?" he asked.

She stared at the boy. Jesse's departure hurt her deeply. But she was afraid it would devastate his son.

Thoughts swirled, her mind tried to drift.

"Santa Fe," she whispered. "The capital is Santa Fe."

"Huh?"

She shook herself. "Nothing. Sorry. Come over here and sit down."

His eyes narrowed. "Jesse really left, didn't he?"

So much for breaking it to him slowly.

"He had to leave, Travis. He has a . . . business problem that he has to deal with. It has nothing to do with you. He wanted to stay."

The words were made up as she went, trying to make the impact less damaging.

"Okay, thanks for letting me know," he said with a quiet nod.

Then he turned and left the kitchen.

"Damn you, Jesse," she said softly.

An hour later, after several frantic phone calls, Kate learned that Jesse really had gotten Harvey Mendle, the Tire King, to replace him. The man had a child in the golf program and was nearly as famous as El Paso's sports stars. He might not have been quite the local hero that the other two were, but he could play golf, and in a pinch he'd have to do.

An hour after that, when she pulled into the golf course parking lot, her stomach roiled. The largest tire she had ever seen, with a house-sized crown gleaming on top, stood in plain sight. The Tire King had arrived, and there wasn't a single soul who wasn't going to know it.

Her cell phone rang.

"What the hell is this I hear about the Tire King advertising in the parking lot?" Julia demanded.

"Hello to you, too."

Julia sighed. "Sorry, sweetie, but something is going on. I've sold advertising at hefty prices, and now the value of those spots is being diluted by El Paso's very own advertising slut."

"Can a man be a slut?"

"Katherine, I'm not in the mood."

"Now it's my turn to be sorry." Kate hesitated, staring up at the black knobby tire that stood as tall as a one-story building, the crown like a gaudy balcony. "I suspect Harvey feels he can do a little advertising."

"Good Lord, why?"

"Probably his price for playing in the tournament."

A long pause sizzled over the airwaves. "You asked him to play?" Julia asked very carefully.

"I didn't. Jesse did. Jesse left town this morning."

"I knew it! That bastard! Oh, sweetie, are you all right?"

The tone of her voice changed to caring so quickly that it brought tears to Kate's eyes. There had been so few people she could count on in her life. But Julia, like Chloe, had always been there for her.

"Hey, don't worry about me. I should have known."

"Oh, Kate. You've always been vulnerable when it

comes to him." Julia sighed. "I'll deal with the other advertisers. Let Mendle have his damn tire. Somehow it all will work out."

Kate wished she was as sure.

The parking lot spilled over, cars lining the streets for miles in every direction. Crowds paid to get a look at the stars.

Bobby Mac was wonderful and gracious, doing his best to make up for the fact that Jesse wasn't there, while Harvey, the Tire King, did more to run people off with his constant sales pitch than get them excited about the event.

Lacey McIntyre squeezed Kate's hand when she learned what had happened, her husband stepping in and saying, "Don't worry about it. I might not be a professional golfer, but I've been known to wow a crowd a time or two."

But Kate could tell that everyone was upset with Jesse. However, it was Travis who broke her heart. The minute he walked up, a group of boys circled him.

"So, Travis, where's your dad?" Then they laughed, as if they didn't for a second expect any dad of his to appear.

Travis shrugged his shoulders, trying not to care. The boys jeered, then headed toward the first tee box to get a good spot.

Kate felt sick watching. But there was nothing she could do about it. She had to put it out of her head. She had a show to tape—with or without Jesse.

She hurried to the ladies' locker room and hastily checked her makeup. She'd have to carry a compact of powder around with her if she wasn't going to shine like an oil slick underneath the hot sun. It was only 8:30 in the morning and already she could tell it was going to be a scorcher.

At 8:55, she stood on the number one tee box, an amazing crowd stretching out along either side of the fairway.

Bobby Mac wore a blue golf shirt with gold trim—his former team colors. He smiled and signed autographs. Harvey Mendle, wearing an eye-shocking orange-and-yellow plaid ensemble with blazing white shoes, gave out coupons for the Tire King.

"Is everyone ready?" she asked.

The men nodded.

"Great, let's get started."

The event consisted of nine holes. An hour and a half of golf that she would edit down into forty-four minutes of highlights with sixteen minutes of ads, all to be shown that afternoon. She had her work cut out for her.

Kate turned to the camera, nodded to Pete, then smiled just as the camera started rolling.

"Good morning, West Texas. We are here at the El Paso Country Club for the first annual golf-off for El Paso's public sports programs." She made the introductions, trying not to cringe at the boos that filtered through the crowd when she announced Jesse Chapman couldn't join them after all. They laughed when she mentioned the Tire King.

The event wasn't off to a great start.

She interviewed each of the men, and after the first minute, she was in her element, asking questions about things that were important to her and El Paso. She sur-

prised herself when she told a joke that made the crowd
laugh. She even managed to make the Tire King sound
interesting. Then she explained that Bobby would be
playing for the football programs, and Harvey would
be playing for the golf programs. A check for $50,000
would be made out to the winner's designated program,
$35,000 to the runner-up's program of choice.

Bobby Mac teed off first, hitting a long and true shot
that flew straight down the fairway. Harvey came up to
the tee box next, addressed the ball, waggled the club,
waggled again and again, until the crowd started to get
antsy. Finally he went into his back swing, the movement awkward, then he followed through in the ugliest
form imaginable. But no one could deny that his ball
went every inch as far as Bobby's.

For good or bad, they were off. Or at least Bobby
was. Harvey, after his one impressive shot, hacked his
way along the course, launching the ball into the crowd,
while Bobby waited patiently and graciously, his second
shot landing pristinely on the green.

Finally, Harvey made it to the rough surrounding the
smooth grass around the number one hole. But they
weren't out of the woods yet. The Tire King, no doubt
flustered or nervous after shanking so many times, shot
the ball clear across the green, scattering the gallery on
the other side.

The crowd groaned. Even Bobby grimaced. Kate told
her TV audience that it was a wonder anyone took up
the game of golf.

Eventually, Harvey sank the ball, two strokes over
par—two strokes behind Bobby Mac. Over the next two
holes, Harvey lost more and more ground. By the time

they approached the fourth tee box, with six holes to go, Harvey was seven strokes behind the football player.

To make matters worse, Travis had walked along not too far from Kate, his golf school buddies jeering and making snide remarks. They had stopped making comments only when she turned around at one point and said, "Is there a problem?"

That shut them up, though if anything, Travis had become more sullen.

The competitors teed up for the fourth hole. Having the best score on the last hole—Kate didn't mention that he'd had the best score on the last three holes—Bobby went first, his ball flying with perfection through the startling blue sky. Kate could practically hear Harvey groan. But no sooner did the Tire King step up to the tee box than a gasp rippled through the crowd.

First one head turned, then another, until the whispering turned into a huge roar that erupted through the gallery.

Everything stopped. Kate forgot the camera.

A spectator called out, "It's Jesse Chapman!" Another shouted, "He's here!"

Kate's mind went still. Her chest tightened. And sure enough, Jesse stepped through the crowd and onto the back side of the tee box.

He shook hands and joked with the gallery, his dark hair shining in the sun. "Sorry I'm late, folks," he said with his famous four-color-magazine smile.

When he saw Kate, he stopped, so tall and muscular, towering over her. He looked beautiful and wonderful and like the person she had loved for a lifetime. But suddenly that smile that had always made her melt wasn't enough. Who knew why he had come back now? A belated sense of responsibility? The realization that he might look worse to the world for not showing up than he would if he played badly? Whatever the reason, he was bad boy Jesse Chapman and he would come and go as he pleased. She would never be enough to keep him. Once and for all, she had to take that to heart and move on with her life.

"It looks like our very own Jesse Chapman has arrived after all," she said into the camera.

"Hallelujah," the Tire King said, walking away from the ball. "Have at it, buddy."

A caddy hurried toward the men's tee with Jesse's clubs. Jesse didn't immediately follow him. He walked over to Travis, and in front of the crowd and TV audience, Jesse crooked his arm around Travis's shoulder. "Are you going to wish your old man good luck?"

The boys from golf camp were impressed. But Travis wasn't so easily won over. Like Kate, he'd had to learn a hard lesson.

"Good luck," he muttered.

But if it hurt Jesse's feelings, he didn't show it. He ruffled the boy's hair, took his driver, then halted in front of Kate. "Miss Katie," he said with a gallant bow for the audience, "I hope I can hit the ball better than we cooked on the last episode of *Getting Real* that I was on."

The women swooned, but Kate just stared at him.

She moved the microphone away from her. "I'm glad you're here. It means a lot to Travis."

He leaned forward so that no one else could hear, every trace of charm gone. "Let's hope like hell neither one of us regrets this."

Then he pulled a golf cap out of his bag, put it on, and walked up to the tee.

The crowd cheered. Bobby and Jesse shook hands and joked. The golf-off suddenly was rife with the anticipation of seeing two great athletes compete.

"Where the heck did you hit your ball, Bobby Mac?" Jesse asked good-naturedly. "I want to know exactly where I need to land in order to beat the cr—" He glanced at the camera. "Crud out of you."

After the laughter died down, Jesse addressed the ball. A hushed silence fell over the gallery. Every eye was trained on this amazing man with his athlete's body holding that driver, muscles tense and rippling as a full-fledged concentration took hold.

But he didn't swing.

He stepped away and wiped his hands on his pants. He laughed, though Kate could see the laughter didn't reach his eyes. And she understood then that this was beyond a shank here or there as she had seen on the video. This was about a man whose life had fallen apart after he got a glimpse of himself as the world saw him: wild, irresponsible, without a care for anything but having fun. Whether it was true or not, that was what he had seen in the short entertainment-news bios that had run. His life had flashed before him, and he hadn't liked what he saw. In that moment, he had lost himself, and didn't know where to go from there.

In her selfish desire to force him to be the man she wanted him to be, she had ignored the fact that what he was experiencing was far deeper than she allowed herself to believe. But he had come here anyway in his attempt to have honor. He was trying to be the kind of man who could be a hero.

Her stomach clenched and her thoughts reeled. What had she done?

Focusing on Jesse, she shoved her microphone into the cameraman's hand. As unobtrusively as she could, she walked up to Jesse as he stood busying himself in his bag, as if he were trying to decide if he should switch clubs. She could see the sweat on his brow, the veins in his temples, the straining tendons in his neck.

"You can do this, Jesse."

Without straightening, he pressed his eyes closed, the brim of his hat hiding his face from the crowd, his fingers fisting around a ball. "Damn it, I can't. Fuck. I knew I shouldn't have come back here."

She leaned close. "You can do it. Take a chance, Jesse, and just hit the ball. Forget about where it will go or what will happen. Take a chance on yourself. Stop blaming yourself for the life you've led."

He looked at her. "What are you talking about?"

"We both know this isn't about the woman, or the golf, or the possibility of shanking. Your game is unraveling because in those news reports you saw a Jesse you didn't want to be—a Jesse you believe doesn't deserve to win one of the majors." She wanted to grab him by the shirt and force him to understand. "You deserve this, Jesse. You are the great golfer and the good man that I've always believed you were."

His gaze grew intense with emotion, then a commotion in the crowd caught their attention as someone pushed through. The always perfectly dressed Derek stepped out wearing a golf shirt and shorts, and looked directly at his younger brother. He walked over, and after a second, he gave Jesse a bone-crushing hug. "Sorry I'm late."

"Late?"

Derek grinned, then glanced at Kate before looking back. "It was brought to my attention that we have some catching up to do. Seems to me that your big brother could start by being your caddy." He hesitated. "If you'll let me."

The two men stood inches apart, Jesse looking as vulnerable as Travis. When Jesse didn't say no, Derek simply nodded his head, then picked up Jesse's bag, telling the original caddy that his services wouldn't be needed. "Well, Jesse, what do you say? Looks like you have a golf-off to win."

Jesse stood there forever, the gallery growing restless. Kate never would have guessed she'd be so glad to hear one of his imaginative oaths.

Jesse swore, took the driver Derek extended, then returned to the tee box. He readdressed the ball, his concentration fierce.

Kate hurried back and got the mike, her heart pounding so hard that blood rushed through her ears. Just when she thought he would give up, her mind racing with possibilities of things she could say to take the blame, he swung. The motion was ragged, especially for a pro, and the follow-through wasn't pretty. But somehow it got the job done.

The crowd cheered. Bobby Mac made some joking comment about spending too much time wooing the ladies. Then Jesse looked back at Kate. This time she saw utter amazement. And joy.

The gallery rushed down the fairway to get a good spot for the next shot. When she lowered the microphone, Jesse smiled. "I did it," he said only for her. "I did it."

She wanted to touch him, hold him in her arms. But she also realized that neither one of them was helping the other. He was tearing her apart, and she had nearly

ruined him. After all this time, she hardly recognized the
thought that they weren't meant to be together—not as
lovers. Not as husband and wife. Maybe not even as
friends.

"I'm sorry I pushed you to this," she said sincerely.

She started to head down the course, but he took her
arm and held her there. "You've been trying to make me
live up to expectations for a lifetime. And it was about
time I did—instead of running from them."

"I had no right, Jesse."

"You had every right. I just hope you can forgive me
for leaving you in the lurch like that."

She could—she did. "But it's not for me to forgive.
That's up to Travis."

Then she hurried away.

He stood there and watched her go. Derek came up
beside him. "It's time I gave you some brotherly advice."
He actually smiled crookedly.

"And that is?"

Derek clapped Jesse on the shoulder. "Do whatever it
takes to keep her this time."

Derek headed down the fairway, the bag banging
against his hip and thigh. Finally, Jesse followed. When
he came to his ball, he pulled out a six iron and lined up
for his second shot. The minute he swung he knew, with
an exhilarating freedom, that it was dead on. The tiny
white ball flew through the air, landing with a satisfying
bounce and roll onto the green. He was faced with a
challenging putt, but one that was doable.

The crowd cheered. Bobby Mac shook his head and
smiled. And suddenly the two men were truly playing,
truly competing. Hole after hole, Jesse closed the dis-

tance between them. By the time they stood on the ninth tee box, Bobby Mac had only a two-stroke lead.

"Looks like we have a close game," Kate said to the camera.

Since Jesse had won the last hole, he went first. He stepped up to the ball and concentrated, and when he swung, he was all about grace in motion. The early tension had melted away, and his follow-through sent his shot rocketing down the fairway with a scientist's precision.

Bobby Mac whistled appreciatively, though he quickly focused. The football player had no interest in losing the golf-off. It might be a charity event, but both athletes wanted to win.

Jesse and Bobby Mac were neck and neck on the last hole, each of them playing like it was the final round of a PGA major tournament. The crowd murmured in anticipation. It was a close game, all right, but to overcome a two-stroke lead in a single hole was exceedingly difficult, even for a professional golfer. Kate didn't know how Jesse could possibly close the gap.

But then the ex-football star hit his shot into the sand trap to the right of the hole. Jesse landed on the green. This was his chance. Kate could see it on his face.

Bobby shrugged for the camera, but it was clear that he wasn't about to give up. The men approached the green, with Kate, the camera, and Travis following. The gallery was hushed when Bobby Mac stepped into the sand pit, trying to decide how best to get out. A tall lip overhung the trap, making the shot directly to the hole nearly impossible. But if he chipped to the side he wouldn't be anywhere close to the pin. The only chance he had to maintain his lead was to go for it.

Which he did, getting out of the trap, but sending the ball sailing to the other side of the green, very nearly into another hazard.

The crowd groaned.

Bobby Mac was lying three in the rough. Jesse was sitting two on the green. Even though Bobby was still in the lead, realistically he still had to chip onto the green, then putt. And given the difficulty of this particular hole, the football star would probably take two strokes to sink his putt. Which meant that if Jesse could one-putt, sinking his ball with a single stroke, he would come from behind to win outright.

Bobby Mac concentrated and made a good shot onto the green. Since his ball was still farther away from the hole, it meant that he had the next shot. The minute Bobby stroked the ball, it looked like it would go in. The gallery's excitement grew with every inch the ball traveled. But just as it rolled close, the ball lost momentum, catching a bad break, and stopped inches from dropping in. A collective groan sounded. Bobby groaned, too, then walked over and tapped the ball in for the double bogie Jesse needed.

Excitement was high when Jesse addressed his shot. All he had to do was make this putt and he would come from behind to win this golf-off—as he should, given his professional status. He could redeem himself for showing up late. He could prove to himself that he still had what it took to win.

It all depended on the putt.

But something caught his eye, an image snagging in his brain. And when he turned around, he saw Travis. The boy stood nearly swallowed by the crowd, but somehow not a part of it, especially not a part of the other kids.

Jesse hated that he had screwed up the summer. Now that the tree house lay in a shambles in Kate's backyard, he had missed the opportunity to give something to Travis that he would always remember. That's when it occurred to Jesse. He could still give something to his son that the boy would always remember.

Stepping back from the ball, Jesse smiled at Travis, then extended the club.

"Hey, T, show us that great putting of yours."

The twelve-year-old's eyes went wide. Kate froze with shock. The crowd couldn't believe it. And the group of snide boys were stunned.

Long seconds ticked by, and Jesse thought Travis would say no. Jesse walked over to him, bending down until they were eye level. "You can do this. I believe in you."

Travis stood there for an eternity before he pulled back his shoulders and took the putter, his gaze determined.

The audience was amazed. And for reasons Jesse didn't understand, his heart beat hard and his palms got sweaty. In all the years he had played the game, he had never cared so much about a single putt. In that second, he didn't think about his own career, or his own reputation. He wanted Travis to make this shot. And it had nothing to do with winning or losing.

The gallery hushed when the boy squatted down to take a look at the angle between his lie and the hole. Then he came over to the ball, took a few practice swings.

Jesse's mind raced, and he realized he should have told Travis that the break was misleading. But it was too late for that. It was all he could do not to close his eyes when his son made the stroke.

The ball headed to the right of the hole, rolling and rolling, the crowd's collective breath held as the ball's path got slightly wider and wider.

Fuck.

Jesse's jaw clenched. But all of a sudden, just when it looked as if it would pass on by, the break kicked in, sending the ball toward the hole.

When the ball dropped with a distinctive clatter, the crowd let out a whooping roar.

With both shock and elation on her face, Kate walked onto the green and got a reaction from Bobby and Jesse. Jesse could see the emotion in her eyes, a genuine caring and excitement for what had happened today. Then she turned to Travis and hugged him. "You were great, T."

He smiled broadly. "Thanks, Kate."

Once she had hugged him, she pulled up the microphone. "Tell us how it felt, Travis?" she asked.

And he did, becoming the star. He gave a blow-by-blow of what was going on in his head from the minute Jesse extended the putter. When the boy finished, he turned to Jesse and looked up at him with an insecure smile. When Travis started to say thanks, Jesse pulled his son to him in a hug. "I couldn't have done it better myself."

The game ended, and Kate motioned for the cameraman to stop rolling. She was swept away with the small crew as the crowd circled around Bobby, Travis, and Jesse. The golfers gave autographs and laughed with the gallery. Jesse kept waiting for Kate to come back. But she never did.

It hadn't occurred to him that returning wouldn't be

enough to show her how he felt. Then he scoffed at himself, understanding that he'd had people clamoring after him for too long. Simply returning wasn't enough to show Kate that he wouldn't leave her again.

He realized that he didn't want to leave again. He wanted to return home for good, surround himself with the very people he had grown up with—the very people who loved him for himself. And he wanted that life to include Travis as well.

But how to make that happen?

To: Katherine Bloom <katherine@ktextv.com>
   Chloe Sinclair <chloe@ktextv.com>
From: Julia Boudreaux <julia@ktextv.com>
Subject: Kate reinvented

Oh, my gosh! The phones are going crazy. Kate! They love you! You were an absolute hit with viewers. And Jesse showing up late. Inspired! Added a bit of drama to the drama! And little Travis ending up the hero. How did you think of all this?

You did it, sugar!

xoxo, j

To: Julia Boudreaux <julia@ktextv.com>
   Katherine Bloom <katherine@ktextv.com>
From: Chloe Sinclair <chloe@ktextv.com>
Subject: Viewers

Julia, advertisers are calling to say we have to do more of this. Kate, as soon as you have a chance, we need to have a brainstorming session.

Congratulations!
C

To: Julia Boudreaux <julia@ktextv.com>
    Chloe Sinclair <chloe@ktextv.com>
From: Katherine Bloom <katherine@ktextv.com>
Subject: Credit

I wish I could take credit, but I have to tell you, not a bit of that
was scripted. Jesse really did leave—just as you predicted,
Julia—then he decided to return, surprising everyone. And the
whole putter thing with Travis—again, a complete surprise. I'm
still amazed that Jesse did it. All I can say is thank goodness T
made the shot. Can you imagine the consequences if he hadn't?
The child never would have forgotten the fact that he had
messed up in front of such a crowd.

Katherine C. Bloom
News Anchor, KTEX TV West Texas

To: Katherine Bloom <katherine@ktextv.com>
    Chloe Sinclair <chloe@ktextv.com>
From: Julia Boudreaux <julia@ktextv.com>
Subject: Defending

Who'd ever imagine that I'd be defending anything Jesse
Chapman did? Certainly not me. But do you think you're being a
little too hard on the guy, Kate? He believed in the kid, and he

showed it. It's just an added bonus for us that it made for great TV.

If you follow the logic that he never should have given Travis the putter for fear that the boy might have failed, you're saying that no one should take chances. Unfortunately, sugar, that's what life is about. Taking chances. And stop being so hard on Jesse.

xoxo, j

To: Julia Boudreaux <julia@ktextv.com>
    Chloe Sinclair <chloe@ktextv.com>
From: Katherine Bloom <katherine@ktextv.com>
Subject: Traitor

Excuse me! Why are you forgetting that I gave Jesse my heart and he threw it back in my face? Whose side are you on anyway?

To: Katherine Bloom <katherine@ktextv.com>
    Chloe Sinclair <chloe@ktextv.com>
From: Julia Boudreaux <julia@ktextv.com>
Subject: Return to sender

I'm not taking sides, and I'm certainly not going to point out that he returned. You have an incredible segment of *Getting Real with Kate* to prove it. As to risking hearts, I am beginning to wonder if the only reason you have been willing to risk yours on Jesse is because deep down you've never believed he'd stay. You haven't been able to believe in love or in forever for as long as I've known you. It's Jesse actually returning that has thrown you for a loop.

xo, j

To: Julia Boudreaux <julia@ktextv.com>
    Chloe Sinclair <chloe@ktextv.com>
From: Katherine Bloom <katherine@ktextv.com>
Subject: That . . .

---

is not true! Tell her, Chloe!

To: Julia Boudreaux <julia@ktextv.com>
    Katherine Bloom <katherine@ktextv.com>
From: Chloe Sinclair <chloe@ktextv.com>
Subject: No middleman, me

I really don't want to get in the middle of this. But, Kate, face it, you only date guys who are unavailable, uninteresting, or certain to leave. Though I can understand why, given your mother. We know it was hard to see those men come and go from her life. But one of these days you have to face up to the fact that some men won't leave—or if they do, they will realize their mistake and come back. I may have doubted Jesse before, but after seeing him these last few days, I'm convinced he's here to stay.

C

twenty-four

Kate stood in the kitchen, looking out into the yard. She had been answering the most astonishing thing . . . fan e-mail. Amazing how things could turn around so suddenly. They loved her. Thought she was funny as well as smart. Level-headed and pretty.

But most of all, they had said she was real. She had finally found her place, her right tone, by truly just being Kate. She smiled at the sappy thought. But she knew it was true.

She'd also read Chloe's and Julia's e-mails.

Were they right? Had she let herself fall in love again with Jesse because deep down she knew that he wouldn't stay? And now that he had returned, was her footing gone?

Was it easier to live in that place where she could simply believe that "forever" wasn't real rather than having to take a chance that Jesse would stay?

The sounds of hammering brought her out of her thoughts. She looked up into the old cottonwood and could just make out Jesse and Travis repairing the damage done by the storm. A lot of damage had been repaired between the two as well.

On the front page of this morning's edition of the *El Paso Tribune* there was a color photo of Jesse and Bobby Mac shaking hands, and another of Travis being held on the shoulders of a group of boys. Kate had never seen Jesse look so proud.

Last night, Jesse had contacted Travis's mother and asked if the boy could stay until school started to give them some time to figure out a path for the future.

Kate was thrilled for Travis, reveled in the joy that brightened the boy's eyes—the difference she saw in him with just the first taste of his father's love and pride.

The sun started to descend in the summer sky. Kate turned away and went to her bath and ran the water, pouring in her favorite bubbles. Securing her curls on top of her head, she slid into the water and sighed as the warmth seeped into her muscles and bones. She closed her eyes, emptying her mind, easing herself deeper.

The house was quiet, and she heard when the hammering stopped, when the back door slammed, and the sound of running water in the kitchen.

Then more silence. No sound—until the bathroom door clicked open.

When she glanced across the room, she found Jesse standing there. He was beautiful, as always—strong and well-defined.

Her pulse sped up, and she had no idea what to expect.

She felt shy beneath the bubbles.

"Where's Travis?" she asked, her voice squeaking.

"I sent him over to Derek and Suzanne's."

"What for?"

"We need to talk."

He shut the door.

Her pulse leaped and she sank a little lower in the tub until the bubbles popped against her chin. "Jesse, what are you doing?"

"Like I said, we need to talk."

"Here? With the door closed?"

He crossed the room and her mouth went dry. She couldn't think where to put her hands. Nervously, she crossed them over her breasts, but he raised a brow. Awkwardly, she set them on the porcelain sides, though that felt a little Queen of Sheba-ish. She let them flutter to the bottom, but that was too casual for sitting naked only a couple of feet away from this man who was sensuality personified. When she started to reposition once again, he grabbed her hand gently. "Kate, stop."

"Easy for you to say. You're dressed."

His lips hitched up at one corner, then he picked up her towel. "Get out."

"What?"

"Come on, get out of the tub."

"Will you ever stop being so bossy?"

He considered. "Probably not. So dry off and get dressed."

"I am not finished with my bath." She humphed for emphasis.

He gave a long-suffering sigh, then said, "Fine." Tossing the towel aside, he started to pull off his T-shirt.

"Now what are you doing?" she demanded.

"If you won't get out, then I'll just have to get in."

"Ack!" Without thinking, she splashed around and stood, bubbles covering her.

But they didn't cover enough.

His gaze darkened. "I'm thinking we should talk in the tub after all."

"Or not! Turn around."

She didn't think he would, but after a second, he retrieved the towel, handed it to her, then turned. The minute she got it around her, he came back and started to dry her off.

She growled. "I can do it."

"Yeah, but that wouldn't be any fun."

The look on his face was so devilishly sweet and teasing that it was hard to hold on to indignation. That always was the way between them, him always breaking through her carefully constructed determination. All he had to do was flash that smile at her and she melted.

But not this time.

"I'm not interested in fun. I'm not speaking to you."

"Good. That'll make things easier."

Before she knew it, he had dried her. After one appreciative glance, he started dressing her in her shorts and T-shirt. Then he pulled her out of the bathroom, through the kitchen, and out the back door to the tree house. He gestured for her to go up first.

"I'm not—"

"You're not speaking to me, remember."

She shot him a scowl, but he merely pushed her up the rungs. At the top, she climbed through the narrow opening into the tree house and sat down Indian style. Jesse was close behind her.

"You and Travis have gotten a good start on rebuilding the sides." She looked out through the partial walls at the trees of the lush river valley.

"We have a lot more to do before we're finished. But that's not why you and I are here."

Slowly, he took her hand and pressed it to the hard planes of his chest. A shiver ran through her as she felt his pulse, steady and strong. She also felt the second the walls of her determination cracked.

"Do you feel that?" he asked with a quiet earnestness that had nothing to do with the media darling Jesse Chapman.

"Yes, I feel it. You know I do. But you can't keep making problems disappear by getting me to feel and forget. Eventually, they all come back."

"Fair enough. But that wasn't what I was trying to do. I wanted you to feel my heart, Katie."

"So we're back to Katie?"

"We never left. Not really." He pulled her hand away, holding it in both of his, tracing the fine bones that fanned out into fingers.

Grudgingly, because she was scared of what he made her feel, she relented. "That was a great thing you did for Travis."

"It was easy."

"No, it wasn't. At a time when you needed proof that you were still a contender in the golf world, you gave him the spotlight. But you gave him more than that. You gave him something he'll always remember—proving that you deserve to be called a hero."

"But do I deserve you?"

Hope, love, excitement, and fear mixed together. "Jesse, don't."

He nodded his head, as if he were conceding to her wishes. But something in his eyes told a different story. The Jesse she had known her whole life, the boy and now the man, was a fighter, someone who refused to give up.

"When I first got here," he continued, "you asked me why I came back."

She pulled her hand away and hugged her knees to her chest. "You said you wanted a vacation."

"I know that's what I said, and I half believed it. But remember when Julia said that she saw me standing out in front of your house that first day?"

She tilted her head, remembering. "Yes."

"I wanted to see you."

She snorted. "Don't start making up stuff now."

"I'm not. I was drawn back here so strongly that I got in my car and drove halfway across the country before I really knew what I was doing. I told myself that it made sense to return to the place where I fell in love with the game. When I arrived, I figured I'd stay in a hotel for a few days, go to the course a few times, then leave. But the next thing I knew I was standing out in front of your house because I wanted to see you. Though I didn't let myself think about why that was. When Julia saw me standing there, she made it all so easy—to see you, to stay with you. To be near you without having to admit to anyone, including myself, why."

"Wanting to be near me? You resisted me from the second you got here."

"I'm sorry for that."

She shook her head. "You shouldn't be." And she meant it. "This whole month has been crazy. Heck, I was so absorbed in my own career concerns that I easily could have made you look horrible on television. I could have ruined you."

"You didn't ruin me. Hell, you saved me. But I resisted you because I *had* women. I simply wanted you. Katie Bloom. I wanted your love, your honesty. Your purity. Selfishly, I wanted your belief in me. If you could still love me, then I could be okay."

He hesitated, then looked her in the eye. "I just didn't recognize it until I was headed out of town. I watched the city limits come, then go, and it wasn't until then that I realized why I had driven all the way to El Paso in the first place."

He stood, pulling her with him, the two of them standing there in that tree house where years ago she had asked him to wait for her to grow up.

He kissed her then, though it wasn't the quick girlish peck she had given him. He kissed her with passion and longing, with reverence and promise.

"I love you, Katie. I have loved you since the day you looked up into my eyes and stopped crying, as if I alone had the ability to do anything and make everything all right. You believed in me—you always have. But that isn't why I love you." He touched her cheek. "You're the most courageous person I know. I love you because you are kind and good. And because you aren't afraid. You aren't a quitter, no matter how tough things get."

Emotion tightened in her throat. She wanted to believe him.

"You are a better person than I will ever be, Kate. But I want you anyway. You are my past and my future. I want nothing more than for you to say you'll marry me."

"Oh, Jesse." Her lips trembled and tears burned in her eyes. "I love you. I'll always love you. But I can't spend my life afraid that you'll leave again."

He leaned forward, much as she had done at the golf-off, his lips so close to her ear that his breath sent shivers down her spine. "Take a chance, Katie Bloom. Take a chance on me. If it takes me the rest of my life, I will prove that I'll never leave you again."

twenty-five

The bright neon Las Vegas night pulsed with heat and excitement. Kate felt them both. She also felt the comforting firmness of Jesse's grip on her hand.

But a second later, she felt a start of surprise when their limousine pulled up in front of My Heart's Desire Wedding Chapel just off the infamous Las Vegas Strip.

"What?" she asked, staring at the tiny replica of a white clapboard church. "What are we doing here?"

Jesse helped her out of the long, white car and gave her one of his heart-stopping smiles, crooked, endearing, and sexy as hell. "You said you'd marry me. I'm not taking a chance you'll change your mind."

The driver popped the trunk and started unloading all sorts of wedding items, then carried everything into the chapel.

Kate was moved and excited. But . . . "How can we get married without family?"

"Travis is here."

"Which is wonderful. You know I want him at our wedding. But what about Julia and Chloe?"

His smile only broadened as he pushed open the chapel doors.

"Surprise!"

Her best friends stood with Travis, Julia in her short skirt and high heels, Chloe with her china doll looks and sensible clothes. Suzanne was there, looking like a society matron, and beside her Derek stood smiling with pride. Then Carlen Chapman stepped out from behind Derek.

The elder Chapman looked older than Kate remembered, more subdued. She knew that these men had a lot to work out, but she was glad to see that all of them were in attendance.

Even Belinda was there, walking up behind her son as the youngest Chapman cast surreptitious glances at his grandfather. But it was Kate's mother who surprised her the most, stepping out from the small crowd, looking like a beautiful earth mother with her long gray hair braided and her gossamer skirts flowing.

She extended her arms. "My baby," she said.

It took only a second for Kate to relax into her mother's embrace. So cherished, so rare.

"Kate, I couldn't be happier for you." Mary Beth reached out for Jesse, tugged him close, then put Kate's hand in his. "Take care of her, Jess."

Jesse assured her that he would. "That is, if she'll let me."

He turned to Kate. "Will you marry me? Here? Now? Not later. I don't want to wait until after the PGA." He went down on one knee in front of the group. "I was serious when I said that I would never leave you again. Marry me now, and be with me forever."

Tears burned in her eyes as she looked around her at the people she loved and who loved her in return. And she knew that they loved the real Kate. Not someone she was trying to be.

"I will," she whispered.

He lifted her up and twirled her around, then she was pulled off to a back room where Julia, Chloe, Suzanne, and her mother prepared her for the wedding. When Belinda seemed at a loss, Kate reached out and pulled her into the circle.

"You're family now, too," she said.

The women dressed Kate in a gown of white silk and low-heeled leather shoes that were soft as butter. They did her hair and fixed her makeup, and when she was ready she could only look in the mirror in awe.

"You're beautiful," her mother said, coming up beside her, hooking their arms together. "This all reminds me of my first wedding. Young. In love. Everything beautiful and perfect." Mary Beth sighed dreamily and launched into a description of her many weddings, of her loves, of her many different lives, as if yet again this event, as with all events, was about her. "I love weddings. Did I tell you I met a new man?"

Kate stared at her mother, panic starting to creep through her. But Jesse must have sensed it, because in minutes he was beside her, ignoring the dictate that the groom not see the bride before the ceremony. He pulled her close and whispered emphatically, "You are not your mother. This will be our one and only wedding."

He kissed her then, holding her secure, and she knew she wanted this, had been waiting for this her entire life.

* * *

An organist played the wedding march, and the handful of pews were filled with her friends and family. Travis stood next to his father at the altar. But it was Jesse whom she saw.

Her heart beat hard as she approached, a mix of fear and hope knotted in her chest. She wanted this man—she had always wanted him. But part of her was still afraid.

Then he did something amazing. He pulled out two rings and handed her one. His. When she caught a glimpse of hers, her mind swirled back in time.

"*We'll marry, you know.*" Her words from what seemed like a thousand years ago. She six, Jesse ten. "*We won't bother with a big, gigantic wedding. It'll just be you and me and our families. But we have to have rings. Real rings. A plain gold one for you so you won't look like a sissy. And I'll have that really great kind with two hands locked together holding a crown.*"

Jesse had remembered, as if he had tucked the memory away until it was time.

It was time. Every doubt washed away, and when they were pronounced man and wife, Kate realized that dreams do come true.

"*I love you, Jesse. Do you love me, too?*" she had asked all those years ago.

And when he kissed her, finally, all these years later, he answered her question.

"Yes, yes, a thousand times yes."

*Turn the page for a sneak peek
at the next book in
Linda Francis Lee's Sexy series*

Sinfully Sexy

On sale October 2004

Chloe Sinclair plunged through the wind in a short glittery dress, high heels, and a tiny purse that was more decorative than practical. She couldn't see a thing, didn't realize she wasn't alone until . . .

She ran into another body. Hard. Jarring them both.

The impact sent her lurching forward, arms extended like she was flying. It happened so fast that she couldn't regain her balance. Her gloved hands hit the pavement first, the tiny chain on the purse like a vice around her wrist. Next, her knees crashed into the ground and pain shot through her. For half a second she lay there stunned.

"Are you all right?"

A man's voice, clear and deep, commanding, came at her in a disjointed muffle through the wind. She tried to pick herself up, but before she could manage, strong hands came around her and he swept her up with amazing ease. She tried to make out who he was, but he was much taller than she, and she couldn't see more than his shirt when he pulled her close, his body blocking the wind.

Huddled together, he propelled them the remaining few steps to the hotel entrance. Despite the pain, she was very aware of the man's touch, of the way his arm was secure around her, the way he controlled her body with ease. She had an altogether foreign thought that she was safe.

Once inside, he swept her through the lobby, but when they came to a set of double doors leading to the hotel bedrooms, she stiffened.

"Where are you taking me?"

"I'm staying here."

"You're taking me here, as in to your . . . your . . ."

"Room?"

"Exactly," she stated primly. "I can't go to your room."

He made some kind of grumbling noise deep in his chest, but instead of guiding her through the doors, he tugged her away and had her inside an elegant ladies' room decorated in marble and brass. Thankfully it was empty. Though not as thankfully, he slid the lock home.

"Now what are you doing?"

"You're bleeding."

"Bleeding?"

He pointed.

"Oh," was all she got out of her mouth when she glanced down at herself and got a really good look. Her once shimmering thigh-high stockings were ripped beyond repair, blood and grit marking both of her knees like a six year old after a playground fall.

On top of that, she had never been all that great with blood.

"Oh," she repeated, this time sort of wobbly.

"Don't go weak willed on me now."

"I am not weak willed," she stated, her spine straightening.

"That's what I like to hear."

Next thing she knew, he had her up on the marble counter as if she didn't weigh anything at all, her skirt riding high. That was when she looked up and saw his face. Her first real look. She wasn't sure if she sucked in her breath or if she sighed. She only knew that her world went still.

They stared at each other, she on the sink with her chin tilted slightly, he standing so close that his thighs touched her knees. He seemed as surprised as she felt.

It seemed like an eternity that their gazes locked, but probably wasn't more than a second.

He looked as commanding as he had acted. He was tall, his dark hair brushed back, his dark eyes filled with intelligence, knowing, and confidence. His autocratic control of the situation was apparent in the hard line of his square jaw. This was a man used to getting what he wanted.

He wore a finely made shirt that molded to broad shoulders and narrowed into a lean waist and long legs. Standing there he appeared to be in charge of his surroundings, not giving a second thought to being in a ladies' bathroom with a woman he didn't know and with the door locked. He didn't smile or say a word, though his gaze seemed to draw her to him. But after another second, his eyes narrowed fractionally and he gave a barely perceptible shake of his head, before he focused on her scrapes.

"Let me look at your hands."

He didn't wait for her to agree. He took each palm,

peeling the shredded gloves away finger by finger. This time she knew she sucked in her breath when his hands cradled hers, large and tanned, hers pale in comparison.

Fortunately, the gloves had protected her palms. Her forearms hadn't been as lucky.

"These have got to hurt," he said, studying them.

Once he said it, she was reminded that they did.

He took one of the paper towels that were stacked in a functional brass holder and soaked it with warm water, the hotel monogram going dark as it got wet. Despite his commanding size, his touch was gentle as he cleaned the blood and grit away. The sting was blocked out by the sizzle of sensation this hard-chiseled man caused. She watched him as he concentrated on the job—the way his head bent close so he could get a better look, before he nodded in approval and started on her other arm.

She was aware of every breath he took, the sound like a caress against her ear. He cradled her arm as he studied the wounds. She couldn't remember the last time she had been touched—by anyone. She grew lightheaded and she swayed.

He glanced up. "How are you doing?"

"Fine," she whispered.

Better than fine. She felt strange, hot tears of yearning burning in her eyes as he nodded his head in approval and moved on to her knees.

But the torn stockings were in the way. Without hesitation, he reached under her dress. She gasped. Like a lover, his strong hands brushed against her legs. Her breath shuddered through her body, feelings that had nothing to do with healing or wounds settling low until she felt the need to press her knees together. But she couldn't because his forearm and hand was in the way.

Her head swam at the feel of his fingers finding the tops of her ruined thigh-highs, first one, his hands so close to the juncture between her legs, then the other as he whisked them down and tossed them in the trash.

The act wasn't intended to be sexual, but when the only physical attention she had received in ages was when she got a manicure, this man's touch made her world tilt even more. It was the sort of feeling, she realized, she had waited a lifetime for. Intense. Like a dream from which you don't want to wake up.

She had hammered her life into the contours she deemed acceptable. But the reality of who she had become made her wonder at the price she had paid.

Feeling this man's hands on her thighs, even innocently, made something flare.

Rebellion against everything she believed to be proper? Imprudence?

No, she realized. Nothing so complicated. It was hot, simple, and unrestrained desire.

But she wasn't about to give in to something like that, least of all with a stranger. She was smart. She was sensible.

"I could have done that," she stated over the staccato dance in her chest, her eyes shifting nervously as she tried to find some place else to look besides the silky waves of his hair.

"No need now."

He concentrated on her knee. She tried to find the old Chloe, the one she knew, the one who would demand that he take his hands off her.

"I was trying to sound intimidating," she said.

He glanced up at her, one dark brow rising. "I guess it was the squeak in your voice that threw me."

"I did not squeak!"

"You did."

Her mouth fell open. "This really isn't going as it should."

"I didn't realize there was a certain way to do this."

"There is."

"I must have missed that day at school."

"Funny."

He smiled then, for the first time, she realized, and her breath caught a little more. It was amazing, like the sun coming through a dark, stormy sky. Then he straightened. "There. One knee done."

Sure enough, one side was cleaned. It still looked horrible, but the grit was gone.

"Are you a doctor?"

"No."

"A paramedic?"

"Not that either."

"Then you just go around saving damsels in distress."

For reasons she couldn't fathom, that wiped every trace of humor off of his face, the clouds returning.

"You've been reading too many fairytales," he said sharply. Then his features settled back into that hard-chiseled command. "Would you rather I had left you in the hotel driveway and continued on to find a cab as I intended? Is that another rule I missed?"

He looked at her, his dark eyes direct as if he could see into her mind, her heart . . . like he could see into her soul. She looked away, then couldn't help herself. She glanced back.

Her voice caught in her throat. "You're laughing at me."

After a second, that half smile of his reappeared, reluctantly, his head tilted every so slightly. "Never."

Then he returned his attention to his project. Her knees.

"This one's a real mess," he said, pressing a new paper towel to the ragged skin.

"Ouch!"

He leaned closer, and she looked down at him, his hair thick and dark. He didn't wear cologne, but he smelled clean and strong. She had a startling image of him leaning close to kiss her. Sensation flashed through her. Hot, sweet, and intense. She thought of touching him. Reaching out. Of being a feline instead of a llama.

This was the sort of man who made a woman feel sexy. Dark and dangerous, commanding the world around him with nothing more than a look and a few words.

A stillness descended over her, fine and crystalline, and she had never been so aware . . . of a man's hand on her knee. Of the way his strong fingers splayed against her inner thigh. And when he looked up she was sure he felt it too.

Their gazes locked, their bodies close. He glanced at her lips and a teasing sweetness made her yearn even more.

But he was a gentleman.

After one last glance at her mouth, he returned his attention to her knee. The outside world was forgotten. She felt cocooned by awareness. She felt every time his thigh brushed against hers.

Everything that wasn't her, everything that wasn't Chloe Sinclair, surged up. Suddenly she wasn't embarrassed at the thought of being sensual. She wasn't afraid of being rejected.

And wasn't that really why she had been afraid to be sexy? The fear of rejection?

Sitting there now, with this man touching her, this stranger with his hands on her body, any sort of embarrassment she felt melted away beneath the terror of what she wanted to do. Give in. Touch him back. Good Girl Chloe Sinclair wanted to be sinfully sexy.

She felt dizzy at the thought, her heart beating hard as she clutched her hands together to keep herself from doing what she knew she'd regret. She thought of splashing cold water on her face. She counted to ten, then twenty. She concentrated on all she had to do over the next few weeks. She had payroll to approve. Find new advertising dollars. Brainstorm new programming options. But when he finished with her knee, he straightened again, his competence and composure disarming.

He stood there studying her, not smiling. Then his eyes drifted down over her body, the dark of his eyes flaring with something hot. No one had ever looked at her that way before, the heat tangible, making her feel both panicked and excited.

Then everything changed.

It happened so fast that she didn't have time to think. One minute she was holding on to being sensible Chloe, smart, sane, safe, her life as it always had been. Then the next she whispered, "Kiss me."

One long beat of silence passed before a tremor raced through him.

She was being forward and inexcusably loose. But like a dam of restraint had finally broken apart, water rushing through crashing at her defenses, she didn't care. She wanted to lose herself in his arms, just this once, with this stranger who would disappear from her life when it was over.

Tonight, just tonight, she didn't want to be sensible or even smart. She wanted to be free and wild, and filled with unchecked desire.

Frustration kicked inside her when he didn't kiss her. He only looked at her, didn't reach out. He took her in, and she cringed at the sudden thought that even made up and not looking anything like her usual boring self, he wasn't attracted to her.

What an idiot to think that a man this strong and handsome and clearly powerful, would want her—even with no names mentioned or strings attached.

"Oh, God, I've completely made a fool of myself. I'm sorry." She tried to get down off the counter, the movement reminding her of the scrapes on her knees.

"You haven't made a fool of yourself," he said, his voice ruggedly insistent, his body blocking her way. "You are beautiful and desirable—"

Her snort was a knee jerk reaction, the old Chloe surging back ruthlessly.

"—but you don't know the first thing about me."

That stopped her. She cocked her head and studied him. Was he testing her?

"You don't know me either," she whispered. She met his eyes, and she bit her lip for a trembling second. "That's the point."

She startled him, and from the look of him she guessed he was rarely surprised.

His brows slammed together. "I could be a . . ."

"What? A murderer?"

"I am not a murderer." He sounded put out.

"Okay, then a Mexican bandit?" She tried to smile.

"Are we living in the same century?"

He looked at her lips again, despite his better intentions, and she could see something that her inexpert eyes swore was desire. Hope surged and she felt an impatient anticipation.

"Would it help," she asked breathlessly, "if I promised that I'm not a bandit?"

She expected him to laugh, or at the very least smile. Instead his gaze darkened. "I'm not so sure about that. With your innocent blue eyes and mouth meant for sin, you look like you could easily steal something I've never been willing to give," he stated cryptically.

But before she could question him, he groaned and cursed. Then this stranger pulled her into his arms.

They clung together, the warmth of his body surrounding her. Their kiss grew instantly hot, their mouths slanting together as if neither of them could get close enough. His hands ran down her spine and she knew with a heady sense of certainty that whatever his reasons for kissing her, this wasn't about pity.

She wrapped her arms around his shoulders. She didn't admit how many times she had imagined something like this. In her dreams, in her fantasies. Giving in to a forbidden passion.

He ran his tongue along her lips, opening her more. Their tongues tasted and probed as she tugged his shirttails from his pants, wanting to feel skin.

"Who are you?" he whispered hoarsely against her ear.

She hesitated for a second then said, "Does it matter?"

She didn't wait for an answer. She ran her hands up his chest, material gathering against her wrists, and after another second he gave in again.

"Wrap your legs around me," he commanded in a gruff voice.

A sharp thrill ran along every nerve ending, centering deep and low. She did as he asked, then felt a shiver of excitement as he unzipped the back of her dress, the beaded skirt riding higher until it came up around her hips, the top sliding lower until it revealed the curve of her breasts.

He picked her up and wheeled her around, pressing her back against the finely papered wall. Then he dipped his head, that dark hair brushing against her as he trailed his lips along her skin.

"God, you are soft."

Lower and lower until he took one nipple in his mouth. He had exuded raw sensuality just tending to her wounds. Now, with his intent purely sexual, there was an animal fierceness to him that scared her as much as it thrilled her.

White hot electricity pulsed through her, every nerve ending tingling. Struggling, she tugged her arms from the restraint of her dress, the beads bunching in cool heaviness against her hips. When she was finally free, she reached up, wrapping her arms around his shoulders as his thumbs found her nipples. She felt hungry and needy in a purely physical way.

She groaned without an ounce of inhibition when his thumb and forefinger closed on one taut peak. She trembled inside and her head fell back against the wall. Then he ripped off his shirt, lowering her just a bit and it was in a moment of gasping surprise that she felt the hard contours of his naked chest against her breasts. She felt alive and captive at the same time, pleasure heightened by the illicitness of what they were doing.

Reaching up, she tangled her fingers in his hair, instinctively arching to him as he seared his mouth across her body. When he gently sucked one breast, her hands knotted and she had to force herself to let go.

Neither of them said a word. They came together in a dance of silence. Slowly, he let her down until she stood, her dress falling to her ankles. His mouth nipped at her skin. He cupped her bottom, the thin edges of a thong she had secretly purchased doing little to separate them. Palms to flesh, his fingertips curled low until she felt him touch the juncture between her spread thighs.

The contact surprised her. At first she felt self-conscious. She started to break free. But that was the old Chloe. The one she'd find again once she walked out the door and never saw this man again. But right now she wanted to let go. While she had the chance. No one ever had to know.

Drawing a breath, she widened her legs. His deep guttural moan brought an answering cry welling up in her. She felt desperate, like this was her only chance. She wanted more of him, wanted to be closer. He must have sensed it in her. He pressed their bodies together. He kissed her again, his hands coming up to frame her face as his mouth reclaimed hers.

He nipped at her lower lip before teasing it open, allowing him in to taste her more intimately. She didn't realize she had moaned until the sound rumbled in her ears. She felt small and cherished, even beautiful. Her hair was wild, but the way he held her made her feel as if he could hold her forever and he'd be lucky.

His hands slid down her neck to her shoulders. The heels of his hands grazed the tops of her breasts, but not lower. The tips of his fingers brushed over her collarbones, back and forth as he kissed her. She thought she would cry out in frustration before he finally cupped her breasts in his palms.

He pressed them high, his fingers brushing over the peaks, circling. She felt his breath against her ear when he ran his tongue along the delicate shell. Then his thumb and forefinger closed with gentle insistence, over her nipple. Pulsing, once, twice, his tongue dancing the same rhythm in her mouth. She felt everything in the core between her legs. Hot and needy.

When she groaned, he secured her spread eagle against the wall, his hands touching her, worshipping her . . . wanting her. Cupping her hips, he pulled her to his hardness, again and again, in that rhythm prescribed by his tongue.

She trembled, stunned by the strength of her need. His breath on her nape was like wind to a fire.

He cupped her jaw, tilting her face to him. "I want you," he whispered.

His voice was laced with the sound of raw hunger. "I want you, too," she answered.

And when he started to undo his belt, she reached down to help, their fingers tangling together.

Frantic, they tugged at the buckle and leather, and the sound of the door banging against the lock didn't reach her at first. Her world consisted of this stranger and his hands on her bare skin. But something must have registered with him because he cursed and tore away from her.

With a sudden flash, she realized people must be gathered just outside of the door. She could hear them talking, some woman complaining that the hotel shouldn't lock the only bathroom they had in the main lobby. Then someone else who told them to step back, followed by a jangle of keys against the lock.

"Oh, my gosh!" she gasped.

Thankfully her stranger wasn't paralyzed. He immediately whipped up her shimmery dress, whirled her around and had her zipped back up with the proficiency of a dresser at a Broadway play. Just as the keys turned in the lock, he had his own clothes back in place.

"Let me handle this," he stated, stepping in front of her to block her from view.

He stood like a warrior, his stance wide, his features dark, his frame massive and forbidding. If anyone could protect her from embarrassment, this man could.

But Chloe was hardly paying attention. With her heart in her throat, she lowered her head, tucking in her chin. Her heart beat like a drum, pulsing through her, and the second the door opened, she flew into action. She wheeled out from behind him, startling the small crowd who had gathered, and dashed for the door.

She felt badly leaving the stranger to deal with the mess, though not badly enough to stay. But just when she got through the crowd, for one quick second, she looked back. He was looking at her, his hard-chiseled face quickly shifting from surprise to anger when he understood what she had done. A shiver of regret raced through her. He didn't look like the type of man any sane person should anger. She prayed she never saw him again.